# HIS BROTHER'S WIFE

www.transworldbooks.co.uk

# HIS BROTHER'S WIFE

Val Wood

# BANTAM PRESS

LONDON · TORONTO · SYDNEY · AUCKLAND · JOHANNESBURG

TRANSWORLD PUBLISHERS
61–63 Uxbridge Road, London W5 5SA
A Random House Group Company
www.transworldbooks.co.uk

First published in Great Britain
in 2013 by Bantam Press
an imprint of Transworld Publishers

Copyright © Valerie Wood 2013

Valerie Wood has asserted her right under the Copyright, Designs and
Patents Act 1988 to be identified as the author of this work.

This book is a work of fiction and, except in the case of historical fact,
any resemblance to actual persons, living or dead, is purely coincidental.

A CIP catalogue record for this book
is available from the British Library.

ISBN 9780593070888

Addresses for Random House Group Ltd companies outside the UK
can be found at: www.randomhouse.co.uk
The Random House Group Ltd Reg. No. 954009

The Random House Group Limited supports the Forest Stewardship
Council® (FSC®), the leading international forest-certification organisation.
Our books carrying the FSC label are printed on FSC®-certified
paper. FSC is the only forest-certification scheme suported by the leading
environmental organisations, including Greenpeace. Our paper procurement
policy can be found at www.randomhouse.co.uk/environment

Typeset in 11½/14½pt New Baskerville by
Kestrel Data, Exeter, Devon.
Printed and bound in Great Britain by
Clays Ltd, Bungay, Suffolk.

2 4 6 8 10 9 7 5 3 1

MIX
Paper from
responsible sources
FSC
www.fsc.org
FSC® C016897

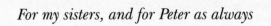

*For my sisters, and for Peter as always*

# AUTHOR'S NOTE

*A man may not marry his brother's wife, nor a woman her husband's brother.* Such unions were forbidden in scripture and in law by the Church of England's Marriage Laws of 1560 until 1921, when the 1907 Marriage Act was amended accordingly, providing the first spouse was deceased.

# PREFACE

The powerful force of a gale far out in the German Ocean abated slightly as the white crests of the high tide rushed towards the yawning mouth of the Humber estuary. The swell lashed the sinuous curve of Spurn Point, and struck again when it reached the reclaimed banks of Sunk Island and Cherry Cobb Sands in Holderness. But they didn't break, and the tide went on to raise the level of the River Hull, already high from the draining of the lowlands, so that many houses sited close by were flooded, as they so often were.

Onward it flowed towards the confluence and wide flat plain of the Ouse and the Trent, the trumpet-shaped channel narrowing as it reached Hessle to create a flood tide that covered the wetlands and salt marsh beyond Brough, Broomfleet and Ellerker Sands and the outlying hamlets and villages in this low-lying and lonely landscape.

# CHAPTER ONE

## Hull, 1860

Harriet trudged up High Street towards the George and Dragon. How she hated this job! The customers with their stinking breath and coarse hands on her backside, who she had to push away with a smile and quizzical eyebrow so as not to upset them, so that they didn't get nasty or complain about her to the landlord. The landlord wasn't so bad; he saw what was going on and didn't blame her for it, but his wife was a harridan.

Still, it was a job and they were hard to come by. She sighed. I suppose I must count my blessings and be thankful that I managed to find extra work at 'hostelry, she thought, but even so I don't see how I can manage to pay 'rent, not if we want to eat. If I'd been nicer to 'mill foreman he might have kept me on full time, but his wandering hands are worse than 'hostelry customers', and him with a wife and four bairns. So he punished me and has put me on half time, until I change my mind, which I won't. Instead, she had taken the job at the George, even though she didn't like being out late in the evening when her mother was so ill. The older woman hadn't eaten for days but even so she still retched, although she brought up nothing but green bile. I'm going to ask if I can leave early tonight. I wish . . . what do I wish?

She turned into the yard. This was an ancient inn, one of the oldest in Hull and in the oldest street in the town, set close by the River Hull where the November fog drifted in from the sea and floated amongst the houses and alleyways. I don't wish for riches, but it would be nice to have enough to eat, and not have to worry about paying 'landlord, and – to have a good man in my life, one who spoke softly, and would look after me and my mother. And I would tek care of him. Was there such a man, she wondered.

Two weeks earlier a stranger had come into the inn. He wasn't local; she knew all the regular customers by sight if not by name, and she hadn't seen this man before. He'd been polite, asked for food as well as ale, and she'd thought . . . well, she'd thought that he seemed pleasant. He'd asked for fresh bread as if he was used to eating good food, and although he hadn't been flippant or saucy he'd seemed interested in her, for she'd caught him glancing to see if she was wearing a wedding ring, and there'd been something he said. What was it, she thought. Something about a husband. That was it: had I a husband to go home to? But I didn't answer; I'm not in 'habit of discussing my life with a stranger. He was in Hull on business, he said, so he must live out of 'district. It would be nice if he came back like he said he would, and then I might find out who he is, does he have a wife, where does he live, is he in regular work? She let out a breath of resignation. But no use daydreaming, Harriet. This is your life, such as it is.

She swung open the door. There was a bright fire burning and already men standing by it warming their backsides. The landlord's wife stood behind the bar counter with an expression so brittle it could shatter glass. 'You're late,' she said.

'I know,' Harriet replied. 'I'm sorry.'

Anger coursed through his veins. It had for as long as he could remember, though he didn't know why; but it was his retaliation, his way of dealing with what he considered to be injustice, his way of coping with long-standing rejection.

Noah Tuke rode the stallion hard, testing its health and strength. He'd bought him cheap, doing a shady deal with the owner who was pressed for money and had cursed him for his meanness. This would be Noah's second visit to Hull and when his quest was done he had no intention of ever going back to the town again.

He'd gone there seeking a wife in the middle of October, and reckoned that he might have found one. With a bit of luck and a few choice words he might get as good a bargain as he had with the stallion.

He needed a woman who could work, and although he could have gone to Goole or Brough, both nearer to his marshland home than Hull, Goole was a new company town of no more than four or five hundred people, built for the shipping industry and attracting few women apart from the dockers' wives; and in the small community of Brough someone might have recognized the son of one of the farmers from the water-logged wastes outside the town, and the last thing he wanted was raised eyebrows or inevitable questions of motive.

He had reckoned that a woman employed in one of the inns and hostelries of Hull would be used to long hours and drudgery; she should be young, but not so young that he'd have to teach her the facts of life. Mature, but no more than twenty-five, and presentable and attractive; not a whore, although he had no problem with previous experience, providing she was clean; and she should have no commitments. No children, no parents, no ties, and no one with claims on her. She should be looking for a chance to better herself and be prepared to leave the town and become a countrywoman.

On the first visit, he had become almost drunk in his search. He hadn't realized just how many inns and beer houses the town held. He'd gone to those that were slightly run down, the kind of place where a woman without family might apply for a job and be prepared to work for a pittance.

Some of the places he tried employed women who in his opinion were nothing more than sluts. Some of them leered at him, giving him toothless grins as they asked if he was new to the area.

'Passing through,' he would mutter, drinking his ale and moving on.

Other hostelries, crowded with seamen, were attended mainly by a landlord and occasionally by a landlord's wife, as tough and mean as they appeared to be, and he would leave swiftly without ordering a drink. The meandering High Street with its courts and alleys, the lanes running off towards the Market Place and narrow staithes leading to the River Hull, was a hotchpotch of ramshackle buildings, fine houses, barbers' shops, workshops and law offices as well as many ancient, crumbling inns. The only way he could retain a sense of direction was by keeping the tower of the Guildhall or the medieval church of St Mary's within his sight.

He had been about to give up his search and go home when he came to the stable yard of an alehouse with a sign of the George and Dragon swinging over the door. A narrow alley with the nameplate George Yard led through from the High Street into Lowgate and he decided to try his luck once more.

It was a cold night but there was a good fire burning in the grate with customers gathered round it; the bar counter was clean, as was the long table in the middle of the room. A woman in her twenties was serving ale from a jug and he saw her skilfully swerve away from a man's hand reaching beneath her skirt.

Mmm, he'd thought. Not a whore then, unless she's playing hard to get. She'd smiled at the man, but not provocatively; no doubt she'd be under orders from the landlord to be nice to the customers.

She might do, he'd thought, providing she wasn't spoken for, and he leaned on the counter and ordered a pint of their best ale. She'd spoken pleasantly, with a trace of the local accent.

'Haven't seen you before, sir,' she said. 'Are you visiting 'town?'

'Aye,' he said. 'A bit o' business here. Went on a bit late. I'll be on my way home after this. Have you got owt I can eat? I missed my supper.'

She hadn't asked him where home was, but said she could rustle up a plate of beef or ham with bread.

'Bread was fresh this morning,' she said. 'It's not stale.'

'Aye, that'll do. I'll not eat stale bread. I like my grub. Did you mek it?'

'No.' She laughed. 'Landlord's wife buys it from 'baker.'

'Bet you know how to mek it though, don't you?' He'd pushed his hat back and watched her as she took bread out of a crock under the counter, sliced it, placed it on a plate and took two thick slices of beef and ham from beneath a covered dish. He noticed she wasn't wearing a wedding ring.

'Course I do,' she said. 'My ma showed me how when I was a bairn. I don't mek it now, though. I don't have a good enough oven, and besides, 'baker's cheap enough. Mustard?' she asked.

'Aye, and plenty of it.'

He ate quickly. It would take at least two hours to get home; he'd left a note on the kitchen table to say he'd be late and reminding Fletcher not to lock him out.

'That were grand,' he commented, when he'd finished. 'I'll come again.'

'Do,' she'd nodded.

'Are you here every night? Or do you have a husband to go home to?'

She'd looked sharply at him and he wondered if he was taking things too fast; he wasn't used to dealing with women and didn't know their foibles or eccentricities, except his mother's and she didn't count.

'I'm allus here,' she told him, leaning on the counter. 'I'm lucky to be in work. Landlord's not bad, not like some I've worked for who expect you to work all 'hours God sends for onny a copper.'

He'd nodded and left it at that, leaving as soon as he'd

finished his ale. She hadn't admitted to having a husband, but he was fairly sure she would have said if she had, if only to warn him off.

Although it was a long shot, she was the reason he was going back now, two weeks later. He'd been tempted to return within a week, but he didn't want to appear eager, only as if he really were there on business. Besides, he didn't want his brother to become suspicious, and he would, he muttered beneath his ragged breath. The heathen would smell a rat and begin muckraking in every dunghill he could find until he discovered what Noah was up to.

They'd had a bet; at least he had challenged Fletcher to a bet. They'd been fighting as they often did as to who should have the last word over how the farm should be run, and as they'd raged at each other their father, Nathaniel, had come out of the house with a shotgun and fired it over their heads.

'Get back to work, both of you,' he'd shouted. 'I give out orders here, nobody else.'

They'd both muttered and growled. They were grown men after all, too old to be taking orders from an old man, even if he was their father. It was that night, as they were going up to bed, that Noah had said, 'If one of us had a wife and some bairns, that'd decide who was to run 'farm.'

Fletcher had glared at him. 'And how would that decide? And what would Ma say to having another woman in 'house?'

Noah had shrugged. 'Nowt,' he said. 'She'd have to put up wi' it.' He'd grinned. 'I'll bet you 'price of a young heifer I'll find a wife afore you do.'

Fletcher hadn't actually agreed to the wager and had turned away with a shrug. He generally avoided confrontation, but Noah thought he'd think about it and turn it over in his mind and decide he didn't want to be beaten by his younger brother.

Tonight Noah rode straight into Hull's High Street, dismounted, and walked to the inn's stable yard. He looked about him. It was very dark and drizzling with rain, and late, about half past ten, yet there were plenty of people about. The doors of the Corn Exchange were open and groups of men were standing on the steps so he guessed there had been a meeting in progress.

There were also some youths hanging about under a street lamp that cast a sickly yellow glow on them; he eyed them up and down, ignored the ones who were making the most noise and pinpointed one who was standing quietly, not joining in with their frivolity but listening as an outsider might.

Noah stared hard at him until the youth, as if aware of his attention, turned his head towards him. Noah indicated with his thumb that he should come over.

'Yes, sir?' the lad mumbled. He looked about twelve or thirteen.

'Are you honest?'

'Yes, sir, as much as most.'

'Is that a yes or a no?' Noah hissed.

The youth took a step back. 'Erm, it's a yes.'

'I need somebody to look after this hoss while I attend a bit o' business. Can you do that?'

'Oh, yeh!' The lad brightened up considerably. 'I can do that all right. That's why we've been hanging about here, to see if any of 'gents wanted any errands running, onny they didn't cos they're all on their way home.'

'This is a valuable hoss.' Noah stared down at him and the youth nodded. 'If owt should happen to him . . .' He bent down so that he was breathing into the boy's face. 'I'll give you a penny now and another two when I come back, and if you're not here or 'hoss has gone, I'll find you and slit your throat. Do you hear me?'

The lad's mouth dropped open, and then he closed it again. He glanced towards the crowd of lads, who were beginning to split up and wander off. He swallowed and licked his lips.

'Yeh,' he whispered. 'He'll be all right wi' me. You can depend on it, mister. I'll wait here in 'yard.'

Noah dropped the penny into the boy's palm and then made a slitting gesture across his own throat and a jabbing

17

gesture with his forefinger. The boy took the reins and led the horse to the yard, away from the eyes of his mates.

Noah hitched up his coat collar and took off his hat, ran his fingers through his long dark hair and pushed open the hostelry door.

# CHAPTER TWO

The girl was behind the bar counter washing glasses; the landlord stood with one foot on a chair, talking to a customer. He put his foot down as Noah came in and wiped his hands on his apron.

'Evening, squire,' he said and Noah nodded.

'Pint of your best,' he told the girl, and she pulled him a full tankard of ale and placed it in front of him. She looked tense, a creased and pinched look about her mouth, but she thanked him civilly when he pulled coins from his pocket and scattered them on the counter.

'Any food tonight?' she asked, and he was flattered that she remembered.

'No thanks. I've had my supper.' He'd eaten before leaving home and had got up abruptly from the table when he'd finished; he'd put on his coat and left the house without saying where he was going, which he knew would annoy his mother.

The girl nodded vaguely and looked across at the landlord, who came across to the counter. 'Go on then,' he grunted. 'Get off, but you stay longer tomorrow to mek up for it.'

'Thank you,' she murmured. 'I will.'

She disappeared through a door behind the counter, re-appearing a minute later wearing a shawl wrapped round her head and shoulders.

Noah drained the tankard and wiped his hand across his

mouth. 'Thanks,' he muttered. 'G'night!' He walked towards the door before the girl did, so that it didn't look too obvious that he was leaving at the same time; but when she followed him he made a show of opening the door for her and saying good night again.

He didn't look back at her but noted which way she went, then hurried across the yard towards the youth still holding the reins.

'You wasn't long,' the boy said. 'I thought you'd be ages yet.'

'Long enough,' Noah muttered. 'Here!' He handed him two more coins.

'Thanks, mister! Any time. I'm allus about round here.'

'Aye, well, I don't know if I'll be this way again.' But on the other hand, he thought, I might be. It might take a bit longer than I expected to capture fair lady.

She had cut down the alley which led into Lowgate, a much wider street than the High Street, and he guessed that a woman would probably feel safer there amongst the traffic and people than on the darker High Street, so close to the river and its narrow lanes.

He saw her a few yards in front of him, walking quite swiftly and purposefully. He led the horse after her, and when he was close enough for her to hear the clatter of hooves she turned her head as if to check who was behind her.

'Hello!' he called. 'I'm not following you. I'm on my way home.'

She turned her head again, but nervously, he thought, and he spoke again.

'Didn't I just see you in 'George and Dragon?'

She turned fully this time, pausing in her stride. 'You might have done.'

'Am I on 'right road to get out of town? I don't know Hull very well.'

She paused again and answered. 'It depends where you want to be.'

'Near Brough. It's alongside 'Humber.'

20

'Sorry, I don't know. Is it east or west? You can meet up with 'toll road if you're going out to Holderness, or when you get to Blackfriargate you can go west on 'road to Hessle.'

'That'll do me then,' he said cheerfully. 'Do you mind my walking alongside you?'

'No,' she said. 'I'd be glad of it. It'll mebbe stop me getting pestered by drunks.'

'Ah, yeh,' he said. 'I suppose you'll get that in a town. Where I live it's very quiet; women can walk safely at night.'

'Can they? That must be a relief to them.'

'Have you far to go?'

'Blackfriargate,' she said. 'One of 'streets off it.' She glanced at him. 'Just past King Billy.'

He shook his head. 'You've lost me.'

'King Billy's statue! It's at 'bottom of Market Place. You can see it from here, look. It shines cos it's made of gold. We live behind 'Shambles. You'd know where you were by 'stink of it, specially in summer.'

*We*, he considered. So who else lives there? 'You must be near to 'river then, are you?'

She sighed. 'Yes. Houses get flooded at least twice a year. It's where 'River Hull flows into 'Humber. Confluence, I think it's called.'

She's not stupid then, he thought. 'Did you finish early at 'inn tonight?' he asked.

'Aye, I did. My ma's sick. I didn't like to leave her on her own, but I need my wages. I expect 'landlord'll dock them, though. He'll not pay me for when I'm not there.'

His spirits dropped. Damn and blast, he swore beneath his breath. 'What's up wi' your ma?'

'Don't know. She's been sick for weeks; can't hold any food down. We can't afford 'doctor.' She sighed again. 'Don't know what I'll do if she doesn't get any better.'

'Haven't you any relatives who can look after her while you're at work?'

She shook her head. 'Nobody. My father's dead. I'm onny

21

one left out of five bairns. Two of my brothers were lost at sea. My sister died when she was a babby and my eldest brother jiggered off to Australia or somewhere.'

'As an immigrant or a convict?' he joked.

'An immigrant,' she said seriously, not hearing his humour. 'About ten years ago. Not heard a word since. My ma's allus asking about him and I make up this tale that he's a farmer and will send for us when he's made his fortune.'

'What's his name?'

'Miles, same as mine. Leonard Miles. If you ever come across him, send him to see me, will you?' Her voice was bitter. 'I'd like to tell him a thing or two.'

'I will, Miss Miles. But what's your first name so that I can tell him his sister was asking about him?'

She laughed then. 'I reckon pigs will fly afore that happens.' She stopped at the corner of another street. 'But I'm Harriet. This is Blackfriargate, where I turn off. Thanks for walking me home.'

'I'll come wi' you,' he said. 'Tek you to your door.'

'There's no need,' she began, but he insisted and she didn't argue as he followed her, with the stallion trailing behind him.

He could smell the blood and guts from the butchers' shambles as they passed, just as she had said, and he could imagine the stench and the flies in the hot summer months.

'You must wish to get away from here,' he said. 'It's dark, too. How do you find your way about?'

'Lived here most of my life,' she said. 'Know it wi' my eyes shut.'

They went down one alley and then another cutting across it. There was another smell now, sweeter than that of the offal sweepings from the butchery.

'Malt,' she said, even though he hadn't asked. 'There's a malt kiln near here. I quite like 'smell of that.'

'Where are we?' he asked, thinking that if he didn't have the name, he'd never find the place again.

'Robson's Entry.' She turned into another narrow entry

packed close with terraced housing. A single lamp post stood at the entrance, shedding a dim light but illuminating the poverty. 'We're here. Third door along. Thank you,' she said again. 'I can't ask you in. We've onny got one room.'

'One room!' He was aghast. Even though his motives were not entirely innocent, he was stunned to think that anyone could live in such a place, cheek by jowl with their neighbours. 'Go and check if your ma's all right. I'll wait here in case you need any help.'

Harriet turned to look at him. She seemed astonished that anyone would care, and of course he didn't, at least not for the reasons that she might be thinking. 'There's nowt to be done even if I do need help,' she muttered. 'I told you, there's no money for a doctor.'

'Go on,' he said. 'Go and see.'

Her lips parted as she considered and he wondered what it would be like to kiss her. Bet not many men have done that, he thought, and yet I'd guess she's ripe for it.

She turned away again and opened the door, which wasn't locked. Nowt to steal, he thought.

He put his ear to the door, which she hadn't shut completely, and heard her voice murmuring, 'Ma, it's me, Harriet. Are you all right? Ma? Are you awake? I'll light a candle. Fire's gone out.'

He pressed his ear closer and then pushed the door a little wider and peered through the crack. It was pitch black inside and he couldn't make out any shapes; then he heard the rasp of a match and saw a short spark of light that instantly went out. She cursed softly and struck again. This time the flame caught and he saw her hand held to a candle stub. In a moment a flickering glow revealed a low bed, with Harriet bent over it.

'Ma,' she said again. 'Are you awake? Speak to me.'

No sound came from the bed, and he held his breath. He hadn't gone through all this palaver for the old woman to be sleeping soundly when he'd hoped she'd snuffed it.

He moved away from the door as Harriet straightened her back and turned. 'Are you still there?' she whispered.

'Yeh. Is she all right?'

'I don't know. I'm worried.' She came to the door and put her hand to her throat. 'I don't know what to do.' She gave a little huff of breath. 'I don't even know your name; why am I bothering you? You don't know us from Adam or Eve.'

There was a catch in her voice and he heard her fear.

'Noah Tuke,' he said. 'Do you want me to come in? I'll tie 'hoss up.'

'Would you? I've no right to ask, but . . .'

He hooked the reins over an iron shoe scraper near the doorstep and stepped inside. 'Have you no more light than this?'

'Just another candle stub,' she said. 'I have to be sparing wi' them.'

He leaned over the bed and saw the woman; her face was wrinkled and sickly yellow, but he thought he saw a slight rise and fall of the blanket that covered her.

'Don't you have a neighbour or anybody, another woman, who'd come and tek a look at her?'

'There's a woman my ma used to know who lives in 'next entry. Ma and her used to stop and talk, in 'days when Ma went out, but I've not seen her in months. Everybody else is like us, living hand to mouth, wi' no time even to stop 'n' pass 'time of day.'

'Why don't you go and see if she'll come? You can't stop here on your own and it wouldn't be right for me to offer.' He made it sound regrettable that he couldn't, because he was a male. 'But I'll stop wi' your ma till you get back.'

Her voice broke as she said, 'I've allus been scared that summat like this might happen. Are you sure you don't mind? I don't like to – but thank you. I'll not be long. No more'n five minutes unless she's in bed, which she might be. It's late.'

He nodded. 'Tek your time. If she can't come, then we'll think o' summat else. It's cold in here. Shall I try to light 'fire?'

She shook her head as she went to the door. 'No wood, no coal, to light it.'

What a life, he thought. Purgatory. She'd be well out of it. He gazed down at the woman in the bed, her head on a thin pillow. They both would. He saw a flicker of eyelids and, startled, he looked closer. The eyes blinked and her mouth moved. She licked her lips and tried to speak.

'Harriet?' It was a mere croak. Her eyes opened wider; they had probably been grey or blue once, but were now glazed, filmy and opaque. 'Who are you?' He could just make out her words. 'Are you . . . a doctor?'

'Yes,' he said. 'I've come to mek you better.'

She gave a shallow sigh and nodded her thanks.

He put his hand beneath her head and gently pulled out the pillow. 'I heard that son o' yours in Australia is doing very nicely, Mrs Miles; Leonard, isn't it? Now, I want you to close your eyes for me.'

She obeyed, giving a little smile, which he covered with the pillow and gently but firmly pressed with both his hands.

# CHAPTER THREE

Harriet sat by her mother's bed, still unable to believe that she had gone so swiftly from this world into the next. It had been three nights since the stranger had walked home with her and offered to wait whilst she ran for a neighbour. He'd been sitting by the hearth when she returned with Mrs Chambers, who had taken one look at her mother and pronounced her dead. He'd risen from the chair and exclaimed, 'No! I swear I heard her make a sound not five minutes since.'

Mrs Chambers had nodded solemnly. 'Her last words, sir, bidding farewell to this life on earth.'

Harriet had moaned, and Mrs Chambers had patted her hand and said her mother was ill no more. 'Not that that's much comfort to you now, m'dear, but what sort o' life was left for her?'

Noah something or other had risen to leave. 'I'm sorry,' he said. 'Sorry to have met you under such circumstances. Is there owt I can do?'

There wasn't, but she thanked him for asking. Mrs Chambers said she would see to everything, and when Harriet had returned from showing the stranger back to the Market Place the woman had smoothed her mother's hair and folded her hands across her chest and she looked very peaceful, less strained than she had done in the last few weeks.

A doctor had called the following morning to write a death certificate and Harriet had taken the rest of the day off work. She sat in the chair all day and night with a blanket wrapped round her, not even bothering to go out and search for kindling to light a fire.

She had gone back to the mill the next day to find that her hours had been cut again, and when she told the foreman she hadn't come in the day before because her mother had just died, he simply said that if she was living alone she wouldn't need as much money as women with families. Then she had returned to the George that evening to find that the landlord had found someone else to take her place. Again she explained, pleading that she needed the money, but he merely shrugged and said, 'Life's a bitch whichever way you look at it, but I dare say you'll survive.'

Survival, she thought, that's all it is; there's nothing else in life, no hope, no money. How do I pay 'rent on less wages? They were already in arrears. She had been buying extra milk and bread to try to build up her mother's strength, but the poor woman had not been able to keep it down. After tomorrow, she thought. After the burial tomorrow, perhaps then I'll be able to think straight.

Harriet had been to Holy Trinity church to ask about interment, praying that her mother could be buried in the churchyard rather than be taken elsewhere. She had heard that the churchyard was full and the vicar had confirmed it, but he was a kind man and knew full well the situation of many of his parishioners.

'We're not churchgoers, sir,' Harriet had told him. 'But my mother was a good woman, a true Christian in every sense. She would never have passed by on the other side of anyone in need.'

He'd nodded sympathetically and told her that he would find a place for her mother and there would be no charge, if she could raise a penny for a candle to light her mother's way to heaven.

She'd done that, taking it from the wages the landlord had given her for the night her mother died, when she had left early. He hadn't knocked anything off and she'd thanked him, asking him to think of her if the job became vacant again. He'd hesitated and then bent to murmur, 'It's 'missis, you see, Harriet. She's a bit jealous of how 'customers like you; she's noticed that 'men like a bit o' banter and you don't seem to mind, even though you keep 'em at arms' length.'

Harriet was astonished. Men were men and they tried to get their hands up the skirts of most women, but not of course the one that the landlord's wife was wearing. It's not that I was in 'front row when looks were given out, she considered. I'm no beauty; quite plain, really. My hair is of no special colour – mouse, mebbe – my skin's pale and my mouth's too wide, though my teeth are good. What's up wi' woman that she should be jealous o' me?

There were no other mourners when she and Mrs Chambers stood in the churchyard over a shallow grave whilst the vicar uttered a few words, which gave her little comfort. He had asked her when she first went to see him if there were any other family members buried in the churchyard. She had shaken her head, and then remembered her baby sister. Surprisingly, he had found the details and the approximate site – for there was no headstone – and so Maria Miles was laid to rest with her long-departed daughter.

'They'll be company for each other,' Mrs Chambers offered encouragingly as they walked back down the Market Place, but Harriet's forehead creased as she considered how that could be.

Realizing that she would have to find more work, she trawled around the public houses the following day and into the evening. She'd washed her hair beneath the communal pump, clenching her teeth as the cold water froze her scalp, and then rubbed it dry on a piece of old towelling and fastened it in the nape of her neck. Then before she opened any alehouse doors she pinched her cheeks to give them colour, lifted her chin and tried to look bright eyed as she asked if there was any work available.

There was none until the last place she tried before returning home; it was a miserable hovel, one room only, not much more than the size of her own, with one table and ale drawn from a cask. It was kept by an unkempt man who leered at her, and said he might be able to offer her one night a week. She babbled that she would consider it and backed away. As she stepped into the street she almost crashed into someone passing by.

'Hello,' he said. 'I've been looking for you.'

'Who is it?' She stepped back into the doorway, but the space was confined and she felt trapped.

'Noah Tuke,' he said. 'We met—'

'Oh!' She breathed out. She could barely see his face, it was so dark in this corner. 'Sorry, I couldn't see. It's – well, there are all sorts of odd coves about. You have to be careful.'

'I went looking for you at 'George and Dragon,' he said. 'I was wondering how you've been since your mother died. Landlord's wife said you'd left.'

'I didn't leave,' she said indignantly. 'I was given 'sack! Landlord's wife didn't care for me, it seems.'

'So are you working here?' He looked curiously at the planked door and grimy window.

'Not if I can help it.' Her voice was bitter. 'But sometimes beggars can't be choosers.'

'Do you fancy summat to eat?' he asked. 'I've missed my supper again. I'd have had it at 'George but 'beef was curling at 'edges and I didn't like 'look of it!'

Harriet hesitated. What did he want in return for a bit of bread and meat? She was hungry, but not that hungry. It was a long time since she'd been with a man and then it had been because of fondness and not because she was down on her luck as she was now.

'What do you say?' he asked. 'There's no ulterior motive.

29

Well . . .' It was his turn to hesitate and he stared right at her. 'There might be, but I'll discuss it wi' you first.'

'Discuss what?' she asked sharply. 'I'm not on 'game, nor ever will be.'

His reply was equally brusque. 'That's not what I'm asking. But there's summat which might be beneficial to us both. But I'm not saying owt down here in this miserable alley. Will you come an' have summat to eat and we can talk face to face?'

That was fair enough, she thought. There'd be no harm in that, and if I don't like what he's proposing then at least I'll have had my supper.

She led him towards a tavern off the Market Place where reputedly the food was wholesome and the ale good. She ordered a meat pie and a glass of ale and he did the same. The smells coming from the kitchen were delicious and she tried not to wolf the food down when it came; the meat was tender, the crust crumbly and the gravy thick. It was served with mashed potatoes and cabbage and she couldn't remember ever having eaten so well.

Noah Tuke eyed her when she was finished and said, 'Do you fancy some apple pie? You seemed hungry.'

She swallowed a small belch and patted her chest. 'I haven't been able to eat since my ma died.' She refrained from telling him she had barely enough money to buy food. 'I didn't have 'heart to cook or eat whilst she was still in 'room wi' me.'

He suppressed a shudder. 'Is 'funeral over wi' now?'

'Yes,' she said softly. 'It's done. So what did you want to talk about?' Better get it over with, she thought.

He turned first to the landlord and ordered two portions of apple pie and two more glasses of ale, and she considered that money or lack of it didn't seem to be a problem to him. Is he softening me up for some purpose?

He waited for the ale to be brought and put his elbows on the table. 'You'll think this odd,' he began. 'And I suppose it is, and you don't know me, but then neither do I know you, so we're on equal footing in that respect. I'd guess that you're on your uppers. Any woman who has to work at night must be. I suppose you work during 'day as well?'

She nodded reluctantly. 'At one of 'flour mills.' She did not tell him that she'd been put on short time.

'An' I gather that you've no husband or bairns either?'

'What's this leading up to?' she broke in. 'Why would you be wanting my history?'

'Cos I want everything straight in my head before I say owt. Your ma's just died, your brother's gone abroad, and you've got nobody. Am I right?'

Her eyes filled with tears and her mouth trembled just as a serving girl put the apple pie in front of them. Harriet stared down at it and knew that no matter how she wanted it, it would choke her if she tried to eat.

She blinked rapidly but couldn't speak and took a sip of ale. She swallowed and then muttered, 'Ma was all I had. I'm devastated that she died so quickly.' She took a deep sobbing breath. 'I don't know what to do.'

His mouth twitched and he looked away, and then picked up his spoon and began to eat.

'Well, this is what I'm proposing,' he said, ignoring her tears. 'I'm unmarried. I told you already that I live further up 'river. I'm a farmer and I'm seeking a wife. I reckon that you'll do well enough. What do you say?'

# CHAPTER FOUR

Harriet gazed at him without speaking. He wasn't exactly handsome; he was of average height and sturdily built with a straight back, a long nose and a firm bristly chin, and his hair was black, which she thought made him look foreign. He wasn't smiling, but had an intent expression in his dark eyes. Looks don't matter when choosing a mate, she thought. Kindness and generosity of spirit were more important in her opinion, but he hadn't mentioned either of those things. It would seem to be a matter of requirement only.

'Why me?' she asked. 'You don't know me. I might be a scold or a harridan.'

'You might be, and I might be a rogue. We'd have to tek a chance on that.' But then he smiled as he looked back at her. 'But I don't think you are. I'd know. I'd be able to tell.'

'What would be 'advantage for me? I'd want to be married in church; mek it proper and binding.'

'Well, I don't hold wi' all that mumbo jumbo, but yes, I'd want it legal and binding, and as for 'advantage to you – you'd have a roof over your head and food on 'table; you'd have to work on 'farm, feeding 'hens an' that, but nowt you couldn't cope wi'. You look strong enough. I wouldn't want a weakling. But more important . . .' His voice dropped. 'I'd want bairns – sons to carry on 'farm.'

'How long have you been looking for a wife?' she asked.

He looked away. 'For a bit. Not seen anybody else that took my eye.'

In spite of herself she was flattered. He wasn't the kind of man she was attracted to, but there were few men who would want a woman of twenty-three, even though she was fit and healthy.

'I'd have to think about it,' she murmured. 'It's a bolt out of 'blue. It's not every day somebody asks me to marry them.'

He shook his head. 'I need to know. What are your options, Harriet? Have you got a line o' suitors waiting? Have you got 'chance o' better work?' He leaned towards her and whispered softly, 'Have you got enough money to pay your rent for that hovel you're living in?'

She hadn't got any of those things, she reflected, her spirits plummeting. 'When do you need to know?'

'Tonight. I don't want to mek any more journeys to this town except for one to fetch you home. Mek arrangements for 'banns to be read, if you agree; it's got to be in your parish.'

'What will 'vicar think?' she murmured. 'I've onny just buried my mother!'

'I shouldn't think he'd care less. An' it's not his business what you do. All he should be concerned wi' is that it's been done right an' proper.'

Harriet put her hand over her mouth. 'I've no clothes to wear for a wedding. Nothing to bring to a marriage.'

'What sort of excuse is that?' he asked. 'If you marry me I'll be responsible for providing for you.'

She gazed at him. What a relief that would be, she thought. No more worrying about where the next crust was coming from. She looked down at the apple pie. The sauce was beginning to cool and form a skin.

'If you agree, I'll give you some money to buy a decent frock or skirt or whatever you need.'

'You'd trust me wi' money? What if I spent it and then disappeared?'

'I'd not give you that much to mek it worthwhile; an' if

you did I'd come an' find you.' He gave a lopsided grin but somehow she didn't think he was joking. He didn't seem the humorous sort.

She looked nervously about her as if the room, the serving girl and the few customers could help her make a decision. Rain was pattering on the windows; it would be cold at home without a fire.

'All right,' she said impulsively. 'I will. I'll see 'vicar tomorrow. He can read 'first banns on Sunday.'

'Good.' He rose from the table and called to the landlord for the bill and Harriet looked at the apple pie again.

'Can I tek this home wi' me?' she asked. 'I can't eat it now. I'll bring 'dish back tomorrow.'

The landlord glanced at her dubiously and then at Noah standing over him. 'Aye,' he said. 'All right, tek it. I'll put a paper bag over it.'

Harriet watched as Noah paid him and left a small tip. It wasn't generous; it was extra but wouldn't cover the price of a pie dish if she didn't return it.

Noah put his arm on her shoulder as he ushered her out. 'I'll set you home,' he said. 'I've left 'hoss at 'George.'

'There's no need,' she began, but he interrupted.

'There's every need,' he said. 'I need to keep you safe, don't I? You know what you have to do? Go an' see your vicar, give notice to 'landlord that you're leaving.' He glanced at her. 'Or are you in arrears?'

'Yes,' she said weakly. 'Three weeks. I'll have to pay him if I give notice.'

He sniffed. 'In that case don't bother telling him. Damned landlords, they mek plenty out o' folks. Just sell whatever stuff you've got.'

'I might bring one or two things,' she said.

'Aye, trinkets mebbe, nowt else. We don't need furniture.'

It began to rain heavily as they walked towards Blackfriargate and Harriet hoped that the alley wasn't flooded. She pulled her shawl over her head, trying at the same time not to drop the pie dish. I'll have that for my breakfast, she thought, before I go to 'church.

Noah was talking. 'So, I'll be back in just over three weeks. Mek 'date on 'Monday after 'third reading of banns. Tell him. Tell him that's 'date you want, in late afternoon. About four. It'll be getting dark by then an' I'll have finished 'jobs on 'farm.'

'I expect you have a busy life?' she offered. 'Allus summat to do.'

'Aye, that's right. This is your entry, isn't it?'

'Yes,' she said. 'Well done. Not everybody can find their way.' She opened her door and he followed her inside.

'I know my way about,' he said. 'Here, give us that.' He took the dish from her and put it on the table. 'Have you got a light?'

'Yes,' she said nervously, slightly afraid now that she was alone with him. She struck a match and lit the stub of candle, shorter now than it had been when he came last time. She'd tried to be sparing with it, but it wouldn't last the night. 'I'm sorry there's no fire.'

He delved into his coat and brought out his pocket book. 'How much will you need for clothes?' he asked. 'And a bucket o' coal?'

'I don't know. I don't ever recall buying any. And coal?' She shrugged. 'I can manage without if I'm leaving in three weeks.'

'I'll give you five shillings. You'll have to pay 'parson for 'banns, I expect.'

'Will I?'

'He's got to live, hasn't he, though I expect he'll have a private income. Barter him down if you can. Buy yourself some food. Don't want you all skin and bone when I tek you home. And get a candle.'

She gave a wan smile; was he being kind or just practical?

He put five shillings on the table. 'That should be enough.'

Harriet closed her eyes. She'd never had so much money;

she must surely be doing the right thing in agreeing to marry him. Then she gasped as he turned and put his arms about her waist.

'A little kiss to seal our commitment, hey?'

She held her face up to his; it was to be expected, she supposed. A pact, and he'd want to know she wasn't a prude.

He kissed her roughly, his stubble scratching her face, and then he lifted her chin and kissed her full on the mouth, his lips covering hers so that she could taste his ale and the meal they had shared.

'You're a fine-lookin' woman, Harriet. How is it that nobody's snatched you up afore? Not strait-laced and frigid, are you?'

'No.' She gave a nervous laugh. 'But neither am I wanton.'

He pulled her closer then swung her round so that she had her back to the wall. 'You can be wanton wi' me, now that we've agreed to marriage.' He pulled up her skirts and spoke softly in her ear. 'I saw a feller at 'George trying to put his hand up your skirt and you fended him off. Let them know that you weren't available to just anybody, didn't you?'

'Yes.' She tried to push him away. 'And – and I'd rather wait till—'

'No,' he said. 'We don't have to wait for 'marriage bed. Not now.'

She gasped as his hands roamed and squeezed her flesh – her buttocks, her belly, her breasts – and then he held her with one firm hand as he unbuttoned his breeches.

'Please don't,' she pleaded. 'I'd want it to be special on our wedding day.'

'Poppycock,' he muttered. 'Anyway, I'm all fired up. I can't stop now. Come on, let's find out what's in front of us.'

She almost screamed as he tore violently into her. It had been five years since she had been with Charlie, before he was lost at sea, and this man was nothing like him. He was rough and hasty, rigorous and unrelenting as he took her with no thought for her feelings or her pain.

He grunted as he finally pulled away from her. 'Phew,' he muttered. 'I was ready for that.'

Like being hungry and then eating your fill, she thought bitterly as he buttoned himself up. Dear God, what have I done?

He took his leave then, saying he had to walk back to collect his horse from where he had left it at the George and Dragon, but she barely listened. All she was aware of was her own heart racing and the tremble in her legs.

'I'll see you in three weeks,' he repeated. 'Remember what you have to do? Be ready. I shan't want to hang about.' He paused for a minute, his hand on the door sneck. 'We'll need witnesses, won't we?'

Harriet shook her head. She didn't know.

'Aw, we'll pull somebody in from 'street,' he said brusquely. 'Give 'em a tanner for a drink, that should satisfy 'em.' He looked closely at her. 'I'll come here to fetch you and we'll go to church together. I'll bring 'trap.'

She nodded. She seemed to have lost the ability to speak.

'Cat got your tongue?' He leaned towards her and lifted her skirt again, squeezing her buttocks. 'You've got a fine behind, Harriet. Nice and rounded, better than I'd hoped for.'

He dropped his hand, opened the door and was gone out into the darkness and the pelting rain.

# CHAPTER FIVE

Harriet wept all night. She wept because of her stupidity, she wept for her mother, and she wept for the plight that she and all women like her were in.

Towards dawn she dropped into an uneasy sleep and was woken later by someone banging on her door. She rolled out of bed and was astonished to realize that she was still wearing her skirt and blouse from the previous day. She must have dropped on to the bed just as she was and curled up in her distress.

'Who is it?' she called.

'Rent!'

She recognized the gruff voice of the landlord's agent and scanned the room. The money left by Noah Tuke was still on the table. 'Just a minute,' she shouted. 'I'm not dressed.'

She scooped up the money, bar sixpence, and put it in her skirt pocket, then ran her fingers through her tousled hair and went to the door.

'All right for some folk,' he commented. 'Nowt to do but stop in bed all day.'

'Tell you what. I'll swap you,' she said. 'You can have my non-existent job o' work and I'll have yours, collecting money from folks who have nowt.'

He opened up the rent book. 'It's not my money.' He raised

his eyes. 'Have you got 'rent? You're in arrears, like everybody else.'

Harriet opened her palm. 'Sixpence,' she said. 'That's all I've got. Either you have it or 'butcher does for some stinking meat.'

He gave a deep sigh and took it and dropped it into his battered leather bag, then glanced up at her again. 'Where's your ma? She's generally here to mek excuses.'

Harriet bit her lip. 'Dead,' she muttered. 'Buried her last week.'

'Oh, sorry. Poor old lass. Pauper funeral, was it?'

Harriet hesitated; she couldn't lie over such a thing. She shook her head. 'Vicar found a place for her in 'churchyard wi' my sister, but he didn't charge, except for a penny to light a candle.'

He nodded sympathetically. 'She's happen better off where she is. Not much future for such as us, is there?'

Harriet felt even more dispirited at his dismal words, but she was surprised and grateful when he put his hand back in the bag and brought out a penny.

'It'll not be missed,' he said, handing it to her with a sly wink. 'I can easy lose a penny.'

'Thank you,' she said. 'I'll do my best for next week.'

'Aye,' he replied. 'Don't worry about it, I might not call. It's no skin off my nose.'

She closed the door and went back to sit on the bed. He's right, she thought. There isn't any future. No work, no rent, no roof. So what do I do? Although Noah Tuke had left her smarting both physically and mentally, she realized that he had offered her a lifeline, an opportunity to climb out of the pit she was in.

I'll ask for 'banns to be read, she decided, even if I don't go through with 'marriage. I've every right to change my mind at 'last minute if I want to. But something told her that if she did default on her promise, then he'd come looking for her to demand his money back. And by then, she considered, it might well be spent.

As she jangled the money in her pocket, she thought that it would be nice to buy a new set of clothes. Well, not exactly new, she amended; there wouldn't be enough for brand new, but good second hand.

She ran through her options. Try for work once more, do the usual rounds of begging for employment in the inns and taverns for night time, and maybe, she thought, I could try for some other work during the day. I'll go to some of the other mills. I've plenty of experience and they'd be pleased to have me. But she knew she was fooling herself; there were others just like her, and they were all chasing the same jobs.

Or I marry him as I promised, in spite of his insufferable behaviour. What sort of man is he to act like that with a woman he's just met, even if he has asked her to marry him? Is he telling me the truth about himself? He obviously has some money, or how could he afford to shell out for supper and ale and give me money to buy clothes and pay for 'banns to be read? But his coat and breeches were nothing special; mebbe he's been saving up for this, mebbe he just decided that 'time had come to look for a wife. He must need somebody to help him on his farm.

She hugged her arms around herself. It's freezing in here. I wonder what sort of farmhouse he lives in? She allowed herself the luxury of imagining a proper brick house in the middle of the country, with chickens at the door and their own cow for milk and a blazing fire in the kitchen grate. But how has he been managing until now? Who's cooked his dinner, and done his washing? He never mentioned a family. Has his ma died, just like mine?

But then, with a jolt, she thought of something else. He could have made her pregnant.

That decided her. She ate the remainder of the apple pie, washed, combed her hair and went out, dropping off the pie dish and then heading towards the church to ask the vicar about the banns.

She approached him nervously and told him in a quavering voice that she was going to be married. He frowned. 'Were you not here for a burial service last week?'

'I was, sir,' she said, 'and now I need 'marriage banns proclaiming or whatever it is has to be done.'

'Rather soon after your mother's death, isn't it?' His voice was disapproving. 'No time for grieving?'

'I'll grieve for 'rest o' my life sir,' she said. 'But I've been offered a chance and I'm going to tek it.' She took in his grim expression. 'It's either marriage or 'workhouse. I've been put on short time at 'mill, I owe rent arrears and I've lost my job at 'alehouse. I could go on 'streets, I suppose,' she said resentfully, 'that's another option. Would it be better to sell my body to several men rather than just one? You tell me, sir. I'm sure you know best.'

He cleared his throat and looked away. 'I'll pray for you,' he murmured, 'and read the banns on Sunday.'

Harriet told him when they wanted the marriage ceremony, adding that as Noah was a farmer it was the only time he could manage; when the vicar asked for her future husband's name, age and place of residence, she told him as much as she knew. Not knowing how old he was, she made up Noah's date of birth, guessing at about twenty-five or -six.

She blew out her cheeks as she left the church, glad the ordeal was over, and as she crossed over to the Market Place she saw a woman she knew from the mill.

'Nancy!' she called. 'Aren't you at work?'

The woman came towards her. 'I've been put on short time, like you. I'm out looking for another job, though God knows how I'll manage wi' two bairns at home.'

'I'm getting married,' Harriet blurted out. 'I've had an offer.'

Nancy's mouth dropped open. 'You must be mad! You'll be in 'family way afore you can blink an eye. Don't,' she urged. 'At least you've onny yourself to look out for.' She heaved a sigh.

'I was allus envious o' you. Just you and your ma, no houseful o' bairns wanting feeding and clothing or a man under your feet all day.'

'Ma's gone,' Harriet felt tears gathering, 'so there's just me now, and it's a lonely life, especially wi' no money.'

'Who is he?' Nancy asked curiously. 'From round here, is he?'

'No.' Harriet shook her head. 'I barely know him. He's from out o' town – a farmer, he says. Lives further up 'estuary.'

'Ah!' Nancy appeared to reconsider. 'Well, I dunno then. You'll have food on 'table, I expect?'

Harriet nodded miserably. 'Hope so. He's given me some money to buy a skirt for 'wedding. Will you be a witness, Nancy?' she asked impulsively. 'He said we could pull somebody in from 'street, but I'd rather it was somebody I knew.'

Nancy licked her lips. 'I've nowt to wear, except what I've got on now.'

'Doesn't matter. Will you come? If you're not working, that is.' She gave her the day and the time and Nancy said she would be there if she could, and then Harriet asked her to come with her now to help choose something suitable to wear.

'Yeh,' she said. 'I'd like to do that, an' I reckon if he's given you money to buy summat for yourself, then he must be all right. There's not many men'd give money to a woman to spend on herself and not on food or rent.'

'Do you think so?' Harriet asked, wanting reassurance.

'I do!' Nancy said emphatically. 'I reckon you've done all right for yourself, Harriet. Wait till I tell 'other lasses when I see 'em. They'll be that jealous.'

They toured the many second-hand clothes shops in the back streets, looking for something clean and serviceable. Harriet thought that if she was to live in the country she wouldn't need anything frivolous, even though she sighed over a green satin skirt. Eventually they found a grey skirt with a circle of black velvet ribbon two inches above the hem, and priced at one shilling. Nancy declared it would be eminently serviceable, and suitable as a mourning garment too.

In another shop Harriet spotted a white cotton blouse and a short grey buttoned jacket and managed to beat the shop-keeper down to a shilling for the two.

'My boots will have to do,' she said, as they came out of the shop. 'I'd rather spend a copper at 'bath house; that would be a treat, wouldn't it?'

'Oh, aye, it would,' Nancy agreed. 'I can't help but think you're doing 'right thing, Harriet.'

Harriet pushed to the back of her mind the fact that she wasn't as sure as Nancy, but thought that she might as well enjoy the frivolity of a smart set of clothes and a hot bath before she took the final step towards marriage with an un-known man; and feeling generous she put her hand into her skirt pocket and brought out the penny the rent man had given her and handed it to Nancy.

'Go an' buy your bairns a penny loaf,' she said. 'You've bucked me up no end.'

'Oh, thanks, Harriet,' Nancy said gratefully. 'I'll see you at 'church door then? In three weeks' time.'

# CHAPTER SIX

By the day of her wedding, Harriet had sold the few belongings that she would no longer need in her new life. The table had gone, and a wooden cupboard containing her mother's few pieces of crockery and pans. She had kept one cracked cup, a single chair and her mattress, but sold the metal frame and springs of the bed.

She put her old skirt, her better skirt, a shawl, and a cotton blouse into a bag. Don't want to mess up these new ones, she thought, looking down with some satisfaction at the grey skirt. Not if I'm feeding chickens or collecting eggs. In spite of her fears she felt a frisson of excitement as she anticipated what might be in front of her.

At half past three, she washed her hands and brushed her hair, put her brush and comb into the bag and sat on the chair to wait. Fifteen minutes later she jumped as the door was sharply rapped. Cautiously, she opened it. He was here.

He stepped inside. 'Are you ready? I've got 'cart out in 'street.'

'Y-yes,' she said nervously. 'Will we be coming back here?'

'What for? There's nowt you need, is there?'

She glanced round. 'Just 'mattress and 'chair.'

'We don't need 'em,' he said brusquely. 'I told you we've plenty o' furniture.' Then he grinned. 'And you'll not need your mattress when you'll be sharing mine. Come on, let's be off. I haven't got all day to hang about.' And he walked out of the door into the entry.

Harriet took a deep huff of breath and glanced round the room. It wasn't much but it had been home and was filled with memories of her mother; but what else to do? She realized that without this marriage, she still wouldn't have been able to stay here. She locked the door and hid the key under a stone and turned away for the last time without looking back.

The horse wasn't the same one as he had ridden previously; this was an old nag which pulled a battered wooden cart. I thought he'd said a trap, Harriet mused as she glanced inside it and saw the muddy interior and gathered up her skirt to climb up to sit beside him.

At Holy Trinity church, Nancy was waiting at the gate. She had a friend with her, someone who also worked at the mill, whom Harriet knew only slightly.

'She offered to come as another witness when I told her,' Nancy whispered, glancing nervously in Noah's direction. 'I don't think she believed me.'

Harriet nodded. 'Can't believe it myself,' she murmured. 'Nancy, if you go to my house afterwards – you'll find 'key under a stone – you can have 'mattress and 'chair that I've left behind. Sell 'em if you don't want 'em.' She indicated with a toss of her head. '*He* says we won't need 'em.'

'Oh, thanks,' Nancy said gratefully. 'You're a pal. I'll get Jack to give me a hand. We can do wi' another mattress for 'bairns to sleep on. We're that squashed in our bed.'

Noah was marching towards the church door and looked impatiently back at Harriet. 'Are you coming or what?'

'I'm coming,' she said, adding under her breath, 'it's now or never.'

The ceremony didn't take long. The vicar seemed as anxious to get it over with and be rid of them as they were to finalize it. As they came out under a grey, darkening sky, Noah looked at the two witnesses, sighed, and put his hand in his pocket. He gave them sixpence each, but didn't speak to them. They both mumbled their thanks and Nancy glanced at Harriet, rolled her eyes and murmured, 'Good luck.'

Harriet was sure that she would need it. She climbed back into the cart, being careful not to catch her skirt on the rough wood, wrapped her shawl around her, for the weather was cold and damp, and hoped they wouldn't have to travel far.

'Where was it you said you lived?' she asked, as he pulled away. 'Brough, was it?'

'No, that's 'nearest town,' he said. 'Farm's further out, between Ellerker Sands an' Broomfleet, near 'river bank.'

'Does it flood?'

'Aye, sometimes. When 'tide's high. We've to dig out ditches regular. House is not so bad; we've dug ditches round it.'

*We?* Dare I ask?

'Who else is there?' she ventured. 'You keep saying *we*.'

'Me brother and me, we keep 'ditches clear. Da helps now and then.' He gave a grunt. 'When he's a mind to.'

'And – erm, where do they live?'

He turned and looked down at her. 'In 'same house. Where d'ya think?'

Harriet closed her eyes tightly. 'Three of you! Does that mean I've three men to look after, to clean and cook for? I wasn't expecting this.'

'What were you expecting? A life o' luxury? I told you that you'd have to help about 'farm. Anyway,' he shook the reins to urge the steed faster, but it didn't make any difference, she still plodded on at her own pace, 'Ma does all 'cooking. She won't want anybody else interfering in her kitchen.'

It gets worse, Harriet reckoned. 'What does she think about you marrying and bringing a wife home?'

He threw back his head and guffawed. 'Ha! They don't know yet. None of 'em know. It's a big surprise for all of 'em. Especially Fletcher.'

'Fletcher?'

'Aye, my brother. We're allus at daggers drawn, arguing about who does which jobs and who's more able on 'farm. So

I says to him, whoever's first to bring a wife home shall have more right to say what's what about 'farm, and if there are any sons, then they'll have 'farm when Da's gone.'

Harriet frowned. 'And did he agree? And what did your father say about it? Surely it's his decision.'

He gave a sly chuckle. 'Whether he agreed or not, it's done now, and as for Da, I never bothered to tell him, but it's not his decision in any case. That's for 'landowner to decide, but I reckoned if I had a houseful o' lads he'd want us to tek over.'

'I don't understand,' Harriet said desperately. 'You told me you were a farmer, with a farm. You never said owt about it belonging to somebody else.'

'I am a farmer,' he said sharply. 'But I never said I was made o' brass! Do you know how much money you'd need to own your own farm? We're tenants; have been for years. My father took it on from 'estate owner when he and Ma were married.'

'I didn't know how it worked,' she said in a small voice. 'But he's not likely to turn you out if you don't pay 'rent?'

'We have to mek it pay; we've to keep it in good order and mek sure 'buildings are looked after, things like that. But he never comes to look at it. As long as we pay him every quarter he's not bothered, though he sends his bailiff to tek a look now and then.'

'Bailiff!' she breathed. 'Oh no!'

'Farm bailiff,' he said. 'He collects 'rent and keeps an eye on things, not like 'bailiffs in town who come to tek your goods if you don't pay 'rent.'

They continued in silence for several miles. Harriet pondered that she might have made the biggest mistake of her life and wondered how she could get out of it. She even considered jumping down from the cart and making her way back to Hull, but thought better of it. I'm legally married and he could drag me back. Besides, we're out of town; it'd be a long walk back.

It's done, she thought as they travelled onward on roads she didn't know. For better for worse: isn't that what I've just promised? The life I'm going to might not be much better, but it could have been worse if I'd stopped in Hull. She sighed and looked about her but there was nothing much to see, only a few lights in distant windows; they must have been travelling for an hour and it was almost dark. She wondered how the horse could know its way home, as Noah was just sitting there holding the reins loosely, his hands between his knees, and whistling between his teeth.

'Are we nearly there?'

'Not yet; we're onny just past Hessle. Coming up to North Ferriby next.'

'It's just that – call o' nature, you know. I can't wait much longer.'

He tugged on the reins and drew up. 'Hop off then. Don't tek long.'

Harriet jumped down and peered about. There would be no one to see her, that was for sure, but where to crouch? She could see the outline of bushes and trees, but otherwise nothing. She took a few steps behind the cart, holding on to it so that she didn't fall, and decided that here would be as good as anywhere. She lifted her skirt and relieved herself, trying not to splash her new skirt.

'You'll not want to wear that fancy skirt when we get home,' he commented as she climbed back up beside him. 'I hope you've brought summat suitable for working in. And you'll need rubber boots as well. There's a good deal o' mud about.'

'I've onny got what I'm wearing,' she said. 'I hadn't any money left for another pair.'

He grunted. 'Mebbe Ma has an old pair that'll fit.'

'Noah,' she said, after a while. 'Look at 'sky!'

He looked up. 'Yeh, what about it?'

'All them stars – hundreds of them!'

The sky was black but sparkling with myriad stars, making her feel dizzy as she stretched her neck to gaze at them.

'Millions, more like,' he said. 'They're allus there, 'cept

when they're hidden by cloud.' He paused, and then muttered, 'That's onny thing that you can be sure of.'

They rattled along, sometimes on a bumpy uphill track, other times on a smoother road, and Harriet ached with sitting so long; she had never travelled so far in the whole of her life.

Presently Noah said. 'Coming up to Welton.'

'What does that mean?'

'One of 'villages. We've to tek a longer route when pulling 'cart. I came quicker riding across 'country tracks.'

Harriet sighed. It seemed as if they were travelling to the ends of the earth.

After what seemed an age he remarked, 'Won't be so long now. We're nearly at Ellerker. Just a few miles more.'

They passed through a small village with cottages set round a green area, and lamps lit in the windows, but when they left it the sky was so low and thick with cloud that she couldn't distinguish anything more and the stars had disappeared. The air smelt fresh yet damp, she thought, just like Robson's Entry, but there was a colder wind here that chilled her bones.

She had no way of knowing how long they had been travelling. She ached everywhere and had a thumping headache; then the mare gave a whinny and quickened her pace.

'Old gal knows we're nearly home,' Noah said briefly. 'She'll be after her supper.'

So am I, Harriet thought, and a warm fire and a bed; she reflected that she would even submit gladly to her husband as long as she could lie down and rest.

'It's salt marsh round here,' Noah informed her, 'so it's a bit damp. But you'll be used to that, I expect, seeing as you've allus lived close to 'river?'

She sighed. 'How can you farm if you're that close to 'estuary?'

'We're set back, well back, and providing 'Humber doesn't break its banks we can keep sheep and a few cattle; we just have

49

to keep 'ditches and drains clear and build up 'embankment to keep water out of bottom field.'

'I see,' she said, but she didn't. She knew nothing about the country, but a lot about floodwater and the damage it could do.

Presently the horse whinnied again and turned on to a rutted track. They racketed along, the cartwheels lurching and jerking in deep cracks, and Harriet held on, fearing the cart might turn over, but Noah just sat there letting the mare dictate the pace, and then with a grim deriding laugh exclaimed, 'Here we are. Marsh Farm. Now for it! Let's see what they've got to say.'

# CHAPTER SEVEN

Harriet stepped down from the cart and Noah unhitched the mare from the traces, letting her amble away across the yard towards what looked like a barn or a shed. The only light in the two-storey house showed through a small downstairs window.

Harriet shivered. She was nervous, but there was also a chill wind blowing from the estuary and she pulled her shawl closer to her.

Noah pushed open a planked door and told her to follow him. She stepped over a high threshold into a small lobby, which had coats hanging on hooks and stank of wet boots. He opened another door, and before Harriet could even glance inside a woman's voice complained sharply, 'And where've you been?'

He held the door for Harriet, and as she moved up beside him he answered, 'Getting wed, that's where I've been. This is my wife, Harriet.'

The woman who had spoken was sitting at a scrubbed wooden table bearing the remains of a meal. In the middle of the table was an oil lamp. Mrs Tuke, if it were she, might have been fifty or possibly younger; she was small and thin, with a lined face and grey hair beneath a pleated cotton bonnet. Sitting opposite her was a man who Harriet guessed was Noah's father. He had a shaggy white beard and was wearing

51

a felt hat and what seemed to be a long cotton shirt with wide sleeves. They both stared at her without speaking.

There was another man at the table and she thought this must be Noah's brother, Fletcher, and wondered at the choice of name. He pushed his chair back and stood up. He was taller and his long hair lighter in colour than his brother's, and he was frowning, though without the glowering expression that Noah wore.

'You got wed without bothering to tell us?' His voice was deep and angry.

Noah grimaced. 'Huh! Would you've come to 'wedding?'

'Doubt it,' his brother muttered. 'But mebbe we'd have liked to be told.'

'Well, I'm telling you now,' Noah jeered. 'Sit down, Harriet.'

There was only one spare chair at the table and Harriet, clenching her lips, pulled it out from the table and sat down. She felt the heat of the fire at her back, which was very comforting. She nodded at Noah's mother and then at his father.

'How d'ya do,' she muttered. 'I'm Harriet M-Miles – or at least I was until this afternoon. Now I'm Harriet Tuke.'

'How much did he pay you?'

Harriet turned to Fletcher Tuke, who had asked the question. 'What? Pay me – what for?'

He gazed at her, his grey-blue eyes piercing into hers. 'To wed him. You surely didn't marry him out of choice?'

Harriet put her chin up. 'It was my choice, yes. I wasn't forced into it, if that's what you mean.'

'It wasn't what I meant.' His voice was steely.

'Where'd you meet her?' This time it was the older man who asked the question of Noah. 'She's not from round here.'

'I'm from Hull,' Harriet responded. 'And I can answer for myself.'

Noah folded his arms across his chest. Harriet thought that he was rather enjoying the situation.

'Can you now?' It was the woman's turn for a question. 'And did he tell you that he was bringing you to live in *my* house?'

Harriet hesitated and licked her lips. She gazed at her mother-in-law's stony expression. 'No,' she admitted. 'He didn't. He didn't tell me owt except that he was a farmer and lived near 'estuary.'

Fletcher guffawed. 'A farmer! Is that what he said? Heaven help us.'

Noah's father pulled off his hat, revealing a thick thatch of white hair. His eyebrows, still black, bristled. 'She'll be after your money.'

Harriet began to laugh, a note of hysteria that she tried to quell as Mrs Tuke broke in, looking first at Harriet and then at Noah with cold grey eyes before saying, 'Why would she marry you?'

Noah didn't answer, but Fletcher broke in. 'Legal, is it? Not over 'broomstick?'

Noah flared up. 'Come outside an' say that.'

'I'm onny asking,' Fletcher claimed. 'But like Ma I'm wondering why she'd choose to marry you and come to live out here.'

Harriet was astonished. There was such an undercurrent of tension, and something more that she couldn't quite fathom, a dislike perhaps, as if not one of them cared a jot for the others. She thought of her mother and their relationship, how they had pulled together in adversity, each of them thinking always of the other's well-being, and the loss of her brought sudden tears to her eyes, but no one noticed her distress, except perhaps Fletcher, who glanced at her and gave a slight puzzled frown.

'Could I have a drink o' water, please?' she asked. 'If it's fresh.'

'If it's fresh!' Mrs Tuke exclaimed. 'We're not in 'habit o' drinking tainted water.'

'Mebbe you're not,' Harriet retaliated. 'But where I lived we had to be careful of what came out of 'pump.'

'Tea?' Fletcher interrupted. 'It's just brewed. Would you like a cup?'

Harriet nodded, noting Mrs Tuke's disapproving expression. 'Yes, please.'

Fletcher wove round the table to the open brick-built fireplace, which contained a four-bar iron range, the like of which Harriet had never seen before. There were racks and spits and a jack attached to the wall and a huge steaming kettle hanging from a hook. He reached up to a shelf in a wall cupboard and took down a cup, then lifted a big brown teapot from a side shelf of the range and placed both on the wooden table.

'Milk?' he offered and she nodded again.

'If you've any to spare.'

'Plenty,' he said. 'We've got our own cows. Didn't he tell you that either?'

Harriet shook her head and glanced at Noah who was still standing, chewing on a piece of loose skin on his thumb. He hadn't told her anything. 'Is there no supper?' he asked.

'You'll have to share yours wi' your *wife*,' his mother spat out. 'We weren't expecting company.'

'She's not company,' Noah roared, making Harriet jump. 'She's my wife and she's stopping!'

Harriet drank the tea. It was hot, but tasted strange, and she realized it was because of the milk. She was used to drinking weak tea on its own or with thin watered-down milk when they could afford to buy it. This was strong tea with globules of fat from the milk floating on top.

Mrs Tuke got up from the table and made a great show of clearing away dirty plates and bowls and stacking them noisily on a wooden draining board at the side of a shallow stone sink. Then she took down two bowls from the cupboard and put them on the table.

'Shift yourself, Mr Tuke,' she snapped. 'Mek room.'

A large iron pot was hanging from one of the hooks over the fire, and taking a thick cloth in her hand Mrs Tuke lifted it down on to a shelf and then filled the bowls with thick soup.

'Do you want bread?' She directed the question to Noah.

'Yeh,' he said, taking Fletcher's seat. 'We both do.'

Harriet ate under the scrutiny of Mr Tuke, who had moved his chair about three inches and sat with his elbows on the table, staring at her. Mrs Tuke poured hot water from the kettle into the sink, but Fletcher left the room and she heard the outside door slam.

The soup was thick with onion and potato and a little meat and tasted hot and nourishing.

'Thank you, Mrs Tuke,' Harriet said. 'This is very nice.'

Mrs Tuke turned round as if startled, or maybe, Harriet thought, she's not used to being thanked.

'How long have you known her?' Noah's father asked. 'Where did you meet? Not in a brothel, was it?'

Harriet took a breath. How dare he? But she noticed that Mrs Tuke stopped her rattling of the dishes and stood poised, waiting for an answer.

Noah pointed a warning finger at his father. 'Don't you dare say such a thing *ever*. Do you hear?'

The old man shrugged. 'Well, why else did you go to Hull? There was no reason to.'

'No. He needn't have gone to Hull if he'd wanted a brothel,' Mrs Tuke butted in. 'He could have found one closer to home.'

'That's enough from you, woman!' her husband shouted back at her. 'Just shut your mouth.'

Mrs Tuke put her hands back in the sink and said nothing more.

'I worked in one of 'hostelries in Hull,' Harriet told him. 'That's where I met Noah; and if you want to know about me, then ask me. I've got a tongue in my head and can speak for myself.'

She didn't mean to be rude and realized that this wasn't a good start to her new life, but she was riled by his asking Noah questions about her and completely ignoring her. She heard a suppressed scoff from Mrs Tuke and so did Mr Tuke, who glanced keenly at his wife's back, muttered something that sounded like 'Sharp an' all', and then shoved his chair back from the table and went to sit in an easy chair close to the fire. She saw then that it wasn't a shirt he was wearing but a smock over his breeches, the kind that she had seen in old books picturing country folk.

Noah gave a sly look at Harriet as if he approved of her comments; then he finished his soup and he too pushed his chair away and got up. 'I'll go an' mek sure we're secure,' he said. 'Then I reckon we'll go up.'

Mr Tuke stared straight at Harriet, then, teasing his beard, gave her a leering grin. 'Aye, do that,' he said. 'An' don't mek a row. We've all to be up early in 'morning.'

Noah shook his fist at him and slammed out of the room, causing his mother to mutter, 'They'll have that door off its hinges.'

'Do they always argue?' Harriet asked her.

Mrs Tuke looked over her shoulder. It seemed to Harriet that she must rarely be engaged in conversation or asked her opinion about anything, for she stood as if contemplating, twisting and squeezing a dish clout in her hands. When she spoke, her voice was cracked and bitter. 'Were they arguing? I didn't notice,' and bent over the sink again.

Harriet sighed. I don't know if I can stand this. She felt nervous, anxious. What an odd family they are. I might high-tail it back to Hull in 'morning. I'd go tonight but I'd get lost and might finish up in 'river.

Noah slammed back into the kitchen again. He was carry-ing Harriet's belongings, which she'd left in the cart. He held them out to her. 'You forgot these,' he said. 'We'll go up.'

'I need 'privy,' she said in a low voice. 'Will you show me where it is?'

He opened the door again to go outside. 'You'll need your shawl. It's bucketing down wi' rain.'

She wrapped her shawl about her shoulders and scurried after him as he went down the yard and into what appeared to be a field, but it was so dark she couldn't see where she was walking. He stopped at a wooden structure and opened the door.

'Here. Can you find your way back?'

'Yes,' she said. 'But I'll remember to bring a lamp another time.'

She felt around in the darkness and located the wooden seat and sat with her elbows on her knees and her chin in her hands. She groaned. 'What have I done? In heaven's name, what have I done? What kind of a madhouse is this? What kind of family have I married into?'

# CHAPTER EIGHT

Before they went upstairs Mrs Tuke opened a door leading to a walk-in cupboard and came out carrying something heavy in a large brown paper bag. 'Here,' she said brusquely. 'You'll mebbe not want to share. I wouldn't.'

Curious, Harriet peered into the bag. It was a cream-coloured chamber pot. 'Oh – thank you.'

'Everybody empties their own,' Mrs Tuke stated. 'Except Mr Tuke and I wouldn't trust him to not spill, but I won't do anybody else's.'

'Quite right, Mrs Tuke. You wouldn't want to.'

'You can empty my piss-pot now, Harriet,' Noah said from where he had one foot on the stairs. 'That'll be one of your wifely duties.'

She stared up at him. 'No, it won't. It says nowt about that in 'marriage vows.'

'And you might get a clout if you're not careful.' He turned to go up the steep staircase.

Harriet glanced back at her parents-in-law, who were looking at her intently. Mr Tuke's lips were lifted in a sneer, but his wife's eyes held hers in a steady expressionless gaze.

'First time he hits me,' Harriet told them calmly, 'I'll hit him back. Just so that you know.'

Mrs Tuke held her look for another brief moment and then

said mechanically, as if she said it every night of the week, 'Time for your bed, Mr Tuke.'

The bedroom where Noah was waiting for her was large, but divided into two by a thin partition which ran from the window almost to the door. Noah's bed was on one side and another bed on the other, each 'room' having half the window. A lamp was lit on Noah's side of the partition.

'Who sleeps in 'other half?' she asked cautiously.

'Fletcher. Ma and Da have a room at 'other end of 'passage.'

'There's no door between us,' she said.

'No.' He was already pulling off his shirt and unfastening his belt. 'That's why I went outside, to tell him to wait a bit afore coming up.'

She swallowed. 'It's raining. He'll not want to wait outside.'

'He'll not want to come up either,' he grinned. 'He's in 'cow-shed.'

'You'll have to fix a door,' she said. 'I don't like to think he's just on 'other side.'

'He'll not listen.' Noah stripped off his breeches. 'Get un-dressed, Harriet. Come on, look sharp.'

She gave a deep sigh. Better get it over with, she thought, pushing the chamber pot under the bed. It probably won't take long.

Noah was demanding, as Harriet guessed he might be, and was quick the first time and fell asleep instantly, but he woke again a few hours later and rolled on top of her. She shushed him. 'Your brother might hear,' she whispered.

'Let him,' he muttered. 'If he don't like it he can sleep some-where else, like in 'cowshed!'

She was sure that Fletcher wasn't sleeping. She heard the springs of his bed creaking as he turned over, so she knew that he must be able to hear Noah grunting and gasping and probably her low whimpering too, for Noah was not gentle, but rough and persistent. She tried her best to keep quiet and not cry out.

The honking croak of a gaggle of geese flying overhead woke her the next morning and she turned over to find Noah's side of the bed empty. She gave a tired sigh and wished she could sleep a little longer, but part of the bargain was that she would help on the farm. So what can I do, she thought as she poured cold water from a jug into a basin on the washstand and washed her hands and face. I'm a town woman; I know nothing about living in 'country.

She dressed in her old skirt and warm jumper and looked out of the half window. It was still not quite light, but as she gazed across the yard and beyond a gated fence she saw a long meadow, a grey sky and flatland and a glint of brown water, which was the estuary.

Downstairs Mrs Tuke was in the kitchen, stirring something in a pan over the fire.

'Morning,' Harriet said, and Mrs Tuke turned round, cast an expressionless glance at her and merely nodded before turning back to the ritual of stirring.

'Can I do anything?' Harriet asked her.

'Like what? I've managed all these years wi'out any help.'

Harriet shrugged. This was not going to be easy. 'My ma and me, we allus shared our tasks,' she said. 'At least we did when we were both working, but lately – well, after Ma became ill, I did most things.'

She knew she was more or less talking to herself as Mrs Tuke appeared to be totally uninterested, but she felt she had to make some sort of effort to bridge the gap between them. She could understand the antipathy that Noah's mother might feel towards her; after all, for her son to bring a complete stranger into her home without so much as a by-your-leave was hardly tolerable.

Harriet wondered how her own mother would have felt if she'd arrived home with a husband without a word; but then, she considered, I wouldn't have got married without discussing it first. I'd have taken a courtship slowly.

'What was 'matter wi' her?'

60

The question interrupted her reverie. 'Sorry, what?'

'Your ma.' Mrs Tuke faced her. 'What was her illness?'

Harriet shook her head. 'I don't know,' she murmured. 'She'd had a cough which settled on her chest.' She put her hand over her eyes and pressed them. 'Then she seemed to get worse. She had no strength, but – but I never expected her to go so fast. When Noah came to 'house . . .' She paused as Mrs Tuke stood looking at her. 'He said he'd wait with her while I ran for a neighbour – I couldn't afford a doctor, you see – and when I came back, she was dead.' She heaved a breath. 'Just like that. I was gone onny a few minutes.'

'Sit down,' Mrs Tuke said. 'Gruel's ready. Men'll be here in a minute. Except for Mr Tuke; he's still abed.' She gave a disparaging twitch of her mouth. 'He'll not be up for another hour.'

Harriet sat down at the table. 'Well, why not?' she responded. 'He can tek it easy when he's got two sons to help him.'

'They'll not do it right for him,' Mrs Tuke declared. 'Never have done.'

The door was flung open and Noah rushed in. 'Breakfast ready?'

'Isn't it always?' his mother muttered.

He gave a grin when he saw Harriet sitting at the table. 'Morning,' he said slyly. 'Glad to see you up bright and early. Have you found her some jobs, Ma?'

'No.' His mother served them both a dish of gruel and put the pan back on to the fire, but lifted it off again as Fletcher came in. He nodded at Harriet, but avoided looking at her directly and sat down opposite Noah.

'Da not up yet?' he asked, as his mother poured the gruel.

'For heaven's sake,' she ranted. 'When is he ever?'

Harriet ate the thick and creamy gruel, but she felt a burning tension in her chest. She avoided catching anybody's eye, feeling like a spare part that didn't belong here, but she also felt that the simmering atmosphere was not wholly down to her presence.

'Are you not eating with us, Mrs Tuke?' she ventured.

'No. I eat when it suits me.'

'Ma doesn't eat wi' us,' Fletcher told her. 'Except at supper. She prefers to eat on her own.'

When the men had finished breakfast and drunk a mug of tea, they both pushed back their chairs and left the table and went out again, and Harriet wondered at their manners. Neither of them had thanked their mother.

She got up too and cleared the dishes and stacked them in the sink.

'Thank you, Mrs Tuke,' she said. 'Can I wash 'dishes, or is there owt else that needs doing?'

Mrs Tuke gave a dispassionate shrug of her narrow shoulders. 'You can let 'hens out,' she mumbled. 'And feed 'em some corn, then look to see if any of 'em have laid.'

'Erm, where's 'hen house?' Harriet said diffidently.

'Bottom of 'yard,' Mrs Tuke answered. 'Near 'field. You'll need to tek 'basket to carry 'eggs in,' she said as Harriet draped her shawl round her shoulders. 'If there are any,' she added. 'They go off lay at this time of 'year.'

'Do they?' Harriet said. 'I didn't know.'

'Don't know much, do you?' She glanced scornfully at her new daughter-in-law.

'Not about country matters, no, I don't,' Harriet responded. 'But I'm a quick learner – given 'chance,' she added.

'Let 'em into 'field wi' 'sheep,' she was told, 'and mek sure you fasten 'gate or else they'll all be off and then there'll be summat to say.'

I don't know how I'm going to be able to stand this, Harriet thought again as she went across the yard. All this tension, nobody wi' a good word to say to anybody. What's up wi' them all?

There was a light drizzle and a chill wind and she shivered as she walked carefully across the muddy yard; she didn't want to skid and land on her backside. She'd forgotten to ask Mrs Tuke if she had a spare pair of rubber boots as Noah had suggested, but even if she had remembered she would have hesitated in case she made a blunder.

Noah and Fletcher weren't about and she wondered where they were and what they were doing, but as she approached the hen house Fletcher appeared from round the back of it with a spade in his hand. They both stopped in their tracks.

Harriet spoke first. 'I've to let 'hens out.'

He gazed at her for a second before asking, 'Do you know what to do?'

'Don't I just open 'door?'

He gave a wry grimace. 'On a day like today they don't allus want to come out.'

'Don't blame 'em,' she said. 'So how do I mek 'em?'

'You'll have to go inside and persuade 'em,' he said, and smiled. 'Give 'em a shove if necessary. Then when they're out, open 'field gate and let them in there. Do you know where 'corn is?'

Silently she shook her head and followed him to a wooden lean-to with a metal bin inside it.

'In here,' he said, taking off the lid to show her the grain. 'But be sure to put the lid back on when you've filled 'bucket, or else we'll lose it all to rats. Onny half fill it,' he added, 'and scatter it over 'grass.'

She grimaced. 'I hate rats,' she said. 'Can't stand 'em.'

'Well, we have to live with 'em,' he said. 'And they have to eat to live, like all creatures do, but scavengers that they are, we have to mek sure they don't eat anything that we want, so everything's to be securely fastened.'

'What about foxes?'

'What about 'em?' He looked straight at her now, not avoiding her glance as he had at breakfast, and today his eyes seemed more blue than grey.

'Well, don't they go after 'hens?'

'Aye, they do, and that's why they've to be shut up every night. Do you want me to help you fetch 'em out?'

'N-no, thanks,' she said. 'I'll manage.'

63

He nodded and walked off and she watched him for a moment, seeing his ponytail swinging across the back of his neck, then she turned to the hen house and unfastened the bolts and turned the iron key which Mrs Tuke had given her.

'Come on then, my beauties,' she cooed, entering the warm, straw-smelling structure. 'Let's be having you.'

# CHAPTER NINE

Apart from being cold, Harriet enjoyed feeding the hens. Some of them were fixed firmly on their perches and she had to lift them down, and though they squawked and fluttered she liked the feel of their soft warm feathery bodies.

They ran after her when she went to the feed bin, getting under her feet in their eagerness. She opened the gate to the field, closing it after her as she had been told, although the few sheep there showed no disposition to escape. They were muddy and bedraggled, with torn fleeces trailing behind them, and she thought maybe they'd been caught up in a hedge.

She scattered the corn and went back to the hen house, again making sure the gate was secure behind her. Don't want to blot my copybook on 'first day, she mused. She found four eggs: two white, one speckled and one brown. I'd like to taste the brown one, she thought. I've never had a brown egg. She told this to Mrs Tuke when she bore in the eggs triumphantly.

'You've never had a brown egg!' Mrs Tuke said in astonishment. 'Well, they don't taste any different from white, but I'd guarantee you've never had a fresh one either.'

'No. Not fresh like these.' Harriet handled the smooth but messy eggs with care, washing them in the sink as she was told, before putting them in a bowl and taking them through a door into the pantry.

The pantry door was off the kitchen, and although she had noticed it this morning she hadn't known what was behind it. Now she walked in and looked round at the limewashed slabs where milk was kept cool and butter lay with a muslin cover over it. A fowl and a joint of beef sat on the bottom shelves with domed mesh covers over them.

I must have done 'right thing coming here, she breathed. At least I'm not going to starve. There's more food here than I've ever seen in my life. Farm must be mekking a profit in spite of looking run down.

'Hurry up and shut 'door,' Mrs Tuke called to her. 'Larders have to be kept cool, don't you know that?'

Harriet came out and turned the large iron key. 'First time I've ever been in one,' she said.

Mrs Tuke gazed at her for a moment then swung the kettle over the fire where it began to steam. 'Sit down,' she said. 'I want to talk to you.'

Harriet did as she was bid and watched as Mrs Tuke made another pot of tea. Two pots of tea in a morning, she marvelled. Ma and me thought we were lucky if we got one a day.

Mrs Tuke poured, and pushed a cup towards her. 'Now then,' she said brusquely. 'Why did you really marry him?'

Harriet sipped the tea and pondered. Not why did you really marry my son, or why did you marry Noah, just plain and simple him. Does he not deserve a name? What's he done to mek her so antagonistic?

Mrs Tuke's eyes narrowed as she waited for an answer.

Harriet sighed. 'If I'm honest, he caught me at a low ebb. Ma was sick, I'd been put on short time at 'mill and then Ma died, like I told you, an' when I went back to 'hostelry where I'd been working at night, I was given 'sack. I saw Noah again a few days later and he treated me to some supper. And then he said he was looking for a wife, an' asked me – asked me if I'd consider marrying him.'

It wasn't quite like that, she thought. It was more of an ultimatum. He said I had to decide there and then.

66

'And you said yes, just like that?' Mrs Tuke said abrasively. 'A man you didn't know? A man you'd onny just met? Did you think he had money? Or were you desperate?' she added with thinly veiled sarcasm.

Harriet sighed. Nobody would understand if they hadn't been at rock bottom as she had been. 'He said I'd have a roof over my head. I had to mek up my mind,' she said. 'I'd no money, no job, and I was in arrears wi' rent.' She pressed her lips together. 'I decided to tek a chance. It was either that or 'workhouse if I couldn't find work. Noah said he wouldn't be coming back to Hull. Time will tell whether or not I've made 'right choice.

'I'm sorry,' she added. 'We've both been caught out. You were not expecting me and I wasn't expecting to find a house full o' people. I thought that Noah was living on his own; he never said he had a family.'

Mrs Tuke sat in silence, gazing into space. It seemed to Harriet that she was mulling something over and debating whether to discuss it, but she said nothing until there was a sound from upstairs, a thump as if someone was getting out of bed. Then she said, 'That'll be Mr Tuke. He'll be wanting his breakfast.' She got up from the table, and then turned back to Harriet. 'If I were you, I'd mek myself scarce for half an hour. He's not in 'best o' tempers first thing.'

Harriet put her shawl on again and headed for the door, but Mrs Tuke called her back. 'You'll find some rubber galoshes in 'porch. There should be a pair to fit you.'

She felt heartened by this small consideration and thought that Mrs Tuke had a fair amount of irksome provocation to deal with herself. She must think that I'm just another addition to it. I don't understand why Noah was in such a hurry to get wed; he must have known that he was going to annoy them all. Did he do it deliberately, she wondered. Was it some devil in him that wanted to rile them?

It had stopped raining so she decided to explore the farm, though she reckoned that was a very grand name for just a

67

clutter of derelict buildings. She found a brick stable with three stalls and two horses, the fine stallion Noah had ridden into Hull and the ancient mare that had brought her here from their wedding. She unbolted the stable door and went inside and stroked both of them. The stallion skittered away from her, but the old mare stood placidly whilst she talked to her and then nuzzled into her hand as if looking for a tit-bit.

She carefully fastened the door behind her when she left and found she was looking down at a black and white dog, who although emitting a low growl was also wagging his tail. 'Hello,' she said. 'Who are you?'

She bent down and allowed him to sniff her skirt and hands but didn't attempt to stroke him. She was wary of dogs, never having had one. When he had finished examining her he sat down at her feet as if waiting for her next move. 'Come on then,' she said. 'Where next?'

Next was a large wooden shed, although she thought it probably had another name. This appeared to be a depository for farming equipment; as well as spades and forks and coils of rope there were various wooden implements she didn't recognize. She couldn't think of a use for any of them, except for one, which was quite large and cumbersome and she thought might have been a plough. There was a waggon and the cart that Noah had driven to fetch her; harnesses and bridles were hanging on the walls and wooden crates and wicker baskets were piled up in a corner.

The dog had been by her side as she looked round but he suddenly gave a low woof and bounded to the door, his tail wagging furiously. Fletcher's broad shoulders filled the door-way, and although she couldn't see his face, as the light was behind him, she felt his scrutiny.

'Looking for summat?'

'No,' she said. 'Just looking. I'm surplus to requirements at 'minute so I thought I'd tek a look round. What's this?' She pointed to the implement she had been examining. 'Is it a plough?'

He came towards her. 'Yeh. Single furrow wooden beam; it's an old ox plough which Da used when he was a lad, but we don't keep oxen now.'

'So – do you grow corn?'

He nodded. 'We haven't much land, and what we have is very wet.' He pointed to the spades on the walls. 'We're constantly working on 'ditches and drains to tek water off 'land, but we grow wheat, oats, beans, turnips and clover. In rotation,' he added. 'Not all at 'same time. We have to feed 'animals as well as ourselves.' His eyes narrowed. 'Did he tell you nowt?'

Harriet shrugged. 'He said he was a farmer. I'm a town woman,' she said. 'He mebbe thought I wouldn't understand country matters.'

Fletcher grunted. 'He could've given you 'benefit of 'doubt.' He shook his head and sighed. 'We're a mixed farm. We've onny a dozen cattle bred for meat, and two milch cows for home use.' He gave a sudden grin that lit up his face and Harriet smiled too as he added, 'We could teach you to milk them. We've a goat in kid too. And a few sheep, bred for market, which you've already seen. And a couple o' pigs for 'table.'

'So does the old horse pull 'plough? She doesn't look strong enough.'

'No. She pulls 'cart and Ma sometimes uses her for going to Brough. We have a plough horse. Noah's out ploughing a fallow field now. It's very wet, but we've to get ready for spring planting. He's using an iron plough; single furrow cos it's onny an acre field.'

She nodded as if she knew what he was talking about. It will all make sense eventually, she thought.

'Sorry, I must get on,' he said, and walked over to the far wall where he exchanged the spade he was carrying for a long iron-tipped wooden one. 'I drew 'short straw this morning; my turn to clear 'drainage channels.' He put the sludge spade over his shoulder. 'At least I'll keep warm.'

Harriet watched him walk away across the yard, the dog following him. He seems friendlier now than when I arrived. Of course it was a shock for them all to have a stranger thrust into their midst. She saw the broad set of his shoulders, his narrow hips and long legs, and an unwitting and wayward thought came unbidden – that had it been Fletcher and not Noah who had come looking for a wife, she would perhaps not have lingered so long over her decision.

She gave herself a derisory shake and went back into the yard to continue her exploration. She found the cowshed, and a pigsty with two snuffling, rooting pigs in the pen. She glanced back at the house and noticed a curtain twitch at the kitchen window, but couldn't make out who was behind it; she turned her back and went into the sheep field, again carefully fastening the gate behind her, and headed off in the direction of the estuary.

The low cloud had lifted and a pale watery sun brightened the sky. Harriet followed the line of the ditch where water was running fast, crossing two more fields. She could see that the estuary, a steely grey colour, was very lively as the incoming high tide caused rippling currents which lashed the banks. Several coal-carrying vessels were steaming westward where the estuary narrowed; over on the south bank, Lincolnshire was a thin dark strip of higher land with tall chimneys spouting thick black smoke.

She stood on the edge of the bank and let her gaze wander over the wide salt marsh, which this morning was covered by the tide, and then up and down the estuary. Her eye was caught by a fluttering of wings where a flock of birds were resting or nesting on what looked like a small island, and she took a deep, satisfying gulp of air. Apart from the rush and lap of the water and the flapping beat of wildfowl, there was a calm and comforting silence; something she was unused to in the bustling town with its constant rattle of traffic and cries of market vendors. If it were not for the friction I appear to have caused in this family I have joined – if it wasn't there already – I think I could like it here.

# CHAPTER TEN

Harriet walked slowly back to the farm, wondering whether Mr Tuke would have finished his breakfast. She was at a loss to know what she could do that might be useful.

Near the side wall of the house she saw Fletcher bent over his spade, his ponytail swinging over his shoulder. She approached him, curious to know what he was doing. He straightened up and raised his eyebrows.

'I wondered how you were getting on,' she said lamely. 'You said you were going to clear 'ditches.'

'I am,' he said briefly. 'I'm enlarging this cut to tek 'water away from 'buildings. You see how 'ground slopes towards 'house? Well, if we don't keep this area clear when we get a lot o' rain we'll be sitting in a lake, so we dug this to meet up with 'other drain' – he pointed to another ditch at the side of the yard – 'so that 'whole lot runs off down towards 'estuary. In 'Netherlands they're experts on land drainage and this is what they do.'

'Oh! Have you been?'

'No, but I've read about it and seen drawings. There was this fellow called Cornelius Vermuyden or some such who dug dykes to stop 'sea flooding 'land, oh,' he drew a breath, 'about two hundred years ago, and then he came to live in England and did 'same here; he diverted 'River Don up near Doncaster and made a new channel ending in 'Ouse near Goole. Called it 'Dutch River. Not everybody agreed with what he did and it turned out to be unsuitable for shipping, but I reckon he had some good ideas.' He kept on digging as he spoke, throwing up the wet clay on to a heap.

'And so – if 'estuary should break its banks, if it was high tide, I mean,' Harriet said, 'shouldn't you have a deep ditch down at 'bottom of 'field to catch it?'

Fletcher straightened up again. 'Aye, or a large pond – washlands, they're called. I think we should, but Da thinks it a waste of time an' energy. He says we can't keep water out no matter what we do.'

'But you could contain it,' she said eagerly. 'Make it less of a threat?'

He gazed keenly at her and then grunted, 'A woman wi' a brain!'

Harriet stiffened indignantly. 'We all have one,' she retaliated. 'Just 'same as men. We don't allus have 'opportunity to use 'em.'

'I didn't mean—' He broke off as Noah appeared round the corner of the barn. The dog was slinking along behind him, his tail between his legs.

'What 'you up to?'

It took Harriet a second before she realized that Noah was talking to her.

'I – I'm discussing drains and dykes,' she said.

'You what!' He scowled, his eyebrows close knit. 'Get yourself inside an' mek me a drink, never mind discussing summat that's got nowt to do wi' you.'

She opened her mouth to argue, but seeing his eyes flash she decided against it and went towards the door. 'What do you want?' she asked. 'Tea? Cocoa?'

He stared at her. 'I want a pint pot o' tea an' I want it in less than five minutes an' I want a piece o' pie or a slice o' fruit cake to go wi' it.'

*Yes, your honour*, she seethed resentfully. No possibility of please or thank you.

Inside the kitchen Mr Tuke was sitting at the table. Mrs Tuke was building up the fire with coal.

'Noah wants a pint pot o' tea and a piece of pie or cake,' Harriet said. 'Is it all right if I mek it?'

'Doesn't Fletcher want one?' Mrs Tuke glanced at her.

'He didn't say if he did or not.' Harriet shrugged. 'I don't know if I'm supposed to guess what they want or to already know their routine.' She was smarting, both at Fletcher's comment and at Noah's demand.

Mrs Tuke's mouth twitched irritably. 'Aye, well, women are supposed to be mind-readers where men are concerned. Haven't you found that out yet?'

'No.' Harriet swung the kettle over the fire. 'But I'm learning.'

'What did she say?' Mr Tuke leaned forward, screwing up his face.

'She didn't say owt, Mr Tuke,' his wife answered. 'At least not to you.'

Mr Tuke continued to stare as Harriet made a large pot of tea and cut a slice from a cake that she found in a tin in the pantry. By the time she'd put them on the table, the door was opening and Noah was stepping inside.

'Boots!' Mrs Tuke said forcibly, and Noah sat down on a wooden chair by the door and took them off. He glanced at Harriet and sat down at the table opposite his father.

'Why'd you bring a woman home?' Mr Tuke said.

Noah took a bite from the cake. 'I told you, she's my wife,' he muttered. 'Not just a woman. It was time I was wed,' he added. 'We need sons here.'

'I've got sons,' the old man said, and Harriet, watching them all, was taken aback by the sudden look of hostility on Mrs Tuke's face, directed not only at her husband but at Noah too.

'Aye, so you have.' Noah took a slurp of tea. 'But we've to prepare for 'next generation.'

So I'm a breeding machine, Harriet thought. But I wonder

74

why there are only two sons? Did the Tukes lose bairns at birth or to illness? I'll find out in time, I suppose.

'You might not have sons,' Mrs Tuke muttered at Noah. 'There's no guarantee.'

Noah gave a mocking grin. 'We'll keep on till we do.'

His father sniggered. 'Best sleep at 'back of 'house then, so's you don't disturb 'rest of us.'

Harriet turned away and headed for the stairs, disgusted by the way the conversation was heading, but Mrs Tuke, in a burst of fury, exclaimed, 'That's enough from 'pair of you. I'll not have such talk in my house.'

'*Your* house?' her husband snarled. 'Since when has it been *your* house?'

She leaned towards him and answered in a sinister whisper. 'Since as long as I was married to you.' She pointed a finger at him. 'And don't forget that it's not yours either, but belongs to Master Hart.'

Harriet paused in the doorway. This was not really about her, she thought. This was an old festering sore and since her arrival it had suddenly burst open.

She was about to leave the room when the kitchen door opened again and Fletcher came in. He sat on the wooden chair and began to unlace his boots, his gaze travelling from one person to another as if assessing the situation.

'Is there a chance of a cup o' tea or shall I go out and come back in when 'storm's abated?' he asked.

'There's tea in 'pot,' his mother said. 'Might as well have it while it's hot.'

Harriet wasn't sure what to do, to stay or to leave. Would it be better if she weren't there so they could discuss the situation and clear the air? No, she thought. Why should I leave? If they're talking about me then I want to be here to find out why. She went to stand with her back to the range and glared at the three men.

'I seem to have caused some discord in this house,' she said. 'And I wouldn't have agreed to come if I'd known that; but I'm here, for better or worse as I agreed in 'marriage ceremony, so I reckon we should have this out in 'open.'

Mrs Tuke looked away, avoiding her gaze, though her husband watched Harriet with an expression she couldn't quite read; he seemed to be sizing her up, appraising her like a recently acquired piece of property or livestock. She held his gaze until with a wry grin he dropped his eyes.

Noah said nothing, just sat back in his chair and watched her with a smirk on his face.

Fletcher cleared his throat. 'You might not think it, but this has nowt to do wi' you. We'd probably have had a row about something else entirely; that's 'way it is in this household.' He paused, and then said, 'Just so that you know what we're like, Noah and me are allus at each other's throats; we have been since we were young lads. I can't remember how it started or why, but as soon as we were big enough to fight, then that's what we did. Da encouraged us and Ma did nowt to stop us.'

Harriet glanced at the parents of these wayward sons. Mr Tuke was tipped back in his chair with his arms folded and looking as if there was a bad smell beneath his nose, but to her astonishment Mrs Tuke seemed to be holding in some emotion. Whether it was anger, frustration or simply unhappiness, Harriet couldn't tell, but her lips were pressed tightly together and her hands held by her side were clenched so hard the knuckles showed white.

'I don't understand why you fight,' Harriet said, her voice strained. 'I'd have thought that living out here in 'middle o' nowhere you'd have relied on each other for companionship, that you'd have pulled together to make life bearable. That's what my mother and I did. We had no one else, so we needed each other. I wouldn't have left her alone to get married, not for a fortune, I wouldn't.' Her voice trembled and then broke. 'If she hadn't died, I – I wouldn't be here. As for Noah not telling you his intentions,' she looked towards where he was sitting, wearing a smug expression, 'I can't explain that.'

'I'll tell you why he didn't say owt to us,' Fletcher broke in. 'He wanted to be sure he'd found someone first. If he'd announced it and then it hadn't happened, he'd have lost face and been laughed at; he'd have been told that nobody would want to marry him.'

'That's no way to talk about your brother,' Harriet protested.

'No?' Fletcher raised his eyebrows. 'And is a *bet* 'best and proper way to find a wife?'

'What do you mean?'

'I mean, *sister-in-law*,' Fletcher's eyes flashed, 'that your husband was determined to find a wife because whichever of us had bairns first would have first claim on 'farm. Never mind that I'm 'eldest son and should have prior right to it; he bet me the price of a young heifer that he'd find a wife afore me and tek over.' He stood up. 'So that's what happened, Mrs Noah Tuke.' He towered over her. 'You're here because you were a prize in a wager and the loser would owe 'price of a heifer.' He raised a finger. 'But I'll tell you that I never agreed to it. I never said yes to such a scheme, but he went ahead anyway, so 'onny way now to resolve this issue and clear the air,' he turned to his brother, 'is for us to decide in our usual way, and that's outside in 'yard.'

Noah got up from the table, slamming back his chair so hard that it toppled over with a crash. 'That's fine by me,' he bellowed. 'Let's sort it out now once and for all.'

The two men grabbed their boots, both hopping and almost falling in their attempt to be the first to put them on and get outside.

'Stop!' Harriet cried out. 'Please. Don't.'

Fletcher turned, hesitating at her voice, but was jostled forward by Noah and then by their father who hustled them both out of the door.

Mrs Tuke put her hand on Harriet's elbow. 'Leave them be,' she muttered. 'They'll not settle it otherwise.'

'But how can you bear it?' Harriet cried. 'They'll hurt each other.' Tears began to stream down her cheeks. 'I want to go home!'

'Apparently, this is your home now,' Mrs Tuke said. 'What was it you said? For better or for worse?' Her words were cutting. 'And what would you be going back to?'

Harriet sat down and wept as if her heart would break. It seemed that she had gone headlong from one desperate situation straight into another. She shook her head. 'I don't know. I don't know.'

# CHAPTER ELEVEN

It had been such a long day, Harriet reflected as she turned back the bedcover that night. Not a good start to married life.

She knew she could never love Noah, that she would only ever tolerate him. He was a boor, devoid of manners just like his father. But I've made my bed, she thought as she climbed into the one that was now hers, and must lie on it.

Wide awake, she waited for Noah to come upstairs. No point in trying to sleep, for she was certain he would wake her. Her thoughts went to her mother-in-law. She seems to have a chip on her shoulder, but once she's used to me being here in her house we're sure to find we have something in common.

The brothers had fought out in the yard; she and Mrs Tuke had sat silently on either side of the range, unwillingly listening to their shouts, and the crashing of wheelbarrows, iron buckets and metal spades that were knocked over as they fell on to each other in their chase around the yard. They could also hear Mr Tuke roaring his encouragement as they battled.

Then the porch door had opened and a minute later closed again; Mrs Tuke took a deep breath and murmured, 'Nearly over.'

Harriet had cast an enquiring glance towards her but then almost jumped out of her skin as the crack of a rifle shot rang out.

She'd gasped and stood up. 'What's that? What's happened?'

Mrs Tuke had shaken her head. 'Nowt to worry about,' she said calmly. 'It's over. They'll be in for their dinner in a minute.' She rose from her chair and, taking a cloth, lifted the lid from a simmering pan hanging over the fire. An aroma of soup filled the room.

Harriet sat down again. She was trembling. A vision of the death of one of the brothers or their father, the idea of a pool of blood staining the muddy yard and the marching feet of the constables, filled her with fear. Never in her life had she or her mother known trouble such as this. Poverty and hardship, yes, but never the fear of murder or the hangman's noose for a perpetrator.

But then the men had returned to the kitchen, Mr Tuke first, triumphantly it seemed, with his shotgun in his hand, which Mrs Tuke ordered him to put away immediately. He'd grinned and propped it up in a corner. Then Noah and Fletcher had come in, both with bloody noses and each sporting a swelling eye. Noah's bottom lip was bleeding profusely.

They'd sat down in their places, saying nothing until their mother had portioned out bowls of soup and put a loaf of bread in the centre of the table. Harriet had vaguely wondered when she had made the soup or baked the bread, for she hadn't seen her do it.

'Sorry, Ma,' Fletcher said, picking up his spoon. 'It was necessary.'

Noah glanced at him and then at his mother but remained silent, merely tearing off a hunk of bread and dropping it into his soup.

After they had eaten, Harriet asked if she could bathe their wounds. Noah laughed. 'Think this is an injury, do you?' he grunted between swollen lips. 'Think I want namby-pambying? Ask Fletcher; he's more likely to succumb to a woman's soft touch, hey Fletch? Just like you did when you were a bairn!'

Noah had gone out again and Fletcher had asked his

mother if she had a piece of raw beef and Harriet was sent to get it from the pantry. Fletcher put his head back to place the meat on it, but Harriet suggested that the eye should first be bathed with warm water; Mrs Tuke had given her a clean soft cloth and Harriet had poured lukewarm water from the kettle into a small bowl. She gently bathed his swollen eye and washed away the blood from his nose, and in the seconds before placing the raw meat on the swelling he'd opened his eyes and gazed searchingly at her.

That unnerved me, she thought now, as she lay in bed; what was he looking at? What was he thinking? And why didn't his mother bathe his injuries, and Noah's too?

She heard Noah's footsteps on the stairs and turned over, pretending to be asleep. The bed creaked as he sat on it to pull off his woollen socks; she could smell his sweat and the muddy earth he'd been ploughing. It creaked again as he stood up to take off his shirt and breeches, but he kept on his undergarments as he had the night before, grey buttoned combinations of long pants and vest.

'You awake, Harriet?' he asked as he got into bed. He shook her shoulder when she didn't answer. She turned towards him and gave a sleepy grunt. 'Mmm?'

'Come on,' he said. 'Wake up. Come on top. I'm dead beat.'

'Go to sleep then,' she murmured.

'I want a son,' he muttered. 'An' then I'll mek his life a misery, just see if I don't.'

Harriet sat up. 'What? Your own son!'

'No, daft bitch. Fletcher! He'll rue this day.'

The next morning Harriet woke to yet another dreary wet day. She washed and dressed and made their bed, and heard Mrs Tuke in the adjoining room. She put her head round the partition and saw her stripping the bed of sheets and blanket, pillow and counterpane.

'Is it washday?' she asked. 'How will 'bedding get dry?' Harriet and her mother used to go to the washhouse on a wet day if they had money to spare.

'Not washday.' Mrs Tuke didn't look at her. 'Fletcher's moving to 'box room.'

Harriet felt her cheeks flushing, but was also aware of huge relief. 'Can I help you? Are you moving 'bed as well?'

'Aye, 'whole lot. Fletcher says he'll move 'bed at dinner time. He said you'd be better having extra space where you can put your things.'

I don't have any things, Harriet thought, but I'm grateful anyway.

'There's a spare chest o' drawers in 'box room that we can move over,' Mrs Tuke went on. 'There's nowt much in it. Onny bits o' linen and suchlike.'

'Thank you,' Harriet said. 'It's good of Fletcher to give up his room.'

'Aye, it is.' Mrs Tuke stood for a moment, contemplating, gazing vacantly out of the window. 'Still, I suppose we've to be prepared,' she muttered. 'You might need 'extra room eventually.'

Harriet didn't answer. They might, she thought. If Noah was so determined to have a son they would be having a night-time ritual until she conceived.

'How would you feel about having a bairn in 'house, Mrs Tuke?' she asked quietly.

'I don't know,' she answered brusquely, and then looked up, frowning. 'Why, surely you're not—'

'No.' Harriet smiled. No sense in telling her that Noah had seduced her that night in Hull when he had walked her home. 'Of course not. There's hardly been time yet.'

Mrs Tuke looked away. 'Sometimes it onny needs just once,' she muttered. 'That's all it teks.' She seemed to gather herself together. 'Come on then, tek that end of 'mattress and we'll shift it to 'other room.'

As they were moving it down the narrow passage another bedroom door opened, revealing Mr Tuke in crumpled grey combinations, his hair and beard dishevelled. Harriet averted her eyes.

'What's going on?' he rasped. 'Can't a man be allowed to sleep?'

'Go back to bed, Mr Tuke,' his wife said. 'It's not yet seven, and besides, you're not half decent.'

When Harriet lifted her eyes again, he leered at her. 'Reckon there's nowt she hasn't seen afore.'

'*Get back to bed!*' Mrs Tuke screeched so loudly that Harriet jumped, and Mr Tuke stepped hastily back into the room and closed the door.

Mrs Tuke's face was like thunder. 'Damned heathen,' she muttered, and she heaved on the mattress with a superhuman strength that sent Harriet staggering.

The box room was very small and she wondered how Fletcher would manage. She reasoned that he would only need to be in there to sleep, but then worried if the bed would fit.

'If it won't,' Mrs Tuke said, when Harriet mentioned it, 'then he'll have to sleep on 'mattress.' She seemed indifferent, as if she had given up caring what any of them did.

When they went downstairs, Harriet helped herself to the gruel that was set on the shelf at the side of the range. She added a pinch of salt but was surprised when Mrs Tuke put a jug of cream on the table.

'I've never had it with cream,' she said. She gave a little laugh. 'I don't ever remember having cream.'

'Try it, then. It's not to everybody's taste. It's too rich for mine.'

Harriet dipped the tip of a clean spoon in the jug, then touched it with her finger and licked it. 'Mmm,' she murmured. 'Not sure. Where's it come from?'

Mrs Tuke stared at her. 'From 'cow, of course. Where else?'

'Shouldn't 'calf be having it?'

'Calf's long gone from its mother,' Mrs Tuke said. 'That's why we're having it.'

Harriet paused with the spoon in her hand. 'You mean it died?'

Mrs Tuke continued to stare at her, and then shook her head in disbelief. 'No,' she said. 'He's in 'top field, grazing on what bit o' grass we've got. When he's older we'll sell him.' She frowned. 'You know nowt about farming or husbandry, do you?'

'No,' Harriet agreed. 'I don't. When I was looking round yesterday, Fletcher said mebbe I could milk 'cows; could I, do you think? I'd like to be useful. I've allus worked.'

The older woman sat down across from her. 'How would you feel about getting up at four in a morning to feed 'em, and then going back an hour later to milk? Then letting 'em into 'field and later in 'day going back out to milk again?'

Harriet expelled a breath. So that's when she makes her bread and prepares the meals, in the early hours after feeding and before milking and before anybody else is up.

'I'd give it a try,' she said. 'You'd have to show me.'

'I'm onny milking one at 'minute. Other one, Dora, hasn't calved yet,' Mrs Tuke told her. 'By 'time she does, Daisy will be dried off and her milk, what's left of it, 'll be given to 'pigs for fattening. Then when Dora has calved, we'll use her milk.'

'Won't her baby want it?'

Mrs Tuke gave a sudden smile and Harriet mused that her mother-in-law looked younger than she had initially thought. She must have been pretty once. Her skin was weathered now, but her grey eyes were large; her hair was hidden beneath her pleated bonnet, with only a few strands showing.

'Calf,' she corrected Harriet. 'We don't call 'em babies in case we get fond of 'em.'

'But you give them names?'

'Aye,' she nodded. 'Milch cows, I do. They're allus Daisy and Dora.'

Harriet had a sudden misgiving. 'What'll happen to Daisy when she's finished giving milk?'

'She'll be put to 'bull. Ready to start calving again.' She must have seen the anxious expression on Harriet's face. 'It's

84

what they do,' she said prosaically. 'That's their function, to produce.'

Harriet looked at her and gave a pensive nod. So, no different from any other female, she reflected. Rich or poor, that's our role.

# CHAPTER TWELVE

The following morning Harriet was downstairs by half past three. Noah was still asleep as she slipped into her old skirt and flannel blouse and put her shawl round her shoulders. Mrs Tuke was already in the kitchen and the kettle was steaming.

'I wasn't sure if you'd come down,' she muttered as she made a pot of tea. 'It's an ungodly sort of morning, but at least it's not raining.'

'I'm not a morning person,' Harriet told her huskily, 'so you'll excuse me if I don't talk much?'

Mrs Tuke nodded. 'Fine,' she agreed. 'I can't be doing with unnecessary conversation.'

They drank their tea in silence. Then the kettle was filled again for the men's breakfast drink and they went out into the dark morning, Harriet first pulling on the borrowed rubber boots over her thick stockings.

Mrs Tuke led the way to the furthest end of the yard where a brick building joined the house wall. Harriet could hear the lowing of cows and the rustling of straw. Mrs Tuke opened the door to the cowshed and spoke softly to the two occupants.

'Now then,' she murmured. 'Ready for your breakfast?' She opened up another stall, and reaching for a hayfork that was leaning in a corner she scooped up a truss of hay and dropped it into a low basket, which the cows could reach. She then opened another door that led into a small brick-floored shed and with a large scoop half filled a wheelbarrow with grain from a wooden chest.

'They have a weekly ration of seven bushels of grain,' she said. 'And they need chopped turnips, but those can be fed to them when they're outside.'

She's remarkably strong for such a tiny woman, Harriet thought. She was a good head shorter than Harriet, and yet she handled the barrow as if it was no weight at all.

'We'll leave 'em to that and have our breakfast and then come back for 'first milking. They're milked twice a day. In 'summer I'd let 'hens out at 'same time, but because it's still dark I daren't risk it cos of 'fox!' She glanced up at Harriet. 'You wouldn't like 'sight of that when 'fox's been at 'em.'

Harriet shuddered. 'No, I wouldn't.'

The door was carefully closed and they went back to the house, where Mrs Tuke cooked bacon, sausage and eggs.

'This is 'best time of 'day,' she said over her shoulder. 'It's quiet. Nobody here but me and my own thoughts.'

'And now I'm here,' Harriet said apologetically. 'Disturbing you.'

Mrs Tuke gave a slight shrug of her shoulders and then dished up the food on to two plates. 'I wouldn't have asked if I'd thought you weren't up to it,' she said. 'But you might not want to do it.'

'I have to do something,' Harriet said, putting cutlery out on the table. 'I'm used to earning my keep. If there's not enough for me to do here, then mebbe there's somewhere else I could work?'

Mrs Tuke looked dubious; she signalled Harriet to sit down and eat. 'There's not much to do round here, except in 'summer, unless you walked into Brough and got work in one of 'hostelries. But Noah wouldn't like that.'

'No.' Harriet shook her head. 'I don't think he would.'

After they'd finished breakfast, Mrs Tuke prepared her bread dough and put it in a large pancheon in the hearth,

covering it over with a clean white cloth. Harriet was reminded of when Noah had asked her if she'd made the bread at the
inn. Was he testing her, she wondered, to find out if she was
capable of making bread, or curious to know whether she had
a husband and children to feed at home.

'Can I scrub potatoes or do owt for dinner?' she asked.

Mrs Tuke thought for a minute. 'Aye. You'll find 'taties in a
sack under 'shelf in 'pantry, and carrots in a box next to 'em.
I'll chop meat for a stew and then we'll go back out and see to
'girls.' She drew in her breath as if caught out in a blunder and
added, 'Cows, I mean.'

It was a shade lighter when they went outside again, but the
cloud still hung low and grey. Mrs Tuke had gathered up two
clean pails and half filled one of them with tepid water.

'I don't like November,' Harriet commented. 'It's such a
dreary month.'

'Aye, it is,' Mrs Tuke agreed. 'But we're almost out of it.
December in a couple o' days.'

'Is it? I've lost track of 'time since my ma died.'

'Do you miss her?'

'Yes. She was all I had. My onny brother went off to Australia,
or somewhere, years ago. Said he had to get out of 'poverty we
were living in.'

'Why didn't you go with him?'

Harriet slid back the bolt on the cowshed. 'Ma was afraid of
going. She didn't want to leave Hull and all that was familiar
to her. I would've gone but I couldn't leave her, not to fend for
herself.'

She felt Mrs Tuke's eyes on her, scrutinizing her. 'She held
you back then?'

'Oh, no!' Harriet exclaimed. 'I never thought of it like that.
She begged me to go, but I said no. I told her that I felt 'same
as her, that I didn't want to leave, that I wouldn't feel that
another country was home.' She took a deep breath. 'But it
wasn't true.'

Mrs Tuke put Daisy in her own stall and gave her a small

amount of grain and extra hay, then dipped a clean cloth into the bucket of water and carefully washed the cow's udder and teats. She showed Harriet how to start the milking, by bumping the udder, as a calf would, she explained. To begin with Harriet was squeamish as she sat on the low stool, her forehead against the cow's warm belly, gently squeezing the teats, but she soon got into the rhythm and felt a surprising satisfaction as the milk began to spout into the milk bucket.

'Goodness,' she said as she stood up to let Mrs Tuke continue. 'I'd never have believed I could do such a thing!'

When the milking was finished Daisy was washed again, and as they came out of the shed Harriet saw two cats sitting outside the door. Mrs Tuke dipped a ladle into the milk bucket and poured the contents into two old saucers.

'That's their treat for catching mice and rats,' she said, watching as the cats lapped with their long rough tongues. 'Now, if you open 'gate into yonder field cows'll find their way through on their own. We take 'milk into 'dairy and cover it wi' a cloth and let it settle and then it's time to cook a second breakfast.'

Harriet did as she was bid and opened the gate, watching as the two cows ambled across the yard and on to the muddy grass. She fastened the gate after them and called, 'What about 'turnips?'

She couldn't be sure from that distance but she thought that Mrs Tuke gave an approving nod. 'Later,' she called back.


After a few weeks Harriet had begun to settle into a routine. She fed the hens each morning and let them into the field, then gathered the eggs, what few there were, and washed them. She helped with the milking three or four times a week, as Mrs Tuke said there was no need for her to do it every morning. Harriet didn't object as she thought that perhaps her mother-in-law liked some time to herself.

One morning Mrs Tuke told Harriet that she would be

taking the trap to Brough to stock up on food supplies. 'It's nearly Christmas,' she reminded her. 'And although we don't mek much of it, I like to have a few extras in.' She chewed on her lower lip and didn't look at Harriet as she muttered, 'Come, if you like.'

'Oh, yes please,' Harriet said eagerly. 'I'd like to. Is it a big town?'

'No. Not like Hull,' Mrs Tuke said. 'Not that I've been there. Brough's not much more than a hamlet, although 'railway train stops there, as it does in Broomfleet. But I know someone who lives down by Brough Haven. She keeps bees and has her own honey and we do a bit of bartering now and again, and – and I like to go sometimes to remind myself that there are other folk in 'world apart from us.'

Harriet thought she caught a touch of wistfulness in her voice, but she continued, 'Brough's an old place; and then there's 'ferry that goes across to Winteringham, and 'road from there will tek you to London, should you ever feel 'need to go.'

The next morning they finished the milking, fed the hens, cleared up after breakfast and at eight o'clock set off, Mrs Tuke having first asked Fletcher to harness the old mare up to the trap. Mr Tuke was still in bed but she had left his breakfast plate sitting on the shelf at the side of the range where he could help himself.

'He'll probably stay there until dinner time,' she said, clicking her tongue at the mare to move off. 'Then at 'end of day he'll think he's missed a meal.'

'What about Noah and Fletcher? Their dinner, I mean?'

'Soup.' Mrs Tuke cracked the whip above the mare's head as they drove up the long rutted drive to the gate. 'It's ready. All they have to do is eat it!'

The day lightened as they bowled eastward in the direction of Brough; the sky was streaked with thin yellow light as the sun rose but there were also flimsy white clouds which Mrs Tuke said meant snow was coming, and it was much colder and sharper than it had been. The raw dampness of the previous weeks had disappeared.

Harriet looked about her at the wooded plantations and copses, the ivy which climbed the silver-rimed hedges and the bright red berries on the holly bushes. She didn't know the country at all, having lived all her life in Hull; she pointed as a rabbit ran across the road and a little later she gave a startled exclamation as an animal like a large dog bounded in front of them, clearing the hedge in a graceful leap.

'What was that?'

'A deer. Have you never seen one before?'

'Never! How lovely it was. So graceful.'

'Aye, they are,' Mrs Tuke agreed. 'Flavoursome too.'

Harriet turned to look at her. 'Oh, but you couldn't kill it!'

'We can't anyway,' she was told. 'They're not ours to kill. They belong to Master Hart.'

'He's your landlord?' Harriet said. 'Is he gentry then?'

'He is. A gentleman through and through.'

'Hah!' Harriet said. 'I don't know if I'd believe that of any man.'

Mrs Tuke didn't answer, but a little further on she said, 'That was his house back there, set amongst 'trees. Did you see it?'

'No. I must have been looking 'other way. Will you point it out on 'way back?'

Her companion nodded, concentrating on the road, and Harriet continued to look about her. There were occasional glimpses of the glinting estuary through the trees, and finally they turned off and took a narrower road which led to Brough Haven.

The small cottage that Mrs Tuke was heading for was close by an inlet leading to the estuary. A track wide enough for a horse and trap, and a ditch with a wooden plank across it, separated the cottage garden from the deep water. Rowing boats and cobles tied up at wooden posts further round the haven were gently dipping and bobbing on the eddying water, rigging clanking and rattling.

An elderly woman came to the door as they pulled up outside her gate. It must be nice here in the summer, Harriet
thought. There was something brown and twiggy growing
up either side of the small wooden porch, which she thought
might be roses. A small garden was filled with grey spriggy
clumps and other small bushes, and there was a tree with
small maggoty apples that she imagined had been left for the
birds.

'Come on in, Ellen,' the woman said. 'I thought I was due a
visit, but I see you've brought somebody wi' you. I didn't think
you knew anybody but me.'

'I don't, Mrs Marshall,' and Harriet, still feeling uneasy
about her position within this hostile family, thought she de-
tected a derisive note as Mrs Tuke answered. 'This is my –
daughter-in-law, Harriet.'

The woman, as round as a barrel, opened and closed her
mouth. 'Are you telling me that that fine son of yourn has got
himself wed at last?'

Mrs Tuke stepped down from the trap and Harriet followed
suit. 'No,' she heard her mutter. 'This is Noah's wife, not
Fletcher's.'

# CHAPTER THIRTEEN

Because of being introduced and then invited into the cottage, it was a moment or two before Harriet absorbed Mrs Tuke's remark. What did she mean? Had Mrs Marshall said Fletcher's name? She tried to recall the exact words, but they evaded her.

The cottage had low wooden beams and a beaten earth floor. A bench stood near the fire, which was set in a shiny black grate on a stone hearth and had a steaming kettle on a long chain hanging over it. A jug of winter greenery sat in the middle of a wooden table, and a curtain was drawn discreetly across a corner of the room. Harriet assumed it was hiding a bed.

'So how are you, Ellen?' Mrs Marshall said.

'I'm well, thank you, Mrs Marshall.' Mrs Tuke lifted the cloth covering the contents of her basket. 'I've brought you a dozen eggs. Hens are not laying many just now.'

'Ah, they'll be going into 'pot afore long, then,' was her friend's reply, and Harriet shuddered.

Mrs Tuke dug deeper in the basket and brought out a plucked chicken wrapped in waxed paper. 'Indeed they will, and I've brought you 'first one. It should be all right until Christmas if you keep it cool.' Then she produced a jar of thick cream, with the top firmly secured.

'Oh, you're too good to me,' Mrs Marshall said. 'I'll put it

93

in 'meat safe outside 'kitchen window. You're not depriving yourself now, are you?'

'No, I've got another hanging in 'shed which I'll pluck in 'morning ready for Christmas Day.'

As they chatted, Harriet realized she was seeing another side to Ellen Tuke: not the dour woman she normally was, but one who could relax and talk in the company of an old friend. Mrs Marshall pulled the chain holding the kettle further down to the fire, and whilst waiting for it to boil brought out a loaf of bread, some cold ham, a jar of horseradish sauce and an apple pie and placed them on the table.

'These are my own apples,' she said. 'That's such a good tree. I've got plenty in store if you'd like to tek some, and plums too from 'back garden.' She turned to Harriet. 'I don't bake so much now as I used to.'

'Mrs Marshall was 'cook at Hart Holme Manor,' Ellen Tuke explained. 'That's how we met, when I was in service.'

'You were in service?' Harriet said. 'Was that at 'house you were telling me about?'

Ellen Tuke nodded. 'Same,' she said, turning her gaze away. 'Until I married Mr Tuke.'

'And how is Mr Tuke?' Mrs Marshall asked. 'I've not seen him in many a year.'

'Much 'same as always, Mrs Marshall, thank you for asking.' Ellen's face was expressionless. 'He doesn't change much; not for 'better, at any rate.'

'No,' the older woman said. 'I don't suppose he does. I seem to recall saying as much the day you said you were going to marry him.' She pressed her lips hard together as she poured boiling water into the teapot. 'Ellen, I says, that's a man that won't change, no matter what.'

'I seem to recall you saying a few other things as well.' Mrs Tuke gave a thin smile. 'And not very complimentary, but there, I—'

'Made your bed and now must lie on it,' Mrs Marshall finished and Mrs Tuke nodded and looked wistful.

They've had this conversation before, Harriet mused as she drank her tea and accepted a slice of ham, a chunk of bread and a spoonful of horseradish sauce, which was hotter than she had ever tasted and brought her out in a sweat. I expect they have 'same discussion on every visit. They must constantly hark back to the old days.

After they had eaten and talked some more, Mrs Marshall put on a pair of rubber boots and took them on a walk by the Haven. A pale sun was partially obscured behind ragged white and grey clouds, throwing moving shadows on the water.

'We'll have snow afore 'week's out,' Mrs Marshall said. 'Mark my words if we don't. I can feel it in my bones.'

'Do you live alone, Mrs Marshall?' Harriet asked. 'It seems a solitary sort of place.'

'Aye, I do, m'dear, but I'm never lonely. Every day there's summat different to look at, a fresh sunrise and sunset every day of 'week, and I defy anybody to say there's a better one anywhere in 'world. A whole rainbow of colours displayed for me every morning and night. Purple, rose, gold and all colours in between. A whole palette o' jewels. And then fishermen come by most days and sometimes they bring me some of their catch and I cook it over 'fire and we share it. And mebbe they'll bring me a sack o' flour or a bag o' corn that they're delivering from down 'river or from 'south bank . . . that's Lincolnshire, you know. After Hart Holme Manor, this is 'best place in 'world,' she repeated, 'that anybody could have 'good fortune to live in.'

Harriet smiled. There was no wonder that Mrs Tuke liked to visit. Mrs Marshall positively exuded good cheer and well-being.

They walked a little way with her and then Mrs Tuke said they ought to be getting back as she wanted to be home before dark. A chill wind had got up, lashing the waters of the Haven into frothy crests.

'You do right, m'dear,' her friend agreed as they turned back to the cottage. 'Darkness soon creeps in at this time of 'year, but afore you go I must give you some of my chutney and preserves. There's a nice batch o' quince jelly and a jar of bramble jam, and for 'fine men in your family a bottle of elderberry wine.'

Harriet looked on in amazement as the eggs, cream and chicken were exchanged for preserves and chutney, apples and plums and a bottle of dark red wine. She had never seen so much food, but realized that it was all home-made, gathered from the earth with effort and satisfaction.

I didn't know, she thought as they climbed back into the cart, I hadn't realized what country folk did. I never guessed that they wouldn't have any shops where they could buy groceries and that they'd have to fall back on their own resources. And that's how they survive.

She said as much to Mrs Tuke as they turned about and headed back to the road, with Mrs Marshall waving them off until they turned a bend and were out of sight.

'Ah, but it's not 'same for everybody,' she replied. 'There's some country folk who can die in a ditch just 'same as folk in town can die in 'gutter. We're lucky that we've got a decent landlord and know how to turn our hand to helping ourselves.' She gave a little shiver. 'If poor folks get turned off their land or can't find work, it's as bad here as anywhere else, especially in winter. But for others . . . well, tek Mrs Marshall, for instance. Master Hart gave her that cottage for a peppercorn rent, and she'll stay there for 'rest of her life. That's his way of payment for good service. She was 'cook for his father afore him.'

'And what about your farm, Mrs Tuke?' Harriet asked because she was interested. 'Does 'same thing apply?'

Mrs Tuke's face tightened. 'We have to mek it pay. And lads'll have to shape up after we're gone. There'll be no favours then.'

They travelled on in silence except when Mrs Tuke urged on the slow-moving mare. 'Come on,' she said irritably. 'Let's be home afore dark or 'rain, whichever comes soonest,' but the old mare simply pricked her ears, snickered, and plodded on at the same pace.

The clouds grew thicker as the sky darkened, and a few drops of sleet fell, but they were not too far from the farm now. Mrs Tuke pointed with her whip and was about to say something when Harriet heard the rattle of wheels and the drum of hoofbeats and turned to look behind her.

'A carriage is coming Mrs Tuke. Should we pull in to let it pass?' It was travelling fast and she didn't think they could get out of the way in time, but it began to slow, the coachman drawing on the reins of four fine horses, as Mrs Tuke drew over to the side of the road. The coachman lifted his whip in acknowledgement, and as they were overtaken Harriet saw a man inside the carriage looking out.

Mrs Tuke sat for a moment, letting it pass by, but it continued to slow until it drew up alongside a pair of open gates. The carriage door opened and a man in a dark overcoat and top hat jumped out and walked towards them.

'What's up?' Harriet said in trepidation. 'We were not in his way.'

'It's all right,' Mrs Tuke said quietly. 'No need to be alarmed.'

The gentleman – Harriet could see that he was no ordinary man by his bearing as much as his dress, and the fact that he was riding in a splendid carriage – walked towards them. Mrs Tuke sat with her hands folded in front of her, the whip lying loosely across her lap. She lifted her chin as the man approached, and although Harriet saw her give a slight smile, she also noticed that her lips were trembling.

The gentleman touched his hat. 'Well, Ellen,' he said. 'I thought it might be you.' He put out his hand and she lifted hers and they touched fingers. 'This is remarkable. How are you? I haven't seen you in such a long time.'

'I'm well, thank you, sir,' she said. 'And yourself?'

He nodded and glanced at Harriet.

'This is Harriet,' Ellen said. 'She's recently married our second son.'

He touched his hat again. 'How do you do?' he said briefly, before turning his attention again to Mrs Tuke. 'Are you on your way home? The weather is turning for the worse; I'm afraid you might get very wet.'

'Yes,' she said. 'We've been visiting Cook – Mrs Marshall,' she added.

'I plan to visit her myself tomorrow. Does she need anything special?' he asked, keeping his eyes on her face.

'I've tekken a fowl for Christmas. Mebbe a sack o' coal or a bundle o' wood would be appreciated.' Ellen Tuke looked down at her hands. 'She seems happy in her cottage.'

He smiled, and Harriet thought how strikingly handsome he was, his eyes grey-blue, his sideburns streaked with silver. 'Good,' he said softly. 'She deserves to be content after a long and loyal working life.' He straightened his shoulders. 'I'll not detain you; you should be getting home, but it's very nice to see you again.'

'And you too, sir,' she replied, looking back at him. 'I trust your wife is well?'

He smiled. 'She is. You knew I'd married again?'

'Yes, sir, I did. Four or five years now, isn't it?'

'Yes. It had been a lonely life for my daughter since her mother died.'

'I was sorry to hear of it. She was well thought of,' Mrs Tuke added, and Harriet saw his eyebrows lift.

'She was,' he answered briefly, before tipping his hat once more and bidding them goodbye. He walked back to the carriage and stepped inside; the driver cracked his whip and they turned through the gates and drove away up the long drive.

'Oh!' Harriet breathed. 'What a charming man. Isn't that unusual in gentry?'

'I suppose it is.' Mrs Tuke gathered up the reins and urged Jinny on again. 'But he allus was, even when he was young. Kind and considerate, too.'

'So what was his name? Hart, did you say?'

'Yes,' she said. 'Christopher Hart, owner of Hart Holme Manor and much of 'land round here, including ours.'

'And, you worked for his mother, did you?'

'For 'family, yes. I was in service there. From being fourteen. I started in 'kitchen and worked my way up to being 'upstairs maid.' She swallowed and her voice became strained. 'I left when I was twenty when I married Mr Tuke. He was one of 'horse lads working on 'estate.'

But Harriet was not thinking about Mr Tuke. She was wondering how Christopher Hart could have known Ellen Tuke well enough to remember her all these years later, and why he would stop and greet her. Surely the son of the estate owner wouldn't have paid any attention to the servants. But Mrs Tuke was still talking.

'Master Hart – Christopher – was one of Mrs Marshall's favourites. He was 'only son; he had four sisters, all older than him, so he was spoilt by everybody, including 'servants; when he was home from school he was always in 'kitchen. He didn't go away to university like his mother wanted him to. He said he wanted to stay at home and learn to run 'estate. So that's what he did, and – and so that's why he knows everybody, like Mrs Marshall – and me.'

# CHAPTER FOURTEEN

'Who was that?' Melissa Hart asked her husband.

'One of the servants from the old days.' Christopher undid the top button of his coat and loosened the stock at his neck.

'The old days?' Melissa smiled. 'You mean in your father's day?'

'Yes. Though I doubt that my father would ever have known her, or any of the house servants, for that matter.'

'But you remembered her? How extraordinary.'

'I recall them all from when I was a boy,' he said gruffly. 'You know I go to visit our old cook.'

Melissa nodded. So he did. He was good at looking after people. Except for me, she thought. I take care of myself as well as his daughter, who doesn't appreciate any effort I make to be nice to her. She sighed. I'm becoming grumpy and bitter, and I don't like myself very much. But she was intrigued that he should recognize and stop to speak to the woman and her companion, or daughter perhaps, in the battered old cart. She wasn't an old servant. She couldn't have been any older than Christopher was himself.

She was pleased to be home, even though she was sure that Amy would have some whining complaint about how late they were and that she had been on her own all day.

They had been attending the funeral of one of Christopher's uncles at Beverley Minster and had been pressed to stay for refreshments afterwards. Melissa had known only a few of the other attendees. She was introduced as Christopher's wife, but knew that she was a poor substitute for the sainted woman who had died ten years before.

If I could produce a son, then I too would be everything that was holy, she thought, but then if I produced a child at all it would be something like a miracle.

The carriage drew up at the steps leading to the front door, which was being opened with exact precision by Boulder, the footman, even before the coachman had let down the step for them to alight.

'Good evening, sir, good evening, madam,' he said woodenly as they went into the hall. 'I trust you had a pleasant journey home.' He helped Christopher off with his coat and took his hat while one of the maids helped Melissa out of her travelling cloak.

'No, we didn't,' Christopher said. 'The weather was cold and the roads were wet. And we'd been to a funeral, if you recall, and the Minster was freezing.'

'Sorry, sir, of course. I beg your pardon.'

'Oh, it's all right, Boulder, we're just glad to be home. Is Miss Amy about?'

'She's in 'sitting room, sir.' The maid answered for Boulder. 'I've just served her tea.' She turned to Melissa. 'Shall I make another pot, ma'am?'

'Oh, please, Alice, if you would, but nothing to eat. I'll wait for dinner.' She raised questioning eyebrows at Christopher.

'Ask Cookson to bring me a hot toddy, Boulder,' he said. 'And I too will wait for dinner. Can we have it a little earlier, Melissa?'

'Ask Cook if it can be ready for seven, Alice, and we'll have time to change.'

Melissa led the way into the sitting room, where Christopher's daughter was sitting by the fire. A tray with a silver teapot, milk jug and sugar basin was set on a small table beside her, and she was sipping tea from a china cup.

'Where on earth have you been?' she asked petulantly. 'Papa? I was beginning to think you were not coming home tonight.'

Her father sighed and sat down on one of the sofas, trailing his arm over the back of it. 'You should have come with us and then you'd know how long these things take. We couldn't rush away; it would have been disrespectful to my aunt and her family.'

'They asked after you, Amy,' Melissa told her. 'They said how much they'd like to see you if you'd care to visit.'

Amy turned a bored expression to her stepmother. 'I'm not going anywhere in this weather,' she stated, and yawned. 'And certainly not all the way to Beverley.'

Melissa sat down opposite her. 'But you were thinking of going to your London aunt, and now you've almost missed the season.'

'I'll go when I'm good and ready,' Amy answered sharply.

Her father frowned. 'Please don't speak to Melissa in that tone of voice, Amy.'

Amy raised her eyebrows and gave a condescending shrug, but they were saved from further comments by the arrival of Alice with more tea, followed by their butler, Cookson, carrying a small tray bearing a glass of hot toddy.

Christopher sipped the toddy, relaxing and pondering on the events of the day; he had found it very trying. He hadn't known his late uncle Felix very well, but he'd got on well with his cousins, Felix's two sons and a daughter, as they were all growing up. The elder boy, Simon, a few years older than him, had grown-up sons already married with children of their own, and if Melissa didn't produce any sons the Hart Holme estate would go to Simon, if he should outlive him, and then to his eldest son.

Perhaps it's me that's at fault, he mused. But it can't be. I've already produced a daughter, and dear Jane suffered several miscarriages and a stillbirth. Poor Melissa. I know she thinks she has failed me, but time is getting on. We've been married for five years now and nothing. Not a sign.

Amy finished her tea in silence and then stood up. 'I'm going to change for dinner,' she said.

'Oh,' her father remarked. 'I thought you might have wanted to talk to us, seeing as you've been on your own for most of the day.'

Amy assumed a bored expression. 'What should we talk about? The funeral? How very dreary. No thank you. I'll see you at dinner.' She walked to the door with her chin up, without making eye contact with either of them.

Christopher shook his head after she had left the room. 'I don't know what to make of her. She used to be such a sweet child. Is this what females are like at her age?'

'It's true that women can feel tense and irritable at certain times, but it's nothing to do with that.' Melissa drew in a breath. 'We must accept it and shouldn't make excuses about it. No, the fact, Christopher, is that she doesn't like me. I don't know if she would have been the same with any other wife you might have brought into her life, but I'm the one here sharing her father, when formerly she had you to herself.'

'But we've been married for five years,' Christopher protested. 'Surely she's accepted you by now?'

'I think not,' Melissa said sadly. And neither do I think she ever will, she thought, and wondered if that might be the reason why she herself was always so tense and thus unable to conceive. It's wrong to blame the girl, I know, she thought, but I am constantly trying to please her and failing totally.

'Should I speak to her?' Christopher said after a few minutes of silence. 'Find out just what it is that's troubling her?'

'She clings to the memory of her mother,' Melissa said softly. 'She endows the remembrance of her with everything that is wonderful. I understand that. Of course I do, but she is almost a woman herself, Christopher; she must put away her childishness. And,' she said with a slight hesitation, 'she should think of you; she should realize that you deserve a life without her mother.'

'That's the top and bottom of it, isn't it?' Christopher murmured. 'She's jealous. I didn't want to admit it before, but I spoiled her; she and I did everything together after Jane died. She was only eight, just a child.'

'And thirteen when we married,' Melissa said. 'Not an easy time for a young girl bordering on womanhood. That I understand too, but I wonder . . .' She paused. 'Would it be a good idea to ask Jane's sister if Amy could go and stay with her for a few weeks after Christmas? She mentioned that she would like to. I'm sure that her cousins would welcome her, being of a similar age.'

Please say yes, she thought fervently, and knew she was probably being selfish in wanting Christopher to herself even for a short time.

'I'm sure she'd be welcomed by any of her aunts, but you're right, she would probably prefer going to Jane's sister than any of mine, for their children are all older and married anyway.' He ran his fingers through his short beard as he considered. 'Shall I suggest it? Or perhaps we should ask Deborah first.'

'Oh, ask first, and I also think it better coming from you, my love. I don't want to appear as the wicked stepmother wanting rid of her.'

He laughed. 'How ridiculous you are, Melissa.' He reached across for her hand. 'But it was your humour that attracted me when I first met you, although how you managed to have any after what you'd gone through I cannot conceive.'

'That and my pretty face,' she said jocularly, though she was aware that she was comely.

'That goes without saying,' he murmured, smiling gently and adding, 'Do you ever think of him?'

She nodded, suddenly reminded of the time before she knew Christopher and of the man she was to have married, who was tragically taken from her. 'Sometimes,' she admitted. 'We'd made so many plans.'

She cast her mind back to the young man she had known since childhood. Their parents had planned their betrothal, they both knew that, but they were happy with the arrangement. They were to be married when she reached twenty-one, but three months before her birthday Alfred was taken ill with influenza and died within a week.

Her sorrow had been deep, but made worse by the anguish of Alfred's parents, and also her own, who proclaimed that she would now never marry and was doomed to spinsterhood with the constant memory of the eternally young, never to be forgotten Alfred. By the time she was twenty-three she had adjusted to life without him, but by then all her friends were married and there were few eligible men left, and she thought that her parents' predictions were proving correct.

But then she met the widowed Christopher and realized that she could love again; he was twenty years older than she and she had thought that as a quiet, rather sad man living with his young daughter he would not find her in the least appealing. But she was wrong. Three months later he declared his love and they were married almost immediately, much to her parents' and Alfred's parents' chagrin. Now, five years later, she still hadn't given Christopher the son he desired above all else and sometimes she asked herself if that were the true reason he had asked her to marry him.

'But,' she added in response to his query, 'I'm happy with you.'

# CHAPTER FIFTEEN

Christopher wrote to his sister-in-law. He'd had a good relationship with Deborah even after Jane died, and he told her of the difficulties he was having with Amy. *I believe she thinks too often of her mother,* he wrote, *and it seems to me that she becomes melancholic at times. I want Amy to enjoy her life, as indeed her mother would have wanted her to. She's at the threshold of womanhood and should be experiencing the joys of it, before one day settling down to what I hope will be a satisfactory married life.*

He closed with the plea that she might be invited to spend time with her cousins, doing whatever young women did – balls, theatres and perhaps even travelling if they so desired – rather than living quietly in the country.

A letter came back almost immediately, with the news that Deborah and her daughters were on the point of sending Amy an invitation to join them for the London winter season and then travel with them to Switzerland, where they would stay for a month, if Christopher agreed.

He called Amy down from her room to tell her of the proposal. Melissa had gone for a walk in the garden, as it was the first sunny day they had had for a week.

'What do you think? Would you like to go? Is it too far, or too long away from home?' he asked.

'It isn't too far, Papa. Of course not,' she answered impetuously. 'I'm not a child, you know. You forget I'm eighteen now. I'm a woman.'

He gave a sad smile. 'I don't forget,' he said softly. 'Every day I'm reminded that you are my grown-up daughter and not the little girl who used to cling to my hand so as not to lose me.'

Immediately she was contrite. 'I'm sorry, Papa. I'm so thoughtless and peevish sometimes, and I don't mean to be, but I can't help myself. I know that you miss Mama as much as I do.'

He chose his words carefully, realizing that whatever he said could be construed as she wished.

'I do miss her, of course, but life must go on, Amy, and I now have Melissa to share mine, as I hope one day you will have someone special to share yours.'

He saw her expression tighten at Melissa's name and knew that his fear that Amy was jealous of Melissa was justified.

She shrugged. It was Amy's most expressive gesture to show that she didn't care one way or another, but he was astonished to hear her say bitterly, '*She* won't mind if I go away, will she? I expect she'll be pleased to see me go.'

'Go where?' Neither had heard the door open or Melissa's footsteps as she came into the room. Her cheeks were pink from the cold and her eyes were bright. 'Someone going somewhere?' she asked artlessly, drawing closer to the fire.

'Amy has had an invitation to visit her London cousins and then travel to Switzerland with them and her aunt.'

'Oh, really?' Melissa sat by the fire, putting her hands towards the flame. 'How kind! But for how long? Can we spare you? We should miss you if you were away too long, Amy. And your papa would worry, wouldn't you, Christopher?'

'Why should he worry? I'm perfectly capable of looking after myself.' Amy drew herself up to her full height of five foot two, an inch shorter than Melissa, which annoyed her. 'Why does everyone treat me like a child, or as though I'm witless?' She looked from one to the other. 'My cousins are more or less the same age as I, and if they are allowed to travel then I see no reason why I shouldn't go too. You must manage as best you can without me.' She gave Melissa a withering look and then smiled sweetly at her father. 'It will do you good to be without me for a while.'

Melissa raised one or two further objections, but was careful not to overdo them in case Amy should change her mind. Finally, she said, 'Well, if you're sure, Amy, but your papa must take you to London himself. I wouldn't settle otherwise. And in the meantime perhaps we should take a look at your wardrobe and go shopping for material to make new gowns. Or we might look at ready-made. We don't want your smart London cousins thinking that we're just country mice who don't know how to dress.'

Amy stared at her, her lips apart. 'Oh,' she breathed. 'Yes, please.'

'Right after Christmas, do you think? I have some catalogues, so we could make a start at looking at styles and fashions.' She smiled at the girl. 'Or we could take the train into Hull. Wouldn't that be fun?'

Their Christmas was quiet. They had no visitors this year but it passed pleasantly enough; there was a flurry of snow on Christmas Eve and they decorated a tree brought in from the estate. The gardener found holly with bright red berries to arrange on the chandeliers, and on Christmas morning they drove to Ellerker to attend the church service.

This, Melissa decided as they sat down for a lunch of goose and accompaniments, was the best Christmas she had enjoyed for a long time. Amy was excited about the anticipated holiday with her cousins and also at the prospect of shopping for new clothes. Have I been at fault here, Melissa wondered as she listened to Amy's chatter, have I indulged her as Christopher's motherless daughter, treating her with kid gloves, when I should have endeavoured to become more of a friend, a confidante?

'So shall we go by train?' Amy asked. 'Into Hull, I mean?'

'Oh yes, I think so, don't you? Chapman could drive us to Brough station.'

'No, no,' Christopher interrupted. 'There have been several accidents. Only a few weeks ago someone was killed on the crossing. I'll drive you through to Hull, or Chapman can.'

'Oh, Christopher,' Melissa complained. 'The accident was the crossing keeper's fault and I hear that he has since been dismissed. We shall be perfectly safe, and neither you nor Chapman will want to wait around whilst we shop. And besides,' she gave Amy a complicit glance, 'we shall go somewhere nice for lunch and maybe even afternoon tea before catching the train home.'

'Oh!' he said, in mock anguish. 'So I'm not invited?'

'No, you are not, Papa.' Amy smiled. 'You know you would hate to kick your heels whilst we shop. This is a ladies only treat.'

And although neither Christopher nor Melissa dared to glance at the other, both felt a great sense not only of relief, but also of warm contentment that perhaps after all they were becoming a complete family and not a divided one.

In the first week of the new year Melissa and Amy travelled to Hull on the train, having finally persuaded Christopher that they would be perfectly safe. They had a carriage to themselves, and although it was cold and they hadn't expected that there would be quite so much soot or smoke, they enjoyed looking out at the countryside and the estuary, seeing it from a different viewpoint.

'The estuary is very muddy, isn't it?' Amy remarked.

Melissa nodded; she had been watching the water birds on the riverbank. The railway line ran very close to the Humber. 'It's sediment, I believe,' she answered. 'I recall my father telling me that the high tide carries it up the estuary from the sea, and that's why we get so many birds. They're searching for food, see.' She pointed to a flock of curlews delving in the muddy water with their long pointed beaks. 'I expect they're looking for worms and other creatures.'

'Yes,' Amy said. 'And fish – and eels! I once went down into the kitchen when Cook was baking an eel pie for the kitchen staff's supper. She asked me if I'd like to try some.' She gave a shudder. 'I refused.'

They were getting along very well, Melissa thought. If they continued in this vein she would be quite sorry to see Amy go off on her holiday. 'Why did you go into the kitchen?' she asked. 'Were you hungry?'

'No,' Amy said. 'It was just that I'd remembered Papa telling me that when he was a boy he often went down to the kitchen and the cook used to give him a slice of pie or a piece of cake. It wasn't the same cook as we have now.' She paused, thoughtfully. 'It was just after Mama had died, when I went down, I mean. Papa was out on the estate and my governess was confined to her room because of a cold. There was no one else in the house I could talk to and – and I had nothing to do except read my text books, as I'd been told I should, but I didn't want to.'

She swallowed and licked her lips and was suddenly jerked about as the train drew to a halt at the next station. 'But Mrs Gorton, who was our housekeeper then, came in and said I shouldn't be there, because I'd disturb the kitchen routine.'

Melissa frowned. A woman without any understanding of a lonely child, for that was what Amy had been. 'And have you been down since?'

Amy shook her head. 'Never,' she said. 'Even though Mrs Gorton left. When I told Papa what she said, he said he would give her immediate notice and I didn't like to go down after that in case they all thought I was a spoilt telltale.'

'Oh, Amy, why didn't you tell me?' Melissa said. 'The kitchen staff would love it if you went down to see them. Not when they were preparing lunch or dinner, of course, but at any other time. I go down quite often. Otherwise they don't know who they are serving; we'd just be names to them and not real people. Owners of the great houses with masses of servants

110

might not know who works for them, but that's not your papa's way.'

The train pulled out again with a screeching whistle and a thick show of steam. 'In fact,' she went on when the noise had died down, 'when we were returning from the funeral before Christmas, your father had Chapman stop the carriage to speak to someone in a horse and cart, and it was someone who used to work here when he was a boy.'

'Really? And Papa remembered him from all that time ago?' Amy was astonished.

'Not a him, a her. And she'd worked in the kitchen when she was a young girl.'

'Papa is so kind, isn't he?' Amy said indulgently. 'He visits their old cook too. Imagine him remembering a servant girl when there must have been so many. She must have been extremely gratified.'

Mmm, Melissa thought, and murmured, 'Yes, I suppose she would have been.'

# CHAPTER SIXTEEN

A brace of pheasants had been delivered from the manor and these, with the addition of the other old hen whose neck Mrs Tuke had wrung, were plucked and stuffed with sausage meat and roasted, making what Harriet considered a sumptuous banquet for Christmas Day. She recalled other Christmas dinners that she and her mother had shared: a small joint of fatty pork, or a thick soup made from marrowbones and vegetables.

But they had enjoyed themselves, she remembered, revelling in being able to stay in bed for an extra hour, and after preparing their meagre meal taking a walk into town to see the grand folk going into church and hearing the joyous peal of the bells. Sometimes they walked down to the pier overlooking the estuary which was what most Hull folk liked to do on their days off; but she also recalled seeing the poor of the town queuing up for the soup kitchen or standing outside the church gates waiting for the congregation to depart and hoping that a coin would be pressed into their outstretched hands.

We were never so poor that we had to degrade ourselves like that, she thought thankfully.

Mrs Tuke placed two jugs of home-made wine on the table, one of elderberry, rich and dark red, the other apple, which smelt sweet and potent. A third jug contained ale. Harriet chose the apple, as did Mrs Tuke, who today appeared to have relaxed her rule of not eating with her family; Noah and Fletcher chose ale and Mr Tuke poured himself a second glass of elderberry.

'You'll be roaring drunk,' Mrs Tuke muttered. 'It's two years old.'

'Not going to waste it.' He took a sip with a puckered mouth and after swallowing drew in his cheeks. 'You get used to 'taste after a glass or two.' He screwed up his lips again and took another mouthful. 'This was my old ma's receipt,' he said to no one in particular, and no one answered or made a comment.

Harriet picked up her glass. 'My ma and me,' she ventured, 'we used to toast 'queen's health in a glass o' beer.'

Everyone looked at her. Mr Tuke scowled, Mrs Tuke cast her gaze down at her plate, Noah began eating, but Fletcher smiled and raised his tankard to her.

'We saw Her Majesty when she came to Hull,' she went on in a quiet voice. 'Whole of 'town was decorated wi' flags and ribbons and flowers.'

Only Fletcher appeared to be interested. 'What did she look like?' he asked.

'Beautiful,' she said. 'Very regal. Prince Albert was with her, and 'rest of 'family. It was such a special day.'

'Waste o' money,' Mr Tuke grunted, stuffing his mouth with pheasant. 'Lot o' fuss about nowt.'

Mrs Tuke cut into a small slice of chicken. 'Some of 'best folk in 'county were there, so I understand. I heard that Mr Hart and his family attended.'

Noah belched. 'Oh aye, they'd be there. They've nowt else to do but grovel afore their so-called betters.'

'How would you know?' Mrs Tuke muttered. 'You don't know 'em.'

'Nor want to,' he contended. 'They're no different from us.'

'Better mannered, for one thing,' she observed.

Harriet felt a tight band around her chest. How could they argue today of all days? It's my fault, she decided. I shouldn't have brought up 'subject of 'queen. I didn't think. Everybody I know was so excited about seeing her, I never thought that some folk might be resentful of her. We weren't, in spite of being poor.

'So, Mrs Tuke,' Fletcher said, and Harriet didn't at first realize he was talking to her and not his mother, although she too looked up. 'It seems that it's just you and me who's toasting Her Majesty's health.' He lifted his tankard again. 'Here's health unto Her Majesty.'

She thought he was mocking her and was ready to give a cutting reply, but he gave her a swift wink and she grasped that he was hoping to provoke his brother and father. She raised her glass. 'Her Majesty,' she murmured, and saw that Mrs Tuke also lifted her glass and sipped, although she didn't utter a toast.

I don't know how much longer I can suffer this atmosphere, she thought. I'm on tenterhooks in case I say summat I shouldn't and set them off arguing.

'That reminds me,' Noah said, putting his fingers in his mouth to remove a piece of meat from his teeth.

'Of what?' Fletcher said.

'That you owe me 'price of a heifer.'

Fletcher put down his knife and fork.

Noah put down his cutlery too and leaned his elbow on the table. He pointed a finger at his brother. 'I bet you 'price of a young heifer that I'd bring a wife home afore you.' He sat back and grinned. 'So you owe me.'

Fletcher's face reddened. 'I didn't agree to any such bet! If you want to choose a wife for 'sake of price of a heifer that's up to you, but don't expect me to fork out for 'expense of it.'

Noah pushed back his chair. 'We'll settle it again then,' he roared, and Fletcher too prepared to rise.

Mrs Tuke banged on the table with a knife. 'If you leave this table now you don't come back to it. There'll be no food on 'table for either of you in future unless you cook it yourselves, cos I'll not be here to do it.'

Fletcher started and turned to his mother. 'Sorry,' he said. 'Sorry, Ma. We'll not fight today.' He glanced at Noah and then at Harriet. 'Not today. Sorry,' he repeated.

Noah guffawed. 'Yellow-belly! Scared o' what your ma thinks!'

'That's enough,' Fletcher warned him. 'Leave it for another day. And don't go upsetting your wife.'

Noah glanced at Harriet and then snarled at his brother. 'Don't you go telling me what to do about my wife. You keep your nose out o' that.' He pointed a finger again. 'That's another score to settle.'

'Sit down!' Mr Tuke bellowed; he seemed to have just woken up, as if what had gone before was nothing to do with him. Then he said, 'Mrs Tuke's full o' threats and promises, she is, but she won't keep to 'em. Mrs Tuke,' he said, 'carve me a slice o' chicken.'

Mrs Tuke did so, and as she placed it on his plate Harriet was horrified to see that her eyes were full of sheer un-adulterated hate, as if she'd just as soon slice him with the knife rather than the chicken.

After they had finished their meal, Fletcher and Noah went out, and Harriet and Mrs Tuke cleared away the dishes. They put the leftovers in the pantry, saving a few pieces of chicken for the dog, and began washing up. Harriet, after glancing towards Mr Tuke, who was snoring in front of the fire, asked, 'Would you really have left? And where would you have gone? It's hard for a woman on her own.'

Mrs Tuke didn't answer for a moment. Then she said, 'Sometimes I think I couldn't be any worse off than I am now. I did threaten once before; that's what Mr Tuke meant.' She picked up a pan and scrubbed at it as if her life depended on it. 'But I didn't go. My conscience wouldn't let me.'

She said no more and Harriet didn't like to pry. 'A con-science is a difficult thing,' she murmured. 'But I could leave now and not feel too badly about it.'

Mrs Tuke again attacked the pan. 'He'd come after you,' she muttered. 'Noah would. He'd be worse than his father. He'd find you no matter if you hid in the deepest of Hull's dark alleyways, and he'd drag you back.'

'Then I have to find another way to cope with this – this situation.' Harriet looked out of the small square window and saw Fletcher running towards the house. 'I feel unnecessary. I've nowt to do but milk 'cow twice a day and gather eggs every morning.'

'Mebbe you should've thought—' Mrs Tuke broke off as Fletcher burst through the door.

'Dora's about to calve,' he announced. 'Do you want to watch?' he asked Harriet. 'You'll have to be quick.'

'Oh!' Harriet grabbed a shawl. 'Yes, please, if I won't be in 'way. Is that all right?' she asked her mother-in-law. 'Leave the rest of 'dirty pans for me.'

Mrs Tuke shrugged, and then said, 'It's like a miracle 'first time you see it.'

Harriet hopped into the rubber boots and dashed after Fletcher. 'Is she all right on her own?'

'Who? Ma?' He turned to look at her, forehead creased. 'Yes, she likes her own company.'

'I meant Dora!' Harriet giggled, and Fletcher gazed at her as if the sound of laughter was new to him. Harriet guessed that there wasn't much merriment in that house or in their lives; but then he laughed too and opened the cowshed door.

Dora lay on the straw grunting and protesting and Fletcher knelt beside her. 'Come on then, old girl,' he murmured. 'Nearly there. Look,' he said suddenly. 'Here come the front feet. Do you want to help her?'

Harriet gasped as she saw first the water sacs and then two feet appear from the cow's vulva. 'What do you want me to do?'

'Just take hold of the feet and when she starts to push, pull gently.'

Harriet felt squeamish as she took hold of the sticky mucus-

116

covered feet and drew in a gasping breath as the cow lumbered to her feet; when Fletcher said 'Now' she pulled and the feet came out further. The legs appeared, followed by a nose and the rest of the head and within a few minutes the shoulders; she felt as if her arms were being pulled out of their sockets. Fletcher's firm hands were on the half in half out body when suddenly the whole wet and glistening calf was lying on the straw.

'It's a female,' Fletcher's voice was triumphant. 'And it's alive. You've delivered your first calf!'

Harriet felt her eyes fill with tears as she saw Fletcher wipe and open the calf's mouth with his fingers so that it could take its first breath. Then she watched as Dora licked it and nudged it with her nose to help it stand; first its head and front legs and then its back legs. The calf stumbled and dropped, stumbled and dropped, getting beneath the cow's legs, until finally it stood on all four feet before falling over again.

'Hey,' Fletcher said softly. 'This is no time for crying. This is a good day.'

'I know.' Harriet snuffled and wiped her cheeks with her shawl. 'But I've not seen anything like it in my life.'

Fletcher gazed at her. 'If you're going to be a farmer's wife you'll get used to it,' he said softly, and then added, 'But 'first time is always special. It didn't tek long because Dora's already had two calves, but with a young heifer it can tek longer. Anyway, we'll leave her to look after it for now. I'll come back in a few minutes and see how they're doing. Come on. We'd better get cleaned up.' He took hold of her elbow to help her up and she jumped as if she had been burned.

'Sorry,' he said, dropping his hand, and she wondered if he had felt it too.

# CHAPTER SEVENTEEN

Harriet's triumph was short-lived, although Mrs Tuke was pleased that it was a female calf that had been delivered. 'We'll keep it,' she said. 'Daisy's getting on a bit, and she'll need replacing in a year or two. We can manage three cows now there's two of us and mebbe mek butter wi' surplus and sell it at 'gate.'

Harriet didn't dare to ask what would eventually happen to Daisy, but when she told Noah she had delivered her first calf he just stared at her and said scathingly. 'Time you were pregnant yourself.'

She flushed, and didn't know how to answer him. It was unfortunate that his father was awake. He looked at her, and giving a lopsided grin commented, 'Not all bitches get pregnant.'

She turned away. How coarse and vulgar he was. Noah had no right to address her in that way in front of him. She was glad that Fletcher wasn't there to hear him; he was outside swilling down under the pump.

'I'm talking to you.' Noah's hard tones made her turn back. 'We've been married nearly a month. Time summat was happening.'

Harriet stared back at him; she was livid with anger. 'Well, if you're going to insist on telling everybody our personal details, perhaps you'd also like to inform them that I've just started my monthly flux, so your manhood has yet to be proved.'

She saw him clench his fist and stayed still. I don't want a black eye so I'd better not provoke him further, she thought cautiously, but then Mrs Tuke brushed past her and confronted her son.

'That's enough,' she said brusquely. 'Take a hint from nature. You should know if you call yourself any sort o' farmer that not all couplings are successful straight away, and sometimes patience is needed. A month is nowt!' She turned to her husband. 'And as for you, Mr Tuke, keep your long nose out of 'trough. This is nowt to do wi' you.'

He simply grunted and turned his face away, but it seemed to Harriet that there was something unspoken between them, a tension or deliberate aggravation that had nothing to do with her or Noah.

Noah shot Harriet a scowl; he didn't answer his mother but simply sat down by the fire opposite his father, blocking out any warmth for anyone else.

Later, Harriet went out again on her own to look at Dora and her calf, and milked Daisy, who had almost dried up. She had been told that very shortly Dora would be milked for the house as well as her calf and that milking her would stimulate more milk; when the calf was big enough to cope with the cold weather they could go outside to join Daisy.

A thick bank of black cloud interspersed with long wave-like strands of grey was travelling swiftly across the estuary from south to north. Looks like rain or snow to me, Harriet thought, but she didn't turn back to the house; the scene was dramatic and compelling to watch, and keeping to the edge of the fields, close by the dyke, she walked down towards the estuary. The water, reflecting the sky, seemed menacing and intimidating as it rose and fell, crested and dipped, hitting the marshy banks of the shore with foaming wash.

In the centre channel where the water was deep a fleet of small boats and barges was heading in the direction of Goole and safe anchorage. This was a powerful and dynamic estuary, the lifeblood of the area, carrying goods and produce to and from not only this coast but the rest of Europe across the German Ocean; today it was not calm and peaceful as it had been when she last walked here, but showing its mettle and strength. The sandbank island she had seen previously was being washed over by the tide, and only the very top of it was showing above the water.

The cloud was now directly above her. She held out her hand, palm uppermost, and felt the sleet begin to patter, sharp, like the points of needles. She turned, picked up her skirt and began to run.

January was bitterly cold, with a sharp frost followed by flurries of snow. Noah and Fletcher were unable to do much work on the land, so they cleared the ditches, which was a constant routine, repaired fences, patched up the walls of the cowshed and stables and climbed up and down wooden ladders keeping the buildings in good repair.

Under Mrs Tuke's instruction, Harriet baked bread, scones and fruit cake, for although she had once told Noah that her mother had shown her how to bake bread she had never had the opportunity to put the lesson into practice. She enjoyed the kneading of dough and the mixing of flour, eggs and butter to make a cake or a scone, but nevertheless was bored. The hens took little looking after now there were fewer of them, and apart from milking Dora and fondling the calf who was now Daisy Two, helping to clean the house and sweeping the yard, there was little to occupy her for the majority of the day.

She stood at the window one afternoon after they had eaten their midday meal and sighed. The day was cold but dry and there were occasional glimpses of bright sky. The brothers had gone outside to fix a length of guttering that had come loose and Mr Tuke as always was snoring by the fire. He's not so old, she thought. Why doesn't he go out and help them?

'You could try up at 'manor,' Mrs Tuke murmured.

Harriet turned towards her. 'Sorry? What? I didn't catch—'

Mrs Tuke glanced at her husband, who had his head back against the chair and his mouth open.

'You could try up at 'manor,' she repeated, 'for temporary work. They'll have tekken on staff at 'hirings, but not everybody stops. It'd be worth your while asking. We allus liked to know who'd be willing to fill in if anybody went off sick, or if there were extra guests coming who didn't bring their own maids.'

'I don't understand,' Harriet said. 'Do you mean 'hiring fair? Those that are held in November?'

'Aye,' Mrs Tuke said. 'Statute Hirings. At Martinmas. Surely they held them in Hull?'

Harriet nodded. 'Aye, they did, but I was at work from 'morning till night so I didn't get to see them.'

'Well, in 'country all 'agriculture workers and some of 'domestics are hired from there. Ours came mostly from Howden or Market Weighton; that's where 'foreman liked to go for new folk. Most of 'farm workers stayed on year in year out, but 'domestics – not all 'young lasses liked being away from home and we used to lose one or two of 'em.'

'So – are you suggesting that they might need someone up at – what's it called? Hart Holme . . .'

Mrs Tuke bent her head so Harriet couldn't see her face for the soft rim of her bonnet. 'Manor,' she said. 'Hart Holme Manor. No harm in asking. But tell 'em it would be temporary.' She chewed on her lip. 'Noah won't like it, but it'd bring extra money in.'

Harriet heaved out a breath. 'I'll do it! When should I go? Today?'

Mrs Tuke permitted herself a small smile. 'No time like 'present,' she murmured. 'Men won't be in again till teatime;

121

they'll mek use of 'fine weather. You could be there and back afore you were missed. And I'd say you'd gone for a walk,' she added.

Harriet dashed upstairs for a warm shawl. 'Am I presentable?' she asked when she came down. She'd brushed her long hair and fastened it in a bun at the back of her neck. 'Where do I go and what do I say?'

'You go up 'front drive past 'formal gardens and afore you reach 'house you'll see a second track veer off to 'left. That leads to 'back of 'house and 'servants' door where deliveries are made.'

They were both speaking quietly because of Mr Tuke, and each held her breath as he gave a sudden snort, licked his lips and went to sleep again.

'Ask for 'cook or 'housekeeper, tell 'em who you are and say you're looking for temporary work but not live-in. Don't forget to bob your knee to 'em, but not to 'maids.'

'How will I know who's who?'

'You'll know,' Mrs Tuke said. 'And if by chance you should see 'master or 'mistress, just stand aside to let 'em pass and bob your knee if they see you.'

Bobbing her knee wasn't anything she'd ever done before and Harriet pondered on this as she slipped away from the house and yard and up the long track that led to the road above. Mrs Tuke had told her that it was about a mile to the gates of the manor.

I never had to bob to 'foreman at 'mill, she thought, nor to 'landlord's wife when I was working in 'hostelry. This'll be a different sort o' life altogether, I should think. I've never met a proper lady or gentleman in my whole life and I'm not sure if I fancy kowtowing to anybody. If I met 'queen, I would curtsey, of course, or to somebody with a title mebbe, but for 'rest, well, are they not 'same as us, onny richer?

There was no one else on the road but she suddenly heard a crashing in the undergrowth and a deer came bolting out of the woodland and crossed the road in front of her, followed swiftly by another, both clearing the hedge and disappearing into a copse.

Well, even if I don't get a job it'll be worth 'walk just to see them, she thought, smiling. It was refreshing, too, to be out in the open, breathing in sharp air, and best of all to be herself, for she found the atmosphere in the house restrictive and confining, especially in the evenings when everyone was inside.

She reached the manor gates, which were partly open; she went through and closed them behind her as she had been told to do at the farm, and set off up the long wide drive. There was well mown grass and trees on either side, and in the distance she could see what to her eyes looked like a good solid house, not overly ostentatious or too grand, with steps leading to a front door with a balcony above it. On the left hand side was an additional wing with a large bay window on the ground floor.

It's lovely, she thought. Imagine living here, or even working here, though I don't expect that 'back will be as handsome as 'front.

As she walked, she glanced about her; over to her right she could see that new flower beds had been dug, although they were empty at present. She turned about and walked backwards to see what the grounds would look like to someone in the house. Oh, yes, she thought, flower beds would be nice. The smooth green lawns were neat and restful to the eye, but flowers would raise the spirits. Roses, she decided. That's what I'd have. I once saw some in a merchant's garden. So sweet-smelling, they were, I could have eaten them.

A rabbit ran across in front of her and she followed its progress, wondering if a keeper would be out with his gun to claim it for the cooking pot. It's a different life out here, she reflected. It's nothing like living in town. Do I like it? Yes, I do, except that I'd like it even better if I wasn't married to Noah and afraid of saying or doing 'wrong thing all 'time.

She lifted her head and looked again towards the manor.

She was almost at the point where the track led off to the servants' quarters, but coming towards her from the direction of the house was a woman, and by her dress – a warm cloak with a hood over a fur hat, gloves and sturdy boots – she most definitely wasn't a servant.

# CHAPTER EIGHTEEN

Harriet thought swiftly. She couldn't dip whilst walking so she'd pause, dip her knee, say 'Good afternoon, ma'am' and walk on.

But she was forestalled by the woman, who on drawing near said, 'Hello. Who are you?'

Melissa Hart knew all the house servants; she'd chosen most of them herself after marrying Christopher. It had been an act of self-defence. She wasn't a mean or calculating woman by any means, but coming to the manor as a new and younger wife she reckoned that the servants who had looked after the lonely widower and his daughter would perhaps be fixed in their habits or adhere too rigidly to the rules laid down by Christopher's first wife. Also, she had thought that having been without a mistress for many years they might well have become used to doing things very much as they wanted.

The first to go had been the cook, Mrs Marshall, who was well past retirement age in any case. When Melissa had told her husband of her intentions, he had at first been horrified, but had then seen the sense of it and said he would find a cottage for her to live in.

'I'm really grateful, ma'am,' Mrs Marshall had said when Melissa gently suggested that she might like to take things a little easier now, and that Mr Hart wanted to show her a cottage by Brough Haven which she could have if she wished.

'Although Hart Holme has been my home for many a year, it isn't mine, and I'd be glad to tek things easy and put my feet up if I had a little place of my own.'

'But you'd help out if ever we were short-handed in the kitchen?' Melissa had asked, without any intention of asking her. 'You have such a good reputation as a cook.'

'Aye, I do, ma'am,' Mrs Marshall agreed, 'but I think not. You and 'master will no doubt be entertaining more, and quite right too, but them days are past for me.'

But she had recommended another cook who worked in Brough and wanted a better place. Melissa had interviewed the woman, younger than Mrs Marshall, and taken her on. Mrs Marshall was gratified that her advice was taken; the new cook, Mrs Lister, was delighted, and everyone was satisfied.

It had not been so easy with the housekeeper. Melissa thought her cold and supercilious, and when she had informed her she was looking for new staff, including an under-housekeeper or senior maid, the woman was rude and arrogant and complained to Christopher that his new wife wanted to change a system that had been working perfectly under her command. He in turn became angry and upset and had dismissed her, giving her a reference that was fair but hardly glowing.

As for the maids, there was a natural reduction; some said they didn't want to work for a new mistress, while those who were conscientious under direction and comfortable working there decided to stay put unless asked to leave.

Melissa then stole her mother's housekeeper, Mrs Clubley, who had always been kind to her and efficient too despite her mistress's constant interference. She jumped at the chance of coming to housekeep for the *young* mistress, and Melissa was grateful to have someone she knew and could rely on.

And so, on seeing a young woman walking along her drive as she was coming to inspect the arrangement of the rose beds she had asked for, she was curious as to who the stranger was. She didn't seem like a humble countrywoman; she walked with an assured air as if on an important errand, and she was looking about her as if she hadn't seen the garden before.

'I'm Harriet M— Tuke, ma'am. I'm mekking for 'servants' hall to ask about a position.'

Melissa raised her fair eyebrows. 'You were going to say something else,' she jested. 'Do you not know who you are?'

Harriet flushed. This was not a good beginning. 'I'm recently married, ma'am. I'm not yet used to my married name. I used to be Harriet Miles, but now I'm Harriet Tuke.'

'Do you live near here?'

'Yes, ma'am. My husband's family have a farm on your land, close by 'estuary.'

Melissa gave a small frown. The only farm by the estuary that belonged to them was a run-down one which Christopher said barely paid its way.

'And – are you not needed at home?' Such a silly question, she chided herself. Perhaps they need her wages.

'My husband's mother looks after 'house so there's not much for me to do, though I collect eggs, when there are any, and I've been taught how to milk 'cows.'

'Well.' Melissa decided to draw the conversation to a close. 'I already have a housekeeper and a cook, so I don't know what—'

'Oh!' Harriet interrupted. 'Nowt – nothing so grand, ma'am. I'm new to domestic work. I used to work in a Hull mill when I was single. I was thinking more of a scullery maid or helping wi' laundry, and I wouldn't want to live in,' she hastened to add. 'My husband wouldn't want . . . well . . .' She paused. 'He doesn't know I'm here.'

'I see.' Melissa didn't really want to know the details of her life. 'Go to the back door, then, and ask for Mrs Clubley or Cook. They might be able to suggest something, maybe on a temporary basis.' She gave Harriet a dismissive nod and began to move away. Then she said, 'Have you been here before?'

'No, ma'am. It's my first time.'

'So you haven't seen the gardens?'

Harriet shook her head. 'They're beautiful,' she said. 'Are you having flower beds, ma'am?'

'Yes, I am, although I don't think the gardener is very impressed with the idea.' Melissa glanced at the bare beds in the distance.

'I think they'd be lovely, ma'am. Roses would be nice. You'd be able to smell 'scent up at 'house, I should think.'

'Exactly,' Melissa murmured. 'My thoughts exactly.' She smiled at Harriet. 'Well, good luck, Mrs Tuke,' she said. 'Tell Mrs Clubley or Cook you've been speaking to me.'

Harriet watched her walk away before she set off down the other path to the kitchen entrance. Fancy her remembering my name, she thought. She's onny young, though. I thought she'd be older. Second wife. I recall Mrs Tuke telling 'master that she was sorry about 'death of his wife. He mentioned a daughter. Poor woman: she'll be playing second fiddle to the girl, I bet. Still, it's not a bad sort of life, I shouldn't think. She looked about her as she approached the back of the house. Although not as grand as the front, it was none the less impressive. The courtyard was clean and well swept, there were tubs outside the kitchen door with green stuff growing in them, and through a gate she saw another garden with regimented plots, a glasshouse and low glass cloches.

Harriet tapped on the door and a young maid opened it. 'I'd like to speak to Mrs Clubley or Cook, please,' Harriet said. 'My name is Harriet Tuke.'

The girl dipped her knee and Harriet was impressed and not a little flattered. I suppose she's told to dip to everybody above her, and everybody is, she thought.

She was asked to come in and wait in the entrance lobby whilst the girl went to enquire. The lobby had outdoor coats hanging on wall hooks and rubber boots standing on low shelving. Walking sticks and black umbrellas were propped in a bucket in the corner. It smelt of carbolic soap.

The girl came back and said that Cook would see her now,

but she was taking her afternoon rest and could only spare ten minutes.

Mrs Lister was sitting in an easy chair and looked up as Harriet entered. 'What can I do for you?' she asked in a not unfriendly voice.

'I'm sorry to disturb you, Cook,' Harriet apologized. 'I'm looking for temporary part-time work and it was suggested that I apply here. I, er, I've just seen 'mistress on 'way up 'drive and she said to ask for you or Mrs Clubley.'

Mrs Lister sat up sharply. 'You asked 'mistress?'

'No, no! She saw me and asked who I was – she was looking at 'garden. I told her I was mekking my way to servants' hall to ask about part-time work, laundry or cleaning . . .' Her voice tailed away. Had she committed a cardinal sin by speaking to the mistress of the house?

Mrs Lister relaxed back against the chair. 'Sit down,' she said, pointing to a stool by the kitchen table. 'Mrs Hart is un-conventional, to say 'least. Some gentlewomen wouldn't even notice 'servants, let alone speak to 'em.' She looked at Harriet and then called to the girl who had let her in. 'Lizzie, mek us a pot o' tea, an' be quick. She's a good enough lass, but a bit slow,' she confided in Harriet. 'Now then, tell me about your-self and I'll tell you if I've any work.'

Harriet gave her the details of her previous jobs. 'I just need something part time,' she said. 'Not necessarily every day, but mebbe a couple o' times a week, if that's possible.'

Mrs Lister slowly nodded her head. 'I'd need to speak to 'housekeeper, but we could do wi' help wi' laundry on a Monday. I've got one woman, but there's too much for just one and 'other girl I had decided it was beneath her and left.'

Harriet smiled. 'She's not been hungry then, has she?'

'No, not yet she hasn't,' Mrs Lister replied, as the maid brought a tray of tea things. 'Don't pour it yet, Lizzie; let it brew. Have you?' she asked Harriet. 'Ever been hungry?'

'Aye,' Harriet said in a low voice, 'I have, many a time. Work's not easy to find in Hull.'

'So can your husband not afford to keep you at home?'

'He doesn't know I'm here,' Harriet said, and found herself explaining her situation.

The inner door opened and another maid came in. She was wearing a crisp white apron and a white cap and carrying a tea tray.

'Alice, this is Mrs Tuke,' Mrs Lister said. 'She's coming to help wi' washing and ironing, wi' Mrs Clubley's approval.'

'Oh, that's a relief.' Alice sat down in a kitchen chair and stretched her legs. 'I helped with 'ironing last time and it's not my favourite occupation. Tuke? My mother used to work here with somebody who married a Tuke. Any relation?'

'My mother-in-law worked here, for Master Hart's mother.'

'It'll be 'same then,' Alice said. 'I don't know her, but I remember Ma talking about them; he used to work here as well, Mr Tuke, I mean.' She laughed. 'It's such a funny name, isn't it? That's why I remembered it. Sounds like Duke.'

'Alice!' Cook said warningly.

'Oh,' Alice put her hand to her mouth. 'Sorry. Didn't mean to be rude.'

'That's all right,' Harriet said, and took a cup of tea from Cook's outstretched hand. 'I quite agree, it's an odd name.' She took a deep breath. She liked it here; it was warm and friendly. 'So,' she said, taking a sip of the strong tea. 'Am I to be tekken on?'

Cook nodded and settled back in her chair. 'As far as I'm concerned you can start next Monday morning. Be here at six o' clock and I'll clear it wi' Mrs Clubley.'

# CHAPTER NINETEEN

Christopher Hart had his lunch and then went into his study, which was just off the hall. He had accounts to attend to, farm rents to check and stock to consider, all meticulously written down by his bailiff Thomson who should have been here to discuss them ten minutes ago.

There seemed to be only one rent account in arrears, Marsh Farm, and he wondered why; to his knowledge they had never been late before. He sat back in his chair and mused on the smallholding down by the river that was rented by the Tukes.

Nobody else would want it, he considered. It's waterlogged, always prone to flooding and yet they manage to scrape a living from it. It was because of him that they had it. He'd never liked Tuke when he worked on the estate as a horse lad. He didn't like the way he treated the horses and was overly subservient, doffing his cap in an ingratiating and servile manner every time he met Christopher, who walked round the estate with his father whenever he was home from school. He wanted to learn as much as he could and eventually take over the running of the estate.

It was when he became twenty-one that his father laid down some rules, and one was that he should start looking for a suitable wife, someone who one day would be able to support him in his position as a landowner, as his own mother helped his father now. One who knew how to handle the affairs of a substantial manor house, who knew all the right people to invite to dinner or for shooting weekends and could deal with the house servants; and it had come as a shock to Christopher as his affections had lain elsewhere.

And a second shock awaited him when Ellen, the dainty, quietly spoken, pretty young maid he had known since she first came to work at the house when she was fourteen and he fifteen told him that she was to be married to the hateful Tuke.

'But why?' he'd implored. 'You surely don't care for him? Not in the way that you care for me?'

She'd gazed at him from her large grey eyes. 'You know that I don't, but there's no future for us, Christopher. Sooner or later you'll have to find a wife,' she'd paused, 'and that can't be me. I'm going to marry Tuke and leave here.' She'd given a sudden sob. 'And you must forget me.'

He'd vowed that he never would, never could, but no matter that he was hurt and upset, he also realized she was right, and thought how strange it was that she should make that decision at the same time as his father. He also knew that he couldn't bear to see Tuke about the place, knowing that he was married to the only woman he would ever care for. He'd been young, of course, he thought now, and youth is full of passion and desire, especially when they involve a forbidden liaison between master and servant girl.

He had been searching for his lost dog one day and had gone out of the gates and down the road and through the undergrowth, calling for Hector. He'd heard him barking and found him with his nose down a rabbit hole, and nearby a derelict cottage with broken-down walls and a roof that had almost collapsed.

It was on Hart Holme land, albeit waterlogged and marshy, being so close to the estuary, but he felt it had potential if the cottage could be repaired, the roof fixed and the land drained, and so he had asked his father if he could take it on as a project.

His father had laughed and asked, 'And then what will you do with it?' and Christopher had answered casually that he would let it. He'd asked his father if he would allow one of the estate workers to help him, and when he had indulgently agreed, he had asked Tuke.

Tuke was at first uninterested, but then one day he had asked Christopher if he might be considered for the tenancy and said that he would work on the house himself in his free time, which was what Christopher was hoping for.

'Me and my wife'd like a little place of our own,' Tuke had said in what Christopher thought at the time was a swaggering manner. 'Especially as she's expecting. We're living with her ma at 'minute and it's not very convenient.'

Christopher heard the news of the forthcoming event with dismay, and any slight hope he might have harboured of calling on Ellen in her cottage when her husband was working elsewhere was dashed for good. But Ellen would be safe with a roof over her head, which was what he desired above all else, so he comforted himself with that thought and set about finding a wife of his own.

He put his elbows on the desk. And poor Jane had been a good wife, and had had much to put up with in their endeavours to produce a son. Perhaps I'm not meant to have sons, he sighed. Nevertheless Melissa had brought him happiness in this second marriage with her unfailing humour and laughter. Melissa, he knew, would never ever consider herself to be anything but his equal.

A sharp rap on the door brought him out of his reverie and he called, 'Enter.'

Mrs Clubley apologized for disturbing him and said she had only just received a message to say that Thomson was laid low with a stomach complaint and couldn't meet him as arranged.

'There's also a tenant asking to see Thomson, sir. Will you see him or shall I ask him to come back another day?'

When he asked who it was and she said Tuke, he almost said no, but then gathered himself together and said he would see him in the rear courtyard in ten minutes. He hadn't seen Tuke for many years; he had left their employ about a year after the cottage was habitable and somehow managed to eke out a living with his stock. Thomson and other bailiffs before him had attended to farm matters, and although from time to time Christopher had called on other tenant farmers, for whatever reasons he ascribed to himself in justification he never did visit Marsh Farm.

Fletcher stood outside the kitchen door. He'd been asked to wait, and although invited in he said he would wait outside. He stood with his back to the door, his arms folded and his feet apart, gazing through the open gateway in the wall that separated the house from the kitchen garden and the stable block. Imagine owning all of this, all because of being born in 'right place and with 'right parentage.

Fletcher knew that his parents had both worked here on the estate and he supposed this was where they had first met, but he had often wondered why they had married, for he couldn't think of two more unlikely people coming together. But his mother spoke little about her girlhood or of her time in service, and his father was a man of few words who generally bellowed when he had something to say.

He had been a stern and unresponsive father; Fletcher could not recall a single kind word or pat on the head from him, though his mother had sometimes been warm and loving when he was a child and often defended him if his father threatened him and Noah with punishment for some minor misdemeanour. It was their father too who encouraged them to fight each other, playing on their differences, of which there were many.

He clasped his hands behind his back and walked about as he waited; he wished now that he hadn't come, but his mother had been anxious that the bailiff hadn't collected the rent a month ago and it was now overdue. Fletcher had finished his jobs for the day and had decided to humour her.

Noah wouldn't have come, he knew, and nor would his father: they would both have blamed the bailiff, not acknowledging that it was up to the tenant to make sure the rent was paid on time. But he also wanted to have a word with Thomson about the possibility of renting extra land and digging another ditch to take off the surplus water.

He looked up at the clock over the stables and thought that in less than an hour it would be dark and he still had to put the cattle back inside; a frost was due and he preferred to have them under cover. Harriet was tending the milch cows and making a good job of it, he admitted, in spite of being a townswoman.

A tall figure hurried round into the courtyard from the front of the house and Fletcher was surprised to see not Thomson but a stranger he guessed was Christopher Hart himself. Hart also seemed to be expecting someone else, for he raised an enquiring eyebrow.

'Sorry to keep you,' he said. 'I . . .' He hesitated. 'I was expecting to see Tuke, one of our tenants.'

'I'm Fletcher Tuke, sir,' Fletcher told him. 'I'm waiting to see Bailiff Thomson.'

'He's sick.' Christopher's eyes flickered over Fletcher. He hadn't met him before. 'Struck down with some malady or other. Fletcher? Your mother's maiden name?'

It was Fletcher's turn to gaze in astonishment at his landlord. 'Yes, that's right.' How on earth did he know? Surely he didn't remember her. One servant in dozens over the years.

'I remember her. When I was a boy I was often in the kitchen being spoiled by Cook.' Christopher spoke casually. 'Your mother and I were of a similar age.'

Fletcher nodded. And you've fared better, he thought. Good living and an army of servants to look after you have kept you in good shape, whereas my mother is tired and weary from looking after two unruly sons and a boorish husband; for that, he thought reluctantly, is 'truth of what he is.

'I've come about 'rent, sir,' he said. 'Thomson didn't collect

135

it last month and my mother was getting anxious about it. She looks after 'accounts.'

Christopher gave a nod, pleased that they were now speaking of the present and not the past. 'I'll remind him,' he said. 'But do tell her she's no need to worry.'

'I will. There's another thing that I wanted to discuss with Thomson, about acquiring another piece of land. Perhaps I should wait until he's out and about again?'

'Good idea,' Christopher said. 'I do have a few other things to attend to today, but when I next see him I'll ask him to look in on you.' He paused, about to take his leave. 'So which son are you? The eldest? Haven't you recently married?'

'No, it's my brother Noah who's married, sir, but I'm 'eldest son.' He gave a rueful grin. 'Unmarried as yet.'

They took their leave of each other and Christopher strode off towards the gardens, where he could see Melissa. Fletcher, however, turned his head as the kitchen door opened and was astonished to see Harriet emerging.

'What 'you doing here?' he asked.

She raised her eyebrows. 'Having a cup o' tea wi' Cook.'

'What? Do you know her?'

'I do now,' she said smugly and smiled at his puzzled expression. They began to walk away from the house and out of the courtyard. 'I've applied for work.'

'Really?' He glanced swiftly at her as if she might be joking. 'Doing what?'

'Laundry.' She returned his glance. 'I haven't told Noah yet, so keep it to yourself, will you, till I've told him?'

'He won't like it.' He shortened his long stride to keep in step with hers.

'I know,' she said, 'but there's not enough for me to do. Your mother's very efficient and doesn't need my help, so she suggested that I try for occasional work at 'manor.'

They began to walk side by side down the long drive and Fletcher accidentally brushed against her. 'Sorry,' he muttered.

Harriet swallowed and murmured something in return.

She again felt that tingling charge and the hairs on the back of her neck prickled. A pulse throbbed in her throat and she risked a glance up at him, but he was staring straight ahead; he'd also widened the gap between them.

'We'd best be home afore dark,' he said.

'Yes,' she murmured. 'I think so.'

Melissa narrowed her eyes as she looked down the drive at the couple walking towards the gate. Christopher also gazed at the retreating pair.

'Who's that?' she said.

'I don't know who the woman is, but the man is Fletcher Tuke. They rent a place by the estuary.'

'Well, the woman is Harriet Tuke and she's applied for work in the kitchen.' She frowned. 'She said her husband didn't know she was here. Has he come to fetch her home?'

Christopher folded his arms in front of him as he watched them. He shook his head. 'He said he wasn't married. She must be his brother's wife.'

'Mmm.' Melissa smiled mischievously. 'They look like a well-matched pair, but they're walking so far apart it's as if there's a barrier between them. It must be hate – or love!'

# CHAPTER TWENTY

They barely spoke on the walk back until they reached the top of the track that led to Marsh Farm, and then Harriet said, 'Your mother told me she used to work at Hart Holme Manor when she was a girl.'

'Aye, she did,' Fletcher replied. 'But she doesn't talk about it much.'

'I don't think she was unhappy, though. She talked to Mrs Marshall, who used to be 'cook there, and they chatted about 'manor.'

'Did they?' He turned to her. 'She's never spoken about it to me, except when I was young and asked her what she did when she was a girl. She allus changed 'subject whenever I asked her anything.'

'Your father worked there too, didn't he?'

'Aye, and he allus has summat to say about it and mostly derogatory. I reckon he was lucky that they gave him 'tenancy here.'

'Your mother said that Master Hart looked after his former employees, that that was 'kind of man he was.'

'Mmm.' Fletcher appeared to ponder and then swiftly put out his hand to catch her as she tripped over a tree root. It was dark on the track due to the overhanging tree branches.

'Sorry,' she said.

He kept his arm on her elbow. 'Yeh, he looks after old

retainers, but my father wasn't old; he was only in his mid-twenties when he and Ma married. He must have asked if he could have Marsh Farm. God knows why,' he said bitterly. 'It's waterlogged, fit for nowt and he doesn't work on it any more. He leaves it all to Noah and me. We're almost home.' He dropped her arm. 'You'd best mek your way ahead on your own. Just tek care you don't fall. Track's rutted.' He paused again, and then explained, 'Noah'll have summat to say if I'm walking with you.'

'Why would he—'

'He doesn't have to have a reason to get into an argument,' he muttered. 'I don't mind fighting wi' him, but there's no need for you to be implicated.'

She turned to look up at him; it was so dark she could barely see his face. 'I'm not,' she said softly, but knew that she could be if she didn't keep her wits about her. 'I've no cause to be.'

'No?' he murmured. 'That's good. Nevertheless, I'd rather you went home first. I'll be right behind you if you feel you'll get lost.'

His face was shadowed; she could see only his eyes and mouth. 'I won't get lost,' she whispered. She saw the gleam of his teeth as he gave a low laugh, and then he gently pushed her in the direction of the house. She walked away from him, turned a corner of the track and walked right into Noah.

She gasped as he grabbed her arm. 'Where've you been?' he demanded. 'I was just coming to look for you.'

'Oh! You made me jump,' she stammered. 'Scared 'living daylights out of me.'

'Where've you been, I said.' Noah shook her arm and she compared his manners with those of his brother.

'I went for a walk,' she told him, recalling what she and Mrs Tuke had agreed. 'Can we go inside? I'm cold.' She also had in mind that Fletcher would be coming down the track at any moment.

'That's what Ma said. Though I don't know where there is to walk to round here. Have you nowt else to do?'

139

'I want to talk to you about that when we get inside. Not out here.'

He kept a firm hold of her arm as they walked towards the house, and she felt as if she had been apprehended. She shook him off a little. 'I wasn't nervous,' she told him, 'if that's what's worrying you. It's not dark on 'top road, onny down 'track. It wouldn't be so gloomy if some of 'branches were cut back. House would be much lighter as well.'

'Oh aye. Mekkin' decisions now, are we? You've not been here five minutes.'

'It was onny a suggestion,' she said. 'Just seems like common sense.'

He almost shoved her into the lobby and she stumbled in her haste to take off her boots and move out of his way.

'Manners,' she muttered. 'Haven't you got any?'

'What?' He stared down at her. 'What 'you on about?'

'Well, don't just shove me,' she snapped. 'What's your hurry?'

'I want my tea,' he bellowed. 'You should be inside wi' kettle on instead o' Ma.'

'Why, where is your ma?' Harriet had a flurry of fear that Mrs Tuke might have left home.

'She's milking. I thought you were supposed to be doing that job now?'

'I have been doing it. I'm not late back; why's your mother doing it early?'

'I don't know. Go and ask her. Mebbe cos 'weather's changing. Cloud's dropping: it's going to rain.'

Harriet pulled on the boots again. 'I'll go and help her.'

'What about my tea?' he bellowed again.

'You'll have to wait,' she retaliated. 'And you'll get nowt by shouting. I'm not deaf!' She pulled on an old shawl that was hanging in the lobby, opened the door and went out, almost crashing into Fletcher. 'And don't you start either,' she said sharply, giving him a conspiratorial glance. 'One of you swing 'kettle over 'fire. It's easy enough to do.'

She heard Fletcher say 'What's going on?' and Noah's

muttered reply as she dashed across the yard, relieved that Fletcher had suggested she come back alone. She realized now what he meant about Noah's not needing an excuse for an argument and she had no desire to get her face in the way of his fist, for she was convinced that if she crossed him he wouldn't think twice about slapping her.

Mrs Tuke was in the cowshed milking Dora, who was contentedly chewing on hay, her calf on the straw beside her. 'I'd have done that,' Harriet said. 'I didn't realize what time it was.'

Mrs Tuke looked up from where she was resting her head against Dora's side. Her skirts were pulled up and a half full pail of milk was beneath her knees. She just nodded, and Harriet wondered when she had last laughed or felt happy. 'It's all right,' she muttered. 'I like milking, and it gives me 'chance to be on my own. Mr Tuke doesn't come in 'milking shed. He says it's women's work, and that's fine by me.'

Harriet crouched down beside her. 'I've got a job up at 'manor,' she told her. 'Laundry. Cook said she'd tek me on but has to check wi' housekeeper first. I've to go up on Monday.'

Mrs Tuke quirked her lips, which Harriet took to be a gesture of approval.

'I met 'mistress, Mrs Hart,' Harriet said. 'She was in 'garden and came to ask who I was.'

'Did she?' Mrs Tuke seemed puzzled by this, and frowned. 'What was she like?'

'I liked her,' Harriet said. 'She seemed very straightforward, and I got 'impression she runs 'house herself and doesn't just leave it to 'housekeeper. She's youngish and pretty. Fair, nice smile. We discussed her garden. She's putting in rose beds.'

'Great heavens,' Mrs Tuke muttered. 'You must have had more conversation in five minutes wi' her than I had wi' Mrs Hart in over five years.' She swiftly corrected herself. 'I mean Master Christopher's mother, of course, not his first wife.'

She got to her feet, carefully moving the milk pail and started to wash the cow's udder. 'Have you told Noah?'

'No,' Harriet said. 'He was coming up 'track to meet me. He

141

was angry that I wasn't at 'house preparing his tea. I told him and Fletcher that one of 'em should put 'kettle on fire while I came to help you.'

Mrs Tuke shook her head. 'Noah won't do it; like his father, he'd think it women's work.' She sighed. 'And generally it is. Menfolk have plenty to do.'

'But it wouldn't hurt now and again,' Harriet interrupted. 'I expect you've helped out at harvest time or, in 'fields?'

'Once I did, but not now. I reckon that wi' three men here there shouldn't be any need for me to do it any more. Although Mr Tuke does little.'

Harriet pondered for a moment and then asked, 'Should I tell Noah about going to work at 'manor in front of everybody, or wait till we're on our own?'

'Even if you tell him when you're on your own, we'll hear about it. He's not going to like it. Wait till we've eaten,' Mrs Tuke said.

They walked back to the house together, Harriet carrying the milk pail and Mrs Tuke the washing bowl, which she emptied in the yard.

Someone had made a pot of tea and the three men were sitting at the table drinking it. Harriet and Mrs Tuke washed their hands and then Mrs Tuke took a pie out of the warming oven.

'Rabbit,' she said briefly, and then turned to take a dish of vegetables out.

She's an amazing woman, Harriet thought. When did she cook that?

'Who brought 'rabbit?' Fletcher asked his mother, and Harriet reflected that he seemed to be the only one of the three men who questioned how food came to the table.

'Horace Sims, early morning,' she said. 'I gave him a jug o' milk in exchange.'

Mr Tuke cackled. 'Bet it was off Mayster Hart's land.' He waited for his wife to serve him with a slice of pie and a helping of vegetables before adding, 'Hope it was.'

'He said he'd been wildfowling down 'estuary, hoping for widgeon,' his wife said. 'But all he got was rabbit.'

When they had finished their meal, and there had been no conversation since the exchange about the rabbit, Harriet cleared her throat. The issue of telling Noah about applying for work at the manor was burning a hole in her chest and she felt she had to spill it out.

'I was up at Hart Holme Manor this afternoon,' she said. 'I – I was passing 'gates when I was out walking and on 'spur of 'moment I thought I'd go and ask if there was any temporary work – you know, just an odd day a week.'

Noah looked at her from across the table and scowled. 'What do you mean? You don't need to work; there's work for you here.'

'I'm used to having a full-time job,' she said. 'I suppose in 'summer there'll be plenty for me to do on 'farm, but at 'minute there isn't, and 'money would be useful, wouldn't it?'

'Aye, it would.' Mrs Tuke suddenly became her ally. 'We could mebbe buy some more laying hens.'

Noah pushed back his chair until it crashed against the wall. 'I'll have no wife o' mine working in servitude.' He flicked his thumb towards the stairs. 'Get upstairs,' he thundered. 'Now! I want to talk to you.'

# CHAPTER TWENTY-ONE

Harriet stared him out. 'We can talk down here.'

'I said upstairs.' Noah began to unbuckle his belt, and Harriet felt a shudder of fear. Mrs Tuke appeared to freeze and Mr Tuke folded his arms and sat back as if about to watch an entertainment.

But it was Fletcher who sat as still and watchful as a cat about to spring.

Harriet picked up a cloth and then the hot pie dish and stood with it in her hands.

'All right,' she said, as mildly as she could. 'If you prefer to talk in private, but I'll clear away 'dishes first. Your ma did 'cooking, it's onny fair I do 'washing up.'

Noah looked puzzled, as if he had somehow been hoodwinked by her apparent agreement, and she guessed that he was normally always ready for a fight. She breathed away her tension. I was ready for him, and he'd have got this dish at his head if he'd touched me. She nodded at him. 'If you really don't want me to work there, I won't,' she said. 'But we'll talk about it, like you say.'

He sat down again and buckled up his belt. Mr Tuke looked disappointed and Mrs Tuke's eyes moved from Harriet to Noah without her moving her head. Then she picked up her fork and stabbed a carrot in the vegetable dish and nibbled on it.

'No pudding tonight, Ma?' Fletcher said softly.

She looked up. 'Oh!' she said vaguely. 'Yes. I forgot. There's apple and bramble pie. I had some pastry over.' She got to her feet. 'I'll get it. It's cold, not hot.'

'I like mine hot,' her husband muttered.

'You can have it hot, Mr Tuke,' she said, on her way to the larder. 'But you'll have to wait for it to warm up.'

Harriet couldn't believe that Noah had capitulated, but when, after washing up and clearing away, she indicated that she was ready to go upstairs and talk, he flourished his hand and said, 'Later. We'll talk about it later,' as if he were still holding the upper hand.

He and Fletcher went out again to finish off some more jobs and nothing more was said about it, until that evening Fletcher mentioned to his mother that he had been up at the manor to pay the rent and heard that Thomson was off sick, which was why he hadn't been to collect it.

'Master Hart said that you'd no need to worry about it. He knows you don't get in arrears.'

'You were up at 'manor?' Noah frowned. 'Did you see Harriet?'

'I stopped and had a cup o' tea wi' Cook in 'kitchen,' Harriet interrupted. 'If I'd known you were there, Fletcher, you could have walked me home. It's dark down that track.'

'Aye, it is. Branches need cutting back,' Fletcher agreed. 'But there's never enough time. Nobody invited me in for a cup o' tea,' he continued in a mock-aggrieved tone, answering Noah's question. 'I talked to Hart out in 'courtyard.' He glanced at his father and then his mother. 'It's a big place, isn't it? Must take a lot o' folk to run it.'

His mother nodded. 'Yes,' she said. 'It allus did.'

Mr Tuke grunted and got up and went to his place by the fire.

Later, in their bedroom, Harriet brought up the subject of her working for the Harts. 'I won't go if you'd rather I didn't,' she said meekly. 'But, you know, 'money'd come in useful, especially for 'bairn, if – when I get pregnant. I'd stop when 'babby came, of course.'

'Mmm.' Noah sat on the edge of the bed to take off his socks and breeches, then pulled his shirt over his head and dropped them all in a heap on the floor. 'That'd have to be 'stipulation. You'd stop as soon as we have a bairn.'

'Oh yes, of course,' she said and thought that they wouldn't want her then anyway. 'So is that all right? Can I tell them that I can start on Monday?'

'Aye. All right. Tell 'em I've agreed to it.' He pulled back the blanket and climbed into bed. 'Onny another time don't go mekkin' decisions afore asking me first.'

Harriet felt quite light-hearted as she set off early on Monday morning. She wrapped her shawl around her; the weather was getting colder. It would be nice to chat with people – if I get the job, she reminded herself; Mrs Tuke was proving to be slightly better for knowing, but she wasn't one for conversation and often seemed remote; no wonder, Harriet mused, living with that miserable man. And they called each other Mr and Mrs, never by their given names. That seemed very strange.

She followed the same path to the kitchen door of the manor and knocked. Lizzie answered and told her that Cook said she'd to go straight to the washhouse, which was further round the side of the house. Harriet smiled: so she'd been taken on after all.

'She said to come in for a cup o' tea at about half past nine,' Lizzie called after her, and Harriet wondered how she would know the time, but then looked up and saw the clock above the archway and another one over the stable block. She found the door to the washhouse and on going in was relieved to find the fire under the boiler already lit and an older woman stoking it with coal.

'Hello. I'm Harriet,' she said cheerfully, and the woman looked up and nodded.

'I'm Mary,' she said. 'I'm deaf.'

146

'Harriet,' Harriet called back, suppressing a groan. Just my luck, she thought. I wanted conversation!

She took off her shawl; it was warm in here, nice to work in during the winter. It was similarly set up to the washhouse she and her mother used to frequent in Hull, except there there had been more boilers. In here, as well as the zinc tub in its brick housing from which steam was already rising, there were two deep side-by-side white sinks, drying racks hanging from the ceiling, wooden clothes horses leaning against the wall, a mangle, and a bright fire burning in a grate. There were also several large wicker baskets full of sheets, pillowcases and towels, and a separate one filled with personal items.

'Which do we do first, Mary?' Harriet shouted.

Mary pointed to the personal items. 'I generally wash this lot first, in 'sink. Tek hot water from boiler wi' that pan.' She pointed to a large iron pan, and Harriet wondered how she would ever lift it. 'Be careful,' Mary went on. 'Don't have 'water too hot for 'mistress's things or you'll shrink 'em. Then we'll put 'sheets in to boil.'

Harriet nodded back at her. If I have to shout all 'time, I shan't be able to speak by 'time we've finished, she thought. There was a pump over the sink and the water ran clear when she worked the handle, not muddy and brown as it sometimes was in Hull. She half filled the sink and then scooped up half a pan of hot water from the boiler and poured it in. Then she took a handful of soft soap from a tin and swished it about to make a lather.

Mrs Hart's petticoats and nightdresses were dainty and edged with lace and Harriet was particularly careful in handling them, as they seemed so fragile. She filled the other sink with cold water for rinsing and popped them in, and then set about washing the other items, mainly men's shirts, under-drawers and nightshirts.

Mary was struggling with the handling of the sheets, so Harriet went to help her. They loaded the first pair into the wash boiler and then poshed them down with the wooden-handled posher. The steam rose from the water and soon Harriet and Mary were perspiring freely. This must be what it's like being in a Turkish steam bath, Harriet thought, wiping sweat from her face.

She rinsed Mrs Hart's underwear again and gently squeezed out the water, then hauled an airer down from the ceiling, wiped it with a clean cloth, placed the clothing on it and hauled it up again. Next they took the sheets out of the boiler with wooden tongs, handling them with extra care as they were red-hot, put them into two clean buckets and tipped them into clean rinsing water in the sinks before putting the next lot of sheets in to boil.

They ran the first lot of sheets through the mangle and draped them over another drying rack; it took the two of them to haul it back up again. They washed another pair of sheets and then they stopped for a breather. 'We can go for a cup of tea at half past nine,' Harriet shouted. 'I'm gasping.'

Mary nodded. 'Let's finish this lot first,' she said, riddling the fire beneath the boiler and adding more coal. 'We'll rinse 'em, put 'em through 'mangle and hang 'em up, put more water in to boil for next lot, and then it'll be about half past.'

Which it was, as Harriet saw on looking up at the clock over the stables as they crossed the yard. Mary obviously had a regular working pattern.

'Have you been working here for long?' Harriet raised her voice as they headed towards the kitchen door.

'Aye,' Mary said. 'Since I was fourteen, off and on. I've given up a few times but they allus ask me back. But there's too much for me on me own, wi' ironing as well. I'm really glad that you've come.'

'I'm onny temporary,' Harriet shouted at her, and clutched at her throat.

'You don't have to shout,' Mary said. 'If you turn to look at me when you're speaking, I can lip-read.'

Thank goodness, Harriet thought, because I couldn't keep up the shouting all morning.

'When do we do 'ironing?' she mouthed. 'Today?'

Mary shook her head. 'I can't stop all day today, but you can if you want.'

They drank their tea in the comfort of the kitchen, but ten minutes later Mary got to her feet. 'Come on,' she said. 'Water'll be boiling. We'll put 'upstairs towels in next, then 'fustian sheets and then 'kitchen towels.' She turned to the cook. 'Give us what you've got, Cook, and your dusters, and they can go in last. We're doing fine now there's another pair of hands.'

It was as they were walking back to the washhouse that Mary posed the question. 'Cook told me 'other day she'd got somebody to help out, but you're not from round here, are you?'

'I'm from Hull,' Harriet said. 'I've onny recently come to live here.'

'How's that then?'

'Got married.' It was easier to speak in short sharp bursts, she decided.

'Who to?'

'Noah Tuke.' She pointed in the direction of the estuary. 'His family have a small farm by 'estuary.'

'I know 'em,' Mary murmured. 'Not seen either of them for a lot o' years. Nathaniel Tuke was a domineering bully of a man who could never call himself a farmer. Never did understand why Ellen Fletcher married him. There were plenty of other lads after her. All of 'stable lads and horse lads. She was a right bonny lass.'

They went back into the warmth of the washhouse. 'She cut herself off from everybody after they were wed,' Mary went on, gathering up an armful of white towels. 'I reckon he stopped her from meeting them she used to know. He was forever boasting that he was well in wi' master just because he rented him a piece o' waterlogged land.' She paused, and then continued, 'I onny saw her a couple o' times after that.'

Harriet shrugged. It was obvious that Nathaniel Tuke was not well liked.

149

'They have two sons,' Mary said. 'Which one did you marry? One of 'em is just like him, so I hear, all shout and bluster. Hope it's not him?'

Harriet forced a smile and shook her head. 'No,' she said. 'Not him.'

# CHAPTER TWENTY-TWO

It was snowing hard when Harriet left the washhouse. Mary had left first, after damping down the fires and emptying the tub of hot water, but leaving a little in the bottom to prevent cracking. Harriet had stayed behind to finish ironing Mrs Hart's nightdresses and petticoats before they became too dry. The room had become hotter and hotter and the sheets on the racks were steaming.

She carefully pressed the collars on the nightdresses, first laying a clean white cloth on them to prevent burning. She used two flat irons, heating them one after the other on the fire bars, then spitting on them to test the heat before wiping them with a damp rag to remove any trace of soot. On removing the cloth she was delighted to see the fragile pattern of the lace emerge from beneath it.

She hung the freshly ironed clothes on the rack, hauled it up with the pulley and left them to air. The lamp was guttering when she had finished and the candles burned down, so there was no more she could do in the dark. She closed the door behind her and scurried off to the kitchen.

'You still here?' Cook was rolling pastry and there was a rich smell of beef coming from one of the ovens. 'Thought you'd gone home.'

'There are still some sheets to iron,' she told her. 'Is it all right to come back tomorrow? I wanted to finish off 'mistress's things before 'lamp went out, but it's too dark to see now.'

'Oh, I should've said.' Cook wiped her forehead with the back of her wrist. 'You can do 'ironing upstairs in 'laundry room. Lizzie'll show you in 'morning. Best get off home now. Lizzie,' she called to the girl. 'Fetch 'cake tin out and cut a slice of fruit cake for Mrs Tuke.'

'Thank you,' Harriet said. 'I am quite hungry, and I'm Harriet, by the way. Mrs Tuke still doesn't sit easy on my shoulders.'

'No, happen not,' Cook said. 'Especially if there're two of you.'

Harriet took a bite of the fruit cake that Lizzie brought her. 'Did you know Ellen Tuke – Ellen Fletcher as was?' she asked.

'No. She'd been long gone when I came here, but Mrs Marshall who was 'cook afore me knew her, and allus spoke highly of her. A pleasant young lass, from all accounts.'

Everybody speaks so well of Mrs Tuke, Harriet thought as she walked home. The snow was thick on the road, but it hadn't settled beneath the trees on the track leading to Marsh Farm and it was very dark. Harriet could barely see where she was walking and she wondered how she could persuade Noah to cut back the branches.

Ellen Tuke glanced up at the clock. She'd finished the milking and shut up the hens before it got dark. She and Harriet had come to an agreement that on a Monday she would do all her old chores if Harriet got the job at the manor. It's no hardship, she'd told her, adding that she'd been doing it all her married life.

'But I want to help,' Harriet had insisted. 'It's onny fair, so can I do 'milking when I'm not at 'manor? That's if I get tekken on.'

She'd obviously got it to have stayed out so long, Ellen thought, starting on another torn shirt. Unless she's jiggered off back to Hull, but I doubt she'd do that in this weather. She looked at Noah, who was sitting opposite his father next to the fire. Fletcher was at the table tinkering with a piece of wood, a screwdriver and a bag of nails.

'Harriet should be back soon,' she remarked.

'Mebbe we can have our tea then,' Mr Tuke grumbled. 'We're late.'

Fletcher looked up at the clock. 'We're on time,' he said. 'It's not yet five.' He glanced at his brother. 'Are you going to meet her? Snow's coming down fast.'

Noah scowled. 'Why should I do that? If she can't walk that bit o' way, she's not going to survive 'winter out here.'

Fletcher shrugged. 'Suit yourself. She's a town lass, that's all. They'll have street lamps in Hull.'

'Not where she lived they haven't,' Noah muttered. 'Well, onny one near 'street end.'

Mr Tuke leaned forward. 'Did you go in 'house?' He gave a sly grin. 'Invite you in, did she?'

Noah cursed. 'Mind your own business,' he barked at his father. 'It's nowt to do wi' you.'

Mr Tuke sat back, looking self-satisfied. 'Bet you did, all 'same.'

Fletcher got up from the table. 'I'll try this on 'stable door. It should fit better than it did.'

'You'll not be able to see,' his mother commented. 'Tek a lamp.'

'I was going to, Ma!' He shook his head at her; she looked up and gave a rueful grimace.

He brought an old oil lamp in from the porch and placed it on the table, turning up the wick and lighting it with a taper from another lamp. 'Won't be long.'

'We'll not eat till Harriet gets back,' his mother murmured. 'It's all ready for dishing up.'

Fletcher went outside. The snow was coming down even faster than it had been earlier and he was glad that they'd made the roofs secure, but instead of heading for the stable he held up the lamp and turned towards the track leading to the road.

'Oh!' Harriet gasped as she skidded. 'Nearly went my length!' The track was slippery underfoot with wet leaves and mud and she huffed out a breath and put out a hand to grab something, but the branches were whippy and not strong enough to hold her if she fell. 'I'll ask if they've got a walking stick or a crook or summat next time I come out,' she muttered. 'I could break a leg and nobody'd know.'

Then she saw the flicker of a light and shouted, 'Hello? Is somebody there?'

'It's me, Fletcher. Stay there, I'm coming.'

She waited. I might have known Noah wouldn't bestir himself to come and meet me, she reflected. He wouldn't even have considered it.

'Are you all right?' Fletcher held up the lamp.

'Yes, I am now, thank you,' she said. 'I almost fell back there. I couldn't see where I was putting my feet.'

'Tek my arm,' he said. 'You need to walk in 'middle of 'track and not under 'trees, but not on 'right hand side where 'ditch is in case you fall in.'

She linked her arm in his. 'The trees . . .' she began. They were both speaking quietly.

'I know – need cutting back. I'll mek a start tomorrow if 'weather doesn't worsen; we'll not be able to do anything else much.'

'Could I borrow a walking stick? For tomorrow when I go back to work? Snow might be deep.'

He lifted the lamp to look at her. 'You're not put off by a snowstorm?'

'No.' She felt the warmth of him through his coat sleeve and felt strangely comforted. 'If I'd been in Hull I'd have had to go to work whatever 'weather was like. If I'd had work, that is.'

'You smell nice,' he told her. 'Fresh, and . . .'

'Soap,' she said. 'I've been in 'washhouse all day. It was lovely and warm; I've to go back tomorrow to finish off 'ironing.'

They were nearing the end of the track; the house walls

154

loomed ahead. Fletcher slowed his steps. 'Best not to tell Noah I met you,' he said. 'I'm supposed to be repairing 'bolt on 'stable door.'

'And instead you came to meet me,' she said softly. 'Thank you. That was – kind of you.'

He lifted the lamp again and looked into her face. 'I didn't like to think you – that is, it's dark and – you might have fallen.'

'Which I almost did,' she whispered and wished he wasn't standing so close, for he might hear her heart hammering.

'I'll leave you here,' he murmured, 'and go back to 'stable. You haven't seen me.'

'No,' she breathed. 'I haven't.'

She stumbled in through the outer door, kicking off her boots and taking off her wet shawl. 'I'm freezing,' she said, as she went into the kitchen. 'It's snowing hard; 'road's thick with it.'

She looked longingly at the fire but neither Noah nor his father offered their chair to let her sit near it. Noah just looked up and nodded.

'Yeh, I know,' he said. 'You're not 'onny one that's been out in it.'

Mr Tuke raised his head. 'Can we eat now?'

'Aye. When Fletcher comes in.' Ellen put down her sewing. 'He'll be in in a minute, I should think.'

'Don't know why he should tek so long to put a bolt on a door,' Mr Tuke grumbled. 'I wouldn't have tekken half so long.'

'Then 'next time there's a job to be done you can do it, Mr Tuke,' his wife said grimly. 'Seeing as you're so very handy.'

'Shall I set 'table, Mrs Tuke?' Harriet asked, anxious to get away from the subject of Fletcher. 'I'm sorry if I've kept you. It's just that it was bad walking.'

Noah pointed a finger at her. 'Don't dare mention them branches. I'm warning you.'

Harriet shrugged. 'Wasn't going to. But don't you need

155

'wood for 'fire? There're piles of dead branches – not that I'm suggesting owt. What would I know?'

'Yes,' Mrs Tuke interrupted, and they all heard the porch door open. 'You can set 'table now. Fletcher's back. Shift your-self, Mr Tuke, if you want to eat, and let me near my oven.'

When Fletcher entered the kitchen Noah put his thumb in the air and then pointed it at Harriet. 'Telled you, didn't I?' he bragged.

'What?' Fletcher asked. 'Telled me what?'

'That she'd find her own way home!' He gave a mocking grin, and looked at Harriet. 'He thought I should come out and meet you and I said you'd find your own way back. That's right, isn't it? You don't need to rely on anybody else, do you?'

She gazed at him. 'Course I don't,' she said. She turned to his brother, and her lips twitched as she said, 'Whatever were you thinking, Fletcher, to suggest such a thing?'

# CHAPTER TWENTY-THREE

Mrs Tuke told Harriet that there was a shepherd's crook in the corner of the shed where the farm tools were kept. 'Mr Tuke bought it,' she said. 'Fancied himself as a shepherd, but we've never kept many sheep and we're hardly climbing up hillsides for him to need it. Tek it. And if you're not sure how deep 'snow is, test it wi' crook first.'

Harriet said she would. The snow had fallen all night and the brothers had been out first thing clearing the yard. The sheep had been in a field shelter, but the cows were kept in their stalls. Mrs Tuke had done the first milking, and as soon as Harriet had finished her breakfast she set off for the manor wearing an old mackintosh she'd found in the porch, her shawl over her head and the borrowed boots over thick stockings.

I feel like an intrepid explorer, she laughed to herself, and was almost ready to admit that she was enjoying being outside.

Walking up the track was easier with the crook, but once she came to the main road the snow was thick and she pressed on gingerly. There was not another soul about; deep snow balanced precariously on low tree branches and the glistening white road was patterned with animal and bird prints. It's beautiful, she thought, looking up into a clear blue sky as a flock of wild duck flew over; just wonderful. I've never in my life seen anything like it.

Her legs were aching by the time she reached the manor gates. The walk had taken her longer than on the previous day and she was relieved to see that a path had been cleared up the middle of the drive, which made walking easier. Somebody was up early to clear this lot, she thought.

She went straight to the washhouse, but on trying the door found it locked. She about-turned and went back towards the kitchen; the courtyard, like the drive, had been cleared and ash put down for easier access.

Harriet sighed. How very agreeable, she thought, to have someone do this for you, without having to stir yourself from your fireside. A young lad came out of the kitchen door and picked up a spade that was leaning against the wall, putting it over his shoulder. He nodded to her as he passed, and began whistling. She reckoned that he'd be pleased to be employed.

Cook told her that the laundry had been taken up to the ironing room. 'Mrs Clubley was right pleased with your ironing,' she said. 'She said it was much better than Mary's. She'll be glad for you to come regular.'

'Thank you,' Harriet said. 'So shall I come once a fortnight?'

'Aye, that'll do, or mebbe weekly in 'summer when we have visitors. And I expect Miss Amy will be home by then; she's 'master's daughter.'

Harriet nodded, and wondered if she would be pregnant by then. But even if I am, she thought, I could still come. She left her boots by the back door, and in her stockinged feet followed Lizzie up the back stairs and down a long corridor to a room which, like the washhouse, had dryers hanging from the ceiling, a wall completely covered in cupboards from floor to ceiling, two ironing boards and a table covered in a thick cloth, and a coal fire burning in a barred grate.

She took off the mackintosh and shawl, rolled up her sleeves, and put the flat irons on the fire bars.

'Sheets are in 'baskets,' Lizzie told her, 'and you can mek starch wi' water from 'jug.' She pointed to a small side table with a jug and bowl on it. 'And Mrs Clubley said to tell you that 'mistress doesn't like 'sheets starched too stiff.'

Harriet had never used starch before. That was a luxury she and her mother hadn't needed with their fustian bedlinen, but these sheets were of the finest linen. She decided to err on the side of caution and mixed it up to a thin consistency and simply sprinkled it along the top and bottom of the sheets. I'm sure somebody'll tell me if it's wrong. And oh, dear, I hope I don't scorch them.

The first hour and a half passed pleasantly. She felt relaxed and her thoughts drifted from being at home with her mother to meeting Noah when she was feeling so very low, her marriage, and coming out to this marshy land. It feels like a foreign country might, she reflected, it's so different from Hull. Her thoughts naturally turned to her new family, and she found that she was constantly thinking of Fletcher rather than her husband.

At half past nine Lizzie brought her a tray with a pot of tea and a plate of biscuits, and she sat on a wooden chair and indulged herself for five minutes. I wouldn't mind working here, she thought. There are worse jobs that I could think of than being near a warm fire and having somebody bring you a tray of tea and biscuits.

She'd just got started on the last pair of sheets and was wondering how long she could stretch out the time when the door opened and a small plump woman in a dark dress and cotton cap came in carrying something draped over her arm.

'I'm Mrs Clubley,' the housekeeper said. 'Mrs Hart sends her compliments on your ironing and asked if you'd freshen up this afternoon gown?'

Harriet just remembered in time about bobbing her knee to her, and said she would take a look at it.

'It's a fine wool,' Mrs Clubley told her. 'So you must be careful not to have 'iron too hot.'

Harriet drew in a breath. It was a lovely blue and so soft that she knew it would drape beautifully on the body. 'I'll use a damp cloth on it, just to be sure,' she said. 'But I must tell you, Mrs Clubley, that I've never done owt like this before. But I'll tek great care.'

She finished the sheets, carefully folding them and putting them away on the shelves of a cupboard as she'd been told to do, and began the gown. She tried to concentrate on what she was doing rather than daydreaming, but no matter how she applied herself, the image of Fletcher, how he looked and the various things he had said, kept coming back to her.

Stop it, she thought. He's nowt to you, and don't compare him with Noah, they're different people. I know they are, she answered herself. He's more thoughtful than Noah, not only of me but of his mother too, and he's not aggressive. Then she began wondering if he would meet her again on the Marsh Farm track, and knew, no matter how she denied it, that she wanted him to.

She was finished before twelve o'clock and very satisfied with the gown. She hung it on a hanger and hooked it over a cupboard doorknob, thinking how it would suit Mrs Hart with her fair hair and pretty features. I hope she's happy, she thought, and I hope Master Hart tells her how lovely she looks in it. She sighed. How nice that must be, to receive a compliment from someone who loves you and not just be a woman there for 'purpose of begetting sons.

Cook expressed surprise that she had finished so quickly and asked her if she'd like to stay and have something to eat. After only a slight hesitation, Harriet said that she would. Cook told her that they would eat before upstairs did, as guests were expected for lunch at one o'clock prompt.

'We're having roast pork,' she said. 'With apple sauce, o' course, duchesse potatoes and winter greens. Just a simple meal, and it's ready to eat now, cos when we've finished my time will be tekken up wi' upstairs. They're having game soup, fresh cod cooked in butter and herbs, and then wild duck wi' juniper berries and thyme for mains. I've made an apple and orange tart flavoured wi' cinnamon for dessert. It's my own recipe,' she said. 'I know what Master likes. He likes his food plain, nowt too fancy.'

'Are you cooking all of that, Mrs Lister?' Harriet exclaimed. 'As well as pork for 'staff?'

'Oh, aye,' she said. 'We've got to eat, haven't we? And there are plenty of us: maids, and Mr Cookson, he's 'butler, you've not met him yet, and Mrs Clubley, and Boulder, he's 'footman, and Johnny is 'boot boy. There'll be nowt left on 'joint o' pork, I can tell you.'

'You forgot me, Cook,' Lizzie piped up.

'Ah, yes,' Cook said and winked at Harriet. 'So I did. Well, there might be a crumb or two left over that you can have, so just hurry up scrubbing them parsnips for upstairs.'

When Harriet left she was not only bursting with food, but also amazed at the speed at which everyone ate, enjoying without appearing to bolt their food, and how Mrs Lister then galvanized the maids to clear away and help her dish up the soup into a tureen, which she sprinkled with chopped parsley. Then she scattered toasted breadcrumbs over the fish and popped it back in the oven to crisp, leaving the duck to rest for five minutes, she explained, whilst she quickly ordered the carrots and Brussels sprouts to be brought to the boil and personally supervised the sauce to glaze the duck.

How does she manage to do all that, Harriet thought as she strode down the drive. She looked back towards the house and saw two carriages at the front door. No doubt the occupants would be sitting down at table enjoying their luncheon. Oh, she breathed, it's another life.

As soon as she reached the top of the track, she noticed something different. The brightness of the morning had disappeared and clouds had developed, yet the track seemed lighter and more open. Then she saw the pile of branches and heard the rasp of a saw.

Noah heeded what I said after all, she thought gleefully. Good, there'll be plenty of kindling and logs for 'fire. But then she remembered that Fletcher had said he'd make a start on them, and halfway down the track was a ladder leaning against a tree and Fletcher at the top of it with a saw in his hand.

He looked down at her. 'There you are, Mrs Tuke. How does this suit you?'

'Thank you.' She smiled. 'It meks such a difference, it's so much lighter. Have you – erm, did you have any help?'

He came down the ladder and scrunched up his shoulders. 'Yeh,' he mocked. 'My father came out to give his advice on how to tackle it, and then Noah came out to look and told me I was wasting my time.'

'I'm sorry,' she began. 'I didn't intend to cause trouble.'

He gave a grim laugh. 'Trouble was here before you arrived, Harriet, but . . .' He paused. 'Your being here might just bring things to a head.'

'What do you mean?'

He gazed at her for a long minute before saying, 'I'm not sure what I mean; I onny know that something's got to change, that we can't go on in 'same manner as we've allus done.'

'I don't understand,' she said.

'No,' he muttered. 'There are things I don't understand either, but now I'm seeing our life here wi' somebody else's eyes and awareness: yours. And there's summat wrong and I don't know what it is.'

# CHAPTER TWENTY-FOUR

I know what Fletcher means, Harriet thought later as she changed into her old skirt and warm jumper ready to help with the milking and put the hens away. Darkness was drawing in and clouds heavy with snow were gathering ominously overhead. At least I think I know. There's a tension in the house, an antagonism between Mr and Mrs Tuke, which rubs off on the brothers. Are they taking sides? Have they always fought? Did Mr Tuke pit them against each other when they were young?

Fletcher seems to be milder, the more tolerant of the two, which is odd as he's 'eldest. Noah is the aggressor, quick to take offence or pick a fight, and not only with Fletcher. I feel that I must be careful of what I say to him. And it seems as if when Noah scores, then so does Mr Tuke, and yet when Noah is rude to his father it bounces off him. But what I don't understand is that Mrs Tuke is almost untouched by what Noah does or says, as if it doesn't concern her. It's so strange and it's very disturbing.

The week dragged. Fletcher and Noah were outside most days, repairing fences, keeping the area around the house and yard clear after each fall of snow, for it kept coming down thick and fast, chopping turnips for the sheep in the shelter in the field nearest the house, and supplying the stock with plenty of straw. And they kept the ditches clear, which seemed to be the most important job of all.

Mrs Tuke showed Harriet how to bake a cake with flour and oats, a small amount of butter, ginger and black treacle. 'It's cheap to mek,' she said, 'and we've allus got 'ingredients in 'larder. Or you can use 'same ingredients and add a couple of eggs and you've got a different kind of cake that'll keep – if it doesn't get eaten.'

As Harriet stirred the mixture she reflected that this was the very first time she had heard any kind of humour coming from Ellen Tuke's lips.

They usually ate their midday meal and supper in silence, until one evening Fletcher suddenly said, 'We should dig out a pond in 'bottom field and let 'water in. Or talk to 'bailiff about it.'

'Don't go on about that again,' his father rebuked him. 'I've said no.'

'It would improve 'land,' Fletcher maintained. 'They're doing it further up 'estuary. It's good river silt.'

'Aye, and how long afore you can use it?' Noah butted in. 'Years! And in meantime you can't use 'land for owt.'

'We can't use it for much now,' Fletcher argued.

'What do you mean by good river silt?' Harriet asked cautiously.

All three men looked at her. 'Keep your nose out.' Noah patted the tip of his own with his forefinger. Mr Tuke guffawed and said, 'Hark at her!'

Fletcher said nothing for a moment, and then answered her. 'At 'mouth of 'estuary what was once an island in the middle of 'river now joins 'mainland. It's been warped; that means that most of 'land is man-made.'

'Not woman-made,' Mr Tuke mocked, but Fletcher ignored him.

'In a nutshell, they dug warping drains and built sluices on 'land and let 'water flood in, then the sluices drain most of 'water out and leave 'sediment behind.' He paused. 'It's 'best

164

farmland in 'county now, but Noah's right, it teks years afore 'land is good enough for planting. But it can be done.'

'You'd have thought that Master Hart would've done it, wouldn't you?' Harriet commented.

'He doesn't need to,' Mrs Tuke broke in. 'He's renting it to us to farm it. He's got plenty of land elsewhere.'

'Aye,' Mr Tuke interrupted. 'He's not bothered about 'bit that we've got, as long as we pay 'rent on time.'

Harriet watched as Mrs Tuke bent over her sewing and saw a wry grimace play momentarily over her lips. Harriet listened and watched, but even after spending time with them when they were confined to the house and yard by the weather, she was no nearer to understanding any of them.

It was a relief when her day for going to the manor came round. The snow had eased, though there were icy pockets on the road where the snow had melted and then frozen again which were treacherous to walk on. But the sun broke through the cloud and Harriet's spirits lifted as she strode out towards the manor.

Mary had sent a message that she was sick and couldn't come, but Lizzie had already filled the washtub with water and lit the fire beneath it and the water was just right for the mistress's delicate underwear, which Harriet washed straight away. She hummed to herself and thought again that she wouldn't at all mind working here. But I'm tied to Noah for life and I've to mek 'best of it. But increasingly, whenever she thought of Noah, Fletcher came unbidden into her mind.

She finished the washing and put it all to dry on the racks and went to tell Cook that she'd have to come back the next day to do the ironing. She was given a cup of tea and ate a slice of bread and beef and then said she would get off back to Marsh Farm as the weather was looking threatening.

'I'll come early tomorrow,' she said. 'About six, and then I'll be finished by dinner time.'

It started to sleet as she got to the road and although she was pleased because the snow would clear, she knew she would be soaked before reaching home. She walked hunched with her head down and wished she had borrowed the mackintosh again. When she glanced up she saw someone in the distance walking towards her. A tall man, moving purposefully. She'd never seen anyone else on the road before and wondered who it was. There were no other houses or farms round here.

She looked up again as he drew nearer. He had a rain cape over his head, but took it off as he approached. It was Fletcher.

Rain dripped off her shawl and hair and down her face and she brushed it away from her eyes. 'Where are you off to?' she asked.

'Nowhere,' he said. 'I've arrived.'

Harriet laughed. 'What do you mean?'

'I've come to meet you.' He unwrapped the cape from his shoulders and put it over her. 'I thought you'd be on your way back.'

'I – do you think you should've done that? What if—'

'Noah's asleep by 'fire. It's too wet to do any jobs outside.' He took her hand and led her toward a shelterbelt of trees at the side of the road.

'What . . . ? For heaven's sake, Fletcher, what 'you doing?'

'I don't know,' he said. 'I just want to talk to you.'

'You can talk to me in 'house. We don't have to talk out here!'

'I can't talk to you in front of everybody. Everything I say is questioned, and you – you can't have an opinion on anything, don't you see that?'

He was standing very close. She could smell the dampness of him. His hair was soaked, as hers was, and it hung damply about his face.

'Noah would have an opinion if he should see us here like this,' she said nervously.

'He won't see us,' he said, leading her deeper into the wood. 'I told you, he's sleeping.'

166

'What do you want of me?' she whispered.

He shook his head. 'I don't know,' he said again. 'But I don't want Noah to have you.'

'I'm his wife,' she pointed out. 'We're married – in church.'

'You don't care for him,' he insisted. 'It's not a marriage made in heaven.'

She scoffed. 'That it's not. But I'm stuck wi' him. For better or for worse, that's what I promised.'

'And you got 'worse,' he murmured.

'I must go,' she insisted. 'I'm frightened.'

'Not of me?' He frowned. 'I don't intend you harm.' He touched her cold cheek with his finger. 'I just want to talk to you.'

'No.' She drew away from him. 'Not of you. Of myself, per-haps, and of being found here with you.'

It was true, she thought. I'm afraid of being alone with him. He's standing too close. He shouldn't touch me like that. I don't feel threatened, but I'm nervous of my feelings towards him. I've never felt like this before.

'What do you want to talk about?' She licked her lips. 'I'm cold.' She shivered.

He put his arms round her. 'I could make you warm,' he said softly. 'Can I kiss you? Just a kiss?'

She said nothing, just looked at him. Her breathing quick-ened and she felt her pulses racing. 'I – don't think you should. I – we'd regret it. If you – we – did, it would mek things different between us. Noah would know.'

'He wouldn't.' He brushed his mouth softly against hers. 'He'd be 'last to notice anything.'

'But it's not right.' She felt her resolve disappearing, melt-ing, just as her bones were doing.

'No, it isn't.' She felt him inch away from her and felt dis-appointment. But he shifted only to bring one hand to her face, to run his fingers round her eyes and lips as he gazed down at her. 'But sometimes doing right seems wrong, and doing wrong feels so right.' He bent his face towards hers and kissed her mouth, and she didn't draw back but let her lips soften in response.

She gave a small moaning breath as he put both hands to her face, holding her fast. 'I've ached to do that since you first arrived,' he whispered. 'How can I bear it that you're my brother's wife?'

# CHAPTER TWENTY-FIVE

For all of January and most of February the weather was bitterly cold, wet and windy, but in spite of that Harriet looked forward to her walk to work at the manor. Although everyone knew their place in the hierarchy, the atmosphere in the kitchen of Hart Holme was friendly, and in the washhouse with Mary, or in the ironing room, she could relax in a way she could not when she was at Marsh Farm: there she was constantly on tenterhooks in case Noah and Fletcher started arguing; she was always aware of Fletcher's presence and couldn't ever meet his eye.

She was jumpy when Mr Tuke was anywhere near her and she never stayed in the house alone with him, but followed Mrs Tuke to the cowshed or the hen house or anywhere else she might go, bar the privy, and then she would go outside and potter about until she came back.

She couldn't recall the exact day when she became conscious that Mr Tuke was watching her more intently than he had done when she'd first arrived, but now she felt increasingly threatened. But whom should she tell about it? Not Mrs Tuke, for in spite of the antipathy apparent between them they were still man and wife; and not Noah, for he was his son after all; and certainly not Fletcher.

But then one morning when Harriet was alone in the kitchen clearing up the breakfast dishes after the brothers had gone outside and Mrs Tuke was letting the hens out, the stairs door opened and Mr Tuke came in. He was earlier than usual and fully dressed in his habitual wear of breeches and smock. He glanced round the kitchen and asked where Mrs Tuke was.

'She'll be back in a minute,' Harriet said nervously. 'She's just letting 'hens out. I'll mek you some tea.' She reached for the kettle to fill it again, but he grabbed her wrist.

'No hurry 'bout that.' He put his hand on her waist. 'We'll have a little chat, shall we, all cosy like?'

'No, I don't think so.' Harriet pulled away from him, but he tightened his grip on her wrist. 'Let go, please,' she said. 'You're hurting me.'

'Don't want to do that, do I?' He leered at her. 'Come on, missy, don't be shy. I'm quite a man, you know.' He bent his face towards her and whispered, 'Bet I could get you in 'family way quicker than that son o' mine can.'

She wrenched away from him, his nails catching her skin. 'Don't you dare touch me,' she hissed. 'I'll tell Noah *and* your wife.'

'Mrs Tuke wouldn't care a jot about you or any woman, and my son'd believe me afore you any day of 'week.' He sneered. 'Don't think I don't know women. I've met a few like you, down on their luck and willing to do a turn for a copper or two.'

She gave his cheek such a smack that his head jerked backwards and he staggered. 'And I've met men like you too, but thankfully not many, and I know how to deal with 'em.' She reached for the kettle again. 'Lay a finger on me once more and you'll feel this scalding water on a very tender place.'

He stepped back, animosity in his eyes. He pointed with his finger. 'You so much as whisper a word and you're out o' my house afore you can blink.'

Before Harriet could reply they both heard the rattle of the latch on the back door. Quickly, he turned and sat down, picking up a knife and fork and holding them upright with his elbows on the table. 'Mrs Tuke,' he bellowed. 'Is that you? What 'you doing, woman? I want my breakfast.'

170

Ellen Tuke was carrying a basket of eggs and her shawl was slipping off her shoulders. She gave a slight nod at Harriet but completely ignored her husband; it was as if he were not there.

'Hens are laying again,' she commented. 'I've gathered a dozen this morning. I've been thinking I might get some ducks. They're very messy, are ducks, but their eggs and meat are good.'

She put the basket down near the sink and then turned back. 'Mr Tuke,' she said as if she had just noticed him. 'What 'you doing up at this hour? Going to help 'lads, are you? What a surprise that'll be.'

She watched Harriet as she went to the sink and pumped water into the kettle, her eyes following her back to the fire as she hung the kettle up again, and then she glanced back at Mr Tuke.

'Harriet, will you just check that I've fastened 'field gate?' she said. 'I'm not sure if I hooked it up properly as I had my hands full.'

Without a word Harriet gathered up her shawl from the back of the door and left the kitchen. She heaved out a breath as she put on the rubber boots and opened the back door, and then she heard Ellen Tuke's menacing voice saying, 'Now then, Mr Tuke, what 'you been up to?'

And his answer, loud but whiny: 'Don't start on me, woman. I haven't done owt, not to anybody, least of all to her.'

'You'd better not let your son catch you,' his wife said. 'And don't think I don't know you and that shifty look o' yourn. I can read you like a book, Nathaniel Tuke, and don't you forget it.'

Harriet escaped to the hen house and sat on the step. She'd have to be more careful to avoid him in future, she thought, but how could she live like this, constantly on the watch; how could she ever be comfortable and feel at home?

A few days later, on a morning which was cold but bright, Mrs Tuke asked Harriet to come to Brough with her. 'I've a bit of shopping to do,' she said. 'I need a sack o' flour and soap and a few other things, so I'll show you 'best places to get 'em, and if there's time we'll drop in and see Mrs Marshall.'

'Oh, yes, please,' Harriet said. Anything to get out of the house. She wasn't due at the manor this week and time was hanging very heavily. And she would not stay alone in the house with Mr Tuke.

Mrs Tuke went upstairs to tell her husband that his breakfast was in the side oven and he must help himself, and asked Harriet to find Fletcher or Noah to tell them they were going out and there was bread and beef for their midday meal.

Harriet couldn't find Noah but she could hear the splintering of wood and guessed correctly that Fletcher was still finishing off the job of thinning out the trees on the track. She turned a corner and saw him. He had his back to her, with one foot on a tree branch and an axe in his hand, about to chop the branch into logs; a large woodpile was nearby.

He lowered the axe and turned. 'I knew you were there, even though I didn't hear you,' he said.

'Alert to danger?' she asked.

'Danger? Aye, mebbe so.' He stood looking at her. 'Or mebbe because I was thinking of you.'

'You mustn't,' she said softly, even though she knew she wanted him to. 'It's – it's not right.' She paused. 'I've onny come to tell you that your ma and me are going to Brough and that there's food left for you and Noah in 'larder.'

He nodded, keeping his eyes on her face. 'Is my father still in bed?'

'Yes. Your mother has left his breakfast in 'oven.'

'He'll not get up for it. He'll stay in bed all morning.' He put down the axe and came towards her.

'No, don't.' She backed away. 'I – I don't know where Noah is – he might come.'

'He won't,' he said. 'He's in 'bottom field.' But he stopped and put his hands up. 'I wasn't going to touch you. I just wanted to be close to you. I'm sorry. I can't help it.'

She studied his face. He looked drawn, as if he hadn't slept. 'I'm so afraid,' she whispered. 'Of Noah and what he would do if he even – even guessed that you—' She exhaled. 'I'm afraid that he'd kill you and then me.'

He smiled, wistfully, she thought, and turned away. 'Enjoy your day,' he muttered. 'It'll do you and Ma good to get out of 'house and see folk.'

They heard the bang of the house door and Ellen's Tuke's voice calling her. Harriet turned back feeling confused and unsure of herself. How good it would be to get away, even for just a few hours.

As they rattled towards Brough, Mrs Tuke said, 'You're quiet. Are you unwell?'

'Just a touch headachy,' Harriet admitted. 'It's nowt much. 'Fresh air will clear it.'

They travelled for another ten minutes before Ellen Tuke, keeping her eyes firmly over the horse's ears, muttered, 'Don't stand for any nonsense from Mr Tuke, will you? He thinks he's God's gift to women, but he'll soon get 'message if you're firm wi' him.'

Harriet turned to her in astonishment. 'Wh— What . . .'

'I know him very well,' she said. 'He can hide nowt from me and I knew as soon as I came in 'kitchen 'other day that he'd been up to summat.'

'I – don't think he meant anything,' Harriet said lamely. 'It was probably onny a bit o' banter.'

'It wasn't,' she replied coldly. 'He'll tek any chance he can get.' She sighed. 'And I'm stuck wi' him just as you're stuck wi' Noah.'

They left the horse and cart outside a shop and Mrs Tuke said that the mare wouldn't run away and she was right, because each time they walked on to another place the horse clip-clopped after them. They only bought a few provisions besides the sack of flour, and it seemed to Harriet that her mother-in-law only really wanted the outing. She must be fed up with being trapped in 'house all day, she thought, just as

173

I am. Indeed, Mrs Tuke seemed to know quite a lot of people and they all stopped to talk to her.

'I lived here with my ma before I went into service,' she explained, 'and for a short time after I married Mr Tuke, although my mother didn't like him.'

They were about to climb back into the cart when a woman came out of one of the cottages. She was clearly a lady by her dress, and she had a maid with her who was carrying several packages.

'It's Mrs Hart, with Alice,' Harriet murmured. 'What's she doing here? She surely doesn't do her own shopping?'

'No,' Ellen Tuke said. 'I reckon she's doing a few good deeds.' She stopped speaking as Melissa Hart approached them, and holding the horse's snaffle she dipped her knee. 'Morning, ma'am,' she murmured.

'Good morning,' Mrs Hart said breezily. Looking at Harriet, she said, 'Good morning, Mrs Tuke. How are you?'

Harriet too dipped her knee. 'Very well, thank you, ma'am. I hope you are too?'

'I am,' she said, her eyes straying back to Ellen.

'This is my mother-in-law, Ellen Tuke,' Harriet said. 'She used to work at 'manor.'

'Did you?' Melissa smiled. 'I'm very pleased to meet you,' she said, not disclosing that she had ever heard of Ellen Tuke. 'It's so nice that there's continuity, isn't it? We've been visiting Alice's mother, who is not well. She also worked at the manor – when my husband was young.'

'Would that be Florence Brown, ma'am?' Ellen glanced at the young maid, who nodded. 'I remember her. She left not long after I did.'

'Really?' Melissa said pleasantly. 'Well, come along, Alice, we have more to do and Cook will be after my skin if I keep you out too long. Good day, Mrs Tuke. Good day, Mrs Tuke – Harriet. Your daughter-in-law has a very good hand with the iron,' she added to Ellen, before drawing away with Alice in tow.

'Well.' Ellen Tuke drew in a breath. 'I've never known anyone quite like her. You wouldn't have caught Master Christopher's mother calling on young maids' mothers, sick or not.' She watched Mrs Hart climbing into a smart trap and taking the reins of a fine horse. 'I don't think Mrs Jane Hart would've done, either. A proper lady she was, from what I gathered.'

'I'm pleased that she does,' Harriet said. 'We're all out of 'same pot, aren't we? It's just an accident of birth whether we end up rich or poor.'

Ellen gazed after the trap as it bowled past them. She huffed. 'Mebbe so.' She clicked her tongue and the old mare moved slowly off. 'I don't think we'll visit Mrs Marshall today. I can feel a headache coming on now.'

# CHAPTER TWENTY-SIX

'Guess who I met in Brough today,' Melissa said gaily, coming to join her husband in the drawing room where he was waiting for the supper bell.

'What were you doing in Brough?' Christopher looked up from his newspaper.

'I took Alice; she told me yesterday that her mother was ill and that she was worried about her, so I said I would drive her in to visit her.'

Christopher frowned. 'Alice?' He searched in his mind for an acquaintance of that name. 'I don't recall anyone called Alice.'

'Yes you do, darling. Our maid, Alice. You see her practically every day.'

'Alice? You mean you drove one of the maids into Brough to see her mother? Why didn't you get one of the men to take her?'

Melissa sighed. 'Because Cook had said she couldn't have the time off and I knew that Cook wouldn't argue with me, and besides, I was curious to know if Alice's mother really was ill or if Alice simply wanted the morning off.'

'And . . . ?' he asked.

Melissa nodded. 'She was ill. Oh, not with anything catching, so don't look so alarmed. She's crippled with arthritis and in a great deal of pain.' She reached to ring the bell on the wall.

'Ah!' he said, returning to his newspaper.

'Don't you want to know who I saw?'

He put down the newspaper. 'You're going to tell me anyhow.' He smiled indulgently. 'Come on then, whom did you see?'

Alice came in answer to the bell and Melissa said, 'Ask Cookson to bring a brandy and soda and a small claret, please, Alice.'

Alice bobbed her knee and went out again.

'That's Alice,' Melissa pointed out.

'I know,' Christopher said patiently. 'And how did you know I wanted a brandy and soda?'

'Because you always like one when we have a chat,' she said.

Christopher sat up straight. 'What are we going to chat about? I'm beginning to feel very nervous, like a schoolboy in front of his headmaster.'

Melissa laughed. 'Silly,' she said. 'I asked you who do you think I saw in Brough?'

He sighed. 'I have absolutely no idea. Really, Melissa, you're worse than Amy. Don't you think it's time she came home?' he added.

'I do, as a matter of fact,' she agreed. 'But she's obviously having a good time and doesn't want to. And that's not what we're talking about.'

He folded his arms. 'So of what or whom *are* we speaking?'

'Mrs Tuke and Mrs Tuke!' she said triumphantly. 'They were in Brough.'

'So? Is that supposed to mean something?'

'I thought you'd be interested! Oh, not about Harriet Tuke because she's new and you don't know her, although you might have noticed how beautifully she irons your shirts and cravats. But your Ellen Tuke. She's the one I met.'

'*My* Ellen Tuke?' He stopped as the butler came in with a tray, mixed him a brandy and soda and then passed Melissa a glass of claret before quietly leaving the room. 'What do you mean?' Christopher went on irritably. 'She's not *my* Ellen

177

Tuke. She used to be Ellen Fletcher when she worked here, before she married Tuke.'

'Were you sweet on her? I think she might have been pretty once, though she's very careworn now.'

He sighed. 'You say the strangest things, Melissa.' Then he considered. 'I suppose I might have been when I was young,' he admitted. 'When my sisters left home to be married there was no one to talk to in the school holidays so I would go down to the kitchen to be spoiled by Cook and the other servants.'

'Including Ellen Fletcher?' she said slyly.

He shook his head. 'She was very shy when she first came to work here.' He paused. 'But you're right, she was pretty then.' He gazed at Melissa. 'She looked rather like you, come to think of it. Fair hair, fair skin, blue-grey eyes, I think.'

'Yours are the bluest eyes I've ever seen,' she said. 'And did you meet her secretly? Did you have a schoolboy crush on her?'

He ran his fingers through his short beard. 'I did,' he answered softly, which quite shocked Melissa as she had only set out to tease him. 'I was too young to know that any liaison was impossible. I couldn't wait to see her each time I came home from school, and then when I finished my schooling and decided I wanted to work on the estate I saw her more often.'

He gazed down at his brandy glass and swirled the liquid around. He breathed deeply, more like a sigh. 'She was the one who eventually broke away. I was just twenty-one.' He gave a self-deprecating laugh. 'My father would have had a fit if he'd known, but it wouldn't have worked and she realized that before I did. I think maybe someone in the kitchen had warned her off.' He sat up straight again. 'And the next thing she was telling me she was going to marry the abominable Tuke. God knows why. Nobody liked him.'

Melissa hadn't expected a confession such as this. He must have been smitten, she thought, to remember so much.

'I didn't think she'd ever be happy with Tuke, and that's the real reason why I gave her the lease on Marsh Farm.'

'Her?' she asked. 'Not him?'

'It's rented to Ellen. Her name is on the lease. I don't know if he knows, he's not very bright, but I didn't trust him to do right by her and I thought that way she'd always have the security of a roof over her head.'

'Why didn't you let it to her at a peppercorn rent?' she asked. 'It's worthless, isn't it, down by the river?'

'Land is never worthless,' he pointed out. 'All land is worth something.'

'Then why not? Like Mrs Marshall,' Melissa said.

He shook his head. 'Mrs Marshall is old and has no one else to look after her. Besides, that was years later, as you know. If I'd asked my father to let Tuke have it for a peppercorn rent he would have wondered why. He didn't know that I'd put Ellen's name on the lease. And Ellen wouldn't have been comfortable either; she'd have considered it a favour and wouldn't have liked that. But the rent is low, in any case, nothing that they can't manage. I put it up every few years now that she has two sons to help farm it.'

Melissa was silent for a moment. Christopher, she thought, must have known Ellen Fletcher very well indeed to know exactly how she would feel about the rent of the house and the land.

'And,' she said hesitantly, 'when you met Jane afterwards, did you love her?'

He looked across at her, and as he smiled at her the supper bell rang. 'It was an arranged marriage, as you very well know,' he said quietly. 'And yes, of course I cared for her.' He rose from the chair and put out his hand to help her up and gently kissed her cheek. 'But it is you I love.'

March blew in and the windows rattled and the guttering shook, but everyone knew that winter was in retreat and spring was on its way. The brothers began sowing and some new lambs were born and Harriet began to look at the farm in a different light. It was no longer so cold, and although the land

179

was still wet a new growth was beginning in the hedgerows, with birds nesting and winter snowdrops and aconites making way for primroses and cowslips, and meadow grass beginning to flourish. The hens began to lay more eggs; Mrs Tuke acquired ducks who, with their wings clipped, plunged their heads into muddy puddles, ignoring the deeper waters of the estuary. They splattered all over the yard so that Harriet was constantly pumping water and brushing to avoid bringing their mess into the house.

The milk yield was flourishing and Ellen made butter and kept it cool in the larder. Harriet wrote signs and nailed them to the gate advertising the surplus of milk and eggs for anyone who might be passing and every other Monday she walked to the manor to do the laundry.

Mrs Hart had left a parcel for Harriet with Alice one day and on opening it she had found a grey wool skirt and two poplin blouses in grey and blue, and a note to say that if they would fit her she would be pleased if she would accept them. They fitted her perfectly and were of a much better quality than she could ever have afforded. Harriet left a note for Mrs Hart to thank her for her kindness.

The days were lengthening and Harriet walked slowly back to Marsh Farm late one afternoon; she felt tired after ironing a big batch of sheets and pillowcases following the departure of visitors from the manor. At the top of the farm track she saw the familiar figure of Fletcher waiting for her and felt a mixed frisson of anxiety and elation; she wanted to see him but worried that Noah might take it into his head to come up the track. The possibility was remote, for he rarely left the homestead, but nevertheless she was nervous and disturbed and not only because he might come across them talking or standing close.

She had tried to avoid any contact with Fletcher for the last few weeks, except when they sat at table during mealtimes, and even then she hardly dared to look at him in case she drew attention to the unspoken communication they shared.

She was sure that Noah or their mother would be able to tell that there was a rapport, an attraction, between them, for if she felt it and Fletcher did too, then surely it must be obvious to everyone else. Whenever he was near she felt an urge to put her fingers to her throat to still the throb of the pulse, so sure was she that others could hear the rapid beat of her heart.

'You shouldn't do this.' Her voice broke as he drew near. 'It's so light now, someone might see—'

'I had to come,' he interrupted. 'I've made my mind up about something and I need to tell you.'

'And I—' she began, but he took hold of her hands and pressed them to his lips.

'No,' he insisted. 'Let me say my piece first. I've had enough. Noah and I – I can't work with him any more. You don't hear half of what he says; he gives out orders as if he's 'master here, and he's not. I am, or should be, but I don't want to lord it over him or we'll fight. We should be able to work together as a team but he won't agree and he keeps on about this damned bet that he says we made.' He shook his head. 'And I'll not have it. But 'worst thing is that I can't bear to think of you being with him, of him touching you, holding you.' His voice dropped to not much more than a whisper. 'It's driving me crazy, Harriet. I can't – I won't stand for it any longer.'

He gently stroked her cheek, and in spite of his roughened fingers it was a tender gesture. 'So I'm leaving. I'm going away – to America.'

Her lips parted and her eyes filled with tears. 'Don't,' she pleaded. 'Please don't leave me.'

'Come with me!' he begged. 'Leave him and come away with me. Stay with him and you'll never be happy. I want you. Come with me, Harriet. I'll allus tek care of you.'

Tears streamed down her face. She could barely speak, and there was so much to say.

'I can't,' she wept. 'I'm pregnant.'

# CHAPTER TWENTY-SEVEN

And apart from that, Harriet thought, as they walked slowly back down the track, their fingers touching, he's my husband's brother and it's forbidden in scripture and in law. What do the Commandments say? Thou shalt not commit adultery – and what's 'other one? Thou shalt not covet thy neighbour's wife. So coveting and committing adultery with your husband's brother must be a hundred times worse. Bound to be, cos women are allus blamed – look at Adam and Eve. She stifled a sob and knew she was wicked because she wanted to; if he'd asked me before to go with him I would have found it hard to say no. But now . . . she swallowed hard. How can I when I'm expecting Noah's child?

She had told Fletcher that Noah didn't yet know she was pregnant, that no one knew, and he in turn said that he hadn't told anyone he was leaving the farm.

'Ma will tek it hard,' he said. 'She won't want me to go, but I must. If I don't break away now then I never will. Before you came,' he said softly, 'I'd often thought of moving on. This place isn't big enough for Noah and me, or Da either. I don't mean in size, I mean because we don't get on. Da was allus a bully when we were bairns. He used to beat Noah, and me too when he could catch me, but Ma was allus there wi' a broom handle to flay him, and if it hadn't been for leaving her with 'pair of them I might have gone sooner.

'Then when you arrived, I wanted to be here where you were; but I can't live like this any more.' He clasped her fingers in his. 'Not now; especially not now. Harriet, this might sound like a terrible thing, but just once before I leave, I want to hold you in my arms. I'd like to know what it's like to kiss you and imagine that you're mine and not Noah's.'

She had had the same feeling, but had known that it was sinful; but would it be wicked, she asked herself, if he was going away and she might never see him again? Would it be so terrible?

'Perhaps we could,' she said, in a shaky voice. 'I don't know. Would it be just a goodbye kiss?'

He smiled and dropped her hand as they neared the end of the track. 'No, I don't think so. And it might mean that I wouldn't want to leave.'

They agreed that Fletcher would be the first to tell the family his news: that he was leaving at the end of the month. After he was gone, they decided, it would make it easier for his mother if she knew a child was expected. 'She'll like that. It'll take her mind off 'fact that she's lost a son.'

He announced it after supper the following day. He stood up from the table and said, 'I've got summat to say and it's not about 'farm or ploughing or sowing, cows or sheep, or ditches and drains.'

Noah leaned back in his chair and muttered, 'Is there owt else that's worth talking about?'

Harriet looked at her husband and felt loathing. Yes, there was, she thought, there was watching the rush of the tide in the estuary when the sun glinted on the water; there was seeing and hearing the hundreds of ducks and geese flying over their rooftop as dawn was breaking. They all had a name, Fletcher had told her. There were the brent geese that she knew by their honking cry, and widgeon and mallard, teal and goldeneye, but as yet she couldn't distinguish which was which. But she now knew the barn owl as it swooped low over the hedges, and could recognize the kestrel when it hovered

183

in silent flight before plunging to kill; she knew the long-beaked dunlin with its curved bill and its funny running walk, and the orange-legged redshank with its persistent cry that scoured the mudflats at low tide, and now as spring was emerging there was the fresh green growth unfolding on the bare tree branches. Noah's seen it all before, she thought, and I haven't, yet it's as if he's unaware of it or it's not important to him.

'Go on then,' Noah said. 'Spit it out.' He gave a sly laugh. 'Is it about that heifer you owe me?'

Fletcher's lip curled. 'That bet you said you'd made; a heifer for a wife, wasn't it?'

Harriet didn't take offence at the remark for she knew what Fletcher meant, but Noah stood up, his fists curling. 'You know what it was,' he said. 'I said as I'd bet you a heifer that I'd have a wife afore you, and I have.'

His father interrupted. 'You didn't get one in calf though, did you? You might have to get another!'

Noah raised his fist at his father and his mother broke in in a shrill voice. 'Stop this. I won't have this kind of talk in my house.'

'Let me finish,' Fletcher roared. 'This is not about Harriet; this is about summat I've been planning for a long time.'

Harriet felt suddenly nauseous and hurriedly rose from the table. She couldn't wait to hear what he was about to tell them and dashed for the back door and out into the yard where she was violently sick.

She was leaning against the house wall, taking deep breaths and looking up into the night sky, counting the myriad stars, when the back door opened. It wasn't Noah come to see if she was all right, but Mrs Tuke, and it wasn't concern for Harriet that had brought her out but her own misery.

'He's leaving,' she said in a low, bitter voice. 'My son, Fletcher. He's leaving and travelling to foreign parts. How can he?' she said hoarsely. 'What shall I do?'

Harriet expressed surprise. 'Why?' she asked.

'He says he can't bear to be here any more when there's so much anger, so much conflict and discontent. Fact is,' Ellen stood with her arms folded, 'he's right. Mr Tuke has always nurtured rivalry between 'em. He's allus encouraged them to fight.'

'Why did he do that?' Harriet leaned her head back and closed her eyes; she felt drained and exhausted.

Ellen Tuke didn't answer straight away, but then said, so softly that Harriet wasn't sure that she'd heard correctly, 'Cos of me, I expect.'

The door opened again and Fletcher stood on the doorstep. 'Ma? Come on in. I want to talk to you.' He stepped out and came towards them. 'Harriet,' he said, reaching for her hand and squeezing it gently. 'I want you to know that I'm leaving. I'm going away, but it's not because of you.'

She returned the touch of his fingers and then dropped his hand. 'Your ma has just said. I'm sorry you're leaving, Fletcher. Won't you change your mind?'

For a second he held her gaze and then shook his head. 'No,' he said. 'I can't. I can't live like this any more. There has to be some peace and harmony somewhere and it's not here.'

His mother suddenly drew herself upright and said, 'Then go! Mek a new life for yourself.' There was a sob in her throat and Harriet reflected that she had never before heard any emotion in Ellen Tuke except anger. 'But come back one day,' she continued, 'or write. Let me know that you're still alive.'

Fletcher touched his mother on the shoulder and Harriet thought of how things might have been, and wondered if Noah might have been tender too if it hadn't been for Mr Tuke's wicked and devious ways. But why was her father-in-law the way he was? He seemed to take pleasure in the conflict within his own four walls, and, she considered fearfully, what would he be like with grandchildren in the house?

Fletcher and his mother went back inside but Harriet stayed out a little longer. He'll not touch my children, she determined. Not Mr Tuke, or Noah either. I'll stand between them and protect them with my own body, my life, if need be, before I'll let them be hurt. Then she thought of what Fletcher had said about his mother defending them with the broom handle, and how strange that Noah had been fashioned by that brutality, but Fletcher hadn't.

She held her hand to her belly, still flat, but all the same containing another life growing inside her. I swear that this child and any other that might come will only know love, not hate. I promise that on my own mother's memory.

# CHAPTER TWENTY-EIGHT

Fletcher, having said that his decision was final and no amount of persuasion would make him change his mind, told them he would leave after completing some jobs on the farm, and a week later he was ready.

He and Harriet did not have their farewell kiss as each had hoped, for his mother followed him about, checking that he had all he needed, including money, clean shirts, trousers, socks and flannel combinations, for she was convinced that America would have nothing that a respectable man could buy as it would be crowded with gold miners, Irish and Red Indians. No persuasion on Fletcher's part could convince her that it was a land of opportunity.

After an initial shouting match Noah said little about his brother's leaving, and what he did say was uttered with a sneer and an attitude of *good riddance*, but Harriet felt that he was shocked by the announcement and not a little put out, for it meant that there'd be no one on whom to vent his anger.

On the Sunday morning Fletcher shook hands with his father, who said nothing, but reluctantly held out a limp hand. 'Not wishing me good luck then, Da?' Fletcher said.

Mr Tuke gazed at him for a moment and then dropped his hand. 'What you do wi' your life is your own affair,' he muttered. 'Nowt to do wi' me.'

'What about you, Noah?' Fletcher turned to him. 'No hard feelings?'

Noah gave a grim laugh. 'I reckon you'll be back in a twelve-month wi' your tail between your legs, but don't expect owt from me. This'll be *my* farm, not yourn.'

'Hey!' their father roared. 'I'm not dead yet. And I'm not planning on going anywhere.'

Noah turned and looked at him and Harriet gave a little shudder at his formidable expression.

'Walk me up to 'top of 'track, Ma,' Fletcher said, hoisting his pack on to his back. 'Mebbe you will too, Harriet?'

'Harriet'll stop where she is,' Noah commanded.

Harriet glared at him. 'I'll walk up wi' your ma,' she said firmly. 'It's 'least I can do, if you won't. It's not every day a son leaves home.'

Noah stared back at her, grunted, and turned away.

Harriet and Ellen walked one on each side of Fletcher. It was a fine bright morning and the air was full of birdsong. Then his mother cleared her throat and asked croakily, 'How do you know which way to go? Which road to travel on?'

Fletcher smiled. 'I'm going to Brough,' he said. 'I'm hitching a ride on a barge with a mate. He'll tek me to Hull and then tomorrow I'm catching a train to Liverpool.'

'You could have caught 'train from Brough, couldn't you?' his mother said tightly. 'No need to go to Hull.'

'They put on special trains to Liverpool, Ma. A lot of immigrants arrive in Hull from Europe and they're not allowed off 'ship until early Monday morning. I want to be 'first in queue to mek sure I get on 'train and find a seat. It's a long journey, six or seven hours at least.'

'So where will you sleep tonight?' she asked, her voice strained.

'Wherever I can find a place to lay my head,' he said. 'Don't worry about me. I'll be fine.'

'That's what my brother said,' Harriet said in a small voice. 'And we never heard from him again.'

He touched her fingers. 'You'll hear from me,' he said quietly. 'Sooner or later.'

'How long will it take to sail to America?' she asked.

'If I can get a steamship, a week to ten days, but if they're full then I'll tek a sailing ship and that can tek four or five weeks, depending on 'weather. But a sailing ship'll be cheaper. I'll tek whatever's on offer.'

They reached the top of the track and Fletcher bent to kiss his mother's cheek. 'Go back now, Ma. Tek care of yourself,' he said softly.

'Aye,' she said on a breath. 'Nobody else will,' and turned to retrace her steps down the track. 'I'll not watch you go.'

But he watched her, a small figure, her head bowed as she walked away, and then he turned to Harriet. 'Kiss me goodbye, Harriet?'

She put her face up to his and felt as if her heart might break. She closed her eyes. 'Come back one day,' she whispered.

He kissed her lips. 'One day,' he said softly. 'And then I'll find you wi' a houseful o' children and you won't want me.'

Harriet drew away from him. How could she answer that? She didn't know what the future held. She would have changed, that was for sure, as he would too.

'Who knows?' she whispered. 'I know that I'll miss you, but who knows what'll happen or what life has in store for us? Our paths have crossed, Fletcher, although perhaps they shouldn't have.'

He gazed down at her. 'I've felt sometimes that it would've been better if we'd never met, and yet having met you I've felt uplifted. Life has tekken on a new meaning and I swear, Harriet, that one day I'll come back and claim you.' He kissed her again, and gently pushed her away from him.

Unlike his mother, she watched him make off along the Brough road, and knew she would always remember the way the wind tossed his long hair, the angle at which he held his head, the breadth of his shoulders and the stride of his long

189

legs as he walked away out of her life, and the fact that he didn't look back.

Mrs Tuke withdrew into herself for over a week. Harriet did most of the milking, fed the cattle and the two goats, let out the hens and shut them away at night, gathered eggs and prepared food for their meals, whilst Ellen, her face expressionless, silently made pastry and baked bread, cooked meat or fowl and served it up, but didn't eat any of it.

Noah and his father didn't comment on her demeanour or the fact that she wasn't eating, but Harriet worried that she'd fade away. It was, she admitted to herself, a selfishness on her part, for she was thinking that without her she wouldn't be able to cope alone, especially not now that she was pregnant. She hadn't yet told anyone, but knew that she must do so soon, for most mornings she was sick, although as she was now first downstairs she could escape outside unseen and heave the contents of her stomach into the ditch.

Mrs Tuke was now the first to bed in the evening, simply departing from the supper table as soon as she'd served the meal and going upstairs without a word. In the morning she rose after Harriet and Noah, but before Mr Tuke, whom she virtually ignored.

Mr Tuke, having made several snide remarks about Fletcher's departure, which fell on deaf ears, now said very little about anything, but placed himself in the same chair at the table at mealtimes and sat waiting with a knife and fork clasped at the ready.

At the beginning of the second week after Fletcher had left, Mrs Tuke came downstairs one morning at her old time, just as Harriet came back inside from the yard, wiping her mouth.

She looked at her. 'Are you not well?' she asked.

It was as good a time as any, Harriet decided, even though she hadn't yet told Noah, and she thought that Ellen might cheer up at the news of a grandchild.

'I'm pregnant,' she said, raising a weak smile. 'Been bilious for 'last day or two.'

'Ah.' Ellen's expression remained blank. 'I hadn't noticed.'

'How are you feeling now?' Harriet murmured, and heard Noah's footsteps in the bedroom above.

'As if someone had died,' she answered abruptly. 'How else would you think I feel?'

'He said he'd come back one day,' Harriet said, though Fletcher had said it to her and not his mother.

'He said he'd write,' Ellen muttered. 'Not that he'd come back.'

Harriet hesitated. The news of her pregnancy hadn't appeared to register with her mother-in-law and she tried again. 'Will 'thought of a grandchild help?'

There was a deep pain in Mrs Tuke's eyes as she answered, and Harriet was hurt and astonished by her answer.

'Why should it?' she said. 'It'll be your child, not mine, and how would you feel if one day you lost it?'

Noah barging through the door saved Harriet from answering, even if she could have thought of an answer, which she couldn't. He looked round the kitchen. The table was laid for breakfast but the tea was not yet made.

'What's going on?' he said brusquely. 'Where's my cup o' tea? Come on, Harriet, look lively. Some folk have work to do. There's onny me now to do everything, you know.'

'You're up early,' she said. 'I was just going to mek 'tea.' The kettle was gently steaming, the teapot was warming on the side shelf and she went to pick it up.

Ellen forestalled her. 'I'll do it,' she said dully. 'You'd best tell your husband 'news he's been waiting on for 'last few months.'

Noah looked from one to the other. 'What?' he said. 'What 'you talking about?'

Harriet stood in front of him. 'I'm pregnant, Noah. Carrying 'child that you wanted.'

He looked her up and down. 'About time,' he said. 'What's tekken you so long?'

Ellen put the teapot on the table next to the milk jug. She looked at Harriet. 'I knew he'd be pleased,' she muttered.

Dismay swept through Harriet. It seemed that nothing would please this man she'd taken for her husband. Nothing. He was incapable of feeling happiness or delight, she realized, and she was therefore surprised when he turned towards her and pointed a stabbing finger.

'It'd better be a lad,' he barked. 'Don't go giving me any daughters.'

# CHAPTER TWENTY-NINE

Melissa woke early. She thought she'd heard a cuckoo, and got out of bed to open a window, the better to hear the elusive bird. She looked across to the woodland at the edge of their land where she thought it had probably nested, having robbed some poor dunnock of its young. She hummed an old tune remembered from her childhood, 'Summer is icumen in', as her eyes travelled across the lawns towards her rose beds, which now in June were beginning to flourish.

She saw Harriet Tuke walking up the long drive and then stop, and although she didn't walk on the grass Melissa could tell that she was looking at the roses. Then she turned and headed in the direction of the kitchen. Melissa frowned slightly: Harriet seemed to be weary and was walking slowly, which was odd, Melissa thought, as she was usually so very brisk. Then Melissa straightened and her eyebrows shot up. There was something different about her bearing. Is she pregnant? She was suddenly dismayed, not on Harriet's account but on her own.

She rang the bell for Alice to come up. 'Tea, please,' she said when the girl knocked and came in. 'And will you fill my bath tub?'

'Yes, ma'am,' Alice gazed at her mistress. Her nightdress was fine and flimsy, and as she stood by the window Alice could see her slim shape quite clearly beneath it.

'I heard the cuckoo,' Melissa said. 'Did you hear it, Alice? It's the forebringer of summer, did you know that?'

'I know it's a summer bird, ma'am. A big grey one.'

'That's the male.' Melissa continued to gaze out of the window. 'He's the one who sings.' Without turning her head, she repeated, 'Tea, please, Alice.'

I wonder why he sings so loudly, she thought. And so joyously; and why doesn't the female? Or maybe she does but we just don't hear her. She sighed and went back to sit on her bed and wait for the tea. Or perhaps, she thought, the female doesn't have as much to sing about as he does.

Christopher had gone to London at the weekend to bring Amy back from her travels and would be home tomorrow after spending some time with his sister-in-law and her husband. He'd wanted Melissa to go with him but she had declined, knowing that Amy would want to have her father to herself on the journey home, so that she could tell him everything that had happened during the months she had been away.

Melissa also wanted time to herself, to get used to the idea of having Amy with them again. She hoped that the girl would have grown up and no longer be the spoilt daughter she had been, although Melissa admitted to herself that following their shopping spree together before Amy left for London the atmosphere had been easier. Perhaps, she thought, I too was to blame for always treating her as a child, when in fact she was verging on womanhood.

She had also hoped that during Amy's absence, when both she and Christopher were more relaxed, she might have become pregnant. But that hadn't happened.

As she sat in bed waiting for Alice to come back, her thoughts wandered to Harriet Tuke. I think I might take a trip to the kitchen to see her. Or no – I'll ask her to come up. She won't talk so easily in front of the other servants. I'll find out if she is pregnant, and if she is – Melissa rested her head on the pillow – will she tell me how she managed it so quickly?

When Alice told her that her bath was ready and helped her

to step into it, Melissa asked casually, 'Is Harriet Tuke here today?'

'Yes, ma'am, she is, it's her day for doing 'washing. Mary's here too.'

'Will you ask her to come up when she has a minute? I want to thank her for her ironing.'

Alice looked surprised, but answered that Harriet took a break at about half past nine and that she could come up then.

'Oh, I don't want to interfere with her routine. When she has finished will do.'

It was lunchtime when Harriet knocked on Mrs Hart's sitting-room door. She came in when Melissa called 'Enter', looking hot and flushed.

'Mrs Tuke – Harriet, come in.' Melissa was sitting by the window, and a soft breeze was ruffling her hair. 'You look very warm. Come here by the window and catch the breeze. Won't you sit down?' She indicated a chair which she had placed strategically opposite her.

'Thank you, ma'am.'

'I'm so sorry,' Melissa said. 'I've interrupted your day; you probably want to get off home, but I wanted to thank you personally for the beautiful ironing.'

'That's all right, ma'am. I'm in no hurry to get back.'

'No? Will your husband not be waiting for his midday meal?'

'His mother's there. She'll have everything ready for him as usual.' But they won't have any conversation, Harriet thought, he'll simply eat and go out again.

'Oh dear, so will you miss your lunch – erm – dinner? You must have something here before you leave.'

'I've eaten, ma'am. Cook generally gives me a slice of bread and beef. I hope that's all right?' Harriet suddenly wondered if feeding casual workers was allowed. 'I didn't have much as I wasn't hungry.'

'No? After all that washing and ironing?'

Harriet smiled. 'I'm ironing in 'morning, ma'am. Except for

the personal things, which I've done already. I like to do them while they're still damp.'

'I see. Do you not find it very tiring? I saw you arrive this morning and I thought you seemed a little weary.'

Harriet was taken aback. She hadn't thought that she would be seen from the house so early in the day. 'I stopped to look at your roses, ma'am. They smell lovely.'

'They do, don't they?' Melissa agreed. 'I'm so pleased that I managed to get my own way over having them. So, you weren't too tired? It isn't too early for you to come to work?'

What's she getting at, Harriet wondered. Why's she brought me up here? 'I'm used to being up early,' she told her. 'It's what I've allus done; when you work for a living it's what you have to do otherwise you wouldn't keep a job, and just because I'm – just because – I'm sometimes a bit tired of a morning . . .'

Her voice trailed away. It's not just because I'm pregnant, she thought. It's because there's no light in my life now that Fletcher's gone.

'Harriet,' Melissa said softly, 'it's all right. I guessed that you might be expecting a child. Am I right?' and at Harriet's silent acquiescence, she said, 'You don't have to worry. Your position here is perfectly safe.'

Harriet wiped her eyes, which had suddenly become moist. 'Thank you, ma'am. I'll keep on working for as long as I can, though I'll have to stop after I've given birth, Noah says.'

Melissa's lips parted. 'Well, I can see that your husband might think it difficult, but what do women do when they have children and need to work to earn money?'

'In town they have child minders, but I'd never do that. Not all of them can be trusted with other people's bairns – children.'

'I see.' Melissa thought for a moment and then said, 'Well, we'll talk about it again, but if he were willing, I don't see why you shouldn't bring the child with you, say to the ironing room? Obviously not the washhouse, as it might not be healthy for a child, but if we had a crib or a basket in the ironing room, might not that be all right?'

Harriet couldn't understand her. She had thought she was going to be dismissed; was there some other reason why Mrs Hart had brought her upstairs? 'It might be, ma'am. I'll ask him, but not yet. I'd have to time it right.'

'Of course.' Melissa smiled. 'It doesn't do to let our husbands know all our little wiles, does it?'

Harriet hadn't heard the term before, but she understood perfectly that she would have to choose her moment carefully to mention to Noah that she'd like to go back to working at the manor after the birth.

'It – erm, it hasn't taken long for you to conceive,' Melissa said cautiously. 'Forgive me for being so forthright, but I long for a child and have not yet had the good fortune. I sometimes think that perhaps I never will.'

'It's not allus the woman's fault,' Harriet said abruptly. 'Men blame them, but they're the ones who supply 'seed and not all seed grows.'

'That's true,' Melissa said softly, but then thought that as Christopher already had a daughter it must be her.

'My husband thought I was barren,' Harriet said bitterly. 'He expected me to get caught straight away after 'first time.' She gave a dry exclamation. 'Some farmer he is!'

'So,' Melissa leaned forward. 'Erm, forgive me,' she murmured again. 'But how often do you think . . .' She put her fingers to her mouth. How could she possibly ask, and of a servant of all people? But then this servant would know the answer better than anyone else she knew.

'Four months!' Harriet declared passionately. 'Four months, and every night, sometimes twice in a night, bar 'time when I was on 'flux, I had to put up wi' him astride me.' Her eyes were fierce as they met Melissa's. 'Even if you loved a man, that's almost too much to bear, but far worse if you know you're onny there to relieve his carnal desires and give him a child.'

197

Melissa was shocked by Harriet's openness and apparent resentment, even though she had wanted to know. 'Do you not love your husband?'

'It was a marriage of convenience, ma'am,' Harriet muttered, knowing she had spoken too freely. Then she murmured, 'Mebbe I'm wrong, mebbe if there's love between you, you'd want to – to . . .' She wanted to say *hold someone in your arms each night*, but she had said too much already and didn't want to give away the secret longing that she wished she had run away with Fletcher, pregnant or not.

*Every* night, Melissa thought. *Every* night! Christopher comes to my bed once a week, and then he treats me with such care and tenderness, as if he doesn't want to hurt me. Is that why I don't conceive? Is our timing wrong – or is it not often enough?

'I'm sorry you appear to be unhappy,' she said quietly. 'I thought it would be a time of great rejoicing.'

'So did I, ma'am,' Harriet murmured. 'And so it should be. Perhaps when I hold this child for 'first time I might feel differently, and if it's a son my husband will be pleased. But if it's not . . .' She gave a little shudder at the prospect of the nightly assault on her body. 'If it's not, then we'll have to start all over again.'

Melissa watched Harriet from her window as she walked back down the drive. 'Poor woman,' she murmured. 'Why did she marry him? Did she think he was her last chance? Did she want the security of marriage, and if so, was it worth the unhappiness she is obviously suffering now?'

She recalled the day, months ago, when she and Christopher had watched Harriet and the other Tuke son walk away together and she'd joked about the gap between them. Then she began to wonder whether Harriet had discovered she'd married the wrong brother.

How silly and romantic you are, Melissa, she chided. You're too old for such girlish thoughts. Nevertheless, she gave a little smile and went to her lingerie drawer, where after lingering over virgin white, soft cream and romantic rose she drew out a pale green nightgown of fine silk and a matching satin chemise, the colour of life and fertility, and draped them across her bed.

# CHAPTER THIRTY

Amy had been away almost six months. No one had thought it would be so long. She had enjoyed the London season, going to parties and balls with her aunt and cousins, and then when the winter became wet and dreary the whole household, apart from Amy's uncle Gerald, had packed up to travel to Switzerland, where they enjoyed the winter sunshine until they returned to London in April.

'We've missed you, Amy,' Melissa said sincerely. 'It has been a long time, and you've grown up whilst you've been away.'

'I missed you both too,' Amy said. Her eyes showed Melissa that she hadn't missed them very much, but it was sweet of her to say so. 'But it's been wonderful,' Amy went on, 'and the time passed so quickly.'

Amy and Melissa were in the sitting room, Christopher having gone to have a word with the bailiff, and it almost felt, Melissa thought, as if Amy might be a visiting relative as she looked round the room or got up to gaze out of the window.

'The rose beds look lovely,' Amy said. 'Were you planning those before I went away?'

'We'd discussed them, don't you remember?'

'Vaguely.' Amy came to sit down again, sighing as she did so.

'So, did you make any new friends?' Melissa asked. 'Did you meet any handsome young men?'

Amy looked at her and then glanced at the door. She dropped her voice. 'I did, as a matter of fact.' She raised her eyebrows and smiled. 'Lots!'

'Oh, lucky girl.' Then, conspiratorially, 'Anyone special?' A shadow of distrust crossed Amy's face, and Melissa blamed herself for assuming they were bosom friends and not step-mother and daughter. 'Or perhaps it's too soon to talk about it?' she added swiftly.

Amy hesitated, and then said, 'It is too soon, but when you met Papa, how long was it before you knew that you wanted to marry him?'

'Oh, immediately!' Melissa said at once, thinking, Heavens, the child is in love. But then she looked at Amy, sitting starry-eyed, and realized that she was no longer a child. She's as old as I was when Alfred and I were planning to marry. 'I fell in love with your father at our first meeting. I don't know if I ever told you, but I was engaged to be married to a childhood sweetheart when I was about your age. Our parents expected us to marry, and we were good friends and very fond of each other, but he died just months before our wedding day, and it wasn't until I met your father that I realized I hadn't been in love with Alfred at all.' Amy was watching her intently, her lips slightly parted. 'Which,' Melissa concluded, 'is most unusual for people like us.' Gently, she added, 'We are expected to make suitable marriages and come to love our husbands or wives over time, as the years go by.'

'That's what Aunt Deborah told me,' Amy said, 'when I said I wanted to marry for love. She said young ladies should look for respectability and security, and . . . that that was what Mama would have wanted for me.'

'Did she?' Melissa was astonished. 'How very conventional of her. I didn't know that she was so very proper. I hadn't been given that impression at all.'

'Well, she didn't appear to be until – until . . .' Amy wavered. 'I met someone I rather liked. We danced together and talked quite a lot and Aunt Deborah thought it rather forward of us

201

both. I think that was why when we went to Switzerland we stayed away longer than I expected.'

'Your aunt would have felt responsible for you, Amy,' Melissa explained. 'It's not easy looking after someone else's daughter.' She hadn't thought of what she was saying until Amy looked at her and then away. 'I'm sorry. Please don't misunderstand me,' she added quickly.

'I don't,' Amy said. 'And I realize now how difficult I must have been. I didn't want Papa to love anyone but me. I was so afraid of losing him, especially after I'd lost Mama.' She smiled at Melissa. 'But now I know that I too can find someone to love, just as Papa found you.'

At supper, Amy regaled them with the tales of where she had been, the sights she had seen in London, the clothes she had bought for the various balls and dances she had attended.

'I've spent quite a lot of money, Papa,' she said blithely, 'but Aunt Deborah said she was sure you wouldn't mind. And by the way, Melissa, they loved the clothes I took with me, and said they had no idea there was anything worth buying out of London.' She giggled, and they both saw the child still hidden there as she added, 'I told a slight white lie when I said you and I often went shopping together in Hull and York. My cousins were quite jealous, I think, because they are only allowed to shop with their mother or a maid.'

Melissa felt a great weight lifting from her shoulders and she thought that Christopher felt the same as he smiled at his daughter's chatter. When he asked if she had met anyone interesting, Amy glanced at Melissa and said, 'Lots of people, Papa, lots and lots. I was wondering if perhaps some time during the summer, if you're not too busy, we could have a house party and invite my aunt and my cousins and a few other people too?'

When he said it was a splendid idea, she took a huge breath and beamed.

That night, as they prepared for bed, Melissa whispered to Christopher that she wanted him to come to her. 'You don't have to get up early in the morning, do you?' she murmured.

Whilst he changed in his dressing room she slipped into her silk nightgown and chemise, and stood by the window looking out.

'Come here,' she said softly when he returned to the bedroom. 'Look at the garden, how beautiful it looks.'

He came to stand beside her and kissed her cheek. 'Not as beautiful as you,' he said. 'What perfume are you wearing?'

She turned to him. 'It's the roses,' she whispered. 'They always smell lovely on the night air.' She reached up to kiss his mouth. 'I missed you whilst you were away,' she murmured, 'and I'm so happy that you're home again.'

He stroked her face. 'So am I, and I think that Amy is pleased to be home.'

'She is,' she agreed. 'But we'll speak of Amy tomorrow. Tonight is our time.'

He ran his hands down the silky gown to her waist, her hips and her thighs, and felt her response. She whispered something in his ear.

'Now?' he asked.

'Yes,' she said softly. 'Now.'

He slipped the chemise from her shoulders and lifted her nightgown, drawing it over her body so that she stood naked before him. 'Melissa!' he murmured, dropping the silk to the floor, but she put her hand over his mouth.

'Don't speak,' she whispered. 'Not a word, except to say that you love me.'

# CHAPTER THIRTY-ONE

Harriet was no longer required in Noah's bed once she had told him of her pregnancy, and as soon as she began to put on weight she asked him if perhaps she should sleep in Fletcher's room so as to give him more space.

'Aye,' Noah said. 'Do that. You disturb me anyway wi' your tossing and turning all night.'

She hadn't been aware that she'd been restless, although her early morning sickness had woken him and he'd turned away in disgust as she retched over the chamber pot.

Now, though, that was over and done with, and although the room was only small she was happy to be in Fletcher's bed, to feel the hollow in the mattress he had carved out with his body and to let her thoughts fly to how it would be if he were lying next to her.

There had been no news from him apart from a single note written to his mother before he left Liverpool on a sailing ship, not a steamship as he had hoped. *The cheapest fare to America is seventy shillings*, he'd written. *So that's what I've taken. I'll be travelling steerage but I shan't mind.*

That was in March and they were now in June, so he should have arrived in New York several weeks ago. New York was to be the first port of call, he had told Harriet before he left, and then he would move on in an attempt to find work. 'Mebbe I'll find gold,' he'd joked to his mother, but she'd answered that wealth didn't mean happiness and he'd made no further attempt to console her.

When Harriet finished her chores each day, she made the most of the fine weather and began to explore her surroundings. During the winter months the weather had been so poor that she was confined mainly to the house, but now the sun shone. Mrs Tuke had acquired a young heifer in calf to continue the milk supply and called it Dora Two, the corn was plumping up, and the new lambs were no longer frolicking but were half grown and contentedly cropping the grass, unaware, Harriet thought thankfully, of what was in front of them. It had taken her some time to come to terms with the reality of animal husbandry, that the cattle, pigs and sheep were for eating and not just to enhance a pleasant pastoral scene.

She walked in the opposite direction to the manor and found farmhouses and cottages, not on the estuary bank as Marsh Farm was, but on the higher side of the road. On her way back one day and feeling thirsty, she had knocked on a cottage door to ask for a drink of water. The door was opened by Mary, who expressed great surprise on seeing her and invited her to come in and have a cup of tea, which Harriet was pleased to do as she had walked too far and her legs were aching.

'I don't get many visitors,' Mary said, 'so I'm glad of a bit o' company.' She poured Harriet a cup of weak tea with a minute drop of milk. 'It's goat's milk,' she said. 'Not everybody likes it.'

'It's not so rich as cow's milk, is it? Settles better on my stomach, but I don't like 'smell of it.'

'Better for you, anyway, now that you're carrying,' Mary said. 'Will you be able to stop on at 'manor? Have you told 'mistress?'

Harriet nodded and sipped her tea. 'She guessed,' she said. 'But she wants me to stay on, and afterwards too, if I can.'

'Oh, you've made a good impression there.' Mary nodded

her head and her jowly chins wobbled. 'Have you made pro-
vision for 'delivery?' she asked. 'For 'babby,' she added, seeing
Harriet's nonplussed expression.

'Oh, no, I haven't.' She had given little thought to it because
it wasn't a procedure she knew anything about, having had no
friends in the same situation. She had vaguely imagined that
Mrs Tuke might help her, having had two sons of her own.

'I can do that, if you'd like me to,' Mary told her. 'I've
brought many a bairn into 'world. Don't do much now as I'm
too far out from 'villages for anybody to fetch me. But I'm not
that far from you if you should want any help. Somebody'd
have to come for me if it's at night, but I can walk during 'day.'

'That's really kind, Mary. I had thought that mebbe Mrs
Tuke – Ellen – might—'

'Not a good idea,' Mary said. 'She had a hard time wi' her
firstborn. Nivver known a woman cry as much as she did.
Not that it was a difficult birth, there were no complications,
but she nivver stopped weeping, even after it were all over.'
She chewed on her bottom lip before adding, 'Don't know
who delivered 'second babby – that'd be your husband – but
it weren't me. I nivver even knew she was expecting till I
happened to hear she'd got another son.'

It wasn't anything Ellen Tuke ever discussed with Harriet;
it was as if she was completely ignoring what was going on in
her household. She had made no comment about her own
pregnancies in connection with Harriet's; neither had she
ever acknowledged that she knew Mary, even though Harriet
had mentioned her by name.

It was a mile walk to Marsh Farm and Harriet decided to
speak to Noah nearer the time when she thought she might be
delivered, and ask him to keep the horse and trap at the ready
to fetch Mary. She was fairly sure now that she would get no
help from her mother-in-law.

But she did ask her one morning if she might borrow the
trap to go on an outing and asked her if she'd like to come
too, but Ellen had replied brusquely that she wouldn't as she

had plenty of other things to do. Harriet apologized and asked if she could do anything to help, but Mrs Tuke shook her head. 'No, you go,' she said, and it seemed to Harriet that perhaps she might be trying to make amends for her indifference when she added, 'Mek 'most of your free time, for you'll have none later on.'

Harriet took a deep breath of air as she drove along the top road, passing Mary's cottage, to an area Mrs Tuke had described as Broomfleet. Ellen had told her that if she drove far enough she would reach the Market Weighton canal, which went through the Broomfleet lock before emptying into the Humber.

'You'll see butterflies and moths along there,' she said, 'and wild flowers in 'meadow grass, though it's mainly agricultural land.'

Harriet gazed at her. It was the first time she had imparted any information about anywhere but their own farmland.

Ellen looked away, as if embarrassed, and said, 'My brothers and me used to walk along 'estuary bank, and 'lads used to swim in 'canal.'

'I didn't realize you had any brothers,' Harriet exclaimed. 'I don't recall you mentioning them before.'

'No, mebbe not.' Ellen clammed up. 'They're long gone, anyway.'

How strange, Harriet mused as she cracked the whip over the old mare's head and they slowly moved off. She seems to have cut herself off from everybody, and doesn't even want to talk about them.

The drive towards the small village of Broomfleet was through flatlands, or marshlands as Ellen Tuke called them, and the estuary was in sight most of the time, with the county of Lincolnshire clearly in view on the other side as the day was bright and sharp without any hint of mist.

The landscape was mainly agricultural, as Ellen had described, but the meadows where cattle grazed were scattered with wild flowers, attracting bees and hundreds of fluttering butterflies: white, orange-tipped, brown tortoiseshell, and some with coloured rings and spots that Harriet hadn't seen before and which filled her with such delight that she kept stopping to look. In the hedgerows pale pink dog roses flourished and there was a rustling and twittering of tiny wrens and busy sparrows; in the ditches she saw violets and golden star-like flowers which she couldn't name, not having seen them before. White flowers gave off the aroma of garlic and mustard, and she caught a glimpse of a twitching snout, beady eyes and a prickly body before their owner swiftly disappeared again.

It was a long meandering drive to the canal and Harriet knew she should be turning back almost as soon as she arrived, but she couldn't resist getting down from the cart and looping the reins round a tree stump so that she could stand by the edge of the water. A grey heron disturbed by her presence flew off in an awkward long-legged flight towards the reed beds. She heard the croak of nesting water birds, mainly black, some with a white head shield and other smaller ones with a scarlet marking. Looking in the other direction she saw the lock gates and the railway bridge in the distance, and she guessed that the bridge carried the waggons and trucks from Brough railway station.

Fletcher had told her that the canal had been dug for drainage and navigational purposes. Over the years, interested parties, mainly farmers, had petitioned for the area to be warped, as Fletcher had wanted to do at Marsh Farm. The additional land would have aided agriculture, but those with navigational interests opposed and blocked the schemes.

She looked down to see the rush of water as it entered the Humber, saw too the busy shipping lanes as barges, keels, sloops and commercial vessels took their contents to and from Hull, Brough, Howden and Goole, across to Lincolnshire and on towards the Trent Falls. To her delight, she also spotted the sleek and shiny head of a seal.

She gave a satisfied sigh as she headed back to Marsh Farm.

At least I now know where I'm living, she thought. I'm not isolated in a small farm on the edge of 'estuary but am part of a wider community. Not a large one, she thought, as she had seen no one but a lone fisherman down by the water's edge, but there are seamen and bargemen on those boats, and lock keepers, and engine drivers on the trains which cross the bridge, and they'll have wives and children living some kind of life, just as I am.

As summer came to a close, Noah became more and more irritable. He shouted at everyone that he was having to do everything himself since his good-for-nothing brother had cleared off, and in the next breath raged that he'd better not come back or he'd find a shotgun waiting to welcome him.

Mr Tuke generally slunk off into some corner where he couldn't be found, but Ellen yelled back at Noah, saying that he was the one who wanted the farm and was now realizing he couldn't manage it alone. She shook a fist at him, saying, 'Now we know who did most of 'work,' which infuriated Noah even more.

By the end of October Harriet had begun to feel sluggish, and although she still rose early Ellen said she'd do the first milking, leaving Harriet to prepare breakfast for Noah and Mr Tuke. Noah barely spoke in a morning, and as she went to bed earlier than he did and slept in Fletcher's box room at the back of the house, she didn't always hear him come up to bed.

But there was one night when she couldn't sleep and went downstairs to sit in the easy chair. She heard the dog bark and the clatter of hooves, and a few minutes later she heard the rattle of the latch and Noah came in. He looked startled to see her sitting in her nightgown and shawl by the banked-up fire.

'What you doing up?' he growled. 'Time you was abed.'

'I couldn't sleep,' she said, and was about to ask him where he'd been, then stopped herself. There was something in his eyes, and a smell of ale on him, that made her decide that discretion would serve better.

But she thought that now might be a good time to suggest that Mary could help her at the birthing but would need collecting from her home. Noah frowned and said wasn't there anyone nearer and wouldn't his mother be able to do what was necessary?

'No,' she said. 'She won't. Perhaps you'd like to deliver it?' She shuddered at the thought. 'You've had experience with animals; it must be 'same.'

His nostrils flared. 'Fletcher used to do that,' he said. 'I can't be doing wi' all o' that fuss. I'll fetch 'midwife when 'time comes.'

That's a relief, she thought, sitting on by the fire as he staggered upstairs. He'd been drinking, she knew, but it was well past midnight, so where else had he been?

# CHAPTER THIRTY-TWO

After that night Harriet became aware that Noah frequently left the farm on Friday and Saturday evenings, but now, if she was awake and had gone to sit downstairs, she made sure that she was back in bed before midnight so that there was no confrontation with him.

She wanted to ask his mother where he might be going, but Ellen was taciturn and didn't encourage conversation and Harriet guessed that she was worrying over Fletcher. She seemed to have no empathy with Noah, which seemed odd to Harriet. I'd have thought she'd be glad to have one son at home.

The time dragged, even though she tried to keep busy and do most of her usual jobs on the farm. I'd have had to keep working if I'd been pregnant in Hull, she thought, and being under the eye of a mill foreman would have been much worse. At least here I can sit down occasionally and take my time over milking and feeding the animals.

One Saturday evening, when they had finished supper and cleared away, Ellen was preparing vegetables by the sink for the next day's meal and Mr Tuke was snoring by the fire. Ellen had given Harriet some white cotton material and she was sewing a layette at the table by the light of the lamp when she became aware of Noah looking at her and chewing on his fingernails.

She attempted a hesitant smile but he didn't respond and simply stared at her, then, abruptly, got to his feet and headed for the door. 'Don't lock up,' he muttered to his mother as he went past her. 'I might be late.'

Mrs Tuke watched his back as he slammed out of the door and silently shook her head, then bent it again to finish what she was doing.

A few minutes later Harriet heard the striking of hooves across the yard and knew it wasn't the old mare that Noah was riding. When Ellen came to sit down opposite her, Harriet murmured, 'Where do you think he'll be going? To 'alehouse?'

'Mebbe.' Ellen glanced at her husband, who was slumped back in the chair with his mouth open. He'd become flabby and corpulent over the summer, demanding larger portions of meat, more butter on his bread and potatoes, more cream on his apple or bramble pies; Ellen turned her face away from him with an expression of distaste. 'Mebbe not.'

'Where then?' Harriet persisted. 'He's tekken 'stallion so he's riding hard.'

Ellen gave an indifferent shrug. 'Reckon that's what he's doing then.' She looked again at Mr Tuke and her lips curled. 'Stallions, 'pair of 'em. Like father, like son.'

Harriet put down her sewing. 'What?' She frowned. 'What do you mean?'

'Are you so innocent that you don't know, or can't guess?' Ellen's voice was cutting.

Harriet put her hand to her mouth. Did she really want to know where her husband had gone on a wet and windy night? Though October had been a mellow month, now they were in November the weather had turned foggy and damp, so what, she wondered, was so urgent or important that Noah had to saddle up and canter off when it was almost bedtime?

Stallions, Mrs Tuke had called her husband and son, although looking at Mr Tuke, sprawled so slovenly in his chair Harriet couldn't imagine him ever being virile or attractive to any woman.

'So,' she murmured. 'Do you think that Noah has gone to meet a woman?'

Ellen Tuke clasped her hands in her lap and didn't speak but gazed at Harriet pityingly, her lips curled. Then she took a heaving breath and said slowly, 'I thought that being a townswoman you'd be worldly, but I gather that you're not.'

'I'm trying not to think about it.' Harriet lifted her eyes to her mother-in-law. 'But if it's not just one woman, then—'

'A brothel,' Ellen stated flatly. 'That's where he'll have gone. No point in beating about 'bush. There's nowhere else he could go. Any half-decent woman will be within her own four walls at this time o' night.'

'So – where?' Harriet whispered. She'd always thought of herself as a woman of the world. She'd met enough men at the various alehouses and hostelries where she'd worked over the years to know when they were on the lookout for a willing woman, and she noted the areas where the brothels were in order to steer clear of them after dark. But she had never thought that she would marry a man who would go looking for such places because his wife wasn't available.

'Where?' Ellen scoffed. 'I could mek a guess at a couple o' places, but there's one in particular where they'll tek any man, young or old, rich or poor, if he dare tek 'chance of coming out unscathed.'

What was it she said when I first arrived? Harriet tried to remember. Something in response to Mr Tuke's probing question to Noah about where they'd met. Was it a brothel, he'd asked, and – yes, Ellen had said there was no need to travel to Hull to find one, that he'd be able to find one closer to home. And Mr Tuke had been angry and told her to shut her mouth.

Was this how she knew? Had Mr Tuke been to a brothel seeking a woman when his wife was pregnant?

Harriet shuddered. If that was where Noah had gone, the worry was what would happen after she'd given birth. Would Noah seek her bed again? Would he pay for a woman's services when he had a wife at home? And if he had been with those

213

women, were they clean? And if they weren't, would he pass on a disease to her?

Mr Tuke suddenly snorted and sat up and looked at them both. 'What?' he rasped. 'What did you say?'

'I said, Mr Tuke,' Ellen responded calmly, 'that you might as well be in bed as snoring by 'fire.'

'I wasn't snoring,' he growled. 'Don't ever snore,' but he heaved himself out of the chair and went to the door and out of the porch, leaving the door wide open so that a cold draught blew into the kitchen. Mrs Tuke tutted and got up to close it after him. He was back within a few minutes and headed for the stairs.

'Nivver snore,' he grunted. 'Nivver in my life.'

Mrs Tuke waited until they heard the bedroom door bang shut and then she said, as if there hadn't been any interruption, 'It used to be in 'centre of Brough, but folk got sick of seeing men going in and out, and men didn't like it either in case their wives found out. So the madam,' she added scathingly, 'found another place on 'outskirts of town and although this was a long time ago, to 'best of my knowledge she's still there.'

'From Mr Tuke's time?' Harriet asked. 'Surely . . .' She wanted to say that the madam would be too old, but that would imply that Mr and Mrs Tuke were old too.

Ellen got up from the table and came to sit in Mr Tuke's chair, motioning Harriet to sit opposite her. She gave several deep lingering sighs, and after a moment or two said, 'I found out that Mr Tuke frequented Miriam Stone's establishment and gave him an ultimatum.' She shifted about in the chair and gazed at the coals in the fire, chewing on her lip. 'It was her bed or mine.' She glanced sideways at Harriet. 'Mebbe you'd mek a different decision, but I don't need to know about it.'

'Of course not,' Harriet said meekly. 'Noah's your son, after all.'

Mrs Tuke, deep in thought, silently shook her head.

Then Harriet had a sudden thought which filled her with dismay. 'I – I suppose it's difficult for young men,' she ventured. 'When they live so far out from other folk; I mean, erm, where do they go to meet decent young women?'

'It's no different for young girls,' Ellen snapped. 'They meet lads at work or on neighbouring farms . . .' She hesitated. 'Like I did.' Then she added, 'You wouldn't catch Fletcher going to places like Miriam Stone's. I warned him off her when he was just a lad.'

Which was what I wanted to know, Harriet thought, but wondered how Ellen would know whether or not Fletcher had visited the place. He wasn't likely to tell her, and if she had warned Fletcher, why hadn't she issued the same warning to Noah?

'Mrs Tuke – Ellen,' she started. 'When my child is born, I hope it'll bring you some happiness.' She paused. 'I know you miss Fletcher, it's onny natural that you'd miss a child when it left home, especially your firstborn, but if Fletcher had been a girl and not a lad she'd have left home to marry by now and you'd mebbe have had grandchildren by her already. I know you'll never think of me as your daughter, and I can't think of you as my mother, having had a good relationship wi' my own . . .' she choked back a sob as she remembered her mother and how special their bond had been, 'but, I hope you'll be able to care for my child, whether it's male or female, because it'll be of your own blood and you'll be 'onny grandparent, apart from Mr Tuke, that it'll have.'

Ellen Tuke stared at Harriet with such intensity that Harriet began to feel uncomfortable, and then she saw a range of emotions pass over the contorted face: confusion, uncertainty, sorrow, pain and finally anger.

'No,' Ellen hissed. 'I won't be able to care for it. I'm sorry for what I'm about to say, and you'll think that I'm an unnatural, unfeeling woman and I'll tell you that I wasn't allus like this, but fate dealt me a nasty blow. I won't love your child because it is *not* of my blood. Noah is not my son.'

# CHAPTER THIRTY-THREE

What? How? Why? With parted lips Harriet silently mouthed the words but couldn't say them, yet comprehension and understanding filtered through her astonishment at the revelation. It explained so clearly why there was so much discord in this family, explained, too, why Mrs Tuke showed no motherly feeling towards Noah.

'Mr Tuke?' she croaked. 'Is he Noah's father?'

'Oh aye,' Ellen muttered. 'Can't you tell?'

Was she not able to carry another child? Harriet dared not ask. But poor Noah. She felt some sympathy for him now – did he know that Ellen Tuke wasn't his mother?

'He's a chip off 'old block all right,' Ellen went on, her voice tight and bitter. 'Mr Tuke made sure o' that. He said I spoiled Fletcher and he wasn't going to let this son grow up to be a spineless namby-pamby. He wouldn't let me teach him anything and that's why – that's why he's 'way he is.'

'So . . .' I have to ask, Harriet thought; I'm carrying Noah's child. 'So – who is Noah's mother? Does she see him? Does he know about her?'

'No!' Ellen Tuke spat out. 'He knows nowt. Neither of 'lads do. They don't know that Mr Tuke turned up with him one night, thrust him at me and said, "Here! Here's another son for you."' She turned her face away from Harriet's gaze, towards the fire. 'I was feeding Fletcher and he grabbed him

216

and put Noah in his place. He was about three or four months old and wouldn't stop crying, and then Fletcher started crying as well because he didn't understand why he'd been pulled away from me.'

Harriet couldn't speak, her thoughts were in such turmoil, but Ellen went on in an intense, simmering voice, 'He said I hadn't to tell Noah he wasn't mine and that I was to treat him as if he was, and if I didn't – if I didn't, well, he threatened me with all kinds of things, like throwing me out of 'house and – and spreading rumours about me. And I was afraid of what he might do.'

What a dreadful man, Harriet thought. How could she bear to live with him? But she must have cared for him once. What made him change?

'Could you not conceive again?' she asked gently. 'After Fletcher?'

Ellen turned to her and her mouth formed a question. 'What?' She moistened her lips. 'Oh. Erm – no. Fletcher was – over a year old and – and nothing was – no. You might as well know,' she muttered, 'that Mr Tuke was allus hanging round me when I worked at 'manor, an' then, well, he seduced me and got me pregnant; that's why we married. I had to, you see, or I'd have been outcast. And then – and then Mr Tuke started going out of a night and I found out that he'd been to 'brothel, and after that I wouldn't have owt to do wi' him. Well, how could I? When he'd been with those women!'

'Noah's mother? She was one of 'women from 'brothel?'

Ellen's eyes looked everywhere but at Harriet. 'He wanted to show me that he was virile and manly and could produce a son – another son – and I was not able to.' She screwed up her mouth into a sneer. 'But I didn't want to. I had a son already. Why would I want another one?'

Harriet was bewildered. Surely having had one son she would have wanted another, or a daughter even? I'd like daughters; you can talk to daughters. And it's odd that Fletcher isn't spoiled rotten if she always made a fuss of him and not

217

Noah. There's no wonder there's so much conflict between them, and yet neither of them know 'reason why. And this is why Ellen's so upset over Fletcher leaving home. She's stuck here with an adopted son she doesn't care for and a husband whom she apparently loathes.

And then I came on 'scene and upset 'apple cart even more. Now she has a stranger, a so-called daughter-in-law, living with her who is about to produce a child who is no relation to her.

Harriet heaved a breath. What a mess. What a hornets' nest they'd all found themselves in.

Harriet tried to be nice to Noah, to be kind to him since Ellen never was or ever had been. But at every friendly word he scowled, or viewed her with suspicion, and on several occasions he asked, 'What's going on? What 'you up to?' when she attempted some pleasantry.

He was still going out at weekends and not arriving back until after midnight, until one day at the beginning of December she asked him if he would stay at home in future.

'Why?' he asked brusquely. 'There's no pleasure here.'

She'd gone outside especially to see him; he was mending a fence and hammering a nail into one of the uprights with great ferocity. 'Because,' she said, 'I think that babby will be here soon, and you'll need to fetch Mary.'

He stood and stared at her, tapping the hammer into the palm of his hand. 'Tekken its time, hasn't it?'

She shrugged and gave a little smile. 'They come when they're ready. You'll need 'trap for Mary,' she reminded him.

'Aye, I know that.'

Harriet huddled into her shawl. It was very cold; a wind was blowing off the estuary, just as it had been when she'd first arrived here. She could barely believe that it was a year since that night.

'Are you pleased?' she asked.

''Bout what?'

'The child!'

218

'Depends,' he grunted. 'Shan't be if it's a lass.'

'Oh, come now, a little girl to spoil?' She was very anxious about the outcome of the pregnancy.

'There'll be no spoiling here,' he said gruffly. 'Whether it's a lad or a lass. Fletcher was allus Ma's favourite; she never had a good word to say to me.'

'Any bairns we have will be treated 'same; no favouritism.' She smiled as she spoke, aiming to assure him that this child wouldn't be the only one, even though he was the last person on earth that she wanted in her bed. She dreaded it. A union without love or caring.

'We'll see,' he said, turning away. 'If it's a lass you can do what you want wi' her. If it's a lad *I'll* decide how he's treated.'

The words filled her with dismay. Her instinct would be to protect the child be it girl or boy.

'Now, get yourself inside,' he ordered. 'And tell Ma she's to do all of 'milking now and you're not to carry any buckets o' feed or milk pails until after you're delivered.'

Harriet walked slowly back to the house. It's what I've allus thought: I'm just one of 'farm animals, a ewe or a heifer or a mare. Just like 'other animals, I've to be tekken care of until such time as a lamb or a calf or a colt is delivered, and in my case a male child.

Her instincts proved to be in good working order, for it was only a few days after asking Noah to stay at home and not go out at night that she began in labour. It was early morning and she continued with tasks about the house; in the afternoon she asked Mrs Tuke if she had some old sheets that she could put on her bed. Ellen gave her a swift glance but didn't comment, and rummaged in a wooden trunk until she found a pair. She also fetched a bar of soap, a large earthenware bowl and a towel and took them upstairs to Harriet's room.

'I'll keep 'kettle on 'boil,' she muttered. 'Do you want him to fetch Mary?'

'I don't know,' Harriet said hesitantly. 'Yes – I think so. Before it gets dark. I'll give him a shout.'

She opened the back door and found Mr Tuke looking about him, whistling tunelessly.

'Mr Tuke,' she said. 'Do you know where Noah is?'

He turned and looked her up and down. 'Yeh. He's in 'barn. What 'you want him for?'

'I need him to fetch Mary,' she said.

'Is it your time?' He continued to scrutinize her.

'Yes.'

He grinned and she noticed he had lost another tooth. 'I'm going to be a granfer then?'

Harriet gave a low laugh. At least he seemed to be pleased, unlike his wife. 'Yes, I hope so. So can you fetch him, please? Ask him to go now.'

He nodded and ambled across the yard, and she called after him, 'And tell him to hurry!' He quickened his step and broke into a trot and she mused that she had never seen him so agile.

She didn't think it was urgent, but how could she know? She wasn't in a great deal of pain: an ache in her lower back, a heaviness in her limbs, a feeling of breathlessness and she was sweating slightly, but apart from that she felt calm and as ready as she could be to face the challenge of bringing a new being into the world. And the greatest feeling of all was happiness, which was a sensation that had been missing from her life for quite some time.

Her thoughts drifted to Fletcher. She was pleased that he wasn't here when she was giving birth to Noah's child. He might have turned against her. His feelings for her might have changed if he'd seen her with his brother's child; might still change when he heard about the birth, if he ever did. And he wouldn't ever know that she cared for him more now that he was gone from her life than she had in the short time they had lived in the same house.

She stifled a sob as she went back indoors, but Ellen heard

it. 'Are you all right? Do you want a drink? Tea? Cool water?'

'I'd love a drink, please. Water will do – if it's fresh,' she added, smiling a little, and Ellen gave her a nod as if she too recalled that first meeting.

Harriet took the cup of water that Ellen had poured from the kettle. It was lukewarm and comforting. 'I think – I'll go up,' she murmured. 'Will you listen out for Noah going, please? I asked Mr Tuke to tell him.'

Then they both heard the rattle of the cart as it went out of the yard, and Ellen commented, 'He won't tek long. It's not that far an' Mary will be ready. She's very reliable.'

She doesn't say how she knows that, Harriet mused. Not once has she mentioned that Mary attended her when she gave birth to Fletcher, nor how she cried at his birth. I won't cry, she thought as she went up to her room. Fletcher's room. Because I'm happy to be having a child. I wonder why Ellen wept as copiously as Mary said she did?

She undressed and slept in her shift for a little while, and woke up feeling decidedly uncomfortable. She got out of bed and reached for the chamber pot just in time. Her waters had broken. She rinsed her hands and face in the washbowl and thought that maybe it wouldn't be long now. Walking up and down the small room and occasionally looking out of the window, she saw that the sun had almost set and the surface of the estuary, reflecting the dark sky, looked like a sheet of shining metal.

Someone knocked on her door and she opened it cautiously. It was Mary, her face red as if she had been standing over the washtub. 'My word,' she panted. 'That husband o' yourn was in a hurry to get me here. I told him that first bairns tek their time, but he wasn't having it, and bundled me into 'cart afore I could get my breath. Just hope it's a lad you're carrying, cos that's what he's expecting.'

'I hope so too,' Harriet said. 'I'd be happy with a girl, but . . .'

'Aye, that's men for you,' Mary agreed. 'They allus want a son and heir, even if there's nowt for them to inherit.'

'I've got – *whoo.*' Harriet winced. 'A bit o' pain. *Whoo.*' She huffed out a breath. 'Yes, definitely summat's happening, Mary. *Hah!*'

'Get on to 'bed,' Mary ordered, shoving a pillow under Harriet's back, 'and let's see what's going on. Oh, my word, this little mite's in a hurry! Come on then, m'darlin', one big push and – Oh!' she exclaimed. 'Here 'babby comes and that's as quick as I've ever known! And a boy just as ordered. Oh,' she said again, 'and he's beautiful, and with – lovely black curly hair.'

# CHAPTER THIRTY-FOUR

That he was beautiful there was no doubt whatsoever. Harriet took him from Mary and gazed in awe. He'd yelled as Mary had gently tipped him upside down and patted his bottom, then carefully wiped his eyes and nose and cut the cord that bound them.

'Hello,' Harriet whispered into his sweet little ear. 'How lovely, how handsome you are. Where did you get hair like that? Not from me, that's for certain.'

'He's a bit jaundiced, I think,' Mary said over her shoulder as she washed her hands in the bowl. 'You'll notice his skin colour'll change in a day or two, after you've fed him.'

Harriet smiled down at her new son. I don't think it will, she thought. I think your grandfather might have something to answer for and I don't know what your father will say. But I don't care. She was suffused with love as she kissed his cheek, and knew that she would love him for ever.

'Thank you, Mary,' she said. 'I'm so grateful that you were here. Is it always so quick?'

'No. Think yourself lucky,' Mary said as she dried her hands. 'I've known a labour go on for days.' She hesitated. 'Do you want me to tell your husband to come up and see his son?'

Better get it over with, Harriet thought. 'Please,' she said. 'But you'll have a cup of tea afore Noah teks you home?'

'Aye, I will. And in a day or two I'll walk over to see how

you're coping,' Mary said. 'No need for your husband to collect me unless there are any difficulties, and I don't think there will be.'

Harriet tucked the babe into the crook of her arm and waited for Noah to come up. She greeted him with a smile. 'Here he is,' she said. 'The son you asked for. Isn't he handsome?'

Noah sat on the edge of the bed and looked at the child and then at her. 'Do all bairns have hair as dark as that?'

'I don't know,' Harriet admitted. 'I've never seen a newborn afore. I think some are born without hair, or very fair. You and I are both dark-haired; but his is very curly, isn't it? Not a bit like ours.'

Noah frowned, and said bluntly, 'If I hadn't known you were a virgin I'd have said you'd been wi' a foreigner. I've seen men on Goole dockside wi' hair like that, so where's it come from?'

Harriet shook her head and breathed an inward sigh of relief that he hadn't lost his temper, nor had he noticed that the first time he'd forced himself upon her she wasn't a virgin. Neither had he accused her of infidelity, or mentioned the fact that she hadn't conceived straight away, for she was certain that if she had he wouldn't have believed it was his child.

'Mebbe from somewhere in our background?' she suggested. 'Grandparents, or great-grandparents? I don't know who mine were.' She carefully deflected any fault from either of them.

'Folks'll talk, and they'll blame you. You realize that, don't you?' He glowered. 'They'll say he's not mine.'

'But we know that he is, don't we?' she said softly. 'How could he possibly belong to anyone else?'

He was floundering. He needed someone to take the blame, someone close at hand, and there was no one.

'Ma's fairish,' he grunted, 'but Da was dark-haired afore he went white.'

'As you are. You're like him, more than your—' She broke off. 'You definitely favour him in every way.'

'Aye.' He looked down at the child. 'What name'll you give him?'

My choice then. 'I thought Daniel Miles,' she said.

He scowled. 'Why burden him wi' two names? One's enough.'

'Onny that Miles was my family name, and there won't be anybody else to carry it on.' She thought of her brother and doubted that she'd ever see him again.

'No.' He stood up. 'Daniel's enough. It's a good name. You can call 'next one Miles.'

'All right.' She smiled and conceded that it was half a battle won, and that she might not have thought of giving her surname to the child if it hadn't been for Ellen's giving Fletcher her own maiden name.

He left then, saying he'd take Mary home, and she asked him to ask his mother if she'd like to come up and see the baby, but a few minutes later she heard the heavy tread of footsteps on the stairs and knew it wasn't Ellen, but Mr Tuke.

She covered her shoulders with a shawl and pulled the sheet up high, leaving the baby's head uncovered. She called for him to come in when he knocked, and he put his head round the door.

He lifted his eyes to stare at her and muttered, 'Mrs Tuke says she'll be up in a minute. She's mekking you a drink. Noah said for me to come up.'

'Would you like to see 'babby?' Harriet asked him. 'I'm not superstitious about anybody seeing him.'

He grunted and moved forward. 'I don't believe in all that mumbo-jumbo about churching and christenings anyway. Noah wasn't christened, though Fletcher was – Mrs Tuke insisted.'

He peered over from the bottom of the bed and gave a start, narrowing his eyes. 'He's a darkie!'

'No he's not!' she admonished. 'He's got black curly hair.' She uncovered the baby's face. 'His skin isn't dark. But he's mebbe got some foreign blood.'

Mr Tuke shook his head adamantly. 'Not from me!' Then

225

he hesitated, his eyes shifting about the room as if he was considering what else to say, unaware that Harriet knew he couldn't blame his wife.

'From somewhere in 'past, mebbe?' Harriet gave him an opportunity to save himself from humiliation.

'Aye, that's it. Mebbe on your side. Lots o' foreigners in Hull, being a port town.'

Harriet laughed. 'Mebbe so, Mr Tuke.' She held his gaze until he turned away, unable to hold the contact. When he reached the door, she called softly, 'He's *my* son, Mr Tuke, and I'll love him no matter who his forebears were. You'll remember that, won't you?'

He looked back at her and licked his lips, then gave a slight nod. She continued to gaze at him and he ran his fingers through his beard, teasing it, as if debating whether she knew the truth about him and Mrs Tuke and Noah.

Downstairs, after Noah had left to take Mary home, Ellen kept herself busy; she tidied the kitchen even though it was never untidy. She filled the kettle and put it over the fire and thought that maybe she should have gone up before Mr Tuke did. But she'd been afraid to. She'd told Noah that she would go up presently and he'd looked at her oddly, as if wondering why she wasn't eager to see the new baby. Then he told his father to wash his hands and go up to see his grandson. He'd said it proudly, and seemed to grow in stature.

Ellen laid a tray and put a cup and saucer, a milk jug and the teapot on it and waited for Mr Tuke to come down. When he did, he went straight to his chair by the fire and sat staring into the flames.

'Well?' she queried. 'Your first grandson, is it?'

'Aye, and not yours!' He turned to face her. 'Did you tell her?'

'Tell her what?'

'You know what I'm talking about, woman. She looked at me all knowing.'

'You're imagining it,' she said, pouring boiling water into

the teapot. 'It's your guilt mekking you think she's seen through you.'

'She'll mek a good mother,' he muttered. 'Better'n you ever did.'

'And your son,' she answered bitterly. 'Will he mek a good father?' She picked up the tray. 'Just like you did,' she scoffed.

She carried the tray up the stairs and along the passage to Harriet's room. The room that Fletcher had decided to make his own after Noah had brought a wife home. She's nowt to me, she thought, but if Fletcher had brought a wife home instead of Noah, how would I have felt? She gave a great sigh. I don't want any more emotion in my life; I don't want to care for anyone ever again. Except for Fletcher, of course, and who knows if I'll ever see him again.

She quietly opened the door and saw that Harriet was sleeping, her cheek gently touching the baby's head. Ellen put down the tray on a small table and tiptoed towards the bed. She took a sudden breath when she saw his dark curls and clutched her hands to her chest. She saw his sweet repose; his soft and luminous skin the colour of cinnamon, and the gentle rise and fall of his breath as he slept, and stifled a sob.

*Oh, Fletcher.* She wept silently for her son and thought of the day he was born. Why did you have to leave?

Harriet opened her eyes and smiled. She looked happy. 'Hello,' she murmured. 'I must have dropped off. Have you – have you seen – my son?'

Ellen cleared her throat. 'I have. You've a fine boy. And so quick, Mary said. I've brought you some tea. You must be gasping. Would you like summat to eat?'

'No, thank you, but I'm thirsty. I could drink a gallon o' water.'

'Have your tea, then, and I'll fetch you some boiled water to sip.' Ellen looked away. 'It'll help wi' your milk.'

Harriet sat up and drank the tea and Ellen sat on the edge of her bed facing her.

'Isn't he 'most beautiful bairn you've ever seen?' Harriet

said softly, looking down at him. 'Or do all mothers think that?'

'I imagine they do,' Ellen replied. 'Fletcher was dark-haired when he was born, but he lost it after a few weeks and when it grew back it was much fairer.'

'Fletcher this and Fletcher that!'

They hadn't heard the bedroom door open, and looked up sharply to see Noah glaring at his mother.

'What about me?' he shouted. 'What colour was my hair? It's allus Fletcher, isn't it? Even on 'very day my son is born you've got to talk about Fletcher. You nivver say Noah did this or that, it's as if I was nivver owt to do wi' you, as if I just appeared out o' nowhere.'

Ellen gazed at him and then clasped her hands together. 'That's because you did.' Her words were plain, without warmth or feeling. 'You were thrust into my arms. I didn't know whose child you were, who your mother was, or owt about you. Your father just said here's another son for you; look after him.'

She held his gaze, which was one of shock and bewilderment. 'And I did, to 'best o' my ability. I fed you, clothed you, sent you to school, just as I did wi' Fletcher. But you were not mine. Never was and never will be. I had a son already and I hadn't asked for another. So if you want to know more about where you came from, then you must ask your father. He fathered you and brought you into 'world, not me, and he's the one who named you and shaped you into what you are. So ask him.'

# CHAPTER THIRTY-FIVE

Ellen got up from the bed and left the room and Noah moved aside to let her pass, not saying a word. He seemed to have had all the breath knocked out of him.

Then he looked at Harriet and his eyes narrowed accusingly and in one stride he was by her bed. 'Did you know?'

She nodded. 'Only recently. I asked her if she was looking forward to having a grandchild.' Harriet suddenly felt very emotional and put her hand across her face. 'She told me no,' she choked. 'Because you were not her son and therefore any child of ours was not of her blood.' She let out a breath. 'I couldn't believe what she was saying, but it was just as she's told you: your father brought you home and gave you to her to look after. He wanted another son and she – it seems she couldn't conceive.'

It would be too cruel, she thought, to tell Noah that his birth mother had worked in a brothel and that Ellen had kept his father from her bed; he'd already suffered a brutal blow discovering that he wasn't Ellen's son, but perhaps it would help him to understand why she always favoured Fletcher.

'But Noah,' she said softly, 'we have a son. Daniel is ours and your father is his grandfather. I think he could be fond of him. He seemed quite proud, although he wondered about his curly hair.' She gave a nervous smile for them to share, a whimsical quip. 'He said it was probably from someone in my family's background.'

'Mebbe it is,' he declared and turned and left the room. She heard him clatter downstairs and then the crash of the back door.

'Not a good start to your new life, Daniel,' she whispered. 'But you won't remember this and I'll try not to let it bother me or my milk might turn sour.'

She got up the next day. She felt fit enough, although tired, as she'd slept only in snatches, restless with jumbled dreams of Noah fighting with his father and Ellen, telling her that he wanted to move away from Marsh Farm, being persuaded to stay as he was the only son at home now that Fletcher had gone. She felt guilty too of not pulling her weight, as if she too was a usurper, just as Noah was.

When she came downstairs Noah barely acknowledged her, and neither was he speaking to his father or Ellen. He was like a simmering kettle on red embers in danger of boiling over.

She'd asked Ellen if it was all right to bring down a chest drawer which she'd lined with a blanket from her bed, and now she found a place for it in the kitchen, away from draughts, not too near the fire, and in a spot where she felt that it wouldn't be under anyone's feet. But when she got up to go outside to collect the eggs and let the hens out, Ellen rebuked her sharply. 'I've seen to 'em.'

'I'll do 'second milking then, shall I?' Harriet suggested.

'No. You can start next week,' Ellen told her. 'If you do ower much in 'first few days your milk might fail and then there'll be a screeching bairn to contend wi'.'

'I need to do something,' Harriet pleaded, but Ellen ignored her.

The atmosphere was almost unbearable. Mr Tuke sat silently by the fire and Ellen seemed to be always at the sink, either scrubbing vegetables or washing pans. Each time Noah came in for a meal he ate what was put in front of him and made no effort to answer Harriet's futile attempts at conversation.

After a week Harriet's nerves were at breaking point and her only pleasure was in taking Daniel upstairs to wash him and feed him and sit with him on her bed as he slept in her arms. She talked soothingly to him when he was awake, and he looked up at her as if understanding her soft words before falling asleep again.

That night she left the kitchen after supper, murmuring good night, and went upstairs. A little while later she heard Noah's footsteps on the treads and got out of bed. Casting a glance at the sleeping Daniel, she slipped barefoot to the room they used to share, gave a soft tap on the door and, after waiting a second, went in.

Noah was sitting crouched on the side of the bed with his elbows on his knees and his hands clenched. He glanced at her but didn't speak.

'Noah,' she whispered, 'we must talk. I can't bear this silence. Nobody is saying anything.'

'Nobody has owt to say.' His voice was flat and low.

'It's driving me crazy,' she told him. 'This should be a happy time for us, but it isn't. We have to resolve this awful mood which is affecting us all.'

'Are you saying it's my fault?' he muttered.

'No! Anybody's but yours. You're innocent in this matter – shame of it is that you weren't told before. You should have been, and mebbe then you'd have accepted it.'

'Do you think that Fletcher knew – knows?'

Harriet shook her head. 'Your ma – Ellen – told me that nobody knew, onny her and your da.'

He grunted. 'And 'woman who gave birth to me.'

'Of course, but we don't know who she is.'

He glanced at her. 'Da must, allus supposing he looked at her while they were begetting me.' His mouth turned down. 'I reckon he did it out of spite, to get back at her.'

'Who?'

231

'Ellen – Mrs Tuke.' It was as if he could no longer call her mother. 'You've seen what a cold woman she is. I bet she kept him from her bed and that's why she couldn't get wi' child.'

Which was true, Harriet thought: on Ellen's own admission she had banned Mr Tuke from her bed on discovering he had been to the brothel.

'We'd be guessing, Noah,' she said simply, 'and what's gone is gone. That was their life. We have to make ours.'

He knitted his black eyebrows together and pondered, then said, 'If I told you that I can't remember a single kind word in my whole life, would you believe me?' Before she could answer, he added, 'No, mebbe just once.' He rubbed his hand over his bristly chin. 'Fletcher. When I was about six or thereabouts, he asked me, in front o' Ma – Ellen – if I wanted to go fishing wi' him. He was going wi' some lads to fish in one of 'field drains. An' she said no, he can't go, I'll not have you being responsible for him, an' then Da came in and asked what was I blubbering about. She told him an' he grabbed me an' said, You don't want to go wi' that beggarly upstart. If you want to go fishing, then I'll tek you. But what I remember most was Fletcher lookin' at both of 'em as if he didn't understand what was going on, and then at me as if mebbe I did. And I didn't.' He swallowed. 'I onny knew that I wanted to go wi' him, an' not wi' Da.'

Harriet sat on the bed next to him and put her hand over his and thought how disgraceful that parents could transfer their hatred of each other to their sons. But why, she thought. Why is there so much discord? There must have been an attraction between the Tukes in the first place, unless of course Mr Tuke had taken advantage of Ellen, as Noah did with me, and she felt compelled to marry him when she found she was pregnant.

She sighed. 'Have you spoken to your father about what you know?' Sullenly, he shook his head, and she said softly, 'I'm sorry, Noah. Would you like to leave this place and find somewhere else? Mebbe Master Hart has another small farm

232

he'd rent you. I'd help. I'm learning all 'time. We could keep enough livestock to earn a living for just us, and then if we have more bairns we could—'

'What?' he scowled. 'We could do what? You mean leave this farm when it's as much mine as it is Fletcher's? No. I'm me farther's son just as much as Fletcher is, even if we've got different mothers, and he's jiggered off to God knows where, an' if he thinks he can come back one day an' tek over just because he's 'eldest, he's got another think coming.'

Well, I tried, Harriet reflected. But 'damage is done. I thought he'd softened a little when he was talking about their childhood, but he hasn't. There's an open wound which animosity has drip-drip-dripped on to like water falling on stone, scouring out a deep cavern which won't ever heal or close over.

# CHAPTER THIRTY-SIX

At Hart Holme Manor preparations were under way for the Christmas house party. The guests included Rebecca Wilkie and her brother Laurence, whom Amy had invited to the summer party back in August, on which occasion both Christopher and Melissa had realized that Laurence Wilkie was the object of Amy's desire, and the reason for much sighing and absent-minded behaviour.

Everyone was due to arrive by Christmas Eve, including Christopher's sister-in-law Deborah, her husband and their daughters and three more young men to even up the numbers, and Melissa couldn't decide whether to tell Christopher their news before the festivities began or after everyone had left the day after Boxing Day.

She hadn't been totally sure of her condition and had not yet consulted a doctor, but after almost six years of counting dates she felt confident that after so much yearning she was at last expecting a child. Her sickness she had passed off as the result of having eaten something that had disagreed with her, and as it hadn't lasted very long Christopher hadn't suspected anything.

There was no doubt in her mind that she had seduced her husband, not nightly, as Harriet Tuke had said of her husband, but several times a week after that first glorious night when he had returned in June from fetching Amy home. She thought that Christopher had at first been rather shocked by her apparent enjoyment of their union, but when on the following evening she had crept naked from her bed and into his during the early hours, he had whispered that he hadn't thought women enjoyed this experience in the same way as men.

'You mean *ladies*, don't you, Christopher?' she'd whispered in his ear, running her hands beneath his nightshirt. 'Ladies of a certain class who have been told by their mamas that this wonderful act of love is to be tolerated and not enjoyed.'

'Why yes,' he'd croaked. 'That is what I was taught to think . . . and it is true that—'

He'd broken off and taken a gasping breath, and Melissa guessed that in spite of what her wandering fingers were doing to him, gentleman that he was he wouldn't give away the fact that his first wife Jane had come from that same restraining background, and *that*, she thought, is why I haven't conceived; he's treated me as if I were made of fragile glass, whereas – she'd smiled in the darkness and arched her body against his – I'm actually as tough as the boots he wears when he's walking his land.

It had been October before she began to suspect and she had delayed telling him, not wanting to disappoint if it should be a false alarm, but now, on the day before their guests were due to arrive, she was perfectly sure and deliriously happy; her waistline had thickened slightly and when she looked in the mirror she saw that her eyes were bright and her skin clear.

'Melissa.' Christopher came into her sitting room where she was sewing. 'Thomson is unwell again and, as it's so bitterly cold, I've decided that I'll deliver the birds to Mrs Marshall and Ellen Tuke myself. But is today too early? I don't want to leave everything until the last minute, even though our guests won't arrive until late tomorrow.'

'I'm quite sure they'll both be delighted to see you today.'

She smiled up at him, revelling in the secret that she would soon disclose. 'If you leave it until tomorrow they might think their birds aren't coming; and Mrs Marshall always likes a chat with you, doesn't she? Tomorrow you'd be in a rush to come home to greet our guests.'

'I would, that's true,' he said. 'Yes, I'll go now and be back for lunch. I'll call on Mrs Marshall first and then go on to the Tukes.'

'Do ask how the young Mrs Tuke is, won't you? I think she'll have been delivered of her child by now, and if you see her, will you ask her to come and see me after Christmas? I want to find out when she can come back to do the ironing.'

'Surely she won't. Not if she's just had a child.'

Melissa set her stitch and then looked up and smiled at him again. 'Oh, I think she will. She'll be glad to get out of the house, I should think. And ask her to bring the baby.'

He bent down and kissed her cheek. 'You're a minx,' he said. 'And you look beautiful. Have I told you that recently?'

'No,' she sighed. 'Not for ages, not since last night in fact. Don't be long,' she added, determining now to give him the news when he came back. 'There's something I'd like to discuss.'

He frowned slightly. 'About Amy?'

'That too,' she said. 'We have to be prepared.' Amy had been mooning about in her room for days, only appearing at mealtimes, and Melissa had told Christopher she was convinced that Laurence Wilkie would ask for her hand in marriage.

Christopher rode first to Brough Haven to call on Mrs Marshall. She hadn't been well the last time he had visited her and he'd had every intention of calling again, but somehow he hadn't and now he felt guilty. He'd been fond of the old lady when he was a boy, and she and Ellen Fletcher, he recalled, had always been as thick as thieves.

The Haven waters were choppy with a deep ground swell and he hoped that the bank would hold, or the flood would tip over and into the cottage, which was slightly lower than the path. The wind was getting up too, whining and whistling as it crossed the quivering water.

Mrs Marshall greeted him warmly but he saw that she had deteriorated since his last visit; she was thinner, and he noticed that her hands were shaking. She offered him tea but he refused, saying he was going on to see Mrs Tuke and that he was expected home for lunch, but he sat down for a few minutes and said he hoped she would be able to use the fowl and asked if she would be able to cook it, for if not he would ask someone to fetch her and she could have Christmas dinner in the kitchen at Hart Holme with the other staff. 'They won't mind in the least,' he told her. 'If you would like to.'

'Oh, no, Master Christopher,' she said. 'I wouldn't, thank you all 'same, and nor would they want me, not after all these years. No, I love my little house and I'm grateful to be here for 'rest of my days. Now, you'll be going to see Ellen Tuke, I expect?'

He repeated that he would and she seemed to consider, chewing on her lip and frowning. 'I was going to ask you to tell her summat from me, but I can't think what it was. Summat about that son of hers, but I've forgotten what it was.'

'She has two sons, Mrs Marshall,' he reminded her. 'One of them is married, and I understand has just had a child.'

'Ah! I don't know if I knew that,' she murmured. 'About 'child, I mean. Perhaps I did; my memory's not what it was. But that'll be Mr Tuke's son, not 'elder one. He's gone away, seemingly.'

'I don't know.' Christopher frowned. 'I don't really know the sons. I've only met one of them. The bailiff generally calls on them.'

She gazed at him from watery brown eyes and then nodded

slowly and sighed. 'I expect that's so,' she murmured. 'That's 'way it's allus been. So Mrs Tuke says, though it's not how she wants it to be.'

He didn't understand her meaning, and after enquiring again if there was anything she needed, which she said that there wasn't, he took his leave of her, shaking her hand and saying he hoped she would have a pleasant and peaceful Christmas. As he was going out of the door he noticed that her woodpile was low and he gathered up some of the wood and brought it inside, placing it in the hearth. 'I'll have some wood sent over,' he said. 'You must keep a good fire; the weather is changing. We'll have snow soon.'

'Aye, that's what 'fishermen say, so it must be so,' she agreed. 'Thank you, Master Christopher sir, and God bless you.'

He mounted his horse and wheeled around and turned to wave goodbye. She was standing in her doorway watching him and lifted one arm in response, the other held stiffly by her side.

He rode back along the road, reaching his gates and being very tempted to go back in for a warming cup of coffee, but he resisted and went on towards Marsh Farm, with the brace of pheasant firmly fastened to his saddlebag. The weather was bitterly cold and definitely worsening and he could hear the surge and swash of the tide, louder here than in the haven as it rushed up the estuary. Clouds were darkening overhead and it seemed more like night than midday. He hoped that the weather would be better tomorrow when their London visitors arrived, for they would be dismayed if they found that they would be confined to the house over Christmas.

As he turned on to the track to Marsh Farm he noticed that some of the trees had been cut back, which he considered was a vast improvement. It had always been a dark and dismal place, with low branches obliterating the sky and hidden tree roots to fall over.

He was almost at the bottom of the track with the farmhouse

in front of him when he heard men shouting. He thought nothing of it at first as men often shouted instructions to one another; but then the voices became rampant, anguished and vociferous, as if in fear, and it was then that he heard the piercing cry of a woman screaming.

# CHAPTER THIRTY-SEVEN

The atmosphere had not improved; the Tukes were not speaking to each other and from time to time Ellen asked Harriet to pass on simple messages to her husband rather than ask him herself. He generally just grunted in answer, but he had a knowing grin on his face which must have irritated his wife.

Sometimes he leaned over the cot to look at his grandson, and although Harriet was grateful that someone was interested in the child she thought that as far as Mr Tuke was concerned it was a case of one-upmanship over Ellen; he was scoring over her, which to Harriet's eyes was probably something new to him as generally his wife seemed to have the upper hand. Now she was the inferior one, which was probably the reason for her hostility.

Noah looked at Daniel from time to time but didn't hold him. When Harriet asked him if he'd like to, he said he'd have an interest in him once he walked and talked, not before.

'But you must be pleased that you have a son,' she pleaded in the privacy of his bedroom. 'Isn't that what you wanted?'

'Aye, that's why I married you, if you remember, and you took your time over it.' He looked keenly at her. 'And I'll expect you back in my bed afore long.'

'But we've onny been married a year,' she protested and tried to ignore the fear she felt at the prospect of sharing his bed again so soon after giving birth. 'Not every woman gets caught straight away.' She tried to lighten the situation. 'Folks'd talk if it was less than three months.'

'I'm not bothered about what other folks think,' he growled, which was contrary to the warning he had given her when Daniel was born. 'Besides, nobody knows you round here, so what does it matter?'

He began to undress and she went swiftly to the door.

'Aye,' he scoffed. 'Scuttle off, but in a week or two I'll want you back in here.'

Harriet turned back from the door. 'Do I mean nowt to you, Noah?' Her voice broke as she spoke. 'Have you no care for me at all? Am I just somebody to satisfy your needs?'

He stared at her and for a second she thought she saw a hesitation in his demeanour, as if he hadn't ever considered her feelings, but then he shrugged it off and said, 'I told you at 'beginning I wanted bairns to carry on at 'farm. I also wanted to be married afore Fletcher – not that it matters now that 'cur's jiggered off; so what do you expect, sweet talk and kisses?' He gave a grim grunt. 'You'll not get that from me.'

No, she thought, closing the door behind her and going to her room, I know I won't, but heaven forbid that I'll finish up like Mrs Tuke. But I'll not refuse him as she did Mr Tuke. I'll give him his bairns, but one day I'll escape and tek 'em with me. I won't leave them to be bullied and unloved like he's been. It's mebbe not his fault that he's 'way he is, but it's too late for him to change. His heart is like stone and can't be melted.

The tension continued, and at the beginning of Christmas week she ventured to ask Ellen if they'd be having a proper Christmas dinner.

'Why wouldn't we?' Ellen said. 'As always. I expect Master Christopher will send us a fowl on Christmas Eve as usual.'

'Oh, good,' Harriet said. 'We'll have something special to celebrate this year.'

Ellen stopped what she was doing. 'Which is?'

Harriet gazed at her in astonishment. 'Daniel's birth! A cause for celebration, surely?'

'Oh!' Ellen turned back to the job in hand. 'Have you thought of being churched and having him baptized?' She paused. 'Or won't you bother? Noah wasn't baptized: Mr Tuke wouldn't allow it.'

'I will,' Harriet said softly. 'I'll have Daniel baptized just as soon as I'm able to walk to 'nearest church to see 'parson.'

'You might find that folk won't have you in their house if you're not churched.'

'Who's going to ask me?' Harriet answered. 'I onny know Mary and them at 'manor. Do you think they'll turn me away?' She had intended going up to the house after Christmas to find out if her ironing job was still open to her, and whether she could take Daniel with her. Mary was doing the washing, which she said she could manage for the time being as long as she didn't have to do all the ironing as well.

'I don't know about 'present mistress.' Ellen gave a disparaging sniff. 'Mrs Hart senior wouldn't have had anybody back after marriage, let alone after giving birth, and neither I imagine would Master Christopher's first wife, but this young mistress, well.' She gave a condescending *tut* of her tongue. 'Mebbe she won't care as she's no bairns of her own.'

Or maybe she will, Harriet mused. She won't want to risk any bad luck, especially as she's desperate for a child; but she didn't voice her thoughts, only wondered how Mrs Tuke came to reason what Melissa Hart would or would not do when she had only met her once.

Harriet was now doing the second milking, and as Dora Two had produced her first calf in November and had plenty of milk she was drinking a jugful every day and Daniel was thriving because of it. There were fewer eggs from the hens and none from the ducks now that the weather was so cold, so Ellen had already commandeered one of them for Christmas Day to supplement whatever Master Hart might send, which had bothered Harriet as she had come to be fond of the ducks' scatty ways and enthusiastic greetings as soon as she stepped out into the yard. However, she knew she would have to get used to the idea that all the stock represented fresh food on her doorstep, either for sale or for home consumption.

Her worst day had been when Noah had asked the pig killer to come and slaughter the young pig they had been fattening up with vegetable parings, leftover food from their table, barley, and snails which had been gathered by the dozens in the wet ditches and added to the feed. Harriet thought she would never forget the sound of its squeals, and she hid in the house until the ordeal was over.

The pig was cut open and hung in the barn until the following day, when it was butchered. Half of it was salted and hung in muslin sacks in Ellen Tuke's larder and the other half cut up into hams and bacon and sold to neighbouring farmers to pay the butcher, with a little profit left over.

I must remember how lucky I am, she'd thought for the umpteenth time as she swilled and brushed the bloody yard. If I'd stayed in Hull I'd have been homeless and starving or living in 'workhouse.

Ellen had made a Christmas pudding in November, which was maturing in the larder, and Harriet had said she'd like to make an apple pie. She had discovered that she had a light hand for pastry, and also found rubbing the lard into the flour very soothing. For those few minutes she could forget the tension that was always simmering in the household. The apples were stored in a wooden box in the barn, high up on a shelf away from rats and mice, and had kept well. She said she'd make the pie the day before Christmas Eve, as Ellen would be building up the fire for a hot oven for a meat and potato pie of her own and the heat wouldn't be wasted.

Noah and his father had had several shouting matches over the last few days, as Noah wanted Nathaniel to get off his backside and come and help him down by the estuary bank. The ditches in the bottom field needed digging out as the high tide had covered the salt marsh and was flowing over the bank. Mr Tuke had refused, saying he had a bad back.

'Bad back! You're just a lazy old goat,' Noah had bawled at him.

He'd asked him again mid-morning when he came in for a hot drink, and Ellen had put her spoke into the argument by saying they should have done as Fletcher had suggested and opened one of the fields to take the excess water at high tide. 'A large pond, he said,' she reminded them, 'and then use what you've dug out to build up 'rest of 'bank.'

There was an uneasy silence, broken when Noah shouted that she didn't know what she was talking about. Then he pointed a finger at Mr Tuke. 'Get your behind off that chair and get outside! There's a flood tide rising an' I'm telling you that we'll lose 'bottom field if it comes over. I can't do everything myself,' he bellowed, and with a great deal of huffing and groaning Mr Tuke pulled himself out of the chair and went into the back porch to get his rubber boots.

'Tide'll slow when it reaches us,' he muttered. 'It allus does once it's in 'narrower channel, after it's passed Hessle.'

'I wish I could help,' Harriet murmured after they'd gone, 'but I don't think I'm strong enough yet to lift a spade, let alone dig a ditch.'

'It's man's work,' Ellen muttered. 'There's enough for women to do in 'house wi'out going outside. They have this argument every winter, but 'bank's not been breached yet.'

But mebbe that's because Fletcher was always out there with his sludge spade, Harriet considered, and recalled what he'd said about the Dutchman with the strange name.

A sudden crack of thunder made them jump. 'Thunder!' Harriet exclaimed. 'I never expected that. I'd better fetch 'apples afore it rains.'

'There's been a storm threatening all morning,' Ellen muttered. 'Bring me a couple of onions while you're there. They're hanging in a bag up on 'wall. I hope it doesn't rain,' she added, 'or them two'll be under my feet for 'rest of 'day.'

244

'All right.' Harriet went first to look at Daniel, who was sleeping in his crib, oblivious of the threatening storms both inside and out. She smiled down at him. He was filling out, his cheeks dimpling, and she was overcome anew by how beautiful he was, his long dark lashes sweeping his olive skin. I can't believe he's mine, she thought, drunk with love.

She put on the rubber boots and draped her shawl over her head and shoulders, and carrying a deep basket she made her way to the barn. The wind was fierce, whistling round the farm buildings and howling through the trees. She bent almost double as it caught her shawl, threatening to rip it off, and had to battle to hold the barn door open as it was almost wrenched out of her grasp.

She closed it behind her when she went in, even though it was dark inside, for she couldn't risk its being blown off its hinges as that would mean another job for Noah and a tongue-lashing for her. She climbed up a short stepladder to reach the apples, putting her hand in the box and hoping there were no mice nesting inside; she brought out three large apples and dropped them into the basket and then looked round for the onion bag, which she saw hanging high up on a nail. She moved the steps and climbed up again, and was putting two onions into the basket when she heard the sound of shouting.

'Oh no,' she groaned. 'Not again. Please!'

'What did I tell you?' Noah yelled at his father. 'If you'd given me a hand afore when I asked you, we might have contained it. Here.' He tossed a spade towards him, but Mr Tuke dropped it and winced as he bent to pick it up.

'I told you I've got a bad back,' he moaned. 'But nobody teks any notice of owt I say.'

'Nivver mind that,' Noah bellowed. 'Look at 'size o' them crests, and now it's damned well raining. Look. Damned sheep have got out. You didn't shut 'blasted gate.'

'Yes, I did,' his father snapped. 'Sneck's faulty. You should've fixed it.'

245

'For God's sake!' The rain was lashing down and Noah wiped his face with his hand. 'Harriet!' he shouted, spotting her outside the barn through the driving rain. 'Try to get 'sheep back up.'

He saw her wave a hand in acknowledgement and put her basket back inside the barn door, then turned back to his father who was just standing there by the bank watching the rising waters as if mesmerized.

'It's no use,' he was muttering. 'There's nowt we can do. It's just us against 'estuary. I'm telling you, that 'tide will slow. It's covered 'salt marsh, I'll give you that, but it won't come any further in. I'll bet you that 'water's no more'n a foot deep. I'll prove it, if you like.'

Noah put his hands to his head in despair and looked towards the middle channel where two sailing barges were tacking to avoid the sandbanks which were so numerous in the Humber and altered the water channels and the flow of the tide as it came up from the river mouth.

'You don't listen, do you?' he snarled at his father. 'You never listen to owt anybody says. You sit all day long in that chair and nivver tek any notice of what anybody's saying. You're wrong! I'm telling you that 'water's deep and it'll come over.'

His father stepped on to the low bank so that he was taller than Noah and looked down at him. 'Just who am I supposed to be listening to?' he jibed. 'Not you, not your ma—'

'Who isn't my ma, from all accounts,' Noah butted in. 'How'd that come about? Didn't want you in her bed? Rejected you, did she, so you had to go elsewhere?' His voice was mocking and offensive.

Nathaniel Tuke turned slowly towards him. 'Why, you – *whoreson*, how dare *you* of all folk say that to me? Me it was who sired you and brought you home and told her to treat you as her own.'

'But she didn't, did she?' Noah bellowed, his throat tightening, his voice hoarse. 'I was allus nobody. Fletcher was 'important one. I nivver stood a chance, not wi' either o' you.' He creased his eyebrows as if suddenly aware of what had been said. '*Whoreson?* What's that supposed to mean?'

'Fletcher? Hah!' His father gave a derisive snort. 'I could tell you a tale or two about him and no mistake, and as for you . . .' He stepped back and searched wildly for a foothold. 'Whoreson, that's what you are.' He cackled with laughter and strove to regain his balance. 'If I should tell—'

He put his foot back to regain his balance, and turning his head jumped off the bank into the water below, the water which he'd bet was only a foot deep, except that it wasn't. It came up above his waist, his feet sinking deep into the mud of the salt marsh.

'You fool, Da!' Noah shouted. 'What did I tell you?' His father was floundering as he tried to keep from falling over. 'Keep still,' he ordered and bent to pull off his boots. 'I'll come in and get you.'

'No,' his father shouted. 'Don't! Look! Watch out!'

Noah gave up on his boots, as the laces were knotted, and he too stepped off the bank almost up to his waist. And as he did so he saw that in the middle of the river was a tide-rip, and as the opposing currents met, the deep and surging wave crests were coming swiftly towards them.

# CHAPTER THIRTY-EIGHT

Harriet began to run towards the stray sheep but realized she was chasing them further down the slope. As she looked towards the bottom field, she saw Mr Tuke step off the bank and disappear.

'He's jumped on to 'salt marsh,' she gasped. 'Why's he done that? Noah told him 'river was running high!'

And then, to her further alarm, she saw Noah jump after him. What are they thinking of? Surely it's dangerous. She sped on until she came to the bank, and let out a scream when she saw Noah and his father struggling in deep water that had completely covered the salt marsh. Noah seemed to be taking lumbering strides and trying to wade, using his arms as oars in an attempt to reach his father, who was up to his neck in the water.

Noah was shouting to him, telling him to stand still, but the old man seemed not to be listening, thrashing about and calling back, and though his voice was getting weaker Harriet could hear him howling, 'I'm sorry – I didn't mean what I said. It wasn't owt to do wi' you, onny her. It wasn't your fault. It was hers. She should never have— Go back. You've a son to think on and a wife who—' His head dipped beneath the water as a wave crest washed over him, and Harriet could hear no more.

Noah's voice was desperate. 'Da! Da! Hold on, I'm coming. It's all right, I'm coming,' but he was knocked over by the same wave, which washed over him, hit the bank and bounced back, covering him once more.

When his head came up again, Harriet shrieked at him. 'Noah! Swim to 'bank! Your da's gone. Save yourself!'

He seemed to hear her for he looked in her direction and called, 'Fetch help.' His mouth filled with river water and he spluttered it out, calling again, 'I – I don't think I can mek it. Current's too strong; it's tekkin' me. I'm sorry, Harriet – 'bout your ma and that. You're a good lass. Look after our lad.'

Harriet screamed, 'Noah, Noah!' But he was carried further out, towards the deep mid-channel, and all she could see was his dark bobbing head and she knew he would have no chance, not when he was wearing his heavy boots, as his father had been too.

She saw the two sailing barges and shouted and screamed to the crews, but they were struggling to keep from capsizing and although she was sure they had seen what was happening below them there was little they could do, for they were trying desperately to save themselves.

'No,' she sobbed. 'No! No! No!'

From the top field a man raced towards her, skidding to a halt beside her, and for a brief crazy second she thought it was Fletcher come back in time to save them.

'What's happened?' Christopher Hart shouted, his breathing laboured, holding his hand to his chest. 'Oh, God! Who's in the water? We must get help.'

He clambered up on to the muddy bank and for a terrifying second Harriet thought he was going to jump in to try to save them. But he slithered back down and turned to her, ashen-faced. 'I fear it might be too late. He's being carried by the tide, unless the barges can pick him up, but they seem to be having difficulties too, and one of them has keeled over. Who is it in the water?'

'My husband,' she wailed. 'He was trying to save his father.'

'There are two of them? God in heaven!' he said in dismay,

clasping his hands to his head. 'I'll ride to the next farm. I think they have a small boat that they can put off.'

'Don't put yourself in danger, sir.' Harriet's voice trembled.

'I won't,' he assured her. 'I'll ask them to alert the port authorities in Goole; see if they'll send out a steam barge. These are very tricky waters and the tide is running exceptionally high. Are you the younger Mrs Tuke?' When she nodded, he took her arm. 'Come along,' he said. 'I'll take you up to the house.'

'No, sir.' Harriet pulled away from him and looked towards the estuary. 'I must wait – wait in case he manages to swim to shore.'

'He won't,' he said softly. 'The tide is against him. You go inside and I'll ride off and do the best I can. Our only hope is that the other barge has picked him up.'

She knew that it hadn't, she had seen the way the sails had dipped into the water, and yet she was still unwilling to leave the estuary bank, as if by being there she might keep some hope alive. But in a daze she allowed him to escort her back, and as they went through the gate the wayward sheep followed them into the top field and huddled in their shelter.

He knocked on the door and opened it without waiting for an answer, ushering Harriet inside. Ellen looked up from the table, where she was rolling pastry. Her face lit up when she saw Christopher Hart, until she cast a glance at Harriet, who was soaked to the skin, her hair in rat-tails.

'What's happened?' she said sharply. 'Christopher – what . . . ?' She stopped.

'There's been a terrible accident, Ellen,' he said slowly and carefully. 'I fear your husband and son have fallen into the estuary and there's a big tide running. Look after your daughter-in-law; she's in need of warm clothes and a hot drink. I'm going to try to get help.'

'But – h-how? What . . . Be careful,' she stammered.

'I'll come back,' he said. 'I can't stop now or it might be too late.'

'But you're wet through. You'll catch your death. Take a mackintosh, if nothing else.'

It seemed to Harriet, who was listening and watching as if through a fog, that Ellen was more concerned about Christopher Hart than she was about Mr Tuke or Noah, but he ignored her suggestion, leaving the kitchen and closing the door behind him.

'Take your wet things off,' she said to Harriet. 'I'll get you a blanket.'

She took a blanket from a chest and handed it to Harriet as she stood by the range stripping off all her clothes right down to her skin. There's no one to see me, she thought dully as she rubbed her hair with a towel, no Mr Tuke leering at me, no Noah, who might want to take me to bed if he saw me naked. What did Noah mean when he said he was sorry? Why did he say he was sorry about my ma? She wrapped the blanket round her and sat trembling in Mr Tuke's chair near the fire; her heart was racing and she felt that at any second she might pass out. She watched as if in a trance as Ellen poured beer into a tankard and heard the sizzle as she placed a hot poker in it.

Then and only then did Ellen Tuke sit opposite her and ask passively, 'What happened? How did they come to fall into 'river? Were they fighting and one pushed 'other in?'

Harriet stared at her wide-eyed. She was only just beginning to comprehend the tragedy herself. 'Is that all you can say?' she said hoarsely. 'Your husband and mine are probably drowned in 'estuary and all you can ask is were they fighting. No.' A sob escaped her throat. 'They were not fighting. Noah was trying to save his father's life.'

Ellen said nothing, though she swallowed hard, and looking away from Harriet's penetrating gaze mechanically shovelled coal from the hod on to the fire. When she spoke again her voice was even and without emotion. 'We'll not think on 'worst until we know for sure. Mebbe a barge or fishing boat'll pick 'em up. Noah's a strong swimmer, though Mr Tuke isn't.'

'Are you not listening to me?' Harriet shuddered. 'They were wearing boots, 'salt marsh is flooded, and I didn't see where Mr Tuke went but Noah was swept out to 'middle of 'river.' She began to sob. 'They don't stand a chance.'

Ellen let her cry, not commiserating or showing any reaction, but after gazing into the flames for a few moments she lifted her head and stared at Harriet. 'They look like real tears,' she declared, her voice flat and detached. 'But you never married for love, onny convenience. You've admitted as much.'

Harriet was shocked. How cold and hardhearted she was, just as Noah had described her. 'I don't understand you,' she whispered, and in her anguish repeated, 'Your husband and mine have been swept away in estuary waters and yet you show no horror, no grief. Have you not taken it in?' Her voice rose to a howl. 'That they're lost?'

Ellen turned away. 'I'll believe it when Master Christopher comes back and tells me it's so. In 'meantime, I've got 'pastry spoiling and a pie to cook.'

'And who'll eat it?' Harriet asked thickly, her energy sapped. 'Not me.'

'You have to eat, you've a babby to feed,' Ellen responded briefly. 'He knows nowt of what's happened.'

As if on cue, Daniel began to wail and Harriet, clutching the blanket round her, went to pick him up. She put her cold cheek against his warm one, which made him cry again. Then she sat down and stretched first one hand and then the other to the fire to warm them, and loosening the blanket put Daniel to her breast.

He's all I've got now, she thought weakly, and in her muddled mind she comprehended that she was now dependent on Ellen Tuke. And I'm nothing to her. She might not want me to stay; she might not even stop here herself, since she can't run 'farm alone. Jumbled thoughts ran unchecked in her head. Master Hart might offer her a cottage like Mrs Marshall's, but he won't offer one to me. Why would he? I'm just somebody who does 'washing and ironing up at his grand house.

She gazed at the child, contentedly feeding. Look after our lad, Noah had cried out. So was he proud of him after all? You're a good lass, he had said, and tears spouted unchecked down her cheeks. Had he always hidden his innermost feelings because no one had ever shown him kindness or understanding, only indifference? As for Mr Tuke, I heard him shout out to Noah that he was sorry. For what? For not being a good father? And why did he say that it was nothing to do wi' Noah, but onny her? Who did he mean? Ellen, or 'woman who gave birth to him?

She took a quivering breath, holding back a sob, and put Daniel to her other breast. We'll never know, for no matter that Ellen Tuke says we must wait to be sure, I saw with my own eyes and know in my heart that they won't be coming back.

# CHAPTER THIRTY-NINE

As he had promised, Christopher Hart came back to Marsh Farm later that afternoon, but the news was predictable. Nothing had been seen of Noah or his father, and word had filtered through via Goole that the crews of two barges were missing.

He sat down by the fire and accepted the offered mulled ale. He was distraught, wet through, his hair soaking as Harriet's had been, and his hands trembled as he took the tankard from Ellen. 'I'm so very sorry,' he said. 'Such a tragedy. I've been promised word if by wondrous chance a miracle might happen.' He shook his head wearily. 'But I fear all hope is gone. It's fearful weather and quite dark and thunderous now, so little can be done until morning. Men will go out at first light to search again.'

'Thank you, sir.' Harriet's voice shook. 'You've been very kind and considerate. Your family must be anxious about you.'

'I sent word to my wife that I'd been held up; she will be very upset when she hears, but it is much worse for both of you, especially with Christmas almost upon us.'

'I'd forgotten,' Harriet murmured, and felt tears welling. 'It was going to be a special Christmas with our new son.' Daniel was sleeping on her knee, and she moved his shawl that Mr Hart might see his face.

He nodded, and Harriet saw that he was very affected

by the sight of him. 'A fine boy.' His voice was choked. 'You must tell me if there's anything I can do to help you in your hour of need. You too, of course, Ellen,' he said, turning to her.

'There is something, Master Hart,' Harriet said, and Ellen looked at her sharply. 'Daniel hasn't been baptized, nor I churched, and as I'm not supposed to go out in public until I am . . .'

'Ah, of course,' he said. 'We'll be seeing the parson over Christmas and I could ask him to visit you. Shall I do that? It will be a few days, I suppose, before he comes, but you'll need time to grieve over your loss, to cope with your sorrow over this terrible tragedy that has come upon you so swiftly, and – and then . . .' He paused. 'Depending on any outcome there will be other arrangements to be discussed.'

He means a funeral, Harriet thought. That's if they ever find them. And 'magistrate to be informed.

He left them, telling them not to get up, that he'd see himself out, but Ellen insisted on taking him to the door. Harriet heard a few murmured words and then the bolt striking home as Ellen locked it after him. Harriet took a deep gasping breath. She would have left it unlocked – just in case. If that act wasn't final proof of an ending she didn't know of another.

'My dear, wherever have you been?' Melissa was astounded at Christopher's appearance. 'You're soaked through! You must have a mustard bath at once.' She reached for the bell to summon Alice, but Christopher put up his hand.

'I've already asked for one to be prepared,' he said. 'I'm so very cold. I'll tell you briefly what's happened, have my bath and go straight up to bed.'

Melissa rose to her feet. This was so unlike him. 'You've been out all day. I was told you'd been held up. What's happened?'

He poured a glass of whisky from the decanter and drank it straight down. 'A terrible tragedy.' He came towards the fire and held his shaking hands towards it. 'I don't know where to begin.'

He told her in short bursts how he'd gone to Marsh Farm and heard a commotion, men shouting and a woman screaming.

'I thought at first it was a family quarrel and hesitated to become involved, but then realized that it was something much worse.' He went on to describe how he'd looked towards the estuary and seen a woman down by the bank in obvious distress.

'Apparently Tuke had fallen into the water and her husband had jumped in to try to save him. But the salt marsh was covered by deep water and they were both washed away by the high tide. I've never seen it so fast and strong.'

Melissa, shocked, gazed at him. 'Don't tell me they're . . .'

He nodded. 'Gone. I did what I could, sent men out on the bank to look for them, alerted the authorities, but it's bad, Melissa. I fear there's no hope for them. And you were right, the young Mrs Tuke has a very young baby, no more than a few weeks old, I should say.'

'Poor girl,' Melissa murmured. 'And the elder Mrs Tuke, what of her? She must be distraught at losing a husband and a son!'

Christopher frowned slightly. 'I'm not sure. I don't think she's taken it in yet. She seemed quite calm, anyway, but then she was always a stoic from what I recall. But she said something rather odd as I was leaving; something I didn't understand. *It's come at last.*'

'There's another son,' Melissa told him. 'You met him when he came to the house earlier in the year, don't you remember? Where was he?'

Christopher shook his head wearily. 'I recall meeting him, but I don't know where he is. He wasn't mentioned.'

Their visitors were due the next day, Christmas Eve, but that morning Christopher rose early and sent a note to the parson asking him to call urgently at Marsh Farm, even though he would be busy preparing for the church services.

'The parson will be the best person to talk to them,' he told Melissa, 'and young Mrs Tuke needs him to baptize the child and church her before she goes out in public.'

'Of course,' Melissa murmured. 'The blessing for safe delivery from childbirth. Did you see the child?' She had already decided that she must keep her own news for a more appropriate time. 'What was it?'

'A son. A beautiful child. Some foreign blood, I'd say; perhaps the father was very dark. He'll be a comfort to her, I hope.'

'Will you visit them again today?'

'Yes. Regardless of whether there's any news. I feel that I should. I'll let them know that if they need any assistance . . .'

Melissa smiled and kissed his cheek. 'You're a saint,' she said. 'May I come with you? Amy can hold the fort here in case everyone arrives early.'

He nodded. 'Thank you. I'd appreciate your being by my side, and I'm sure they will too.'

They heard the ring of the doorbell. 'That might be news,' Christopher said, heading for the hall. 'If it is, we'll go to the Tukes straight after breakfast.'

It was the bailiff bringing word that a bargeman's body had been found near the port of Goole; his partner had managed to swim to shore and walk to safety, and the second barge had been rescued with both crewmen safe. There had been no sighting of Noah or his father.

Christopher was glad to have Melissa with him as they drove to Marsh Farm. He'd been disturbed by Ellen's behaviour as he'd left the previous day. She had appeared to be unaffected by the loss of her husband and son. He had put her un-emotional behaviour down to shock, but as he was leaving and she had accompanied him to the door, she had clasped his hand and whispered the words he'd repeated to Melissa and he didn't understand her meaning in the slightest.

He knocked and they entered, as no one seemed to have

heard them. Harriet was sitting gazing into the fire with her child on her knee and a warm shawl covering them both. She looked up, startled, and saw them in the doorway.

She attempted to stand, but Melissa hurried towards her. 'Please don't get up, Harriet,' she said softly. 'I've come to offer my condolences. I'm so dreadfully sorry. Words cannot express—'

'Thank you, ma'am,' Harriet whispered. 'I'm sorry; I seem to have lost my voice. Mrs Tuke is milking in 'shed. She'll not be more than five minutes. Can I offer you a cup of tea?'

'No, thank you,' Melissa said. 'My husband has something to tell you.'

Christopher's fingers ran round the rim of his top hat. 'There's no trace of your husband or his father,' he told her. 'One bargeman has drowned, the others are safe. I'm so sorry that I haven't any better news for you.'

Harriet shook her head. 'I didn't expect any, sir,' she said huskily. 'Not after what I saw. Here's Mrs Tuke coming in.' She had heard the click of the door sneck.

Ellen had seen the horse and trap outside and her expression was composed, until she saw Mrs Hart standing by Harriet and then it froze, though she dipped her knee.

'Good morning, ma'am, Master Christopher,' she said formally. 'Thank you for coming. I don't suppose you have anything new to tell us?'

'I'm afraid not, Ellen,' Christopher said. 'It's a terrible tragedy. Do you have any other family we can get in touch with?' He glanced at Harriet, who shook her head and mouthed, 'No, sir.'

Ellen crossed her hands. 'No, but I'd be obliged if you'd send a message to Mrs Marshall to acquaint her with what's happened.'

Christopher, saying that he would, cursed himself for forgetting that he'd intended to send a sack of logs to the old lady. It's Christmas Eve, he thought; everybody will be busy. I wonder if she has enough fuel to manage over Christmas?

'You must let us know if there's anything you need for yourself or your child.' Melissa spoke directly to Harriet. 'May I see him?'

Harriet smiled, though her mouth trembled. 'Yes, ma'am.' She drew away the shawl. Daniel gave a yawn and opened his dark eyes, which were fringed with the longest lashes Melissa had ever seen, and looked about him as if observing his surroundings.

'Oh!' Melissa sighed. 'He's *beautiful*. Quite, quite beautiful. I don't know many babies, but I'm sure there are none who can match him.'

'Thank you, ma'am,' Harriet whispered. 'I thought it was just me being biased.'

'I think not,' Melissa said gently, and turned to Ellen Tuke. 'You must both be so very proud. The child will give you comfort in these dark days.'

'Quite so, ma'am,' Ellen said stiffly.

The Harts left them and headed for home. 'What a very cold fish your Ellen Tuke is,' Melissa commented when they reached the road. 'I don't think it's only shock that has made her so. I feel she has some rancour eating away any generosity of spirit.'

Christopher gave a deep sigh. 'I think you may be right. She is certainly not the person I once knew.'

# CHAPTER FORTY

Christmas Day felt very strange and Harriet was unwell, spending most of the day sitting by the fire in a daze, gazing into the flames. Ellen milked the cows, fed the sheep and cattle and brought in the eggs. Then she cooked just one of the pheasants, baked potatoes, and boiled carrots and cabbage. They ate very little, and although Ellen had steamed the Christmas pudding Harriet couldn't eat any of it.

After she had cleared away, Ellen suggested Harriet went to bed. 'If you're ill we can't cope,' she said bluntly. 'Nor can you feed 'babby. If we're to survive here you have to be fit.'

Harriet heard her words but was barely listening; she felt as though she were existing in a bubble. She gathered Daniel up from his cot and went silently upstairs. Five minutes later Ellen brought up a stone hot water bottle to warm her bed and a cup of hot milk sprinkled with cinnamon.

After drinking the milk and with Daniel tucked up beside her, she fell asleep almost immediately and was woken in late afternoon by Mrs Tuke shaking her.

'Parson's here,' she said, 'an' asking to see you. Shall I ask him to come up or will you come down?'

Harriet felt dizzy but slightly better after her long and deep sleep. 'Could he come up, do you think?' Her voice was still croaky. 'Will you stay with him?'

'Of course I will,' she answered sharply. 'He'll not want to be in a young woman's bedroom on his own.'

Harriet reached for her hairbrush and attempted to straighten her mussed-up hair. Sitting up in bed, she draped her shawl around her shoulders and waited.

The parson offered his commiserations, gave her God's blessing and asked for her to be given strength in her present difficulties. Then he baptized Daniel, to whom she gave the middle name of Miles after all, for recalling Noah's saying that they'd call another son by that name, she thought sorrowfully that she might never have any more children.

She went downstairs after he had left. Ellen was making tea and cutting into a Christmas cake, and Harriet allowed herself the uncharitable thought that apart from the absence of Noah and Mr Tuke from the table, Ellen was behaving much as usual. She shivered, even though the room was warm. 'I was thinking,' she croaked. 'It's a pity we can't get in touch with Fletcher. He might want to come home.'

Ellen poured the tea and sat opposite her at the table. 'He's gone to mek his fortune,' she said bluntly. 'He'll come home when he's good 'n' ready.'

'But if he knew what had happened to his father and Noah he'd want to come back and support you.'

'Mebbe,' Ellen answered, tight-lipped. 'But he doesn't know.'

Harriet sipped her tea and nibbled on a small piece of cake. 'Would you like me to stay?' she asked. 'Or should I leave, seeing as I'm no relation to you, and neither is my son.'

Ellen stared at her. 'Do you think I'm so callous that I'd turn you out in 'middle o' winter?'

Harriet gazed into space before answering throatily, 'I don't know what I think. I don't feel capable of thinking about anything.'

'Then I'll tell you.' Ellen leaned towards her. 'They're not coming back, so we have to mek 'best o' things. When you're well again we'll work out a plan for 'New Year. We'll sell 'cattle for we can't raise 'em, but keep one milch cow; that'll be as much as we'll need. We'll sell off 'sheep – they're more bother than they're worth – but raise a litter o' pigs and sell 'em at six months. We'll keep the goats to keep 'grass down, and sell hosses – we should get a good price for 'stallion and plough hoss, but we'll keep 'old mare for 'time being. We'll buy more hens and ducks wi' money we mek, and then we'll have eggs and meat.' She sat back and folded her arms. 'We'll manage,' she said.

She's already made plans, Harriet thought, and wanted to ask what about the maintenance of the farm, the fences and gates and – she gave a little shudder – the estuary bank. We can't do those things; or can we? Mebbe when I'm feeling better and winter is over I'll be able to do more, but I wish, oh, how I wish that Fletcher would come home. I just want to see him. I know there can be nothing more than a loving friendship between us but I just want to know that he's near.

On the day after Boxing Day, Christopher Hart came to their door to tell Ellen that Mrs Marshall was ill.

'I sent a man round on Christmas Eve with a sack of wood and to tell her of your misfortune,' he said. 'He came back to tell me that a boatman who had shipped up in the Haven had called in to see her and found her unwell. I'm sorry I couldn't come before, but I've had a houseful of guests. I've sent someone with provisions and she seems to be coping. It's, erm, perhaps not good for her to be alone.'

Ellen thanked him for coming, but it seemed to Harriet that she was more upset over her old friend's illness than she had been over her husband or Noah.

When Harriet felt stronger, she began to do more work about the house and farm. Neither Noah nor his father had yet been discovered, and some of the men from neighbouring farms who called in to offer sympathy and a helping hand if needed remarked that they might never be found.

'Could've been washed out to sea on 'following tide,' one

pronounced dourly. 'Or trapped under a sandbank. Sorry to say, I reckon you've seen 'last of 'em.'

Which is no comfort at all, Harriet thought as she gazed out at the now gentle flow of the Humber.

Frequently, after finishing her chores, she walked up the track to the top road to check if there had been any letters delivered to the post box, but it was always empty, and she realized that on the rare occasions when there had been a delivery Mrs Tuke had already collected it. She must be checking first thing, before starting the milking.

January was very cold, with thick snow that came halfway up the door, and they kept a spade inside the house to dig their way out if they should need to. The sheep were sold, though there was little profit on them, but there was sufficient bedding left now to keep the pigs and Daisy warm. Ellen wrung the necks of the older hens and there were enough eggs from the others to keep them supplied until the weather improved.

By March the two women had a regular routine, but Harriet hankered after going back to the manor, and she broached the subject with Ellen one day.

'Mrs Hart said that she'd be glad to have me back,' she told her. 'And 'money would be handy if we're going to buy more livestock. I could go up after 'first milking if you'd do second, rather than 'other way round as we do now.'

Ellen considered silently for a few moments and then said, 'What about 'bairn?'

She never speaks of him by name, Harriet thought, just as she never did with Noah. In fact, she reflected, she never even mentions Noah or his father.

'I'd tek him with me,' Harriet told her. 'I'll onny be doing 'ironing anyway, not washing, so he'll be quite safe. And it'll onny be once a week at 'most.'

Ellen nodded and agreed. She didn't offer to look after Daniel, not that Harriet would have wanted her to. She wanted her child to be loved and she didn't think Ellen Tuke was capable of that.

The following Monday Harriet was up early; she did the first milking and then fed Daniel, who was thriving. He followed her with his eyes and chuckled and crowed when she talked to him. His cheeks were dimpled and he had a little round belly, which she gently tickled. As she dressed him she told him that they were going up to the big house where they would see Cook and Alice and lots of other people, and he gurgled at her as if he was taking in every word.

'He doesn't understand what you're saying, you know.' Ellen had her back to her as she stirred the porridge.

'I know that,' Harriet said, 'but I want him to hear me talking, so he can begin to copy me when he's ready. Surely you used to talk to Fletcher when he was a babby?'

Ellen didn't answer. It was as if she hadn't heard her, but Harriet knew that she had.

As she strode along the top road with Daniel strapped to her, she felt a huge uplifting of her spirits at being away from Ellen Tuke's depressing temperament. She leaches away any happiness, and I have some now that I have Daniel to love, and am coming to terms with the loss of Noah and his father, which was such a terrible waste of life however difficult they were.

Although she hadn't loved Noah, nor even, if she was honest, felt any fondness for him, she understood him better now that she knew how badly treated he had been as a child. He never knew love, she thought, and I do wonder whether if his real mother had kept him he would have turned out differently.

And why didn't she keep him? Was she too young? Did Mr Tuke tell her he wanted a child and she obliged because she simply had no feeling towards him? She's Daniel's grandmother, she thought. Perhaps one day I'll try to find out.

Nearing the manor gates, she saw the postman walking towards her. "Morning, Mrs Tuke, how 'you doing?'

'Much better, thank you.' She smiled. 'Have you owt for us?'

'Aye, I have,' he said. 'And if I can give it to you I can save meself a bit o' walkin'.' He peered short-sightedly at the envelope. 'It's addressed to Mrs Tuke, so that'll be you or 'other missus, and it's another o' them wi' a foreign stamp.'

Harriet blinked and took it. 'Oh,' she said. 'Thank you.'

'Righty-ho,' he said. 'I'll be on me way.'

'Yes,' Harriet said vaguely. 'Be seeing you.'

She walked on, clutching the envelope, but as soon as she turned a bend in the road she stopped and looked at it. It was a foreign stamp, an American one. What had the postie meant – another of them? Did he mean that he'd delivered another letter from abroad to someone else, or had he delivered others to Marsh Farm with American stamps? She couldn't really be sure that it was from Fletcher, for she had never seen his handwriting, but she couldn't think who else it might be.

It was addressed to Mrs N. Tuke, and she sighed. If it was indeed from Fletcher it would certainly be intended for his mother; he had no way of knowing that Noah and his father were dead, and would think that Noah would be angry and suspicious if she received a letter from him.

She turned it over in her hand and there it was, his name and an address in big bold handwriting.

Melissa glanced out of her bedroom window and smiled when she saw Harriet Tuke cutting down the side drive to the servants' entrance.

Ah, she's back, she thought. And she's brought her baby with her. I'll slip along to the ironing room later and take another look at him, and apprise her of my own pregnancy. I don't in the least mind who knows of it, and I have no intention of shutting myself away until after the birth. It is a cause for celebration, and Christopher thinks the same.

She had told him of the forthcoming happy event after their guests had left. The tragedy of the double drowning had cast a cloud over them both, although they had been as hospitable as possible and not let it interfere with their guests' enjoyment.

Laurence Wilkie had spoken privately to Christopher on Boxing Day, to tell him of his affection for Amy and express the hope that he might begin correspondence with her, which if she were willing, and with Christopher's approval, might lead to something permanent. They'd liked him immensely, and Christopher's sister-in-law had spoken of him favourably. She had told them that he was very well connected and his father's only son and heir; Christopher's only complaint was that if they should marry, Amy would be whisked away to live in London.

'But it will be so nice to be able to visit them in their London house, darling,' Melissa said, when he'd voiced his fears after everyone had departed. 'And besides, we are going to be very busy ourselves.'

He'd looked at her enquiringly, and she had then given him the news that made him the happiest man in Yorkshire.

# CHAPTER FORTY-ONE

Some of the laundry was already drying in the ironing room when Harriet arrived, but first she had to show Daniel off to the kitchen staff and the other servants.

They all oohed and aahed over him and he obligingly laughed and chortled at them, but Harriet could tell they were curious about his olive skin and dark eyes. Understanding that in the circumstances they would be unwilling to broach the subject, she decided that it was best to air the matter at once.

'You'll all have heard that we have had a terrible tragedy thrust upon us and that I'm now a widow,' she began. 'My beautiful child will never know his da or grandfather, or who any of his forebears were, but as you can see,' she smiled down at him, 'there might have been a trace of foreign blood somewhere in his past. Or it might be in mine, for how can we tell? Unless 'knowledge is handed down by word o' mouth there's no knowing where any of us come from.'

'You're quite right there, Mrs Tuke,' Mrs Lister said. 'I thought I was Yorkshire through and through, until one o' my ma's relations showed up and it turned out we were part Irish!'

Harriet had been told that she might use one of the linen drawers in the ironing room as a makeshift cot. Someone had loaded pillowslips on a clothes horse, and stood it in front of the fire, so Harriet took them off and replaced them with linen sheets, which took a lot of drying. She folded the slips and put the irons on the fire to heat. Then she sat on a chair and started to feed Daniel, sure that afterwards he would sleep for a few hours. She began to relax, her tension unravelling, and thought about the letter residing in her skirt pocket.

She wondered about its contents whilst ironing, and from time to time took it out of her pocket and looked at it. I wish I were brave enough to steam it open, she thought, turning it over in her hand. One corner wasn't properly closed; it wouldn't take much, she thought, and then chastised herself for even considering such an immoral act.

When the door opened she quickly stuffed it back in her pocket, surprised to see Melissa Hart here in the servants' quarters.

'Hello, Harriet,' she said. 'I'm so pleased you were able to come back to us. How are you feeling now? The parson told us you were quite unwell when he visited you.'

Harriet dipped her knee. 'I was, ma'am. It was 'shock of everything, I suppose, and seeing it happen right in front of my eyes.'

Melissa nodded. 'I don't know how you'd ever get over such a thing,' she said gently. 'And your mother-in-law, how is she?'

'Coping well, ma'am,' Harriet told her. 'She's just getting on wi' looking after animals: milking cow an' feeding pigs and so on. We got rid of 'cattle an' sheep and just kept what we could manage. Do you think . . .' She hesitated. It wasn't really her place to ask, but she decided to; it was something she had worried about and needed to know. 'Do you think that Master Hart will let Mrs Tuke continue wi' tenancy of 'farm? She allus looks after 'books, so she tells me, so he needn't worry that she doesn't understand 'em, and I'm sure we can mek it pay if . . .' She wanted to say *if she lets me stay*, but that would raise more questions about Noah. 'If we work together,' she concluded.

'But *I* don't understand why you would need to ask,' her

employer said, frowning a little. 'As far as I know, the tenancy is in Mrs Tuke's name and always has been.'

But – I don't understand, Harriet thought. What about when Ellen said that Mr Tuke had threatened to throw her out of the house if she didn't look after Noah?

'Oh. I must have misunderstood her, ma'am. Oh, well, that's a relief.'

Melissa sat down on the chair and looked down at Daniel, who was sleeping soundly. Then she glanced up at Harriet. 'In case you haven't guessed,' she said softly, 'I am at last with child.'

Harriet carefully put down the iron, unsure whether to continue with the ironing. 'I'm very pleased for you, ma'am. You and Master Hart must be delighted.'

'We are.' Melissa laughed. 'Don't tell a soul, but I took your advice.'

Harriet wrinkled her eyebrows. '*My* advice, ma'am?'

'Yes.' Melissa dropped her voice confidentially. 'Do you recall when I asked you how long it had taken for you to become pregnant? You said – was it four months? And every night!'

Harriet blushed and put her hand over her mouth. Had she really told her that?

Melissa laughed again. 'I realized then why I wasn't getting pregnant. Am I shocking you, Harriet? Women – ladies like me – don't talk of such things, do we? Or at least we are expected not to, and I certainly wouldn't discuss it with anyone else I know.' She raised her eyebrows. 'But I don't think I shock you, do I?'

Harriet smiled. 'No, ma'am, you don't.' Then she considered. 'Do you think I might ask you a question?' At Melissa's nod, she murmured, 'Do you think that doing something which might be considered wrong – if it hurts nobody – could be . . .' She searched for the right word.

'Justified?' Melissa suggested.

'Aye, yes, that's it.'

'It would depend on what kind of wrongdoing, I suppose,'

269

Melissa said thoughtfully, 'and what effect it would have on the person committing the act.'

'It would be in search of 'truth,' Harriet said. 'Nothing else, really.'

'Then I would say yes, it could be justified.' Her eyes sparkled. 'But as I'm quite devious myself, perhaps I'm not the best person to give such advice.'

'I'd reckon you are, ma'am.' In view of the fact that Ellen had misled her over the tenancy, Harriet decided to steam open the envelope before leaving the ironing room.

The letter was a revelation, for it seemed it was written in reply to one that Ellen had sent to Fletcher in January, after the Christmas tragedy, for he began by saying how nice it was to hear from her; yet judging by the tone of the rest of the letter she hadn't mentioned the deaths of Mr Tuke or Noah. He asked how his father was and hoped that Noah was managing and harboured no hard feelings towards him, and trusted that Harriet was in good health. He added that he hoped they'd had a reasonable winter and asked if there were many spring lambs. He went on to say that America was a huge country and money could be made there, *but as money isn't my main reason for being here I'm not too sure about staying. I'm used to a small neighbourhood, I suppose,* he concluded, and sent his regards to everyone.

Harriet was horrified that Ellen hadn't told him about the tragic loss of his father and Noah. Why hadn't she? Why would she keep such a thing from him? The letter, she decided, after all her deliberations on the rights or wrongs of opening it, had left more questions than answers.

She carefully put the letter back inside the envelope and closed it up, then put a piece of old linen over it, pressed it firmly with the iron and put it back in her pocket. Then as an afterthought she brought it out and looked again at Fletcher's address, and memorized it.

\*

She handed the letter to Ellen on arriving back at the farm and told her that she'd met the postman on her way to the manor, which was perfectly true. 'He thought it was for me,' she added, telling a small white lie.

Ellen snatched it from her. 'It says Mrs N. Tuke,' she snapped. 'It's obvious it's for me.'

'I'm Mrs N. Tuke too,' Harriet reminded her. 'But I knew it was for you because I saw 'American postage stamp. Of course,' she said in a vague manner, 'my brother might have been writing to let me know he'd left Australia, except that—'

'He wouldn't know your married name or where you live,' Ellen butted in sharply. She put the envelope in her pocket.

No, he wouldn't, Harriet thought. More's the pity. It would be nice to have someone from my own family to talk to. But I must accept that Leonard's gone and never likely to come back. 'Are you not anxious to read the letter?' she asked. She shook her head and sighed. 'Poor Fletcher. He'll be very upset when you give him 'news about his da and Noah.'

Ellen was about to get something out of the oven, but she turned at that. 'What meks you think I'm going to tell him?'

'Surely?' Harriet exclaimed. 'Surely it's his right to know? He might want to come home.'

'I'll tell him when I'm good an' ready,' Ellen muttered between clenched lips, 'and not afore.'

Not for the first time, Harriet wondered how she could continue living here with Ellen Tuke, who rarely spoke to her unless it was about household or farm matters. But she knew she had no option at present but to stay. Where else could I go with a young child? There'd be no work for me, not even at the manor once Daniel begins to walk, unless I can find a child minder. But that idea was abhorrent to her. She could never trust a stranger.

She suggested to Ellen that she might ask Mary if she knew

271

anyone who would farm the second field rather than leaving it fallow, and after thinking about it Ellen agreed. 'Tell her if she knows somebody they can rent it for free but that we'll share 'profit, if there is any. There's still time to sow another crop, or somebody can use it for grazing as long as they look after 'animals.'

I'd prefer that, Harriet thought as she walked up to Mary's cottage. I like to see cattle or sheep in 'fields. Cows with their tails swishing away 'flies, and 'sheep grazing so peacefully.

Mary was always pleased to see her and they sat chatting over a cup of tea, with Mary bouncing Daniel gently on her knee, and Harriet wishing that Mary were Daniel's grandmother rather than pretending that Ellen was.

'I do know somebody who wants a bit o' land as it happens,' Mary said, when Harriet asked her. 'My nephew. He's a bargeman. An' come to think of it, I know a couple o' farm labourers who need a strip big enough to grow their own vegetables and a bit o' corn. In fact they could mek it like 'old strip farming from long back, and there'd still be room for a few sheep or goats. I'll ask for you. Have you heard owt from Mrs Tuke's other son? Him that went away?'

Harriet shook her head. 'I haven't,' she said. 'But he's written to his mother. He's in America.'

'America!' Mary exclaimed. 'You'll not be seeing him again then?'

'Probably not,' Harriet agreed, suppressing a sigh, for Ellen hadn't disclosed anything about the letter she'd received, and had Harriet not steamed it open she would have known nothing at all about him.

She recalled the comment that Noah had made when Fletcher had told them that he was leaving; Noah had tauntingly said he'd give it twelve months and Fletcher would be back with his tail between his legs.

Will he be back, as Noah said? Has he been waiting until the twelve months are gone by to prove his brother wrong? He doesn't know that Noah is no longer here to mock him;

neither does he know that Noah is only his half-brother, but that doesn't matter either, for even if he still feels 'same way about me as I do about him, I'm still his brother's widow. And because of that, legally, and morally as it says in 'Bible, we can never be together.

# CHAPTER FORTY-TWO

The year progressed; two labourers and Mary's nephew, Tom, came forward in response to Harriet's request. They were planning to work together to produce vegetables for their own consumption; on a small area of land they'd grow turnips for animal feed, and keep another patch for half a dozen sheep and a similar number of goats.

Harriet chatted to them whenever they came to tend the field, always taking Daniel out with her, strapped to her in a shawl. She also called on Mary in her cottage. She enjoyed her company and she knew the older woman liked to see Daniel; one day when she was there Mary gave her a parcel of woollen coats and leggings she had made for the baby. 'I know you don't have much time to knit,' she had remarked, 'and I've allus liked to do it.'

She regularly walked down to the estuary bank. She wanted to defeat her memories of the day when Noah and his father had been lost. I have to confront my fears, she thought, but also treat the estuary with respect.

When the tide was low, the salt marsh was beautiful, fine-leafed sea grasses colonizing the rivulet bed, reeds swaying gently, making soft rustling whispers when the breeze ran through them. There were daisies and sea pinks, which the labourers called asters and thrift. They called the marshy land flats and carr.

She was beginning now to recognize the wading birds by their cries as they searched the mud: the *ack-ack-ack* of the colourful shelduck, the chuckling chorus of the dabbling teal, the bubbling trill of the curlew and the wailing *peewit* of the lapwing as they flew erratically above her.

Tom, the bargeman, who also owned his own coggy boat, hammered a stake into the bank and tied the boat to it. He told Harriet he liked to fish in the estuary and said he'd bring her the odd flounder or young salmon, which he did, often. He also worked the land during the week, depending on what shift he was on.

She was feeding the pigs one day when she saw him in the other field. He waved to her and she walked across to talk to him. They spoke of the weather, which was warm but had been wet, and of how the crops were doing, and then he startled her by asking about Fletcher. 'Have you heard from him lately?'

She was shocked into wordlessness. 'Erm.' She cleared her throat. 'I – erm, he writes to his mother, not to me. How do you know Fletcher?'

He grinned. 'Oh, everybody knows everybody else round here. I've known him and Noah since we were bairns. It was me that set Fletcher off on his travels. I took him in 'barge from Brough down to Hull to catch 'train.'

'I see,' she breathed. 'And, so – have you heard from him?'

'Aye, a while back. I had a letter, oh, 'end o' last year.' He leaned on his spade. 'But I didn't get round to writing back till mebbe March, when I told him I was sorry about his da and brother not being found. Not heard owt since,' he mused, frowning a little. 'Course, he might have moved on and not received 'letter.'

Harriet asked him where had he written to and he said somewhere in Ohio, so she knew it was the same town she'd seen on Ellen's letter.

So now he knows, Harriet pondered as she walked back to the house. I wonder what he'll do? She decided that she wouldn't mention anything to Ellen. Two can play at that game, she thought. It's like cat and mouse and I'm not comfortable with it, but I can't afford to antagonize her; she has 'upper hand.

On a hot day in late July, Ellen decided to drive into Brough. 'I'm going to call in and see Mrs Marshall,' she said. 'I haven't seen her since she was ill, and I need to buy flour and I'll tek some eggs to sell. We've more than we need now that they're laying so well.'

Harriet nodded. It would be nice to have the house to herself, she thought, just her and Daniel. She'd put him on the floor on a blanket and let him stretch and kick his limbs without the risk of being trodden on.

She helped Ellen to bring out the cart and mentioned that the old mare was looking thin and scraggy. Ellen fastened her bonnet but didn't comment, just cracked the whip and moved off.

'Yes, well, enjoy yourself,' Harriet muttered to Ellen's back as the cart turned up the track. Sighing, she turned to go back into the house, but as it was such a lovely day, instead of playing inside with Daniel, she carried him into the field and spread a blanket on the grass and they both lay on their backs with the sun beaming down on them.

Ellen clattered along the top road but pulled up when she saw the postman walking towards her. 'Owt for me?' she asked tersely.

'Not today, mum,' he said. 'Waiting on a letter from your son, are you?'

'That's not your concern,' she said sharply, and saw his eyebrows lift. 'And I'd be obliged if you'll put any correspondence addressed to me in 'post box and not give it to anybody else.' She cracked the whip and the mare moved slowly off again, leaving the postman staring after her.

'Come on,' she urged the horse. 'I haven't got all day.' This hoss'll have to go, she thought. She's served us well but she's

276

past her prime. With money I've saved from 'stallion and 'plough hoss I'll buy another mare.

She was driving towards Hart Holme Manor and her thoughts turned to Christopher Hart as they so often did, especially now that Nathaniel wasn't there to intrude upon them. I could mek some bother there, she contemplated, a twisted smile on her lips. But I won't just yet. I'll bide a while; his wife isn't going to produce a son for him, that's obvious, so when 'time is right and Fletcher comes home, as he will when I tell him that them two have gone for ever, then 'way is clear.

Course, I'll have to get rid of her and her son first. They're nowt to me, but for now it suits me to have her here. She works well, I'll give her that, but I'll not have her giving 'eye to Fletcher. Thinks I didn't notice owt afore, but I did. 'No,' she muttered. 'I've got other plans for Fletcher that have tekken a lot o' years to come to fruition.'

She was almost at the manor gates when she screwed up her eyes and slowed the mare. Someone was walking purposefully along the road towards her. Christopher! She smiled. How did he know she would be driving along here when she so rarely did? He wasn't wearing his hat and his long hair shone bright in the sunlight.

She waved and shouted. 'Christopher! Christopher, it's me – Ellen!'

He raised a hand, continuing to stride towards her. 'I'm so pleased to see you,' she called. 'I was just thinking about you.'

She drew the mare to a standstill. She still loved him. Had always loved him, and had thought he loved her once, in spite of their differences. She sighed, recalling how she had taken advantage of him that one time when he'd been slightly drunk and she'd persuaded him into the garden; but a few weeks later she had heard in the manor kitchen, that hotbed of gossip, that his father had told him he must look for a wife. It was Cook, Mrs Marshall, who had warned her and she hadn't minded his first wife, for she realized that his parents had chosen her for him, and of course he was expected to marry well.

But this second wife, she was young and fair-complexioned and pretty, just as she herself had once been, she thought bitterly, and that, she had decided, was why he had chosen to marry her.

'Ma?'

What was he saying? Why did he say that? And why was he dressed like a common working man instead of in his fine clothes?

'Ma,' Fletcher repeated. 'Are you all right?'

She stared at her son. Her son! *Fletcher.* Not Christopher after all. What was he doing here? This wasn't part of the plan.

Fletcher put his hand over hers, which still clasped the reins. 'It's Fletcher, Ma. Who did you think it was?'

She shook her head. 'I don't know,' she whispered. 'I – I wasn't expecting you. I thought – I thought . . .' How has this trick been played? I'm not ready. I haven't got everything settled in my mind.

'Why didn't you tell me?' he asked, and when she looked vaguely at him he added softly, 'About Da and Noah. Why didn't you tell me in your letter?'

'Who told you?' she snapped. 'It was her, wasn't it? She'd no right!'

'Who do you mean? Harriet? No.' He gazed at her worriedly, wondering if her mind had turned because of the disaster. 'It was Tom Bolton; you remember Tom? He wrote to say he was sorry about Da and Noah. He told me he'd been in 'search party that had gone out lookin' for them. He said that 'Humber could be treacherous if you didn't know it. But they did know it, Ma, we all did, so what happened?'

She couldn't tell him and seemed confused at seeing him, so he took hold of the reins, which she was gripping so tightly, and turned about and headed back home. And it was there, as they pulled up in the yard, that he saw Harriet with grass in her hair and a child in her arms and he smiled and thought it was the most beautiful sight he had seen in a long, long time.

# CHAPTER FORTY-THREE

Harriet wanted to rush forward and take him in her arms but she had to hold back, aware that Ellen was watching. But Ellen seemed vague, looking at Fletcher as if she wasn't sure who he was or why he was there.

'Fletcher!' Harriet walked towards him and he kissed her cheek. 'This is a surprise.' Her voice dropped. 'It's good to see you, though we're a sad household.' She glanced at Ellen, who was watching her intently. 'Your ma will have told you about your da and Noah?'

Fletcher swallowed. 'I'd heard,' he said. 'I heard from an old pal, Tom Bolton. He'd been out on 'river wi' search party. Why didn't somebody write and tell me? I'd have come home straight away.'

Harriet gave a slight shake of her head. 'We – we didn't . . .' How could she say that his mother didn't want him to know? 'It was such a terrible time.' Tears came unbidden to her eyes. 'Such a shock to lose them both.'

'And not yet found?'

'No. Over six months and nothing,' she choked, and didn't know if her tears were for Noah and his father or emotion at seeing Fletcher again.

'Are we going to have a cup o' tea, Ma?' he called to his mother. 'I'll put 'hoss away.' Ellen muttered something and went indoors.

'Harriet,' he breathed. 'I couldn't bear to be away from you any longer. I thought before that I couldn't live with you so close and belonging to Noah, but never to see you was worse. I was thinking of coming home when I heard from Tom.' He stepped nearer and gazed at Daniel in her arms. 'A girl or a boy? No, he's far too beautiful to be a boy.'

She smiled. 'But he's a boy. Daniel was onny two weeks old when Noah – when Noah drowned. He never got 'chance to know him.'

'Can I hold him?' he asked.

'Onny for a minute,' she said softly. 'Your ma won't like it.'

'What?' He frowned. 'What do you mean?' He held the baby for a moment, then kissed him on the forehead and handed him back to her. 'He's not like Noah, except for his eyes. Noah's were dark. But his complexion . . .'

'Fletcher – there are things to tell you, but not yet. It's – not been easy.'

He nodded. 'It never was, Harriet, but one thing at a time. Let's go inside. I want to know how Da and Noah came to fall into 'river. They've lived alongside it all of their lives.'

'I think your da fell in, and Noah went in and tried to save him.' She spoke swiftly. 'But Ellen,' she choked back a sob that came with the retelling of it, 'your ma won't have it that that's how it happened. But I was there,' she said defiantly. 'I saw what happened.'

They sat silently drinking tea in the kitchen, Fletcher eating cake. He scooped up some crumbs and popped them in his mouth. 'Good to have some home-made grub, Ma.'

She glanced at him. 'That's not mine. Harriet made it. We're out o' flour now. That's where I was going when . . . when . . .' She looked round the kitchen. 'I was going to Brough,' she added.

'When you saw me coming towards you,' Fletcher prompted. 'But you thought I was someone else, didn't you?'

'No,' she said sharply. 'I thought I was seeing a ghost. You should have been— I thought you were in America.'

'I wanted to leave as soon as I heard 'news from Tom,' he told them. 'But I was working on a farm and had to work an extra month before I could set off for New York. It's a long story,' he said wearily. 'I had to wait for a berth. It took longer than I anticipated.'

'It's a long way,' Harriet murmured.

'But I'm home now and we need to talk,' he said. 'Not only about what happened, but what's going to happen next. I'll have to see 'bailiff or Master Hart about changing 'tenancy agreement to my name instead of Da's. Has owt been mentioned about it?'

Harriet watched Ellen to capture her expression at this question, but it didn't alter as she said, 'No. But don't worry about that just now. I'll speak to 'bailiff 'next time 'rent's due, or I might go up to see Master Christopher myself. I know him well enough. He won't mind.'

Harriet wondered why Ellen didn't tell Fletcher that the tenancy was hers and not Mr Tuke's. Why was she avoiding telling him the truth? But she only added, 'Master Hart was very kind and helpful. He was here on 'day it happened. He was bringing 'Christmas bird. He rode up to 'next farm to try and get help.'

'Did he?' Fletcher murmured, his expression thoughtful.

Ellen nodded in agreement, her eyes bright. 'It was typical of him,' she said. 'He's not altered since he was just a young man. Still 'same as ever he was.'

'So you'll be staying, will you, Fletcher?' Harriet asked. 'America didn't pull you up from your roots?'

'I can't leave you both on your own now, can I?' he said, glancing at her, leaving her unsure if he meant her and Daniel or her and Ellen. 'Besides, I was ready to come back. It's such a huge country I felt swamped somehow. But . . .' he hesitated. 'Well, mebbe I'll talk to 'landowner. Mebbe we should move further back from 'estuary. It's so wet down here.'

Ellen's eyes were darting about as he spoke. 'This is my

home,' she hissed. 'Don't be mekkin' plans wi'out consulting me first.'

'I won't, Ma,' he said in a conciliatory tone. 'Don't you worry 'bout that.' He smiled across at Daniel and put out his hand to him and the child grabbed his fingers. 'But we have to think of future generation, like Daniel here. We need land that's productive so we can earn a living from it.'

'We made a living wi' three menfolk afore,' his mother snapped. 'We're two men less now.'

Fletcher winced at her sharp words and Harriet turned her head away, closing her eyes in reproach.

'We scratched a living, Ma,' Fletcher said. 'That's all. We'd nowt left for luxuries like buying a new cart or waggon.'

'Anyway,' Ellen continued as if he hadn't spoken. 'Harriet might not want to stop. What's to keep her and her child here now that she's no husband to look out for her?'

So here it is, Harriet thought. I knew that sooner or later she would say something to Fletcher about Noah, but I didn't think it would be so soon after he arrived home. She held Daniel close to her to protect him and for comfort.

Fletcher's gaze on his mother was one of astonishment and outrage. 'Ma,' he croaked. 'What 'you on about? This is Noah's wife, Noah's child. Of course she'll stay.'

Harriet's voice trembled as she spoke. 'I think you'll find that your ma has summat to say about that. Haven't you, Mrs Tuke?'

Ellen stared at her. Confronted now, she had to tell Fletcher the truth about Noah or for ever live the lie, but she was confused, it seemed, as to whether this was the right time. She swallowed hard. 'It won't look right,' she muttered at last. 'Folk will talk. A young widow here wi' a single man.'

Fletcher gave a short harsh exclamation. 'But you're here,' he exclaimed. He glanced at Harriet. 'Folk might talk, an' talk they can if it suits 'em.'

'That isn't what your ma meant, Fletcher,' Harriet disclosed, determined now to have everything in the open. 'She has summat to tell you about Noah and your da.'

Ellen Tuke gazed at her with something like loathing and then spat out. 'It won't mek any difference, you know. I know what you're up to.'

Fletcher stood up. 'Enough! What's going on?'

'Noah wasn't my son,' Ellen said bitterly. 'He was Mr Tuke's, not mine. Mr Tuke brought him to me when he was a babby an' told me to bring him up as if he was my own.'

Fletcher was struck into silence and sat down again, silently contemplating. Then he frowned and said slowly, 'Is that why – is that why you never took his side? You never had a kind word to say to him. I noticed. I knew there was a difference between us, and . . .' Again he was silent. He shook his head. 'Summat's allus bothered me. I remember – I think I remember – my first memory of Noah was when I was lifted off your knee and he was put there in my place.'

He gazed at Daniel, who had his head on one side and was regarding him with interest. 'I can remember crying,' he murmured, 'and Da shouting.' He turned to Ellen. 'So who was Noah's mother? Was it someone you knew?'

Ellen's lip curled. 'Nobody I knew,' she scoffed. 'Just some whore from a brothel.'


Harriet went upstairs to feed Daniel and consider their future. Fletcher would have to contemplate his own future, too, and for the moment it couldn't include her. She was still in mourning, for one thing, and for another . . . She sighed dejectedly. They could never marry even if they wanted to. She was his brother's widow, and although according to Ellen Noah was only his half-brother, it was still illegal in the eyes of the law and the scriptures, and, in the eyes of the world, morally wrong.

But I care for him, she thought. And I think he cares for me; but is he strong enough to resist his mother? I know she wants me gone. She wants her precious son to herself now

284

that her wayward husband and poor unwelcome Noah have departed.

She stroked Daniel's cheek and he gurgled up at her with his milk-washed lips. 'I think,' she murmured to him, 'that we must set out and try to find out about your other grandmother.' Daniel chortled and kicked his chubby legs. 'I can tell you about one,' she told him, 'and she would have loved you to bits if she'd been here, but she isn't.' She felt sad again when she thought of her mother. 'And maybe this other one won't want to know you, if by chance I can find her, but on 'other hand, she might be curious to know about 'son she gave away.'

But what Harriet also considered was whether Noah's mother had known anything about him over the years. Had Mr Tuke spoken of him on his visits to the ill-famed house of disrepute? And had she heard that her son had died in the estuary, along with his father?

Daniel crowed up at her and then buried his face in her breast. So that's what I'll do, she thought. I'll try to find out who Noah's mother is, or was, if anyone's willing to tell me. Then at least I'll know a little more about my own son's heritage.

# CHAPTER FORTY-FOUR

Harriet and Ellen had had a working arrangement in place before Fletcher arrived. Each had her own jobs to do, Harriet doing the first milking and letting out the hens and ducks. Ellen prepared breakfast for the two of them, which they ate mostly in silence, and later did the second milking. They looked after the goat and pigs in turn and generally worked in unison. Harriet still contributed to the household accounts with her ironing at the manor. It was the only money she ever held in her hand, and she kept some of it back before giving the majority to Ellen, who put it in a purse in a drawer to which she held the only key.

However, now that Fletcher was home, Ellen gave Harriet jobs to do which she was sure were meant to keep her away from Fletcher. He had gone back to his customary routine of keeping the ditches clear and mending fences and gates that had fallen into disrepair since Noah drowned.

On the first ironing morning after his return, Harriet was dressing Daniel before they left when Fletcher asked why she was wrapping him in a shawl. 'Surely you're not tekkin' him with you?'

She nodded. 'I allus do. They don't mind. He sits in a little chair or he sleeps whilst I'm ironing.'

'But why don't you leave him here? Or – oh, I suppose you have to feed him while you're out?'

'I do, when I get there. Then I know that he'll be good. He watches me' – she smiled at the thought – 'or he falls asleep.'

Ellen had gone outside, and Fletcher dropped his voice. 'Does my mother never offer to look after him?'

Harriet didn't look at him but concentrated on wrapping Daniel up. 'Never,' she said. 'Never has, nor do I want her to.'

'I see.'

'No, you don't, Fletcher. Your mother doesn't want us.' Harriet took a deep breath. 'I was useful to her before you came back and admittedly she wouldn't have turned me out during 'winter. Also, I don't think she wanted to be alone.' She looked straight at him. 'But now that you're back, I think she sees me as a threat.'

'I think her mind has turned since my da and Noah drowned,' he murmured.

Harriet didn't comment, but she didn't agree. She was convinced that Ellen had some plan up her sleeve and that she and Daniel were not included in it.

As she walked towards the manor, she toyed with the idea of asking Mary if she'd ever thought of taking in a lodger. She mused over the idea that if she and Daniel could live with her, Mary might look after Daniel whilst Harriet did all the washing and ironing for the Harts. I could even ask for a job in 'kitchen, she considered, but sleep out.

She didn't see Mrs Hart that day, but a parcel had been left for her in the ironing room, containing a blouse and skirt and a heavy woollen shawl. Mary popped her head in to see her after she'd finished the washing and told her that the sheets were almost dry enough for ironing.

'I'll come over to see you one day, Mary.' Harriet raised her voice. 'We haven't had a chat for a while.'

Mary smiled and said that she mustn't forget to bring Daniel too, and Harriet felt a warm glow and wished once again that Mary were Daniel's grandmother.

It was nearly five o'clock, and as Harriet walked back she felt a despondency settling more heavily on her the nearer she came to Marsh Farm. And then she saw Fletcher waiting for her at the top of the track. It seemed at that moment as if he had never been away. Nevertheless, she thought, neither of them was free; the constraints of Noah and Mr Tuke and Fletcher's mother held them as fast as any rope.

He led her into the cover of the trees, where they were sheltered by the fresh new growth produced by his harsh pruning before he left on his travels. In the safety of her arms, Daniel cooed and babbled at the rustling of leaves and lifted a plump hand to catch them. Fletcher kissed her cheek and then her lips and then caught Daniel's hand and blew his lips on it, making a purring sound. The child laughed delightedly.

'I love him,' he whispered to her. 'I want him to be mine, as I want you to be too. What can we do?'

'I don't know,' she whispered back. 'Nothing. It's not possible. You and Noah have 'same father; it's against 'law and 'church.'

He kissed her again. 'There must be something – or else we must live in sin.'


Two days later she suggested that she might travel to Brough to buy some items they needed: flour, sewing thread and soap. Ellen eagerly agreed and Harriet knew that she didn't want to go herself and leave her alone with Fletcher. Ellen made her a long shopping list and gave her some money, and also packed up some bread and cheese in case she became hungry.

'No need to rush back,' she told her. 'You enjoy your day out.' She sighed then, and added, 'I must go and see Mrs Marshall when I have time. She'll be wondering what's happened to me.'

When Harriet had left in the cart, with Daniel strapped into a chair that Fletcher had fashioned out of a wooden potato box and packed with a blanket, Ellen rushed into the house, set the table for two and put the kettle on the fire again. Then she called Fletcher inside.

'I want to talk to you now that we're on our own,' she said eagerly.

Fletcher frowned. 'You can say owt you want in front of Harriet,' he told her. 'I've no secrets from her. She's family.'

'Not mine, she's not,' his mother said smugly. Sitting down at the table, she folded her arms across her thin chest. 'I need to talk to you and it's nowt to do wi' her. It's onny to do wi' you and me.'

He sat opposite her. 'Before you say owt, Ma, I want to tell you that I'm very fond of Harriet, and she is of me.'

His mother leaned towards him and her eyes glistened. 'You'll not want owt to do wi' her when I tell you what I've kept secret. I've got plans for you, Fletcher. Had plans for years and years and could never see how they'd come to pass.' She gave a chuckle, and again Fletcher frowned. She was behaving very oddly. 'But my prayers have been answered. When 'waters took Mr Tuke and his son—'

'Don't call him Mr Tuke,' Fletcher exploded. 'He was your husband and my father and even if he wasn't a very good one he should be treated wi' respect now that he's not here to answer back! And Noah was my brother and I'll have nowt said against him either. Besides,' he added, 'I've got plans too. I'm a grown man; I can mek my own!'

She seemed startled by his response, but the kettle started to steam and she got up to pour water into the teapot whilst Fletcher sighed impatiently, tapping his fingers on the table.

'There're jobs waiting to be done, Ma,' he said. 'Won't this keep until later?'

'No, it won't.' She sat down again and warmed her hands on the teapot. 'You'll see. Your whole life'll begin to change when I say what I'm going to say. Your prospects will increase one hundredfold, you mark my words.'

And what she said gave him cause to think that her mind really might be wandering, although if she was telling the truth then she was giving him the freedom to do what he wanted, but also presenting him with a huge dilemma.

# CHAPTER FORTY-FIVE

Harriet heaved a deep sigh as she drove away from the farm. It was such a relief to be away from the strained tension between her and Ellen. She seemed to be softening towards me at one time, but now she's just as she was when I first arrived as Noah's wife.

The day was glorious, sunny and warm with a sweet smell of newly mown hay; the hedgerows were abundant with dog roses, honey-scented meadowsweet, wild garlic and red campion and swarming with bees and butterflies fluttering from flower to flower. She wanted to weep, for she knew that under other circumstances she could be happy here – she *was* happy here, but this happiness couldn't last. She would have to move on; she couldn't live under the same roof as Fletcher.

Brough, Alice in the manor kitchen had told her, had once been an important Roman town, but now, although still designated as a town, it was really little more than a village, certainly not as large as Hull, Harriet thought as she drove the cart through the streets. But it still had a working ferry across the Humber to Winteringham on the southern shore, and from there a good straight road ran to Lincoln and eventually to London. Not that I will ever go there, she mused. That journey is not for me.

She finished her shopping for the items on her list and asked the elderly shopkeeper if she knew the whereabouts of

Mrs Miriam Stone. The woman looked startled at her question.

'Why, m'dear, why ever would you wish to visit her?' She looked Harriet up and down. 'You'd do well to keep away from such a person.'

'Oh?' Harriet pretended astonishment. 'I've been asked to leave her a message. Is she not a worthy woman?'

'I believe she leads a quiet life nowadays, but she has a – well, I'll say a poor reputation, for I wouldn't wish to heap any further denigration on her name, no matter that it might be deserved.'

'I see,' Harriet said thoughtfully. 'I wonder what I should do? Perhaps post it? But then I don't have an address.' She stood with her hand to her face as if thinking.

'Is 'message important? Would it be known if you didn't deliver it?'

'I don't know. If I should be asked then I couldn't lie.'

'Indeed not,' the woman agreed. 'Well, I do know where she lives.' She too pondered. 'If I should write it down, then perhaps you could slip it into her letter box and then you could say you'd carried out 'errand. My word,' she added, 'you must be careful of 'people who give you such messages to deliver.'

'She's a poor servant girl who fell on hard times.'

'And you're helping her out? Well, that's a very Christian thing to do. I hope she's now found a better life?'

'She has,' Harriet said. 'I'm very much obliged to you for coming up with such a splendid solution. Thank you.'

The shopkeeper appeared astonished at her unintended entanglement, but set about searching for a scrap of notepaper and scribbled down an address. 'I haven't put her name on it,' she whispered. 'So no one will ever know.'

Harriet nodded and said softly, 'I'll tear it into shreds once 'message is delivered. It won't ever be needed again.'

She climbed into the trap and drove further up the street and turned a corner. Then, glancing at the address, she asked the first person she saw for directions.

The cottage was tucked into an obscure corner away from the main thoroughfare and seemed neat enough, with clean curtains at the window and a well-brushed doorstep, but when Harriet knocked she saw the curtains twitch. A moment later a woman of indeterminate age, but perhaps in her early fifties, with dyed reddish hair, bright lipstick, and rouge on her pale cheeks, came to open the door.

She gazed at Harriet and then at Daniel. 'Yes?'

'Mrs Stone?'

The woman put one hand on her hip. 'Who wants her?'

'I want to ask you a question about a child.'

Miriam Stone glanced at Daniel again and Harriet hastily said, 'Not this child, he's mine. I want to ask about his father, my husband.'

'Your husband? I don't tell tales.'

'I'm not asking you to,' Harriet said firmly. 'And my husband is dead. But seemingly he was born here and I onny want to know about *his* mother – my husband's mother.'

Miriam Stone heaved an impatient sigh and opened the door wider. 'You'd better come in.'

The house was small but very colourful, with bright cushions on the sofa and chairs and a glass bowl of artificial fruit and flowers on the polished table. There was a strong smell of perfume.

'Sit down,' Harriet was told brusquely. 'So what's this about?'

Harriet sat down and unfastened Daniel's shawl and bonnet. He gurgled up at Mrs Stone, who appeared immune to his charm.

'As you will see, Mrs Stone, my child does not have an English skin. I've been told that my husband was born to a woman who worked here and I simply want to know so that—'

'What was her name?'

'I don't know. My husband was named Noah, and his father . . .' Harriet hesitated. Maybe Miriam Stone didn't know the names of her customers, and Ellen Tuke would be furious if anyone else found out that Mr Tuke had visited a brothel.

'Noah!' Miriam Stone gave a whimsical smile. 'Oh, yes, I remember Noah, and his mother. Rosie. Pretty little thing she was then. Gone very matronly since.' She gave a derisory grunt. 'Didn't like working here, thought she was a cut above 'rest of us.' She sat back in her chair and surveyed Harriet. 'And you thought your bairn might tek after her? She was fair; fair-haired, fair skin. Noah wasn't a handsome bairn, except for his dark eyes. Did his skin go darker?'

Harriet was pondering that she'd come to a full stop. Mr Tuke had dark hair once; she couldn't recall what colour his eyes were but didn't remember them as being remarkable. She glanced at Miriam Stone. 'Noah's skin?' she said vaguely. 'No, not especially. Didn't you – didn't you ever see him again?'

Mrs Stone shook her head. 'Never. Well, I might have passed him in 'street but I wouldn't have known him.' Her lips curled. 'He never came here. Not like Mr Tuke, his da.' She laughed again, coarsely. 'Oh aye, he was allus here. A regular, he was. His wife wouldn't have him in her bed, so he said. Not at all after their first son was born, but he badly wanted another. He was determined to have one, an obsession it was, and he asked if any of my girls'd oblige.'

She wiped her eyes. 'Oh aye, we had many a laugh about it, poor devil.' She bent down and gazed at Daniel, who stared back at her from his beautiful eyes. 'He's a right bonny bairn,' she admitted. 'Not that I've much interest in 'em, not in my line o' business. Did you say Noah was dead?' she asked suddenly.

'Yes,' Harriet murmured. 'Last Christmas. Noah and Mr Tuke both drowned in 'estuary. They've not yet been found.'

'Ah! I think I did hear summat about it a father and son drowning. Well,' she sighed. 'I suppose it don't matter too much now, cos although you might find it surprising, I never talked about 'men who used to come here. Their wives might have heard about it and stopped 'em coming!'

Mrs Tuke knew, Harriet thought, or did she guess? She also

suggested that Noah came too, but seemingly he didn't, and I'm pleased about that.

'But you're barking up 'wrong tree, I'm afraid,' Mrs Stone went on and again she laughed, a harsh grating sound which wasn't at all humorous or pleasant. 'Like I say, Tuke came regular in the hope of begetting a son. What you must understand is that my girls were not in 'way of mekkin' babbies if they could help it, but sometimes they got caught out and we had to mek, shall we say, *arrangements*. But Rosie left it too late and said she wanted to have 'bairn; then, after she'd had him, she realized that she wouldn't be able to look after him and that she couldn't stop here if she kept him. So we told Tuke it was his.' She shook her head and put her hand to her mouth to hide a grin. 'Poor Tuke. Poor feller. He was thrilled to bits. But 'bairn wasn't his. He couldn't even raise a smile, never mind owt else!'

Before she left the house, though her thoughts were whirling in confusion, Harriet managed to persuade Mrs Stone to say where Rosie was living now; at first she insisted that she didn't know, but Harriet had remembered she had said that Rosie was now very matronly and asked if she was still living in Brough.

'Don't tell her it was me that told you,' Miriam Stone urged. 'She's a married woman and won't want her husband to know what she did to earn a shilling when she was young. Not that there's owt wrong with it,' she maintained with a touch of pride. 'It's an age-old profession and fills a need.'

Harriet drove to the Haven and ate her bread and cheese as she sat by the lapping water and meditated on the news she had been given. She felt an overwhelming sense of joy and release flooding through her. Noah and Fletcher are not brothers; they don't share either a mother *or* a father. But I must be sure, and I can only be certain by speaking to Rosie.

The thought of what this information could mean made her feel hot and cold, excited and apprehensive at once. What if

Rosie won't admit the truth? And if she does, what will Fletcher make of it when I tell him? Will he believe it? And more to the point, will his mother believe it?

And, she thought worriedly, how could they prove it, if for instance Fletcher wanted her to marry him when her mourning was over? And what if he didn't really want that? Doubts and uncertainties crowded her mind. He was a man, after all. What if he was only saying these things because he knew that it was impossible? What then? Would she still have to leave Marsh Farm? Without a shadow of a doubt she knew that she would, because her position in the household would be unacceptable. She would be a stranger in the house, unrelated to anybody.

Daniel began to yell with hunger and she unfastened her blouse and started to feed him. She looked down at him and smiled; how could anyone give away a child? Poor Rosie, she thought. She must have been desperate.

When she knocked on the door of the address she'd been given a maid answered it. Harriet asked for Rosie, for she hadn't been given a surname.

The maid looked at her blankly. 'There's no Rosie here,' she said. 'This is Mrs John Gilbank's house.'

'I'm sorry. I must have 'wrong address,' Harriet began, and then hesitated as she heard a woman's voice call out, 'Who is it, Edie?'

'Would your mistress know?' Harriet asked. 'Perhaps it was a previous householder.'

'Don't think so,' she said. 'Mistress has been here for years; but just a minute and I'll ask.'

She retreated to the end of a small hall and stood in a doorway and Harriet heard the murmur of voices. Then the maid turned and went through another door as a woman dressed very plainly in a dark gown – and, as Mrs Stone had said, rather matronly – came down the hall towards her.

'Yes?' she said. 'Who is it you're looking for?'

It had to be her, Harriet thought. She was fair, though now

her hair was lightly streaked with grey, and despite the round-ness she had small hands and feet denoting a once slimmer young woman. Her anxious-looking blue eyes were taking in Harriet and, more searchingly, Daniel, who was sitting up in Harriet's arms and gazing cautiously at her.

'I'm looking for someone who used to be called Rosie,' Harriet said softly. 'I don't know her surname. I was told that she lived here. I'm not here to cause her trouble, but I need to ask her a question. One that's very important to my son, and to me,' she added pleadingly, her voice catching slightly as she considered with some emotion that this might be Daniel's grandmother.

The woman licked her lips, but Harriet could see that her eyes were moist as they strayed to Daniel once more, and as if this might have been a pre-arranged visit she opened the door wider.

'Please come in,' she said. 'I'm Rosie.'

# CHAPTER FORTY-SIX

Mrs Gilbank took Harriet through to her parlour and asked her to take a seat, then called for her maid and asked her to make tea. When it arrived she told the girl she might go and that she'd see her the following morning.

'She doesn't live in,' she explained. 'I prefer my own company.' She paused for a moment and sipped her tea from a fine china teacup.

If this is Rosie, Harriet thought as she drank her tea, then she's done very well for herself, considering her previous employment. The room was cosy, with a glowing fire, gleaming brass candlesticks and a wooden clock on the mantelpiece; the chairs were comfortable and a small round chenille-covered table stood in the window with ornaments and flowers set neatly and precisely upon it.

Mrs Gilbank asked how Harriet had found her: was it through Miriam Stone? When Harriet reluctantly admitted that it was, but that Mrs Stone had only given her Rosie's name and address because of Daniel, she sighed.

'I guessed this would happen eventually,' she remarked. 'Truth will out. In fact I've expected a visit from someone for years. But had anyone come previously,' she hesitated briefly, 'when my husband was still alive, then they might not have been totally welcome.'

'I don't understand,' Harriet said. 'How do you know who I am?'

Mrs Gilbank gazed at her. 'I don't know who you are, but I know who the child is. He's Noah's son, no doubt about it.' She gave a wistful smile. 'You don't see many dark eyes like that around here.'

Harriet hadn't realized that she had been holding her breath until she breathed out. 'Then – then you are Noah's mother?'

Rosie nodded. 'I am – was – Noah's mother.' A fleeting shadow crossed her face. 'But I heard that he'd died. Bad news travels fast, and when I learned that a father and son had drowned in 'estuary I somehow knew that it was Nathaniel Tuke and Noah.' She gave a little shrug. 'I don't know how I knew, but I did, and when I made enquiries I discovered that they'd lived further up 'river, and that 'younger man had a wife and newborn child.'

'Did you ever see him?' Harriet thought it incredible that finding Noah's mother had been so easy. Here she had been, merely a few miles away from him, all along.

'Onny once,' she murmured. 'I saw Nathaniel with a young lad in Brough, and I guessed it was Noah. I followed them up 'street for a while to be sure.'

She took another sip from her cup. 'Nathaniel didn't recognize me. He used to come to Mrs Stone's after he'd tekken 'child, but never to me; I couldn't face him knowing that we'd lied to him. Mrs Stone will have told you that Noah wasn't his? Poor man,' she said softly. 'He was sad, I think. No love given to him in his life, and I imagine he didn't give it either.'

'No,' Harriet murmured. 'He didn't. He was allus angry. Do you think he knew?'

Mrs Gilbank shook her head. 'I don't know. It's possible.'

They sat in silence for a while, the only sound the crackling of the fire and the ticking of the clock, then Harriet shifted in her seat.

'So – who was Noah's father?' she asked, and thought how impertinent it must have sounded to this modest woman.

'His name was Marco,' Mrs Gilbank said softly. 'I think he was Italian, or from a hot country, anyway. His ship had docked in Hull and some local men had brought him to Brough to stay with them for a day or two, and they came to visit Mrs Stone's. I was given him to – entertain. He was young, mebbe eighteen or nineteen, not much older than me, and he didn't speak English.' She smiled at the remembrance. 'He was lovely,' she whispered. 'Innocent. He came back on his own a few days later and asked for me.'

She bent her head. 'When he left, he said – I think somebody had taught him 'words – he said, "I come back." But of course he didn't. But that's why I wanted to keep 'child. I knew it was his. We were taught to be careful.' A smile flickered about her lips. 'But that time I wasn't.'

Again they were silent as Harriet digested the information. But then Mrs Gilbank turned to her and asked abruptly, 'So what do you want from me?'

'Want?' Harriet faltered. It hadn't occurred to her that Noah's mother would question her reason for arriving on her doorstep, but of course she'd think there was an ulterior motive. 'I don't want anything,' she stammered. 'I was onny seeking out 'truth. For my son's sake.'

'How did you know?' Mrs Gilbank asked keenly. 'Who told you that Noah wasn't Mrs Tuke's son? Nathaniel paid Miriam Stone for keeping quiet and not telling anybody; he said it was 'onny way that Mrs Tuke would accept 'bairn.'

'It was Mrs Tuke who told me,' Harriet admitted. 'But she never accepted Noah as her own, and she onny told me because I asked her if she was pleased about 'forthcoming grandchild. She said she wasn't, cos it wouldn't be her grandchild because Noah wasn't her son. He was Mr Tuke's. And,' Harriet was close to tears, 'she's wanted nowt to do wi' Daniel since 'day he was born.'

Mrs Gilbank shook her head in disbelief, and then said, 'Can I hold him?'

Harriet smiled weakly and handed Daniel to her. He grabbed the jet beads at Mrs Gilbank's neck and attempted to eat them.

'Oh.' Mrs Gilbank's eyes were awash with tears. 'Never did I think . . .' She swallowed. 'Never did I think that I'd hold Noah's own bairn in my arms.' She started to weep. 'He was my precious child, and not a day went by but I thought of him and wondered what kind of man he'd become. We, my husband and me, we didn't have any bairns of our own. If we had, mebbe 'pain would have lessened.'

She looked at Harriet. 'He died in January, not long after Noah was lost. He was a good man,' she said, wiping her eyes. 'He never knew about my past, which you might think surprising as this is such a small town. But 'customers never spoke about Mrs Stone's establishment, and I left not long after I gave Noah away and eventually nobody recognized me. I hated that place and was desperately upset about losing my child, and I took what other work I could find until by chance I met Mr Gilbank. He was a Hull man. He'd come to live in Brough after his first wife died. He was nearly twenty years older than me and I knew I'd have security wi' him. But I never told him about my former life or about Noah, for I wasn't sure how he would have felt about it.' Her gaze travelled round the room, touching on her furniture, her ornaments, all her treasured possessions. 'I kept house for him to begin with, and we became fond of each other. And I was content wi' that. Security means a lot when you've been at rock bottom, as I'd been for most of my life.'

Harriet nodded. It did. She knew that, for wasn't that why she had agreed to marry Noah?

'What was he like?' Mrs Gilbank asked, gently rocking Daniel on her knee. 'Noah. What kind of man did he become?'

Harriet hesitated for only a second. She wanted to say that he would have been a better one if Mrs Gilbank had brought him up. He would have had love in his life, which he hadn't had from Mrs Tuke, and so he had grown up feeling unwanted. But she didn't say any of it. Why would she disappoint this woman who had nurtured him in her heart for all these years?

She reached for Mrs Gilbank's hand and gently squeezed it. 'He was a fine man,' she said. 'A son to be proud of.'

As Harriet drove back to Marsh Farm her feelings were in turmoil. Mrs Gilbank – Rosie – had told her that Mr Gilbank always referred to her as Rosamund and that was the name she preferred. 'Rosie disappeared a long time ago,' she'd said.

What she also said, or at least asked, was whether Harriet would call again, for she would like to see more of Daniel. Harriet felt sad at the thought that here was a woman who had been deprived of her own child when she had had love to give, but happy that she had accepted Daniel as her grandson without question. But there was a proviso; Mrs Gilbank would not admit to anyone else that Noah was her son. 'I'm known as a respectable widow,' she told Harriet. 'I don't want to lose that esteem. I hope you understand that?'

Harriet did understand and told her that she would visit again, and also said that if she wished she could write to her care of Mrs Christopher Hart at Hart Holme Manor; but what was on her mind most of all was that although she now knew for certain that Noah and Fletcher were not related by blood, she had no proof. Rosamund Gilbank did not want anyone to know that she had given birth to an illegitimate child, and Mrs Tuke would not admit to anyone that Noah had been born in a house of ill repute. Noah and I were married legitimately in the eyes of 'church and 'law, but more to 'point, in the eyes of the world Fletcher and Noah were brothers and a woman cannot marry her husband's brother. Even Fletcher had said that they would have to live in sin.

She was within sight of the gates of the manor when she saw Fletcher sitting on a nearby fence. Her spirits lifted when she saw him wave and walk towards her, and yet she feared telling him all she had discovered.

'Where've you been?' he asked, jumping on to the cart. 'I was getting worried.'

'Were you?' she murmured. 'What are you doing up here?' She didn't answer his question and wondered why he was out on the road so close to the manor.

'I kept looking out for you,' he said, 'and then started walking. I needed to think. Where've you been?' he asked again.

'Brough,' she said. 'You knew that.'

'It doesn't take all day!'

'I know, but I thought you and your mother needed time alone and – and I sat by 'Haven for a while to eat my dinner.'

'Pull in,' he said. 'I need to talk to you.'

They sat quietly, not speaking, gazing over the Harts' meadowland above the road.

'All this belongs to Christopher Hart, did you know?' he asked.

'Yes,' she answered perfunctorily.

'And he has no sons.'

'No, he has a daughter by his first wife.' She hesitated. 'Mrs Hart is pregnant, but it's not generally known yet.'

He turned to her, his face suddenly alert. 'How do you know?'

She smiled. 'She told me.'

'Really?' He seemed surprised at that. 'Well in with her, are you?'

'No,' she said. 'But I like her. She's straightforward and direct, and although she's a lady she's not pompous and seems to treat everybody equally.'

'Huh,' he said. 'I don't know if I can believe that.'

'Fletcher, why are we sitting here discussing Mrs Hart?'

He folded his arms. 'I didn't intend to talk about Mrs Hart. It's Christopher Hart that I find interesting.'

Harriet waited. It was time for Daniel's feed. She was feeling tired and emotional after the events of the day.

302

'I think my mother's going off her head.'

'What? What are you talking about? Fletcher, talk sense! I'm tired and hungry and I want to get back.' She almost said *back home*, but increasingly she had begun to think that it wasn't, not any more, if indeed it ever had been.

He turned to look at her. 'She's told me something and in one way it frees us to marry – if you'll have me,' he added wistfully, taking her hand in his. 'But on 'other hand, she's opened up Pandora's box and a whole load o' trouble has come my way.'

'I've things to tell you too,' Harriet said. 'Perhaps I should explain first, for it's important.' She saw that he was listening and went on. 'I met Noah's real mother today. That's why I went to Brough. I'd hoped to find out about her, but I met her, and what I found out . . .' She didn't tell him that it was Miriam Stone, the madam, who had blurted out the truth about Mr Tuke, 'What I found out was that your da was not Noah's father; someone else was. You're not even half-brothers. You're not related at all!'

Fletcher sat as still as stone, looking into the distance. Then he put his head back and began to laugh, but it was laughter without mirth, and he quickly sobered up. 'Poor old Da. Poor old devil. To be cuckolded once is bad enough, but twice!'

'What do you mean? You're not mekkin' sense.' She shook his hand off. 'Tell me what you mean.'

He covered his face with his hands and pressed his fingers hard against his forehead.

'I mean,' he said slowly, lowering his hands and facing her, 'that Ma has told me that *I'm* not Da's son either, that Christopher Hart is my father. And that's why I say she's gone off her head, for she's saying that I must tell him, and if I don't then she will, so that he knows that I'm his son and heir.'

# CHAPTER FORTY-SEVEN

'Oh,' Harriet gasped. 'Surely not! Can that be true? She told me— But mebbe that's why – that's another reason she's allus made so much more of you than she did of Noah. But . . .' Her lips parted as she thought of Melissa Hart, pregnant at last after waiting so long. 'You can't tell them. His wife's expecting a child.'

'I don't intend to,' he said slowly, 'because I'm not sure if I believe her, and how can I accuse him, a man in his position? And what proof is there?'

Ellen has told so many lies, Harriet reasoned, how can we believe anything she says? She told me that Mr Tuke had seduced her and made her pregnant. She said he'd threatened to turn her out of 'farm if she didn't treat Noah as her own, and yet I discovered that 'tenancy is in her name; even Fletcher doesn't know that. She's blamed Mr Tuke for so many things, and she told me that Noah would be going to 'brothel when I was pregnant and now I know that's not true, not that it matters now.

'What will you do?' she asked. 'You must stop her from going to see 'Harts herself and causing trouble.'

'How do I stop her – and what if it is true?' he said angrily. 'What then? I want nothing from him. And if it is true and he doesn't know, why has she waited till now to tell me – and him?'

'Because your da is dead,' she said softly. 'Your ma can say anything she wants and there's nobody to question it. She told me,' Harriet hesitated and her voice dropped even further, 'she told me, when I was expecting Daniel, that Mr Tuke had seduced her and made her pregnant and that's why they got married.'

Fletcher heaved a breath. 'What a mess!' He clutched her hand. 'But it meks no difference to you and me, Harriet, not with what you've found out from Noah's real mother. We're free to marry once you are out of mourning. You will marry me, Harriet? Please. Say that you will.'

She wanted to say yes. Desperately she wanted to say yes. Yet she hesitated. She leaned her head against him. 'I do love you, Fletcher,' she murmured. 'But we have obstacles in our way. How do we prove that we're free to marry? Your mother married Nathaniel Tuke and gave birth to a son, *you*, in his name. In 'church register it's recorded that I married your brother, Noah Tuke. In 'eyes of 'world you are my husband's brother.'

He listened to what she was saying, and then said, 'I've never seen my birth certificate and I don't know if my birth was registered. Mebbe it wasn't. When I went to America I asked Ma if I could have it, just for proof of who I was, you know, but she said she couldn't remember where it was.'

Harriet sat and thought over their options and came to the conclusion that at the moment the problems were insurmountable. They needed time to decide what was the best thing to do.

'We mustn't rush into summat we might regret,' she murmured. 'This is a small community. News would spread, rumours would gather and we'd be ostracized.'

'I wouldn't care about that,' he muttered. 'I just want us to be together.'

Harriet shook her head. 'We can't live in isolation. We'd have to think about 'bairns we might have; whatever we did would reflect on them too. No, we must tek this carefully. First think about all 'possibilities and then decide.'

\*

Fletcher wasn't entirely happy about her suggestion but finally agreed that she was right. Gradually, too, he saw for himself how his mother was pushing Harriet out and making her feel unwanted: just little things at first, such as collecting the eggs herself rather than letting Harriet do it; telling Harriet there was no need for her to help with the milking because she could manage alone now there was only one cow; not allowing Harriet to cook or bake, for 'I've allus done it myself; why would I need anybody else to do it?'

'I'm totally spare,' Harriet whispered to Fletcher on one of the few occasions when they were alone. 'And I'm going to do summat about it.'

The following washday at the manor, when she and Mary were taking a rest from the laundry, she put her question.

'Mary.' She spoke clearly. 'Have you ever thought of taking a lodger? Would you have room?'

Mary looked across at her. 'Why, m'dear! Is it you you're thinking of? Are you not happy wi' Mrs Tuke? Or is it your husband's brother that's 'problem?'

'Oh, no,' she said hastily. 'Fletcher isn't a problem at all, quite 'opposite, he can see what's going on.' She decided to confide. 'I think that Mrs Tuke wants him to herself now that he's home again, and – and she sees me as a threat. And she won't let me help in 'house or on 'farm. I feel useless.'

'Yes, I see.' Mary rubbed at her cheek. 'You'd think that Ellen Tuke'd welcome another woman's company, especially when it's a daughter-in-law.' There was a glint in her eyes as she surveyed Harriet. 'And especially wi' a grandson.'

She knows, Harriet thought; or suspects that something's not quite what it seems. She's very shrewd.

'So would it be for long?' Mary asked. 'I haven't a great deal o' space, as you'll have seen, but,' she kept her gaze focused on Harriet, 'if it's just a temporary difficulty, you can stay wi' me until you've made up your mind what else to do.'

'Oh, Mary! Thank you. Thank you so much. Would you –

would you even consider looking after Daniel sometimes and I'll do your work here at 'manor? And pay you, of course.'

'Oh my, but I would, gladly.' Mary's face lit up in a huge beam. 'Until he's walking, which won't be yet awhile, and I'd keep my eyes on him all 'time, you needn't fear that I wouldn't because of my being hard o' hearing. When would you like to come?'

Fletcher was furious when Harriet told him she was going to live with Mary. 'There's no need for this,' he protested. 'I'll talk to my mother.'

'I don't want you to,' Harriet said stubbornly. 'I'll tell her myself, and you'll see her reaction. I'm going to do it, Fletcher. We'll both have 'chance of thinking over what we want to do.'

'I know what I want,' he asserted. 'I want to be wi' you for ever, and I thought you wanted 'same.'

'I do,' she murmured and touched his cheek with her fingers but dropped her hand as she heard the back door open. 'But right now we can't have what we want.'

Ellen came into the kitchen. She looked from one to the other and frowned. 'What? What's happened?'

'I was just telling Fletcher that I'm moving on. I'm tekkin' lodgings elsewhere.' Harriet read the swift look of triumph on Ellen's face and was sure that Fletcher must have seen it too.

'Well, if you must,' Ellen said in a moderate voice, which to Harriet sounded like an attempt to hide her delight. 'You must do what you think best. And as I've said before, it's not healthy having an unmarried man and a young widow living under 'same roof.'

'Ma—' Fletcher began.

Harriet was sure that Fletcher was about to object, and interrupted. 'You're quite right,' she answered in the same tone. 'Just what I've been thinking, and I was explaining to Fletcher that I was sure you wouldn't feel hurt or offended, as he thought you might be.'

307

'No, no,' Ellen said. 'Of course not. Where will you go? Back to Hull, I suppose?'

'Oh, no. I love it out here in 'country and being by 'estuary. I'm going to lodge wi' Mary and keep on working at 'manor; she'll help me wi' Daniel.' She gave a chuckle. 'There'll be plenty o' washing and ironing to do when 'mistress is delivered of her babby.'

The look of victory was wiped off Ellen's face. The change in her was palpable and she clutched the back of a chair.

'Are you unwell, Ma?' Fletcher took her arm to help her sit down. 'What is it? You're as white as a sheet.'

Ellen brushed him away. 'Nothing. Get off, it's nowt.' But it was, for she put her hand to her throat as her breathing quickened. Harriet brought her a cup of water, which she took and sipped. She handed it back and asked croakily, 'When? When does she expect a bairn? How do you know?'

'She told me herself,' Harriet answered. 'I don't know when it's due, but I do know that she and Mr Hart are delighted. Such good news, isn't it?'

Fletcher took her to Mary's the next day. She didn't have many belongings to pack, having arrived at Marsh Farm with virtually nothing. Ellen stood at the door to wave them off.

Harriet gave a wry grimace as they drove up the track. 'Your ma's mekkin' sure that I'm on my way,' she said sourly. 'Though I'm surprised she's agreed that you can tek me.'

'Don't be like that, Harriet,' he muttered. 'It's not like you.'

'I know,' she agreed, 'and I'm sorry, but I see now how one person can influence another.' She turned to him and added, 'I hope she doesn't change you, Fletcher. When Noah was a buffer between you she could put all of her anger on to him.' She sighed. 'Who knows what she might do now.'

'You're speaking of my mother, don't forget,' Fletcher said, his voice full of misery.

Harriet put her hand over his. 'I'm sorry,' she said again. 'This seems like our first disagreement.'

Mary was at the cottage door to greet them and for Harriet it was exhilarating to be welcomed so warmly.

'Come along in,' she said. 'You'll stop for a cup o' tea, young man?'

'Thanks, I will,' Fletcher said, though his forehead creased at the unaccustomed offer of hospitality.

Harriet smiled. Now he'll see how normal people behave, she thought, when there's no hidden suspicion or distrust.

'I remember you when you were a little lad,' Mary told him as she busied herself with the kettle. 'And mebbe you won't know this, but I delivered you.'

Fletcher laughed. 'I didn't know that!'

'Oh aye,' Mary chuckled. 'You were a bonny bairn, but then they all are. You didn't have much hair, not like this bairn.' She nodded fondly towards Daniel. 'He's going to break some hearts, if I'm not mistaken.'

'And what about Noah?' Fletcher glanced swiftly at Harriet. 'He'd have been much darker, was he?'

Mary didn't answer immediately, but put the teapot on the table and reached to get crockery down from a cupboard.

'Erm – I didn't deliver him,' she prevaricated. 'I think I onny saw him a couple o' times when you were bairns playing wi' our Tom out in 'meadow. But funny, isn't it,' she said, concentrating on cutting into a fruit cake, 'how brothers and sisters can differ in colouring? Summat from way back, I expect.'

When Fletcher had finished his tea, Harriet walked back to the cart with him, leaving Daniel with Mary. The old mare was cropping the grass on the verge.

'She's very discreet, isn't she?' Fletcher said. 'She knows summat, but she's not telling.'

'Yes,' Harriet agreed. 'She told me once that she didn't know about Noah's existence until somebody told her your ma had had another son.'

Fletcher nodded and gazed across at the estuary, a soft muddy brown today with creamy heads on slow-moving

309

troughs. It was open here, with few trees; Mary's cottage was set within a small garden and had a paddock overlooking the sandbanks. He breathed deeply. 'I recall coming here now. A gang of us lads coming with Tom to visit his auntie Mary and allus getting cake and lemonade.' He leaned towards Harriet and kissed her cheek. 'Don't get too comfortable, will you, Harriet? I want you back in my life.'

# CHAPTER FORTY-EIGHT

Although Harriet was more relaxed in the comforting atmosphere of Mary's house she was nevertheless sad. Fletcher was at home with his mother, and although he had come regularly to visit her when she had first left the farm, he had not been near for over a week. Perhaps, she mused, he's having second thoughts about wanting to be with me; Ellen's influence might be stronger than he imagined.

She and Mary were sitting by the fire. Daniel was asleep in a cot that Mary had fashioned from a large wicker basket and lined with a soft wool blanket, Mary was knitting and Harriet was gazing into the fire, busy with her thoughts.

'You know m'dear,' Mary murmured, 'life's too short to waste, and if, like me, you think it's 'onny life we get – although,' she added hastily, 'you might believe that 'good Lord has other ideas for us – mebbe you should think on doing things to change it.'

Harriet gazed vaguely at her. 'Change it? Change my life, do you mean? How?'

'That's summat you'd have to fathom out for yourself.' Mary counted her stitches and started another line of knitting. 'I never married, as you'll have gathered. But that's not because I wasn't asked; oh, no, indeed I was. I had a young man once and he was very keen on marrying me, but my father was dead set against him – as indeed, I came to realize later, he would've

311

been against any other man who might have been interested in me. My mother was dead, you see, and I was 'onny daughter left at home to look after 'house, and of course my da didn't want to lose me. So I refused my young man and he married another. I've not been unhappy – I like my little house, but it was when I came to help other young women to birth their bairns that I thought of what I was missing. My father lived to be very old, and by then it was too late to change my life and much too late to have children of my own.'

She folded her knitting on her knee and looked across at Harriet. 'So what I'm saying is, don't leave it too late. You'll soon be out of mourning and you're too young to stay in widows' weeds for ever. Tek a chance on finding some happiness afore it's too late. Otherwise, one day, when your son is grown, he'll leave you for another and you'll be alone. Best to find love wi' somebody else.' She smiled, picking up the knitting again. 'An' I reckon there's somebody waiting for you.'

Harriet thought of Ellen, who would be alone if Fletcher left; was that what he was thinking too? A mother's bond was strong; but she also thought she would never hold Daniel back if he wanted to test the world for himself. Her own mother hadn't: she had wished Leonard Godspeed as he set off on his travels, never to return.

'There is someone,' she murmured, keeping her face towards Mary so that she could read her lips. 'But there are obstacles in our path.'

Mary nodded. 'I know,' she said. 'But sometimes obstacles are there for a reason, a sort of test,' she suggested. 'Like a gate or a fence to be jumped over, but oft times you'll find that 'gate has a sneck to be lifted and 'fence has a stile, and it isn't so difficult after all.' She raised her grey, bushy eyebrows. 'I'm sure that you'll both find a way if you think on it.'

Harriet cast her an enquiring glance. 'Meaning?'

'I saw you out of 'window that day you saw him off. He's fond o' you, that young man. It's not allus possible to hide your feelings, not when you're young, at any rate. Sometimes older people can hide all sorts o' things, especially if they've had a lifetime to practise.'

'I don't understand,' Harriet leaned towards her. 'Who do you mean?'

'I mean that Ellen Tuke hasn't allus told 'truth, but that's none o' my business.' Mary looked down and continued knitting. 'But it might be yours and her son's.'

'Mary, look at me.' Harriet lifted Mary's chin so that she was gazing straight at her. 'What do you know about Ellen Tuke? I've discovered things which I believe no one else knows about, but what can I do?'

'Without proof,' Mary agreed. 'Aye, I know that too. But a lot of them that knew her think that your late husband Noah, Ellen's second son, was not hers but born to another woman.'

Fletcher had to get away from Marsh Farm. His mother was getting more vocal every day, constantly and vehemently urging him to go to Hart Holme Manor and confront Christopher Hart, and never mind that his wife was expecting a child.

'Why should he believe you?' He'd actually shouted at her, for the first time in his life. He'd been cruel, he admitted to himself as he marched along the top road, recalling what he'd said. 'I dare say that men like him are constantly being accused of fathering their servant girls' children,' and he'd seen her flinch.

And mebbe it was true, he thought. It must have been tempting for a young man of means to have these young girls so close, and maybe willing too. But she hadn't said that he'd taken advantage of her: she'd said that she loved him and he'd loved her; she'd wanted his child and assumed that he would take care of her, until she'd heard in the kitchen that his parents were looking for a bride for him.

'So poor old Da,' he'd accused her. 'You tricked him.'

'What if I did?' she'd answered coldly. 'He got this farm, didn't he? He'd never've made owt of himself without me.'

Fletcher was so disgusted that he turned about and charged

313

out of the house, and was now heading in the direction of the manor. I have to do summat about this situation, he raged. If Harriet will agree, we'll go back to America where no one knows us. We have 'same name. We can be man and wife.

It was ten thirty and Christopher Hart was drinking a second cup of coffee at Melissa's bedside whilst she ate her break-fast. Melissa had been advised by her doctor to stay in bed of a morning, now that her time of giving birth was getting closer. He had also told her to take a walk outside only if the weather was clement enough, so that she didn't catch a chill. She chafed against his advice; she felt well and healthy, but she was so very large that Christopher now always slept in his own bedroom.

'I shall get up shortly,' she told him, 'and take a walk round the garden this afternoon. I need the exercise. Harriet Tuke worked up to the last minute, and I'm—' She was going to say *as fit as her*, but Christopher interrupted.

'She's a working woman,' he said. 'Much stronger than you are. You do nothing more than admire your roses.'

'I prune and deadhead them too,' she said. 'You didn't know that, did you? I'm stronger than you all think. Old – what's his name, the gardener – Parrish – he almost had apoplexy when he saw me!'

'I know that you are strong, my darling,' he said soothingly. 'But you must be careful. Childbirth is not to be taken lightly, and I don't want anything to happen to you.' Although he wouldn't have dreamed of telling her, he was terrified of losing her. 'I was thinking,' he went on, determined to change the subject, 'and your mention of Harriet Tuke has reminded me . . . Does she still work here, by the way?'

'She does.' She smiled. 'Have you not noticed your beauti-fully ironed shirts?'

'Ah, yes! Well, I was wondering about Marsh Farm and what to do about it now that Ellen Tuke and Harriet are alone there.' He saw that Melissa was about to say something, but he continued anyway. 'It's too large for them to farm it on their own, and the house would be better suited to a family, but on the other hand, the land is so wet that I've spoken to Thomson about the possibility of warping – land reclamation. It would take some years for it to be good growing land, but it would work. They've done it at Broomfleet, and with very good results at the eastern end of the Humber, Sunk Island in particular.'

Melissa raised her eyebrows. Christopher didn't as a rule discuss farming with her before he made a decision, although he quite often told her what had been decided.

'And your reason for telling me this is?'

'Because you talk to Harriet Tuke.' He seemed a trifle apprehensive, Melissa thought curiously. 'I wondered if she might have any thoughts on it if I told them I was considering moving them elsewhere.'

'If you decide to do what you suggest,' she answered pragmatically, 'of course you must tell them that that is what you are going to do. It's your land and you must do whatever you think fit with it. I think it would be very generous of you to offer them other accommodation. However,' she took a tiny bite of toast, 'from what I understand from my spies, the elder son has returned and Harriet has taken lodgings elsewhere.'

It was almost midday and Christopher was in his study. Thomson had been in and again they had discussed Marsh Farm and the possibility of warping. Christopher mentioned that he'd heard that the elder son had returned.

'Yes, I'd heard that too,' Thomson had said. 'Apparently he came back a few weeks ago after he'd had news of the death of his father and brother. It's possible that he might want to stay on. He was always the one with ideas. I recall him mentioning land reclamation some years ago.'

'I see,' Christopher had said thoughtfully. 'Well, we must give it further thought. He wouldn't make much of a living whilst we were working on it, would he?'

He had his head bent over farm tenancy agreements when one of the maids knocked on his open door. 'I'm sorry to bother you, sir.' She dipped her knee. 'Fletcher Tuke is at 'back door, asking to speak to you with regard to a tenancy. I said he should talk to Mr Thomson, but he's gone and Mr Tuke says he needs to speak to you urgently.'

Christopher frowned. Drat! I seem to have been forestalled. I haven't yet made a decision, but still . . . I'll have to discuss it with him eventually. He cleared his throat. 'Show him through, will you?'

'In here, sir?'

'Yes,' he said abruptly. 'In here.'

Fletcher was astonished to be invited in: he had assumed that, like last time, Hart would come out to the yard to speak to him. Instead he was ushered through the kitchen, where there was a good smell of roast beef, up the back stairs, across a wide hall and towards the open door of a room where Christopher Hart was sitting at a desk.

Christopher looked up as the young maid knocked. Fletcher touched his forehead. 'I'm sorry to disturb you, sir, if it's inconvenient. I'd lost track of time and didn't realize it was so near to dinner time.' He gave a sudden grin. 'It was 'smell of roast beef that reminded me.'

'Goodness. Is it?' Christopher glanced at the clock on the wall. 'No, not yet. We eat at one. Do sit down. I'm behind with the time too. I hadn't realized you'd come home until this morning; oddly enough I'd been discussing Marsh Farm with my bailiff and, erm, he told me of your return. I'm so very sorry about your father and brother,' he added. 'A dreadful business; you must have been very shocked when you heard?'

'I was,' Fletcher admitted. 'But I didn't hear 'news immediately or I would have returned straight away. A friend wrote with commiserations,' he said, rather bitterly, Christopher thought. 'My mother, for reasons best known to herself, chose not to tell me.'

'Really?' Christopher was astounded, but after a moment he said, 'I think she – quite naturally, of course – was not at all herself after it happened, was very shocked and unnerved. My wife and I commented on it, and your brother's wife took to her bed; we asked the parson to visit her to baptize the child.' He recalled too that Melissa had said that she thought Ellen Tuke was a very cold fish.

'That was kind of you, sir, very much appreciated.' Fletcher glanced unobtrusively at Christopher Hart to discover any resemblance to himself, but found none. They were both tall and fair-haired, but that was the only similarity as far as he could tell. He gave a quiet sigh. His mother was lying.

Christopher brushed away his thanks and continued, 'As I mentioned, I have been discussing Marsh Farm with Thomson. We've given some thought to flooding the bottom field to increase the acreage; it will be expensive, involving having to build sluices and drains and so on, as you know, to keep the sediment in, but I think it will pay off eventually and make good growing land. I'd considered offering your mother and her daughter-in-law a tenancy elsewhere, somewhere they could manage more easily, but then I discovered that you were back.' He hesitated, Melissa's additional information in mind, but decided not to mention it. 'Which slightly changes things, although I must tell you that that is what I have decided to do.'

Fletcher heaved out a breath of deliverance. He'd arrived at the manor anxious and tense and with no clear idea of what he was going to say; he certainly wasn't going to confront Christopher Hart with a question about his own paternity, no matter what his mother said. But now he knew what was important to him.

'Warping is something I've thought about for years, sir, though in practice I knew we could never afford it. But what I came to say was that I won't be staying on at Marsh Farm. My brother's widow has already moved out and tekken other lodgings; two women in 'same house . . .' He shook his head and grimaced. 'Not a good combination. But Ma can't stay on 'farm on her own, it's far too big, and I came to ask if you've a cottage that she could rent.'

Christopher too felt a release of concern; Ellen Tuke's whispered words when he had called to see her after the tragedy had disturbed him more than he might have admitted. He leaned towards Fletcher. 'I think I have the very place.'

Melissa came slowly down the stairs. Pausing by the newel post, she saw through the open door of the study that Christopher was talking confidentially to someone. They turned and looked towards her, suddenly aware of her presence, and both stood up.

She gripped the post more firmly. She saw their similar height and build, their hair the same colour and texture except that Christopher's was streaked with grey, their open honest faces and wide smiling mouths, and she began to tremble.

# CHAPTER FORTY-NINE

Melissa waited until luncheon before bringing up the subject of Fletcher Tuke. She had only seen his back that day last year as he'd walked down the drive next to Harriet, but today she had known instantly who he was, and was extremely disturbed. Christopher hasn't told me everything about Ellen Tuke, she thought as she sat in the sitting room waiting for the luncheon bell. I suppose that young men are expected to sow their wild oats, which I think is extremely unfair, for if society women should do so they would be considered slatternly and vulgar, and ostracized by their peers and family.

But women like Ellen, what of them? Was she willing? Surely Christopher wouldn't have forced her. He is the kindest, most gentle man, but now I wonder if I really know him. What worried her most of all was why Ellen Tuke's son might have come here. Was he a potential threat to her unborn child?

When they had finished dessert and were sitting drinking coffee, Melissa casually asked, 'Who was that who called this morning?'

'Mmm? When?' Christopher seemed vague. 'Did someone call? Oh, you mean young Tuke? That was a coincidence, wasn't it, when we'd been talking about Marsh Farm? I'd been discussing it with Thomson, too.'

He lifted the pot to offer Melissa more coffee but she shook her head and he poured himself another cup. 'Strange business,' he said. 'It seems that he's only recently returned from America; his mother hadn't told him about his father and brother being drowned. He learned the news from someone else.'

'I said she was odd,' Melissa muttered. 'Any normal woman would have wanted her other son to be with her, unless of course her daughter-in-law was a comfort to her.'

'No,' Christopher said. 'Seemingly that's why she's moved out. They don't get on.'

Melissa pressed her lips together; she wasn't interested in the minutiae of Ellen Tuke's life, only in the plans of her son. 'So why did he come to see you?' She watched Christopher's expression closely for signs of guilt or anxiety, but there were none as he replied.

'Hah! He's saved me a good deal of bother. He came to tell me he wouldn't be staying on at Marsh Farm and wouldn't want the tenancy. He wanted to ask if I would accommodate his mother in another cottage when he moves out. And there's another odd thing.' Christopher put down his cup. 'He didn't know that the tenancy was in his mother's name. He'd always assumed it was in his father's.'

Melissa gave a small sigh; perhaps it was going to be all right after all.

'He seemed like a good sort,' Christopher commented. 'Honest and reliable, the kind of man you could trust. I wouldn't mind him working here, maybe as bailiff if ever Thomson moved on. Anyway, he asked if I would give his mother the news about Marsh Farm. He seemed to think she would take it better from me than from him, and he's yet to tell her that he's moving out.' He paused, and then stood up. 'I got the feeling that he has other plans which don't include her.' He bent to kiss her forehead. 'Must go. Don't overdo things, my darling. You look a little pale.'

'It's because I've been in bed all morning,' she said crossly. 'That's why I'm pale!'

When he had gone, she put on a warm cape to cover her,

for it was a cold though sunny day, and walked into her garden. She had been delighted with her roses, the perfume from them suffusing the air, and although the flowers were almost finished some of them clung on and she stooped to admire their velvety petals and rich jewel colours. I must ask the gardener to bring a seat here for next spring, she thought, so that I may sit and enjoy them; and she thought too that she wouldn't be alone, but would have a child and a nursemaid with her. There would also be guests, for Amy was to be married in May and the reception would be held at the manor.

She heard the crunch of gravel and looked up to see Harriet walking away from the servants' entrance towards the drive. Melissa called to her.

Harriet looked up and came towards her. 'Ma'am.' She dipped her knee as she approached.

'No baby with you today?'

'No, ma'am. Mary's looking after him. We've, erm, made an arrangement. I'm – I'm staying with her at present.'

'I see.' Melissa knew this already, but not from Harriet's lips. 'Do come over here,' she said. 'We can't have a conversation when we're twelve feet apart. Or are you in a hurry to be off?'

'No, ma'am.' Harriet stepped on to the grass and came towards her. 'I know he's well looked after while Mary has him.'

Melissa frowned, nonplussed. 'Mary? But what about feeding him? Or does he take a bottle?'

Harriet flushed slightly. 'I feed him afore I leave and Mary has a bottle o' goat's milk to last him till I get back.'

'Oh,' Melissa said thoughtfully. 'That's how it's done.' She lifted her shoulders. 'I've read in books about all the different ways to manage, but it's still rather a mystery to me.'

'Perhaps you should talk to Mary,' Harriet suggested. 'She's a midwife as well as a washerwoman. She delivered Daniel.'

Melissa thought that she wouldn't be expected to feed her child herself, but would perhaps employ a wet nurse. 'Did she?

Well, perhaps I might,' she said, adding, 'She wouldn't think I was terribly ignorant, would she?'

Harriet smiled. 'No, ma'am. She's very kind; and we're all inexperienced wi' our first babby. Ma'am,' she said quickly. 'Could I speak confidentially?'

'Now?' Melissa was startled and somewhat apprehensive. 'It's nothing personal, is it? I wouldn't want . . .' What if she wants to discuss the question of her brother-in-law's origins, she thought uneasily. What could I say?

'It's about my husband's parentage, ma'am. I need some advice.'

Melissa was confused. Her husband's parentage? Not her brother-in-law's? What a very strange family the Tukes were, so much mystery.

'Come on to the terrace,' she suggested. 'We can sit and speak privately there. I must definitely ask the gardener to bring a seat down here,' she murmured.

Harriet recounted as succinctly as possible her discovery of Noah's birth mother and what she had been told about his real father, although she did not mention where he was born. 'So Noah wasn't the child of either Mr or Mrs Tuke,' she explained, 'which means that Fletcher and I could marry eventually, which is what we both want. The difficulty is, we've no proof that Noah and Fletcher are not brothers, because Noah's real mother told me she won't admit her story to anyone else; she was very young, you see, ma'am, and he was born out of wedlock, and although she's now widowed she doesn't want to lose her respectability.'

'Of course not,' Melissa murmured. 'Poor dear. But would Mrs Tuke not say? She adopted him and brought him up as their own, which was a very honourable thing to do for the child. She needn't say who the parents were.'

Harriet sighed. 'It's not so simple . . .'

Before she left, Harriet told Melissa that she hoped that she didn't mind that she had given her name in confidence to Noah's real mother so that if she should change her mind

322

about disclosing Noah's true background, she could write to Harriet at the manor. 'I don't want any correspondence going to Mrs Tuke,' she explained.

Melissa nodded. 'You don't trust her? Have you thought that you and Fletcher could leave the district and live together anyway?' she said. 'Or does that shock you? You would have the same name, no one would know.'

'That's what Fletcher said. But I have to think of Daniel. What would I tell him when he asked about his family? Do I lie and tell him that 'Tukes are his grandparents? And then what would he think of us? Of Fletcher and me?'

'Indeed,' Melissa said quietly. 'What indeed?'

Christopher was on his way to tell Ellen of his decision to offer her the tenancy of another cottage. He went over and over in his mind how to break the news that she would have to leave Marsh Farm. Whatever I say, she's not going to like it, he thought. She can be outspoken when she wants to be; Ellen's not the quiet shy person she seems. He recalled the days when they were young and used to meet secretly. It was always her idea, he remembered. She was the one who came up with a time and place where they wouldn't be seen, and he was the one who was nervous of being found out. Mrs Marshall too played a part, covering for Ellen if ever they were late back.

That was one of the reasons why he took care of the old lady, in case at some time she might let slip how he and Ellen used to meet. Not that there was anything really serious, he thought, remembering how sensible Ellen had been when she heard that his parents were inviting eligible young women to meet him. Still, it was a shock when she told him that she had decided to marry Nathaniel Tuke, although in a way it was quite a timely relief. She was becoming a little too passionate, he recalled, which was difficult for a young man, especially one in his position.

The thought that he might have had an ardent liaison with a servant girl would never have entered his first wife's head, but Melissa, well, she was totally different. That's why he had been so attracted to her; she was so much more worldly. She would have smelt a rat immediately, and dealt with it.

He hoped that Fletcher Tuke would be at home, but he wasn't. As he entered the cottage, Ellen greeted him effusively.

'I'm so pleased to see you, Christopher,' she said. 'I don't see you often enough.'

'Well,' he said, embarrassed, 'I don't have a great deal of time. The estate . . .'

'I know,' she sympathized. 'You do far too much, I'm sure. Would you like tea? And cake? I haven't lost my touch at baking.'

'I'm sure you haven't, but I mustn't stay long. Ellen . . .' He paused. 'I've come to tell you something.' He saw her eyes light up and she put her fingers to her chin. 'It's about Marsh Farm. I won't be renewing your tenancy agreement in November. The property is too big for you now, and I've decided to offer you another cottage instead. At a peppercorn rent.'

'But . . .' She stared at him. 'Fletcher can work it. It's not too big for him.'

'I have other plans for the land,' he explained. 'I'm going to start warping the bottom field, which means they'll be digging drains and building sluices; the land can't be farmed whilst that's going on.'

'But that's what Fletcher wants to do,' she insisted, her voice rising. 'He's allus said that that's what he'd do if 'land was his.'

'But it's not his, nor does he have the tenancy,' he said gently. 'It's in your name, Ellen. It always has been, as you know, and I'm sorry but I won't be renewing it.'

'You're pushing me out!' Her eyes flared and a flush reddened her thin cheeks. 'You can't. A cottage! I need space for hens and a cow. And then there's Fletcher to think of.'

'I can,' he said patiently. 'And you don't need more than a few hens. The cottage is nearer to Brough. You'll know it; old Mrs Hall used to live in it. There's room for a goat,' he added, and wondered why he was even discussing it. 'Do you want it or not?'

'I don't know,' she said stubbornly. 'I'll have to speak to Fletcher.' She glared at him as she spoke and nodded significantly. 'I'll see what he wants to do.'

And as Christopher spoke again, no sooner were the words out of his mouth than he regretted them. 'Well, perhaps I'm wrong, but I understood from what Fletcher said that he had other plans. He told me that he didn't want Marsh Farm.'

'What?' she whispered.

There was no going back. 'He, erm, he thought that the tenancy was in your husband's name and was under the impression it would come to him if he wanted it. He was surprised to hear that it was in yours.' Christopher stood up to leave. 'There's plenty of time for you to think about the cottage. It's very cosy, and not so close to the estuary. I'll keep it for you until Martinmas. But I've nothing else to offer you, Ellen,' he added. 'So think seriously about it, won't you?'

# CHAPTER FIFTY

Ellen stewed for a week over Christopher Hart's news and hardly spoke to Fletcher. She didn't want to hear from his own lips that he wasn't staying at Marsh Farm; neither did she want to hear that he might be considering a life with Harriet. Not that she thought of her by name, but only as that woman who had married Noah. Least of all did she want to be shuffled off to the small cottage where Mrs Hall had lived.

Then, in a sudden fit of pique she got dressed in her out-door clothes, put the old horse in the cart and didn't answer Fletcher when he asked where she was going.

'Nowhere that concerns you,' she said sharply. She climbed into the cart, cracked the reins and left, leaving him baffled and staring after her from the door.

She headed towards Brough Haven and Mrs Marshall; she wanted to chew over the position she found herself in with her old friend, but also wondered what she would have to say about the long absence since her last visit. She'll understand, I expect. She'll think of how upset I've been after being widowed so suddenly. She'll know how my life's been turned upside down.

But she wasn't expecting to find the door closed when it was usually open, or to find her old friend sitting by a low fire instead of bustling about in her usual manner.

'Whatever's happened, Mrs Marshall? Are you sick?'

Mrs Marshall's head was at a funny sideways angle but she managed to nod. 'Had a funny turn,' she mumbled. 'I was hoping somebody'd come. Managed to keep 'fire in, but it's burning dull.'

Ellen put down her basket and took off her coat, and then went outside to bring in some wood. 'Soon have a blaze going,' she said. 'Would you like a cuppa tea?' She bent towards her old friend and spoke loudly. 'Good thing I brought some provisions; eggs and a fruit cake. Is there any milk?'

'No,' Mrs Marshall answered slowly, as if she had to think about it. 'Somebody knocked yesterday – I thought it might be wi' milk, but they didn't hear me shout – and went away again.'

Ellen Tuke stood back and considered. It was strange, she thought, how life could hit you hard, but then gave you an unexpected lift. She made weak tea, as there was no milk, and poured a cup for each of them, and when she saw that Mrs Marshall was having difficulty holding the cup with one hand she held it for her as she sipped. Then she broke off a small piece of cake and fed it into her open mouth.

'What I'm going to do, Mrs Marshall,' she told her, 'I'm going to mek you comfortable for today, then I'm going home, and tomorrow I'll bring some more food, milk 'n' that, and a mattress from 'spare bed, an' I'm going to stop here until you're on your feet again. How does that sound?'

Mrs Marshall emitted a small sigh. 'You was allus a good lass, Ellen,' she mumbled. 'And it allus seemed – that I was 'onny one who ever knew it.'

Fletcher had his second argument with his mother when she announced that she was going to stay with Mrs Marshall the following day and didn't know when she would be back; she also said that she would be taking the horse and cart, a mattress and several other things with her.

'I'll drive you,' he said. 'I'll need Jinny and 'cart. In any case, you can't keep 'hoss there. There's no stabling, is there?'

'She'll be all right,' his mother insisted. 'I'll put her in 'back garden.'

'She won't,' Fletcher said adamantly. 'She's an old hoss; she likes her comforts.'

'She's ready for 'knacker's yard,' his mother countered.

'I'll tek you,' Fletcher raised his voice, 'and that's 'end of it.'

He was curious as to why his mother was insisting that she would stay with Mrs Marshall until she was better, but on entering the cottage the next morning he realized why. It was a neat, warm place with a woodpile stacked at the side of the house, a vegetable patch, and a water pump and privy in the back garden. She's going to settle in, he thought as he turned for home. She won't ever leave and she'll think she's had 'last word, not only over me but over Christopher Hart too, and if he objects to her being there she can spread the rumour that he ousted her from Marsh Farm. He bit his lips anxiously. But whether she'll ever tell that she gave birth to his child, if it is the truth, is another matter altogether.

Despondency crept over him as he drove back, and he didn't take much notice of people hurrying towards the Haven. He only thought of the jobs he must do. He'd have to sell off the remaining farm stock, and clear the obsolete machinery out of the sheds and barn. He'd a few weeks yet before the end of the tenancy agreement, and Tom Bolton had made an appealing suggestion that he was thinking over very seriously; in the meantime he and Harriet had to make a decision about their future. Should they leave the district or brazen out the gossip that would ensue if they simply lived together?

Harriet hadn't said much about that, but his view was that she wasn't very happy about it. We haven't really talked it through, he thought. Mebbe it's too soon. It's not a year yet since Noah died. Is that it? Is that why she's reluctant to mek a decision? Or is she having second thoughts about marrying me? Has she changed her mind?

\*

328

Melissa called Mary into her bedroom for a talk. 'Harriet Tuke suggested I discuss my condition with you,' she began, remembering Harriet's advice to face Mary when speaking. 'My doctor says very little, and also he lives in Brough, which is rather a long way if I should need him urgently.'

'There's generally plenty o' time, ma'am, especially wi' a first pregnancy,' Mary told her. 'But I understand it's not easy to discuss women's concerns wi' a man.' She clasped her hands in front of her ample body and smiled gently. 'So is something bothering you, ma'am?'

'Well, it's just that I don't know what to expect!' Melissa said petulantly. 'No one ever talks about such things. I'm very well, I think, but my husband thinks that I shouldn't go out and should rest in bed most of the day. And then I'm so *large!*'

'You're also trussed up like a chicken,' Mary frowned, 'and that's not doing either you or 'child any good. Will you permit me to loosen your corset, ma'am?'

'Oh, please do,' Melissa begged. 'That's one of the reasons why I agree to stay in bed so often. I'm so much more comfortable in my bedgown.'

'There's no reason why you shouldn't stay in your bedgown all day if you want to, ma'am. Who's to say that you shouldn't?'

The buttons on Melissa's morning gown ran from the back of her neck to her waist and Mary began to unfasten them, tutting to herself as she did so. At last she slipped it down over her shoulders and then unlaced her corset. Melissa let out a huge breath. 'Oh,' she sighed. 'That's so much better. You know, I have actually refused to wear the crinoline. It's bad enough trying to sit down without being girdled by steel rings!'

'Quite right, ma'am,' Mary agreed. 'Shall I ring for your maid to fetch your bedgown?'

'No. I can get it for myself,' Melissa said. 'And from now on I shall only wear what's comfortable. Just help me off with all this paraphernalia, please, and then we can talk.'

But as Melissa asked questions, and then Mary asked

questions, it began to dawn on Mary that perhaps it wouldn't be too long before the birth. She asked Melissa to lie on the bed and gently ran her fingers over her abdomen.

'If it pleases you, ma'am,' she said quietly, 'I could stay here until you're delivered. I don't think 'housekeeper'd mind if I shared a room wi' one of 'maids. And I think, just as a precaution, mebbe Master Hart would ask 'doctor to call.' She made this suggestion in a mild-mannered way as if there was no hurry at all.

'Oh, if you think so, of course we'll send for him,' Melissa said. 'And certainly you can stay. I should feel much more at ease if you would.'

'There's no rush, sir,' Mary told Christopher Hart as she prepared to leave the house. 'But if 'doctor could call in tomorrow to give his expert opinion . . .'

'Tomorrow? But you said there was no rush,' Christopher exclaimed. 'Is the birth imminent?'

'In another week or so, I think,' Mary said calmly. 'I'm going home to fetch a few things and then I'll come straight back. Mrs Hart said she'd like me to stop till after she's given birth.'

Christopher gasped. 'I'll get somebody to take you home and bring you back, then he can go immediately for the doctor.'

'I said there was no rush, sir,' Mary repeated. 'But 'reason I want 'doctor to come is that I think Mrs Hart might be expecting twins.'

'I'll look after things here,' Harriet assured Mary as the older woman gathered what she needed into a large black bag. The carriage driver was sitting outside waiting for her. 'I hope Mrs Hart will be all right.'

'She's a healthy woman, I've no fears on that score, but as it might be two babbies, I'd rather that 'doctor came to check on her.' She snapped closed the clasp on the bag. 'I'll see you when it's over,' she said. 'It's a good thing it's midweek and we've done all 'washing, cos there'll be plenty later on!'

Harriet watched her being driven away and was pleased that she had suggested Mary's services to Mrs Hart; the mistress would be in good hands. She turned her attention to Daniel, who had crawled across the rug and was attempting to pull himself up by grabbing a chair leg.

How quickly the time has gone, she thought. It seems no time at all since he was a helpless baby in his swaddling clouts, and now he's crawling and trying to stand and I must watch him every minute. She thought then of Noah and wondered how he would have dealt with having a child at his feet. Having had no love in his own life, would he have been able to give any to his son? And what was it he had said? "If it's a lad *I'll* decide how he's treated."'

She sighed heavily. What decisions would they have been, Noah? That he would be subject only to you? Would he have been given 'strap if he didn't obey you? Would he have been allowed to mek his own choices in life? She thought then about Fletcher, who had made his own decision to leave his home, because he couldn't bear to see her living with his brother. Soon I'll have to mek my own decision about living with Fletcher, who isn't, and can never be, my husband.

She suppressed a sob. Am I wicked to think that I want him to be, when Noah has not yet been found?

A sharp knock on the door startled her and made Daniel cry. She picked him up, soothing him. 'It's all right. It's all right.'

It was Tom Bolton, Mary's nephew. He scraped his boots on the iron scraper at the door when she invited him in, and doffed his cap.

'Your aunt Mary isn't here,' Harriet began to explain. 'She's up at 'manor.'

'No. No, it's you that I called to see.' He slapped his cap idly against his knees. 'Though I'd hoped she might be here. It's, erm, well, it might be nowt and be somebody else, but I thought to warn you afore rumours get about.'

'What?' She stared at him, hardly breathing. 'Is it Noah?'

'It might be,' he mumbled. 'But, well, it'll be difficult to tell. I heard out on 'river that a body was seen in Brough Haven last night. I'm on my way to tell Fletcher. I thought we'd go together. After all, I knew Noah as well as anybody.'

'Did you?' Harriet felt shaky and abruptly sat down. She had known that this moment might come one day, but after all this time she still wasn't prepared for it.

'Oh aye. We had some grand drinking sessions together when you were – when you were . . .' He glanced at Daniel, who looked back suspiciously and then turned his gaze away and buried his face in Harriet's neck. 'When you were expecting 'babby.'

'Oh!' she breathed. 'Did you? I didn't know.'

'Course,' Tom went on, 'it might not be him. It could be Mr Tuke or anybody, so don't get your hopes up.'

'I won't,' she said softly. But it'll be somebody's husband, she thought, somebody's father or son, and, for some family, a conclusion. An end of waiting and a chance to say goodbye.

# CHAPTER FIFTY-ONE

There was a flurry of activity in Brough as news spread that a
body had been seen in the Haven the previous evening, and
soon a small group of interested onlookers began to make
their way down to the waterside.

A gusty chill wind tossed the quivering water on to the bank
and then snatched it back again to rush and surge in a plunging vortex towards the middle of the Haven, where it swirled
and eddied against the tide; ragged cloud hung beneath
deeper rain clouds which scudded across the grey-blue sky,
obliterating any light and turning day to night.

At first light that morning two men had taken out a rowing
boat and boat hook to where it was said the body had been
seen, but had found nothing. 'Might have been a dead dog,'
said one. 'Aye,' agreed his companion, 'and been washed away
again. Or mebbe a tree branch. Folks see all kinds o' things in
'dark. Could've been owt.'

Now they were searching again, knowing that two men were
missing and feared drowned from almost a year ago, and this
time there was a constable waiting on shore and a couple of
fishermen sitting in a coggy boat in their long boots, as well
as the crowd of onlookers, some with a reason for being there
and others simply ghoulish bystanders.

Two women were watching separately, though only a few
feet apart from each other. One gave up after about fifteen

minutes and made her way back to a riverside cottage, where she went inside and closed the door firmly behind her. The other, a shawl wrapped round her, hiding her face, her head low and buried deep within her coat collar, stayed and kept vigil.

One of the men in the rowing boat put his hand up in the air to signify that they had found something, the coggy boat put off and the crowd drew in a collective breath. The lone woman turned her head as if uncertain whether to go or stay, but then impulsively drew further back into the crowd, hiding in obscurity.

Fletcher, who had been met by Tom on his journey back from depositing his mother at Mrs Marshall's, hurried down to the water's edge to tell the constable who he was. Everyone watched as the boat hook was dipped into the water to catch hold of something, and saw one of the men turn his face as gaseous bubbles rose to the surface.

The constable cleared the crowd away, telling them that only those who had a genuine cause for staying could do so. He paused at the woman, but before he could say anything she turned, shaking her head and putting her hands to her eyes as she walked away.

'It's him,' Fletcher told the constable when they brought the body to shore. 'Noah. I recognize his jacket, what's left of it.'

'Yeh,' Tom murmured. 'So do I. Come on, lad. We can do no more here. We need to tell Harriet, and your ma.'

'Ah, yes, my mother.' He glanced along the path that led towards Mrs Marshall's cottage. 'She needs to know. But not today. I'll tell her tomorrow.'

Harriet and Fletcher sat opposite each other at Mary's fireside. Tom, at ease in his aunt's house, made them both tea with plenty of sugar and chatted to fill the silence, telling Harriet that Aunt Mary's cottage had been his second home when he was a lad. He built up the fire before taking his leave,

334

saying, 'You'll have plenty to talk about.' Which they had, but neither could find a word to say.

Eventually, when Harriet had put Daniel to sleep and dusk was falling, Fletcher rose to go. 'I'd better get off,' he said reluctantly. 'You'll need time to yourself.'

She paused for a moment, gazing at him, before putting out her hand to grasp his. 'No. Don't,' she said. 'Please stay. I don't want to be alone.'

The doctor gazed at Mary over the top of his gold-rimmed eyeglasses. 'You did well, Mrs Boyle, to spot the twin pregnancy. Very well indeed.'

'Comes of experience, sir.' Mary wasn't going to succumb to his patronizing praise. She knew what she knew. 'I've delivered a few in my time.'

'Well done.' He smiled condescendingly. 'And Mrs Hart wants you to stay until after the birth? Well, I'm quite happy to go along with that if it eases the mother's mind, but be sure to send for me if there's as much as an inkling that the birth is imminent.' She thought he looked as though he was about to pat her on the head and bridled instinctively as he added, 'But it won't be yet awhile.'

'Very good, sir,' she concurred, wondering why he hadn't noticed the other baby himself, and also why he hadn't mentioned to Mrs Hart that sometimes a twin birth was early, as this one might be.

'Is my wife going to be all right?' Christopher asked her after the doctor had gone. 'Two babies! I never expected that.'

'There can be complications, sir,' Mary told him. 'And I won't pretend it will be easy for Mrs Hart, but she's a strong healthy woman and I'll do my best for her.'

He put his hand on her shoulder – she didn't mind that – and said, 'I'm sure you will. I'm relying on you.'

She was given her own room after all, and didn't have to share with a maid. It had been Christopher's and then Amy's nanny's room and was furnished with a bed and a sofa, easy chair, table and chairs, and had a bright fire burning in the hearth with a pricked rug in front of it, and a window overlooking the kitchen garden.

Perfect, she thought, looking round with a satisfied smile. I could be very comfortable here.


Noah's funeral couldn't be held until all official certificates were issued, and these were delayed until formal identification was complete. Fletcher was bolstered by Tom's presence as he signed documents, and he in turn supported Harriet.

It was a week later that a messenger from the manor came to the door and handed Harriet a letter. 'Mrs Hart sent this,' the young lad said. 'She said I had to be quick as it was urgent.'

Inside the envelope was another envelope addressed to Harriet, and a note from Melissa Hart that read, *I trust this is good news for you following the distress you have recently undergone, for which I send my sincere condolences and pray that you can find solace.* In a postscript she added, *I hope that shortly I will have my own dreams fulfilled.*

Harriet sat down. Daniel was sleeping and Fletcher was at Marsh Farm continuing the clearance of the outbuildings, for November was coming up fast. She turned the envelope over in her hand. It could only be from one person. Rosamund – Rosie, as was. She would have heard about Noah. So had Ellen, for Fletcher had been to tell her. She had said little, except that she hoped his soul would rest in peace.

'Is that all?' he'd said. 'Have you no sorrow for your adopted son?'

Ellen had thought for a moment before saying, 'I'm onny sorry that he didn't find a mother to care for him. His own mother should have done that and not given him to someone else.' She'd paused for a moment before adding, 'But I'm sorry for a life passing.'

Fletcher had shaken his head and left, realizing how little he had known her. When he told Harriet she had simply murmured, 'Poor Noah.'

But now, what had Rosie to say? Was she too going to deny her son's existence? Would she say that her precious name wasn't to be mentioned, that reputation was more important to her than her son?

Harriet reached for a table knife to slit the envelope. She drew out two sheets of paper written on with a neat hand, and within them another sheet of folded paper.

Dear Harriet,

I hope you don't mind if I use your given name. I've thought often of you and your son, Daniel, and have had many mixed emotions since your visit. The child, of course, is of my blood too and that of the man I feel sure I could have loved, given the opportunity, but because of my circumstances could not.

I was there at Brough Haven when Noah was discovered and I suffered great distress; on my way home I found myself in the vicinity of Mrs Stone's house and knocked on her door. In spite of her background and past way of life, she can be kind, as she was on this occasion, and she took me in and let me talk. Her sound advice was that if I wanted to rid myself of the terrible guilt I felt then, and have felt for most of my life, I should put things right, and that is what I intend to do. The first step is to send you Noah's birth certificate. When he was born, I registered him as mine and Marco's.

With trembling fingers, Harriet opened the other sheet of paper, which was divided into sections; here was the name of the male child, Noah; the name of the mother, Rosamund Morley, and the father's name, Marco Orsini, and occupation, seaman.

Harriet covered her face with her hands and began to weep. Noah Morley, or Noah Orsini, if his father had come back to claim him as his own; not Tuke at all.

After she had calmed down and stopped crying, she

finished reading the letter. Rosie said she would like to make up for the loss of so much that was precious by arranging a funeral for Noah, which she would pay for, at which she would acknowledge Noah as her son. She completed the letter by saying she hoped that Harriet would allow her to play a small part in Daniel's life.

When Fletcher called later that day, he saw a change in Harriet. She seemed brighter, and although there was sadness in her eyes, she smiled. 'You've summat to tell me?' he asked.

When she nodded, he said, 'Can I tell you my news first? I haven't said owt before, because I wasn't sure how you'd feel about it, but after 'other night, that night when we'd found Noah . . .' He hesitated. 'I thought – I thought that mebbe you – well, mebbe there might be some hope for me. That you wanted me in your life, even if we couldn't be married.'

'Do you want to marry me, Fletcher?' she asked huskily.

He took hold of her hand. 'You know I do, more than anything else in 'world, if onny we could.'

'So what news were you going to tell me that can't wait for me to tell mine?'

'It's Tom Bolton,' he said. 'He's asked if I'll join wi' him and buy a plot o' land up at Elloughton Dale. You'll mebbe not know it, but it's not far from here. I've a bit of money that I earned in America, not much, but enough, and he has too, being a single man; and I've thought it through and I'd like to. But I can't do it without you, Harriet – you and Daniel. If you'd rather, we'll go and live elsewhere. We could even go to America.'

Harriet smiled and handed him Rosie's letter and Noah's birth certificate. 'We'll have to be patient for a little bit longer,' she whispered, her tears falling fast. 'Noah deserves that at least, and we're in no hurry.'

Fletcher finished reading and put his arms round her. He kissed her wet cheeks, and with his own eyes streaming and a lump in his throat he said, 'No, we're not in a hurry, not in a hurry at all.' He kissed her again, on her forehead, and both cheeks, and then her lips. 'Well,' he gave her a watery smile and another kiss, 'not too much of a hurry, anyway.'

'Come along, Mrs Hart,' Mary cajoled. 'One more push, m'dear, and we're nearly there. That's it – easy now, good girl, and here we are – one babby, one handsome son to please your husband. Here now, tek a look at him.' She wrapped the newborn in a soft blanket and gently tipped him up until he yelled in protest, and then turned him towards his mother. 'Aye, a proper lad, letting himself be heard.'

Melissa lifted her head to take a better look at her son, but was gently pushed back again by Mary's firm hand. 'Hold him for a minute,' she said, putting him in Melissa's arms. 'Just so's he can get 'smell of you, but then I want you to tek a rest ready for 'next one.'

'Goodness,' Melissa said weakly, gazing down at him. 'I don't know if I've got the strength to go through that again.'

'Course you have.' Mary took the baby from her and put him on his side in the prepared bassinet. 'Next one will be easier and quicker. Close your eyes and tek some nice deep breaths for ten minutes.'

She ran her hand over Melissa's belly and gently pressed. 'Won't be long. It's starting to turn,' she said softly, and fifteen minutes later, easing out into a whole new world, came her daughter.

'Oh, Mary.' Melissa wept with joy as she held her babies one on each side of her. 'Will you stay? Will you stay and be the children's nanny? Help me to look after them? Please say that you will.'

Mary thought for a mere heartbeat. Her response was im-mediate but she didn't want Mrs Hart to think her too eager. It was what she had wished for, and even on her first night at the manor hopeful plans had already been forming. Her nephew Tom could have her cottage. He'd always liked it there and mebbe one day he'd find a nice young woman to share it with, whilst she would be deliriously happy in the nanny's room, her meals provided, her washing done for her, a coal fire lit every day, and the extra joy of caring for two babies who would be almost like her own.

'Well, ma'am,' she hedged. 'That sounds like a very nice proposition.'

'Oh, please!' Melissa implored. 'However will I manage without you?'

'Well, that would be very nice, thank you, ma'am.' Mary beamed. 'I'd like that very much.'

# ENDING

Daniel was a toddler of two and a half when the marriage of Harriet and Fletcher took place on a warm and sunny June day in the old church of St Mary's in Elloughton. They had waited eighteen months, as was right and proper, befitting a young widow after bereavement, and until the purchase of the Elloughton Dale farmland had gone through and the house Fletcher was building for his and Harriet's life together was nearing completion. During this time Harriet had stayed in Mary's cottage and now Tom was planning to move in after she and Fletcher were married.

The new farmhouse windows overlooked meadows and woodland, and in the near distance the villages of Elloughton and Brough and the familiar waters of the Humber, gleaming like silver in the sun or on darker days rich chestnut brown, could be clearly seen. The land at Marsh Farm was being prepared for warping; ditches had been dug and sluices built, and soon the estuary waters would be allowed in. But the old house that had harboured such resentment and loathing was, without maintenance, slowly disintegrating. The roof had fallen in, the walls were beginning to crumble and no one seemed to care. Nathaniel Tuke had not yet been found.

Tom Bolton was Fletcher's best man. Rosie Gilbank, loving her role as a grandmother, sat in a front pew with Daniel on her knee, but Ellen Tuke sent a message to say she wouldn't be attending the ceremony, giving the excuse that she couldn't leave her old friend Mrs Marshall whose health was failing. Only a few people had been invited, as they wanted a quiet, simple ceremony, but the Harts' carriage had made a detour and stopped at the church gate as Mary had asked if they might, for the Harts, with the twins and Mary and a nursemaid, were travelling that day on a long visit to see Christopher Hart's daughter Amy and her new baby.

Harriet was wearing a new blue flowered muslin gown and matching bonnet that Fletcher insisted they bought for such a special occasion, and she thought as she prepared for her wedding that Noah would have thought the expenditure wasteful and unnecessary. She thought of Noah with wistful understanding now, and didn't blame him for his behaviour after the ill-usage he had suffered. And as for her marriage to him, she had no regrets, for it had brought her to Fletcher and given her Daniel. It had also brought her a good friend in Rosie, who had declared her life was richer because of her grandson, whom she loved dearly.

When they left the church after their vows, Harriet, with Fletcher and Rosie, watched as Daniel placed a rose from her bouquet on his father Noah's grave. The headstone, which Rosie had paid for, simply said *Noah Morley-Orsini, known as Noah Tuke.*

'That will confuse everyone for years to come,' Fletcher remarked wryly, and Rosie smiled and agreed.

As they walked back to the church door the Harts were waiting with Mary and the children to give their best wishes. Christopher raised his top hat, Mary beamed and waved, and Melissa looked keenly at Fletcher, who, Harriet considered, was looking particularly handsome in his black trousers, grey frock coat and waistcoat and white cravat, his hair cut short and curling about his collar. But Harriet thought she saw concern in Melissa's scrutiny. As their eyes met, Harriet gave a slight bob of her knee and a smile of warmth, understanding and reassurance. We are what we are, she seemed to convey, and what has gone before is in the past. She glanced fondly at the children, the Hart twins, Christopher Charles and Beatrice, and Daniel who had rushed over to join them, and thought: this is a sort of ending, but also a beginning; a life of love and caring is in the future now.

# SOURCES

Books for general reading:

*A Dynamic Estuary: Man, Nature and the Humber,* Hull University Press, 1988, edited by N. V. Jones
*Humber Perspectives. A Region through the Ages,* Hull University Press, 1990, edited by S. Ellis and D. R. Crowther

You can read more of Ellen Tuke's story in
Val Wood's exclusive ebook novella:

# THE
# MAID'S SECRET

Available now from all good e-tailers